THE WOMAN SHE LEFT BEHIND

A NOVEL

TOM HUGGLER

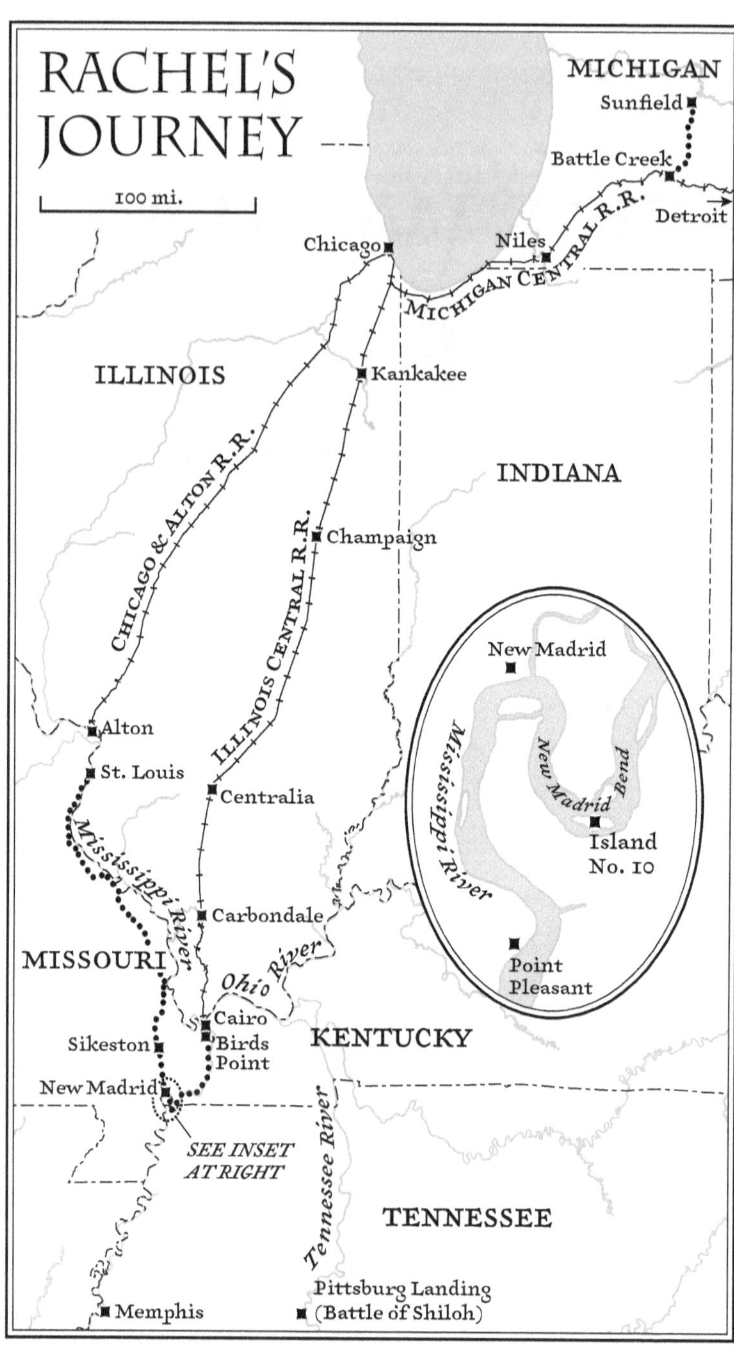

RACHEL'S JOURNEY
100 mi.
MICHIGAN
Sunfield
Battle Creek
Detroit
Chicago
Niles
MICHIGAN CENTRAL R.R.
ILLINOIS
Kankakee
INDIANA
CHICAGO & ALTON R.R.
ILLINOIS CENTRAL R.R.
Champaign
Alton
St. Louis
Centralia
Mississippi River
Carbondale
MISSOURI
Ohio River
Cairo
Birds
Point
KENTUCKY
Sikeston
New Madrid
SEE INSET
AT RIGHT
Tennessee River
TENNESSEE
Memphis
Pittsburg Landing
(Battle of Shiloh)
New Madrid
Mississippi River
New Madrid Bend
Island
No. 10
Point
Pleasant

THE WOMAN SHE LEFT BEHIND

A NOVEL

TOM HUGGLER

SUNACUMEN PRESS

Designed by Marj Charlier, Sunacumen Press
Author photo by J Photography, Grand Rapids, Michigan.
The front cover image is AI-inspired.
Map by Nat Case, INCase, LLC

Sunacumen Press
Colorado Springs, CO
Printed in U.S.A.

ISBN: 979-8-218-77561-2

For Laura,
for being there, every step of the way

PROLOGUE

January 1862
Shaytown Road, Sunfield, Michigan

In the gloaming of a winter's day, a woman traipses through crusted snow in a tiny cemetery carved from a family farm. Songbirds deserted this place long ago. The night will be cold, and neighborhood crows have fled to their pine roost. Who comes here, alone, to visit the only resident in a stone-cold burial ground?

Rachel Barnum does.

Widowed going on four years, Rachel still finds it hard to let Willis go. She keeps vigil from her kitchen window a half-furlong (as he would say) from his final place of rest. Watching the sun brighten the smooth granite headstone assures Rachel that he is there, a bit of comfort to her restless spirit.

Even on days of poor weather, Rachel may lace boots and don mittens, cap, and woolen coat and pay Willis a visit. There, she sits in his chair—the parlor chair he had favored so and often carried to the dining table—for a few minutes, maybe an hour, and talks to him. Their seventeen years of matrimony produced four children, yielded abundant crops, and found them wanting for nothing, in spite of rising inflation fed by rumors of war.

The exertion required to traverse hardened snow has warmed Rachel's tired body, and she needs to rest. Reaching the chair, she shakes it to break free its ice-trapped legs. When one of the wooden back slats separates and lands atop the snow, a pang of despair stings like the prick of a sewing needle. She should not have been so careless. After long exposure the chair has seen better days. She will ask John Welch, her hired man, for canvas to protect the chair. If Mr. Welch came to the cemetery, which she doubts he ever has, and saw the chair in such a state, he would offer to repair it. Rachel cancels that thought, however, because she doesn't want the hired man to feel obligated, especially when the subject has to do with her husband. Life with Willis had nothing to do with John Welch, even though Rachel trusts him implicitly and has grown ever fond of him.

She had laid out the burial plot after Willis passed, months before she met the man she would hire. It was good to keep personal matters private.

After the funeral, Rachel had told her children the grave was sacred ground. "I don't mind you playing over there, and you can go see Poppa any time you wish, but you must be respectful. He was a great man, a devoted father to each of you, and I will not have him forgotten. Or his place of rest disturbed in any way. Do you understand how Mama feels?"

Recalling the reaction of her twin daughters, six years old then, prompts a little smile. Bobbing their heads dramatically, they had reminded Rachel of the chickens she had roaming through the yard.

Gingerly, Rachel eases her body onto the chair, afraid it might collapse in spite of her petite frame. She hasn't sat on it since last week's storm. Assured the cold, brittle wood won't come apart, she folds hands on her lap and reads the chiseled words for the thousandth time since writing them on a stonemason's order sheet:

WILLIS BARNUM
B. FEB. 10, 1819
D. JULY 26, 1859
40 YRS 5 MOS. 16 DAYS

CHAPTER 1

A voice is heard in Ramah,
mourning and great weeping.
Rachel weeping for her children;
and refusing to be comforted
because her children are no more.
Jeremiah 31:15

Four months earlier, September 1861
Sunfield, Michigan

Imagining he was riding with a stampede of other troopers, young Dwight Barnum spurred his cherished Morgan breed and charged into battle. As he and Blaze cut a bloody swath through ranks of a faceless enemy, Dwight gripped the reins in his left hand. His right hand brandished a carbine; a holstered pistol slapped the saddle. When the daydream abruptly faded, Dwight opened his fist to knead stiff fingers with those of his writing hand. Doing so, he imagined ink from a feather nub while signing Dwight Barnum on the document that declared him to be a fighting horse soldier in the Michigan 2nd Calvary.

The voice of the Army recruiter jarred Dwight back to reality. "Horse soldiers are a special breed!" Henry Shaw bellowed from a raised platform. "If you can't ride, or don't want to ride as patriots for your country, there's always the infantry, which I don't mean to disparage. The Union needs soldiers of every kind. This includes artillerymen, boys to hitch up the caissons and stoke the cannons."

The little man with the big voice paused to let his words take root.

"The Army can use snipers and scouts and wagon drivers, too. But those of you who know me know how much I love horses, which is why I asked the governor of the great state of Michigan for authority to raise a company of calvary." He paused, allowing his words to sink in.

After the nation's shocking defeat at Bull Run in July past and the president's call for three hundred thousand new troops to quell the Rebellion, a flock of Army recruiters invaded the North's hinterland. Handbills encouraging men eighteen years and older to enlist appeared throughout Eaton County in southcentral Lower Michigan. In early September a team led by Captain Henry Shaw arrived in Sunfield, a fledgling village between Lansing and Grand Rapids, and Dwight was among several farm boys, most of whom he knew, who came to town to hear the passionate orators. The stirring calls for volunteers to come to arms made Dwight's heart race and his temples throb.

Speakers before Shaw had urged all able-bodied young men to preserve the union, end the insurrection, free those held in bondage, and end slavery forever. But it was the captain's appeal, a pledge to raise an Eaton County company of one hundred cavalrymen, that inspired Dwight to take action. "Our neighboring counties are also assembling cavalry units," Shaw shouted, "but only you Eaton County boys will be called Company B. You will muster into service at the Grand Rapids fairgrounds where twelve companies will form a regiment. A colonel or brigadier general will command this regiment."

Shaw explained he was a horse breeder who raised Morgans on his farm near Eaton Rapids, a morning's ride from Sunfield. When asked for a show of hands from those who owned a young, strong gelding or filly, broken to saddle and thoroughly biddable, Dwight and a dozen others stood tall with arms held high. "If your horses are healthy and intelligent," Shaw boomed, "they will go with you to Grand Rapids for training in marching drills and combat formations. Then you're off to beat the Rebels in the East or West War Theater. You'll serve where your country needs you most."

Arms aloft, Shaw's voice became a roar. "Wherever you Eaton County boys go, your horses go with you! And if there's a patriot here today, man or boy, who wants to serve his country on the back of a horse, but who doesn't own a horse, I will see to it you are paired with an admirable steed, either one of my very own or one provided by the United States Army!"

At this concluding remark, the audience burst into cheers and the thunderous clapping of hands. Before the sun dropped below the tree line of Sunfield village's western boundary, seventeen of the twenty-two young men in attendance had signed three-year enlistments for a salary of eleven dollars per month. Later, a seated Henry Shaw, pouring over papers at the documents table, saw the name "Dwight Barnum" and stood to appraise the sober-looking lad before him. "Barnum, you say? Are you related to the late Willis Barnum?"

"He was my father, sir."

"Lord Almighty, I knew your pa! Sold him one of the finest geldings I ever raised. Beautiful Morgan horse. Chestnut in color. Distinctive white mark on his forehead."

"Yes, sir. That's Blaze." Dwight grinned, his chest swelling with pride. He pointed to a long rail that held his and others' mounts. "I rode him in from the farm. He's right over there."

"If your father was here today, he would be proud. You are going to be a fine soldier on one mighty fine horse." Recruiter Shaw thrust forward a hand. "Young man, welcome to the United States Cavalry!"

March 25, 1862
Along the Ionia Trail near Sunfield

Only a fool lets a *working horse drink its fill*.

Father's warning, a memory from childhood, distracted Rachel as her team stretched powerful necks for more water. With reins coiled around wrists, Rachel forced their heads up, away from the creek, swollen with snowmelt and churning around the horses' knees. "Bill, no!" she ordered. "No, Sam. Upon my word, I said, no!"

When Sam, the older, larger Belgian, snorted and shook himself, Rachel caught the pungent odor of wet leather mingled with sweat. Over forty years of farm life, Rachel had never found this singular smell offensive, a simple testament to honest work done well. The team had already pulled her creaking wagon five miles from home, through the rutted Ionia Trail. It was a soft path, a quagmire in places, from the release of frost in these dying throes of a Michigan winter.

Flank muscles on Bill, Sam's son, quivered from exertion or the frigid creek or both. Despite her impatience, Rachel knew it was good to stop and let the team blow a bit. And she had remembered her father's advice about soaking wagon wheels on a long journey like this one. Water swelled the wood and helped to prevent separation from the iron rims or, worse, a hickory spoke from breaking free.

She clucked and snapped the reins. The startled horses tossed their heads and leaned into the traces until Rachel stopped them with gentle firmness. A bright male cardinal flitted through streamside willows, a drop of living blood in a cold world leeched gray as morning ashes on the hearth at home.

"Whoa, Bill. Easy there, Sam." The exposed wheel dripped as water the color of sarsaparilla purled through spokes.

Wisps of steam rising from the horses' backs dissolved into the cold air, as Rachel shivered and pulled her shawl closer. Young Bill, almost as large as Sam and nearly as strong, would soon feel the plow's bite across that sturdy back for the first time. But not before the new field had dried and the trip was over and Rachel had gone home.

On this morning in late March, she studied the brooding sky and the dark clouds heavy with rain or snow and wondered *when* she would again see her family there. The answer had to do with the hidden telegram tucked into a pocket she had sewn into her dress. A sudden twinge of fear and she chirruped the horses forward. The wagon quaked and Bill slipped a little as he stepped from the solid creek bottom into black muck on the other side, a disturbance that released the sharp scent of skunk cabbage.

"TAKE THE TEAM, MRS. BARNUM," John Welch, the hired man, had said. "Winter's been bad, and it ain't over yet. The road above Vermontville's hardly passable for a wagon. Who knows what lies beyond? Take them both in case one goes lame. We can't work your fields for a month nohow."

Thoughtful, careful Mr. Welch, Rachel had thought even as he spoke. Yesterday, while she packed and arranged her affairs, he had ridden ahead to this very place to evaluate the creek that ran through the swamp known as Barber's Woods. And later, over supper at the dining table with her twin daughters and son, he gave the report, a frown hidden beneath his full, sable beard.

"You can get across the Scipio Creek and through Barber's Woods, but only if it don't rain no more tonight. Mrs. Barnum, I do wish you'd let me drive you over to Charlotte! You can take the stagecoach down from there and have no team to tend and to put up somewhere."

His kind face flashed through Rachel's mind. She knew the offer was not only generous, it was practical, sensible. Still, she couldn't accept. "That coach is not reliable. By the time I got to Charlotte and waited for it to come in, load up, and leave again, I could be long past Kalamo. Maybe as far as Bellevue."

"But you said you never been to Kalamo, never even got below Vermontville. And you don't know what that trail is like beyond town, and then ..." Avoiding her insistent stare, John Welch stopped talking.

Rachel knew his mind. "There's a hotel in Kalamo, another in Bellevue, and surely a livery. There are certainly places to stay if no one offers along the way. An early start tomorrow and I'll be in Battle Creek, Michigan, the next day by the dinner hour. In plenty of time before the afternoon train leaves for Chicago."

Perturbed anew, the hired man shook his head. "It's more than thirty miles. Mrs. Barnum, be reasonable."

"It's forty miles, or more, by way of Charlotte. Mr. Welch, I'm not waiting for a coach that cannot bring the mail on time. I'm going straight down to Battle Creek for that train!"

The children stopped eating the supper stew of beef and vegetables. Seeing them exchange tense glances, Rachel paused and when no one spoke, her tone was less combative. "I do thank you for appraising the road this afternoon, Mr. Welch, and I'm more than grateful for your seeing to the family's needs while I'm gone." And with that, she remembered the piece of cornbread pinched between fingers and swiped at her plate of gravy.

"But, Mama, how will you find him, alone?" asked Hester. "And if you do find him, how can you bring him home all by yourself?"

The questions befuddled Rachel because she had no ready answer. She adjusted the knot of dark hair pulled into a bun and looked at her ten-year-old daughters, whose hair was chocolate-brown like hers. How could look-alike twins be so different? Hester always talking, Helena so quiet. And Rachel's mind reeled back four decades, as it often did, to her own twin sister, Helen, Helena's namesake. Rachel wondered if Helen had been the brassy one when they were little, or had she been the mouth for both of them? Like this girl, her own daughter, Hester.

While the single oil lamp wavered, Rachel's gaze took in the far end of the dimly lighted table past the hired man to the girls' brother, Watson, sixteen already and so like his father Willis—the high forehead, the small mouth. Watson was staring at the hired man, and the boy's mouth was moving, a sign of agitation that Rachel knew stemmed from her son's dislike of John Welch. Her heart quickened, her palms grew damp as events of the past four years rushed to mind like the speed of a thunderclap: *My husband gone! The War, come. And, now, terrifying news of Dwight, my older boy!* Wiping her fingers dry, she put hands to head and thought, Sweet Mother of Jesus, have mercy on what remains of my family.

A lump had formed in her throat. She blinked away stinging tears. Sucking in her lower lip, the words were soft: "I'll bring your brother home if the Good Lord will let me." Eyes widened, her voice inched higher as though to convince herself. "I cannot … will not … leave him *there.* I will bring Dwight home where he belongs."

ON THE HIGH GROUND A mile above Vermontville, the road firmed a little and a stone jolted the wagon. It freed Rachel's mind, and optimism returned. She knew where her ailing son was. The War Department telegram that had come to her on the church steps, after worship service the day before yesterday, was clear. Finding Dwight was less of a problem than getting to where he was.

But was that true? For ten years now, the Michigan Central had plied the rail tracks that stitched Detroit to Chicago. Passenger trains and freight trains pulled troop cars during the Rebellion, and they always stopped in Battle Creek, didn't they? She would take the train from Battle Creek to Chicago. In Chicago, she would board the Illinois Central and journey south, most likely to St. Louis, at least to southern Illinois. Then, a train from St. Louis or Cairo to New Madrid. If there was no train, she would rent a new team! She would find the way. Hadn't her father found a way through the wilderness, bringing his family to this place from New York years ago when she was not yet grown?

"How many roads can there be to New Madrid, Missouri?" she had asked John Welch.

He scanned her children and said, "Then go," in a tone of voice that signaled resignation. "I know you have to do this." Pushing aside his supper plate, he stood up and went outside to finish evening chores.

Then she recalled John's later words, last night when they had talked in the yard, a safe distance from her family. The night was black, and a sliver of moon slipped through gaps in the clouds. A brief waft of warm air hinted at new vegetation and spring. Tree frogs sang in full chorus from the seep across Shaytown Road.

"Mrs. Barnum … Rachel, you don't understand. They're fightin' down there, and you'll be in the thick of it. It ain't peaceful like it is here."

Her fingers curled into fists. "I know, John. I *do* know that. But I have to go."

"It ain't safe. I'm telling you I know what men do when their women are gone. I cut timber all winter long in a lumber camp. And I know what the boys do when the pay comes and they get to town. They're like bulls turned loose at breeding time. The womenfolk ain't safe then. Can't you see what I'm trying to say?"

In the darkness Rachel stared at her hired man with intense interest, as though trying to identify a stranger. *Why was he being so insistent?* "Yes, I know what you mean, John. Last night at supper you said you knew I had to go." Rachel dug a boot heel into the soft earth. "What has changed with you?"

Waiting for a reply, Rachel considered her words.

Why would he understand? He has no children. And I was so lost when he came here I couldn't make simple decisions, even whether to replace those two hens lost to winter. He was a Godsend to me. He still is, but I'm more clear-sighted now.

She heard him suck in a deep breath, hold it a moment,

and release with a sigh. "It's worse with the soldiers. I know this, too. They can be a hellish bunch, like most of the Rebels our boys are fighting. A soldier in wartime's got nothing to lose. Except his life. And if someone's not shooting at him, he don't think about that too much."

Her eyes narrowed. "They're boys, just like Dwight."

"Oh, not all of them, ma'am. They're men after that first big fight. Once they seen the elephant, they're men, and they will do what men want to do."

Something had welled up inside her. It tasted like copper. "I know how to manage my affairs. I grew up with three brothers. All older. I can take care of myself. Why do you argue so? This is my decision, not yours."

Rachel thought he studied the moon, presumably for inspiration before replying. Surely, he mistook her confidence for arrogance. That being cocksure was a false bravado. Eyes returning to earth, her thoughts went dark …

A band of robbers waiting along a deserted stretch of road stops the team. Seizing her by the arms, two men force her into the wagon. Thrown on her back, she fights hard, locking her knees together like a vice. They pin her arms to the rough boards of the wagon bed. A third man fumbles as he ….

She struggled to drive the horror from her mind. *Must stay fixed on the now! If I dwell only on what could be, I will never go.*

John finally spoke. "Yes, it's your decision, but it affects everyone who cares about you. Including me."

During the ensuing silence between them, the tree frogs grew louder. From somewhere in the flimsy shadows, a screech owl quavered, its tremolo like that of a neighing horse.

Touching her shoulder, John spoke again. "I'll go for you, Rachel. It won't be so hard, so dangerous, if I was to go in your place. Besides, I wouldn't have to worry about you then."

The implications of what he said brought moisture to her dark eyes. "Oh, John Welch, you are indeed a treasure, a kind and true friend. But you have work to do here. Repairs are needed. We must get ready for planting."

"I already replaced those boards Bill kicked out of his stall. Rebuilt that busted gate, too. Yesterday I sharpened the colter and blade on your plow." This was not news to her. Every morning she directed much of his work. "But," he continued, "I need to cut those dead elm at the back of the sheep pasture and buck 'em up for next year's firewood. Still plenty of time for that, though."

"Speaking of sheep, how many ewes are left?"

"Oh. Well, seven have lambed. Only three—no, four—to go. Watson can handle them. He knows how to do it now. I made him help the last ewe on his own."

Rachel knew his offer to go in her place was sincere. "Now you are the one who doesn't understand," she said quietly. "I thank you, John Welch, truly I do." Her voice was gentle and reasonable and oddly reassuring. "I *am* going, don't you see? I'm going alone to bring my boy home."

Night grew close. Rachel looked up toward the face of the trustworthy man who had worked her farm for three years. She found his hand and squeezed it. "If you would tend to things while I'm gone, I would be forever grateful."

"I'll do my best. I think you know that, don't you?"

"Yes, I know. If you need help with the children, my husband's cousin Betsey is just down the road." Nothing more needed to be said. Rachel returned to the house, and the hired man left to lock the chicken coop.

RACHEL ENTERED THE HAMLET OF Vermontville, the hooves

of her horses striking the plank road of the village square. Driving past the New England House Hotel, the general store, and E.W. Hyde's wagon shop, she nodded to a woman who came out of the shop to stare at her. Rachel thought the curious onlooker wondered who she was. Or why a man wasn't driving the team. Rachel took in the viscous clouds, still squirming, and thought it might be two or perhaps three o'clock but with no hint of sun, was unsure. Then she remembered Willis' pocket watch. Removing gloves, she withdrew the gold-encased timepiece from the canvas bag of belongings at her feet, opened the clasp, and saw it was 2:45.

She examined the watch a moment and faintly smiled, recalling her younger son's comment. "Mama, I'll take off the chain for you," Watson had offered. "If anyone sees that gold chain, they might try to steal Poppa's watch."

She crossed the Thornapple River, the bridge of logs and boards sagging under the heft of her Belgians. Released from winter, the slick stream ran cold and dark with its freight of tree limbs and sundry detritus but had stayed within its banks. A little more and the Ionia Trail skewed east a quarter mile like a snake-shied horse before resuming the line south. As the team bent into this curve, the first skirmish of rain struck. Those few, frigid drops spattered Rachel who quickly tied the shawl around her head like a bonnet, wrapped the blanket about her upper body, and lunged for the roll of waxed canvas at her feet. But Rachel had failed to untie the knot earlier and now was afraid to drop the reins and attempt it.

Before the wagon came out of the bend, the rain ushered in a fierce squall that tore at the gray blanket. Billowing, it looked like an enormous pillow cover on the washing line.

The first boom of thunder was a cannon shot, and it

discharged a palpable tremor along Rachel's spine. A panicked Bill tried to break from his harness. "No, Bill!" she shouted above the wind. "Easy, Sam, easy!" and the veteran Sam pulled in place, and Bill began to calm and soon fell back into the plodding walk of his partner.

The storm, as though battle-infused, ruled the moment. Warning raindrops became a hardened volley of sleet, and the sleet turned into small hail that sheeted down from the troubled sky. The stinging ice pelted the open wagon, bounced from the horses' backs, and smarted Rachel's uncovered hands. Gripping the reins, she glanced left and right for any form of shelter. The trail changed to a muddied path, dimpled by hooves and creased by wheel ruts—the ruts closing as fast as they had opened—and the floating stones of hail washed away to either side. Rachel slowed the horses even more.

Making herself small within the blanket, she felt the storm wick through the thick wool and into her simple calico dress, causing an uncontrolled shudder. There was nowhere to go but straight on. With some distance to go before Kalamo, the hailstorm spent but the rain still drumming, she shouted "Halloooo!" before a log structure on the west side of the road. Realizing the unfinished cabin had no roof, Rachel drove the team on. As tears of anxiety mixed with rain dripped from the bonnet and onto her face, she prayed that somewhere along this treacherous path of mud the color of spent coffee grounds she would find shelter.

CHAPTER 2

Ionia Trail, south of Vermontville

> *Date: Mar. 21, 1862*
> *To: Rachel Barnum, Sunfield Mich.*
> *From: War Dept. U.S. Army regiment hosp.*
> *New Madrid, Missouri*
> *Re: 2nd Mich Cav., Co. B, Pvt. D. Barnum.*
> *"DWIGHT SICK WITH FEVER. FAILING."*
> *(signed) M.J. Dickenson, 2nd Lt.*

It didn't matter if the pocketed telegram, pressed to Rachel's bosom, was wet or even if she happened to lose it on the journey. The words on that yellow scrap of paper would never fade from memory. She also knew that she must get to Battle Creek as soon as possible. Today was Tuesday. The telegram was written on Friday. Forwarded by post, the message had come to her on Sunday, two days later, now two days ago. Rachel wished she had sent a second letter back to Charlotte with the young man who had raced to her farmhouse and, finding no one home, rode his horse farther up the Shaytown Road. Singing prompted him to dismount before the Methodist Episcopal church and wait near the entrance for the closing hymn to end.

They were singing "What a Friend We Have in Jesus." He didn't know which voice was hers. "Mrs. Barnum?" the rider asked each woman filing out the door. "Rachel Barnum?"

Assured by a nod, he removed his hat and handed Rachel the envelope. "It's from the telegraph office in Battle Creek, ma'am. Came in on the mail run last night. Knew it had to be urgent, ma'am. Rode out here fast as I could this morning." Looking away as she withdrew the message, he watched several crows, gossiping in a barren field across from the church, fly off amidst raucous chatter.

Hester was on the steps with Rachel. "What is it, Mama? What does it say?"

Shocked speechless, Rachel did not look up. Her bowed head resembled a drooping flower, a heavy blossom threatening to snap its stem. She steadied herself with one hand on the iron rail of the church steps, the discarded envelope at her feet. The other hand, clutching the message, shook.

"Ma'am, is there something I can do for you?" the rider asked, his voice subdued.

Rachel looked up, but did not see, could not get a deep breath. She was oblivious to the twins and their brother and to the small group of parishioners that pressed close and whispered. These people—their identities foreign, their voices unfamiliar—were like a still-life in a daguerreotype. "Come to the house!" she gasped, surfacing for air. "I will pay you there. I'll write a letter for you to return."

The specter of her son, unmoving and lying prone on a red field of battle—that horrific image—a cursed thief that had stolen countless hours of sleep since October last, was now a reality that struck her with all its power. The five long months since Dwight had saddled Blaze and ridden away from the farm for Grand Rapids had unsettled her so. The depression Rachel knew after he left was a constant reminder of the ache she had borne when Willis passed. At the farmhouse, with the aid of weak light from her kitchen window, Rachel sat at the table and wrote the letter she had conjured every day over the long, cold months since Dwight went away, leaving her to worry and to weep, alone.

> *To: 2nd Lt. Marshall J. Dickenson, U.S. Army, 2nd*
> *Mich. Cavalry, Comp. B New Madrid Missouri*
> *Dearest Marshall,*
> *"If God takes him, do not bury! I am coming. The Lord*
> *bless you & keep you safe."*
> *(signed) R. Barnum*

The terse message had written itself. Rachel stood up and gazed out the window beyond the naked apple trees to the creek where Dwight and the neighborhood farm boys, some of whom also went to war with her son, had played as children. So recently, so long ago. She paused at the knoll and the single headstone there, above where the creek turned crooked.

Is Dwight next to join his father? That fixated thought made torturous by five words—"DWIGHT, SICK WITH FEVER. FAILING"—on a yellow scrap of paper.

The quiet young man waiting patiently coughed and shifted his stance, and she pulled back from the trance and saw him standing there in her kitchen. "Forgive me," she cried out to him and to no one.

With effusive thanks, he pocketed the coins Rachel tendered, reminding her there was no mail coach on Sunday. Absently, she followed him through the door. He swung a leg over his bay and settled into the saddle. "Your letter should make the telegraph depot in Battle Creek by tomorrow afternoon." A darkened band of sweat had crept behind the saddle. It nearly touched the animal's tail. "When I get back to Charlotte, I'll see that it's posted right pronto for Battle Creek, Michigan."

Rachel nodded. "Thank you for coming. I know it's Sunday. And I know you have a long ride back."

"Thirteen miles. Only two hours."

"Please don't break that horse. The race may not be to the swift. As you said, the mail will not travel today."

A second letter, had her frenzied imagination considered writing it, might have assured her a seat on the train. Would that lack of forethought prevent her from leaving Michigan? And what if the timetable, the one announced each week in the *Eaton County Republican*, had changed? What then?

"Worry words," Peter van Houten, her father, had called such negative rumination. "They are chains that bind good men and hold them from success. And they bind good women, too."

So, Rachel tried to push away the frightful image of a ghost train silently entering the station without stopping and leaving her standing, alone, on the platform while it vanished into fog. She tried to erase the scene in the same way she had scrubbed clean the teacher's blackboard as a primary-grade student in New York.

Every morning brings a new day. Rachel remembered the chant Miss van Royken repeated after prayer. That birdsong voice Rachel could never quite remember and never quite forget: "We can do nothing about yesterday. We can do something about today. And we must never lose our hope for a better tomorrow. Now, who will wipe the slate today?"

A lifetime ago, to be sure, and yet Rachel knew this was not only the way of the Hollanders. The others, especially the first ones—the Irish and English, the Danes and Germans and Swiss and other Europeans—who also came to Michigan and cleared land and built homes and survived the hard times—the ague, the loneliness, the brutal winters, the lack of markets and money—could ill afford Pessimism and its ever-present attendants: Sadness, Depression, Despair.

Yet how could it be otherwise with Dwight? He had been the first-born son after the miscarriage. His birth was too early, the midwife had said, and he was too small and so frail and helpless. Hearing Willis pacing back and forth over the wooden floor in the parlor, she had known how tormented her husband had been, and when it was over and Dwight had cried aloud with the redeeming proof of life, how relieved she and Willis had been. She remembered then how they'd prayed together, on their knees, and thanked God through tears of joy for blessing them. And she could never forget how proud, how beside himself, Willis had been that his firstborn was a boy.

And so, what was a little tempest on this mission to fulfill her promise? Some discomfort, to be sure. A brief chill, yes, that, too. The storm was over, and with its passing, Optimism was returning. There, on the east side of the road, even as the dark sky appeared to brighten, was a clearing and the beginning of a fence. When Sam blew, a horse snorted in response from somewhere in the enclosure.

Their hooves made squishy sounds along the sodden trail as Rachel's team approached human habitation, a frame house that appeared new and unpainted. A moving figure blocked the glow of lantern light coming from a window. When the shadow passed, the glow returned, and a woman's voice shouted a greeting. "Traveler, I have a fire! Will't please you to come warm yourself?"

"It would indeed," Rachel said without hesitation. "Your offer is most kind, and I am obliged to you for it." This friendly woman seemed taken aback that the voice of gratitude belonged to a woman.

Lifting her dress, the woman sidestepped fresh puddles and hurried to the wagon. "I am Lucy McConnel," she said. "My dear, you're wet through! Here, take my hand. Let me help you down. Your hands are cold, near frozen, I declare. You must come with me, into the house." Lucy turned and shouted. "Emerson! Come tend to these horses!"

"But don't unhitch them." Rachel passed the reins to a shoeless boy of twelve or so. "I cannot stay long."

"Oh, no, my dear, you must get dry. You'll catch the chills if you don't. The fever, too." Towering above her diminutive guest, Lucy was a large woman with a loud voice that complemented her size. Escorting Rachel by the elbow, Lucy dismissed two young girls from the doorway and led Rachel inside. She entered the warm shelter without further deliberation.

Consumed in a hearth fire, a round of dried oak crackled. Rachel stood before the fire's glorious warmth and felt doubt leave her body. She ate a succulent wedge of meat and potato pie while sipping hot sassafras tea from her benefactor's sole piece of china. It was a delicate cup embellished with tiny roses, vines girdling the thin handle, and she knew a momentary peace rarely experienced since Willis' passing.

An hour later, Rachel gathered her spread blanket, which had stopped steaming between two chairs before the fire. "Mrs. McConnel, I don't know how to repay such kindness, and I apologize if this seems rude. But I must get to Bellevue before dark."

Lucy rolled her eyes. "Why, it's nearly ten miles! You know how horrible the trail is. Mrs. Barnum, you should not travel alone in weather that can't decide what to do. You must stay the night here. Emerson will see to it that your horses are fed and bedded."

"Kalamo can't be far. Surely the hotel there has rooms to rent." Rachel hoped she sounded sure of herself, to be authoritative but not discourteous.

"The Herring Hotel? Oh, no, Mrs. Barnum. It burned before Christmas. You didn't know?"

"There was no mention of it in the paper."

"Which one is that?"

"The *Republican*."

"Yes, the Eaton County weekly. Kalamo's in Eaton County. I saw the story."

"And Bellevue?" Rachel asked. "There are hotels there, aren't there?"

"Well, yes, the Eagle and the Exchange, too. It's owned by Mr. Flint. He has land between Kalamo and Bellevue." She looked directly into Rachel's eyes. "Mrs. Barnum, do stay with us. You can leave as early as you wish tomorrow."

"And a livery?"

"Yes. Campbell's Stable." Lucy's brow shot up, underscoring a growing incredulity. "It's next to the Exchange. Mrs. Barnum, I simply don't understand why you would leave so soon."

When Rachel didn't respond, she saw Lucy look out the only window at drops of rain chasing each other like tears down an inscrutable face. Noticing remnants of a summer garden with its withered vines and papery cornstalks, Rachel broke the uncomfortable silence, her voice low, the words trailing off. "A relative suffers from a grave illness. I must get to Battle Creek as quick as possible. God bless you, Mrs. McConnel."

Lucy's answer was immediate. "Emerson," she announced, "put up Mrs. Barnum's team. I'll hear no more of it, ma'am. Mr. McConnel would say as much. He took wheat to the mill in Bellevue this very morning."

The flicker of panic Rachel often knew with the loss of control was like flour sinking through a sifter. Time was not to waste, but it was not in her power to manage. She wanted to leave. She needed to stay.

"He may make it home yet tonight, but I will not have you on that wicked road in this weather. Mrs. Barnum, you can leave early in the morning. The family is always up at first light."

Rachel's fleeting smile was one of forbearance. "Thank you," she said. "I am indebted to you. And I have grain in the wagon."

Rachel didn't like having her plans compromised, but she also knew this kind, charitable woman was right. She accepted the comforter that Lucy offered. Kneeling in prayer with Lucy's daughters—curly-haired, blond girls of four and six—she climbed into bed between them and slept so soundly she did not hear Mrs. McConnel's husband arrive late into the night.

Wednesday, March 26

Awakening in the dark, Rachel dressed by candlelight. She ate warm porridge laced with maple syrup with Lucy and her children, made to be quiet so their father could sleep undisturbed. The light of dawn revealed a cloudless sky promising sunshine and a better travel day. While Emerson prepared her team, Rachel bade farewell to the McConnel girls, insisting they were the best bed partners she had ever known, and thanked Lucy, who waved away any thought of payment, for her hospitality. When Lucy hugged her and prayed briefly for travel mercies, Rachel deliberated whether to share the true purpose of her journey. She knew Lucy would be sympathetic but didn't need such support, at least not this morning. The urge to be on her way again left no time for explanation. Willis' watch was ticking away in her satchel, and she had miles to go. A train would be there. She dared not miss it.

It was late afternoon when Rachel left the Ionia Trail and turned onto the Lansing-to-Battle Creek Road. Entering Bellevue, she saw the stage and four horses coming along swiftly, presumably from Charlotte. The driver, wearing a black-oiled slicker and bee gum hat as wide as his shoulders, half-rose from his perch high above the swaying compartment to ride the wooden brake and slow the horses.

"Heah now!" he bellowed, tightening his hold on the reins with both hands. "Slow, boys, slow. Whoa there!" The coach shook to a stop in front of the Eagle Hotel. The driver scampered down and seized a mail pouch offered by someone inside the coach. Swinging the leather sack over his shoulder, he attacked the wooden steps in two bounds and disappeared behind a swinging door into the hotel. When he burst forth a moment later, Rachel was waiting on the stairs.

"Do you have room for another passenger?" she asked. "To Battle Creek."

"Who?" He smelled of leather and tobacco.

"Me. You are going to Battle Creek?"

"Yes'm. And I got a seat. You ready now?"

"I just have to turn in my team at the livery and make arrangements for them."

"Ain't got no time for that, lady. I'm runnin' late already."

"I need fifteen minutes," Rachel countered. "Ten minutes," she added, noticing the frown.

"The bridge was out on the Butternut Creek," the driver snarled. "Had to ford it and a couple other flooded spots, too. Lucky I didn't break an axle or flip the coach. What you doin' traveling alone anyhow?"

Rachel experienced an immediate flush of heat and a sudden pulse in her throat. "What concern is that to you? Are you the sheriff?" She thought of her letter written Sunday afternoon. *Did it get to Battle Creek yesterday? Is it on this stage, now?*

With a grunt, the driver scaled the steps to his perch high above the horses, an action that caused Rachel to feel discharged, insignificant. "Ma'am," he gave a little jerk of his head and touched the flopping hat brim.

"You're stopping at the telegraph station, aren't you?" she demanded. Hands on hips, she stood erect.

"In Battle Creek? My last stop after Pennfield Post Office. Got two letters aboard for the wire."

"Will you kindly ask them to reserve a seat to Chicago? On the 2:48 train tomorrow afternoon?"

The horses, sensing urgency, were already pulling away. The driver drew his whip from its socket. "Don't need to. Train's full only when the troops are moving. Fort Dowling sent its last reg'ment out last week." His whip cracked like a rifle shot. "Git on, boys!"

Rachel watched the coach grow small and melt to nothing as the road swallowed it. She could have been a passenger on that coach, gruff driver or not. Maybe her hired man was right. Maybe she should have listened to John Welch. Her heart sank as she thought about the road that lay ahead. Then, she considered what had just occurred in a positive way: Her letter might be one of the pair bound for the Battle Creek wire, and there was a chance, a decent chance, that it was already there. Why, it might have gone out already, along with what she assumed was a flurry of war correspondence.

And, if that surly driver was right, she wouldn't need a reservation after all.

A chill was coming with the diminishing light. Having traveled twenty-two miles in two days, Rachel was tired and cold. She reached down to flick away a wad of mud from her boot, checked the knots on the hitching post, and stepped inside the hotel. With room secured, she untied the hungry team and walked them down the dirt lane past the blacksmith shop to H. Campbell Livery and turned them over to a stable boy. "Give them an extra scoop of oats," she told the youngster. "They're big draft horses. They pulled hard today."

Back at the hotel, Rachel carried a bowl of cabbage soup with chunks of pork upstairs to her room. In front of the small fireplace, she ate the soup. It tasted salty but was delicious. Opening the woolen blanket, damp again from a spastic morning shower, as close to the fire as safety allowed, she removed her dress and hung it on a chair. Pulling the flannel nightgown over her head, she dropped to knees and, with hands together on the bed, prayed for Dwight and the children and John Welch. The brief prayer over, she opened her bible and sat next to the fire.

Reading before falling asleep had long been Rachel's habit. It helped to ease the day's troubles, calmed her mind, and gave hope to whatever trials tomorrow might bring. She felt closest to God when alone, in bed, at night. For as long as she could recall, Rachel had believed that dying in one's sleep was better than dying during the day. Reading the holy words of promise helped to prepare one for the hour that comes to all. And it was most timely to be taken at night when one is already gone to the world of dreams. She hoped that time was not tonight, for her sake and for her son's.

Placing the kerosene lamp on a reading table next to her, Rachel turned to Psalm 132:3, her favorite:

He who dwells in the shelter of the most high will rest in the shadow of the Almighty. I will say of the Lord, He is my refuge and my fortress, my God, and in whom I trust.

Reading until eyelids grew weary, she added two logs to the fire and squirmed beneath the heavy blanket. Her mind wandered to the twins—Hester and Helena would be washing supper dishes by now. Watson, ever aloof, always keeping to himself, was reading before the parlor hearth fire. There was John Welch, packing his pipe with the sweet-smelling tobacco before going outside to smoke. Although Rachel disapproved of alcohol and tobacco, she didn't begrudge the hired hand this simple pleasure, a habit he had adopted in the lumber camp before turning up at her farm, the winter after Willis died. Mr. Welch, a good man she thought, was looking for work.

Her mind shifted to the way Watson behaved toward John Welch, now three years on. Was her son distant, reluctant to engage with this hired man, because he felt threatened for some reason? With the father gone from this life and the only brother gone to the War, she expected that

Watson would naturally grow into the role of manly authority, but that had yet to happen. Now, alone with her thoughts in a rented room, Rachel wondered why.

She sensed Watson viewed John Welch as an interloper, but did he also see him as a competitor for Rachel's attention? Well, how could that be? Although she had grown ever closer to gentle John Welch, there was no easy familiarity that lovers share, no manifest flash of intimacy, between them. It was true that for a couple of years John had taken his meals at the dinner table with her and the family, which to some degree, he seemed to have adopted as his own. Or did she have that wrong? Was it the other way, that she and the children had adopted John Welch?

The truth she could accept was that Watson had changed. Knowing him as the quiet one, the boy who kept his feelings to himself, she had nevertheless observed in recent months that Watson had grown more distant from her and sometimes was belligerent with his sisters. Was that because she had invited Mr. Welch to abandon his room in the granary and come inside with the family? And to occupy, in reality to usurp, Dwight's empty bed in the room he had shared with his younger brother?

She could see Watson now, the mouth moving as though chewing away on something, and wondered if he ground his teeth while sleeping.

And what of those other possibilities? Was Watson angry, or jealous, because Dwight was old enough to enlist and Watson was stuck at home with three females, made to do chores and work with a man he didn't like, harnessed to school lessons for months of the year until he quit going altogether? She remembered how restless her older brothers had grown with the torpor of farm work, the dreariness of home life, and how Cornelius, the oldest one, had dreamed of signing onto a whaling ship or joining the merchant marine trade before the van Houten family left New York for Michigan.

Rachel was keenly aware that she, and to a lesser degree her late husband, had favored Dwight over Watson. But was that not true of all firstborns? Even so, was it the tender solicitude, the ready attention they had provided Dwight over the growing years? Well, that was due to his frailty, to the pervasive fear of someday losing this pale, often sickly child. Yes, of course, that was the reason they had smothered Dwight with what some might opine was the fawning behavior of indulgent parents. Her thoughts went to a rationalization: Such parental discretion was normal. It was to be expected. Anyone could see that. After all, the healthy are supposed to care more deeply for those less fortunate. Who is to judge that wrong?

And now—why scarcely a month ago—Dwight had reached his nineteenth year and was a proud horse soldier in the Union Army and had come into his own strength and was his own man! When Dwight was born, she was but nineteen herself, a jog of memory that pleased. And then Rachel's mind severed its happy tether and affixed to how she had nursed Dwight long into his second year and how she had removed Watson from her bruised and depleted breast sooner, much sooner, and that, even though this child, this second son—so healthy, so full of living energy—would turn red with rage whenever the nipple withdrew and the milk was no more.

Such deliberation never failed to prompt the familiar and discomfiting surge of unease in her stomach, that lance of agony upon recalling how Watson struggled with changing from baby to boy and now from boy to man. Rachel could see him, the mouth working furiously without food, without speech. She had realized for a long time that Watson held much love for his father and kept feelings of affection for his mother in reserve, sealed somewhere inside, and she wondered if the boy's general unhappiness, his surliness at times, was because Father was gone and John Welch was not only with them but with them in the house Willis had built, sleeping in the same bed the boy's father had made from birchwood.

Deep reflection was never conducive for sleeping, and so Rachel closed this disturbing curtain to the past and opened it again to herself in the garden with the twins. It was spring, her favorite season. Birds were singing. The pasture next to Shaytown Road was green, the sunshine warm like melted butterscotch, and the girls were helping to plant potatoes and corn, and then Rachel saw Hester milking the cow and Helena walking to the henhouse with the empty egg basket, the new one John Welch had made from basswood.

The happy images helped but did not resolve the vexing questions about Dwight's condition: *Would she get to him in time? Was he already gone?*

CHAPTER 3

Thursday, March 27

When a child cries out, a mother awakens. A farm wife is the first to hear the rooster eager for day, the milk cow bawling from a swollen udder. This morning it was someone tapping on a door down the hall from Rachel's room. Fearing she had overslept, Rachel bolted upright in bed. The thin ray of sunlight invading the room allayed her fear: It was early but none too early to be on the way again.

The fire was dead; stirred, its gray ashes powder-like. The floor was cold to bare feet. Rachel dressed and arranged her few possessions in the canvas bag brought from home. Downstairs, she paid for her lodging and food and asked the clerk for someone to fetch the team while she nibbled on a biscuit and drank black coffee. Sitting at a small table before the window while waiting for her horses, Rachel sipped away at a second cup and watched the town come to life.

A horse and buggy stopped at a café across the street.

Lifting a basket of eggs from the seat next to him, a farmer climbed down and went inside. Walking past the window were a woman and little girl, the mother carrying a loaf of bakery bread, her daughter murmuring a tune unfamiliar to Rachel. A young man of twenty or so on crutches crossed the street, the right leg of his brown, homespun trousers knotted at the knee. Rachel wondered if he had lost the leg to a farm accident or a Rebel's musket. She thought about how normal such a scene could become if the War dragged on. Imagining her son, limping along like that young man, sparked a quiver of fear, and her hand began to tremble. Cradling her coffee with both hands, she tried not to spill it.

Seeing her team coming, Rachel drained the cup, collected her things, and went outside. It was cold this morning but thankfully dry. On the road to Battle Creek, she gathered her shawl about her and pondered yet again what terrible fate had befallen Dwight. Assuredly it was serious; after all, she had never received a telegram in her life. Not even the Army officers, some of whom had access to the wire, would dare send a telegram to exchange simple news or pleasantries.

"DWIGHT SICK WITH FEVER." What sickness? What fever? Both he and Watson had survived measles as children. Consumption, though possible, infected its victims slowly and was, therefore, unlikely. Her son's last letter, written on February 26, his birthday, made no mention of illness. Besides, consumption took months to invade the lungs and destroy the body, as it had with her mother.

"FAILING." Again, a sickening fear seized her, and she felt the beginning of distress below. Dwight must be dying, but why? Did he have cholera? Yellow fever? No, it was the wrong time of year for those diseases. But he is sick with a fever. Is it typhoid? The newspaper said that's what killed

President Lincoln's son, Willie, only a month ago. What if Dwight has typhoid fever?

Her qualms leapt to smallpox. Has Dwight caught the pox from someone? He's never been vaccinated for that pestilence unless the Army did it. But then he would have told her in one of his letters.

Chronic diarrhea. Now, there was a candidate! Bertie Mathews' son, Wilson, got chronic diarrhea in Kentucky, didn't he? Poor Wilson lay sick in an Army hospital bed for weeks before they sent him home. Was that because the doctors could do no more for him? Wilson made it on the train to Albion and there he died—less than fifty miles from his mother's arms—but Mrs. Mathews said it was the pneumonia that took Wilson, not the chronic diarrhea. When the body can't hold itself together, it grows too weak to fight a cough. Or worse.

Does Dwight have chronic diarrhea? Rest, proper food, and a mother's care would cure him of that. If she could just reach him in time. Such were the myriad thoughts racing through Rachel's mind.

Another possibility: What if Dwight has been wounded, and there is now an infection? Rachel knew—from her son's letters, from other soldiers' correspondence and furloughs, and from dispatches appearing in the Chicago papers, which she sometimes received a week or two late from a cousin who lived there—that Gen. Pope's Army of the Mississippi was campaigning in the West. Dwight hoped to come home sometime in the summer, but only if they could rid the river corridor of Rebels by then. With twenty-five thousand men under his command, Gen. Pope had already shelled New Madrid into surrendering on March 14, not two weeks ago.

The paper said some fifty Union men had been killed or wounded in the brief campaign. Had Dwight been shot during the siege of New Madrid or in one of those skirmishes with guerrillas in the area? Why didn't Marshall Dickenson say he had been injured?

Why is Dwight sick with fever? Why is he failing? That unsettled feeling, that sinking spell of helplessness that could overtake her whenever knowledge was insufficient or when she must relinquish control was back. At such times she was wont to turn to prayer; so she made a long, plaintive appeal to God, as tears spread along her cheeks, to spare her elder son from whatever terrible misfortune he suffered. And while Rachel prayed, the wagon squeaked along, and her methodical team pulled to a cadence of their own.

The road from Lansing to Battle Creek was in much better condition than the Ionia Trail. Rachel was making good time. By ten o'clock she reached Pennfield. She rested the horses for twenty minutes while she went into the small general store that also served as a post office. According to the kindly postmaster, Battle Creek was less than five miles away. Having never seen Battle Creek, she took in the man's comment that it was "a busy city these days, what with the War and all."

Back on the wide road, Rachel overtook an old man driving a wagon heaped with fresh-sawn lumber. She smelled resin and knew the boards were pine. A pair of walking oxen drew the wagon while a tethered beef steer, probably destined for market, plodded behind. She bade "Good morning" to the old man, who looked up from studying his hands and nodded. They were not alone: walkers, riders, and other teams were also on the move. The wagons, groaning from wooden barrels of maple syrup and farm products bound for the city, and the occasional team returning with factory goods produced there, reminded her of the merchant trade in New York City, which she had experienced for the first time as a child.

Rachel had gone with her father and oldest brother Cornelius to deliver the vegetables and fruit they grew on their small farm a mile from the bridge to Manhattan Island. Her other brothers, Henry and John, had stayed home to weed corn and tie up tomato vines spreading through the spacious garden. The soil was good, the brothers were strong, and their father knew how to grow potatoes, corn, beans, squash, and other produce the restaurants and food vendors favored. The van Houtens had earned a reputation for producing beautiful, fresh food and for its timely delivery. Rare was the day when they'd return home with unsold stock, and even then, a piece of horehound candy might have found its way into her small and earnest hand.

TEN-YEAR-OLD RACHEL LICKED HER STICKY palm, having sucked away the sweet candy flavor. She loved these family excursions to the Big City where everything was in motion: drays coming and going, workers loading and unloading wagon freight, people everywhere, some on horses, others walking. And the noise! What a hubbub of sounds. Merchants hawking wares, the clip-clop of shod hooves, men shouting, whistle shrieks from locomotives, the rumble of trains entering and leaving the teeming city, the shunting of railcars from track to track. Such were the overwhelming sights and sounds to young eyes and ears.

How awesome was Manhattan Island with its cacophony of foreign voices, but how intimidating, too! The city's unbridled energy, its raw power, thrilled and frightened Rachel at once. She noticed how some people seemed to have a disregard, a callousness of sorts, for each other. It was so different from life on the farm where neighbors were friendly, where no one was a stranger.

Her father was not standoffish like these city people. He liked others and was as good at selling as he was at farming. Ever the talker, Peter van Houten easily engaged those he didn't know, and was not above helping a stranger in need. But he was not careless with his trust. Rachel would never forget what he said to Cornelius that day she first saw the Big City.

"Take the team around back. It's better to offload behind this café, not in front."

Cornelius was surprised. "Why, Pa?" I can pull right up in front there with no problem."

"Do that and there *will be* a problem. Too many people in the street today. You only have two eyes, Son."

"Rachel's here. She can watch while I help unload."

"No. This is her first time. I don't want her to have a bad go of it."

"I was your lookout about her age."

"Yes, and you were about as big then as you are now. You were almost a man. She's not. Never will be."

Rachel always felt safe in the presence of her father.

Some city people, men wearing bowler hats and neckties, hoop-skirted ladies with colorful hats trailing bright feather plumes, fascinated Rachel. She imagined that one day she would dress like these women and would walk sprightly with such confidence. She remembered wondering what it was like to be rich. To know your mind. To be important, like that lady with someone to carry her things.

Others were not like those well-to-do people. Dressed in dirty clothing, much of it tattered, they were the city's have-nots. Rachel knew they were the wretched poor, not to be trusted around a wagon full of farm produce. These creatures could be dangerous! Rachel imagined the ones with rheumy eyes, sunken cheeks, or rotting teeth were the very hobgoblins her mother had warded off by making a cross with the hearth andirons every evening before retiring while the simpering hearth fire turned to ash.

After that first venture, whenever she came to the city with her father, sometimes with one or more of the brothers, Rachel saw the desperate people on the crowded streets that reeked of manure from horses and mules. One time, Henry struck a hobgoblin with the horsewhip when the ragged man tried to steal a melon. Rachel grew accustomed to seeing the "ghost people," as she came to think of them, and her dread, of those she recognized at least, began to wane. Her father's habit of acknowledging the harmless ones with a nod or a smile helped to normalize their presence. Occasionally, Peter gave the ghost people a potato or an apple. One time he handed a pork pie from their dinner pail to a dispirited woman whose filthy hand clutched a hungry urchin.

That was the day she asked her father if she could give the little boy a piece of her candy.

"Yes, Rachel. That would be a kind thing to do. God bless you, child." She would never forget that day.

THINKING OF THOSE CHILDHOOD EXPERIENCES now as her team lumbered along the road to Battle Creek, a city much smaller than New York but also awaiting her discovery, Rachel felt a little charge of excitement percolate through her body.

Her thoughts fixed on family. She knew the van Houten history well, having heard various interpretations from her brothers and sister and from their parents, too. Peter van

Houten had begun adult life as a cobbler, having learned the trade in New Jersey while an apprentice to his father's stepbrother. But Peter had not enjoyed this work. Rarely had he made shoes beyond the needs of his wife and their six children. A decorated veteran of the War of 1812, Peter's first love had been, and still was, farming. After the passing of their father, Rachel's grandfather, Peter, and his twin brother, William, had worked their widowed mother's farm in New Jersey for many years, turning it into a profitable enterprise in spite of the brothers' many differences.

Rachel remembered the grim, unsmiling uncle, identical in appearance to Peter but so unlike him in behavior. Uncle William had not gone beyond what he had professed to know. Corn must be sown on the first day in June, not a day before, and never late. Plowing a field in the fall weakened the soil and was a prescription for failure the next growing season.

Uncle William had never used his rudimentary education to better himself. Because he read no books, he lacked imagination. Unlike Rachel's father, who had gone beyond the pictures in the farming catalogs to understand the theory and practice of tillage and crop rotation and the benefits of grafting orchard fruit, Uncle William had remained ignorant of many exciting discoveries at that time.

Their mother, Rachel's grandmother, had dismissed many of Peter's ideas as the wild dreams of a man too curious, much too willing to throw off the rule of tradition, the yoke of assignment. While her wagon rolled on, Rachel imagined her grandmother. Building upon a vague and early memory, she saw her, severe-looking in a simple black dress with white collar, the face pinched and disapproving beneath a white skullcap, her frown perpetual. Rachel could almost hear her voice telling Peter in that thick, halting English of hers: "You are a shoemaker, not a farmer. And you will never be a farmer of any true success."

And so, Grandmother had agreed with William, the practical one, that throwing manure on a field of corn was unGodly, "a waste of work that brings nary a bushel of corn but many a load of weeds."

Wheels rasping as they turned, Rachel slipped further into reverie. Yes, Father was a dreamer. Praise God that he still lives and can dream on! Were it not for his imagination, his focus on the possibilities of a future life, and planning for that life, he would not have removed his family to New York City soon after Rachel's grandmother passed away.

Rachel remembered family legend about how her father had sold his half of the farm inheritance to Uncle William: "Fifty percent of the appraised value. Not a penny more. Not a penny less!"

That remembrance stirred a smile and a chuckle. "Such are the Dutch." She spoke aloud because no one was near enough to hear. While the team clomped on, she wondered anew what had become of the bachelor uncle, whom she had not seen nor heard any news about for thirty years. The letters Peter had mailed to his brother from New York had brought no response. Later, the ones he sent from Michigan came back to him with "unable to deliver" written on the dirty, wrinkled envelopes.

Had Uncle William ever married? Was the woman dour, like him and Grandmother, or was she cheerful and hopeful? Had William and his pretend wife raised children—indeed twins, as Peter and Ann had done—or was that gift reserved for Peter and his progeny alone?

Rachel knew the story well. William and Peter, so alike in appearance, so unlike in temperament, were the last children of an immigrant woman who had borne five daughters and whose husband, who had prayed for sons, hadn't lived to see his twin boys born.

Why do twins run in my family? Rachel had asked that question many times of Margaret, and because she knew her sister's response by heart, she repeated the words aloud to herself. "It's in God's hands, Rachel. We have no part in what the Lord decides."

The thought always made Rachel laugh inside. "Well, somebody decided to lie down with somebody else, Margaret. Or is it possible there's more than one Immaculate Conception?"

"Oh, Rachel, don't be silly. You know very well what I mean!"

"I do. It's just funny to hear you explain it that way."

Rachel's thoughts again drifted to their parents. Peter and Ann had married young. "Margreet," as Grandmother had insisted on calling their first child, had come ten months later in the spring. The earth had been warm, all the way to the second joint of a probing finger, the right time for planting. Rachel remembered her father's tale of how he had tired of repairing shoes all winter, of how he had wanted to grow things instead of fix things. He and Ann had turned the new granary on his mother's farm into a home, and Peter had joined his recalcitrant brother William in partnership. After Margaret, every two years a boy had arrived. First Cornelius, then Henry followed by John, until Ann's last pregnancy had resulted in a special blessing—Rachel and Helen—living proof that God's grace brings abundant recompense to those who believe and are faithful.

And so it had been with Rachel and Willis: the initial miscarriage, followed by first-born Dwight, and then Watson. Next, had come another stillborn, and, at last, daughter Hester with identical twin Helena close upon. In memory of her own beloved sister, taken so many years before, Rachel and Willis had named their last child "Helena."

Thoughts of family brought to life the image of her beautiful mother. Rachel remembered the tresses of shining brown hair that tumbled from the fasteners when Mother had unloosed them, a joy she had not permitted herself for years after little Helen went to live with Jesus. Rachel had been about four, the unclear memories like swamp vapors. But she could never erase that one image, the bowed heads of her people: the dark and brooding faces of Uncle William and Grandmother, the plain wooden box with the child inside, her dear sister and best friend, fading away into the earth, and then the sadness always enveloped her like the wrap about her shoulders, which failed to bring warmth this cold March morning.

CHAPTER 4

Battle Creek, Michigan

Rachel arrived in Battle Creek at half past the noon meal hour. The city was bigger than Charlotte or Bellevue or any of the other towns she had known since coming to Michigan. But even with its new two-storied buildings, Battle Creek was no Buffalo or Detroit, the only real cities she had seen since leaving New York. The Lansing-to-Battle Creek Road became Maple Street and then Jefferson Street before crossing the rails and the river. Experience with city life suggested the railway would lead to her destination, and Rachel found the telegraph office without asking for directions. Assured her wire message had gone out the day before, she drove the horses across the bridge to Main Street and D. J. Downs Livery where she arranged for their care.

"How long do I need to feed 'em, ma'am," inquired the stable hand, admiring the handsome sorrel team from his seat at a desk. A jovial young man, he was about the age of her own boys.

Rachel hesitated. "I don't know. A week, I'm sure. Longer? Yes. It could be two weeks, maybe more."

Seeing her uncertainty, the clerk wrote a receipt for three dollars and fifty cents, looked up from his desk, and handed it to her. "Well now, if it's more than a week, you can just pay up when you come back." A mischievous grin spread over his smooth face. Cocking head to the side as though speaking to someone else, he shrugged. "Whenever that might be. And if you don't come back, say, after two weeks," he conspired with a giggle, "why, we'll just keep 'em!" Laughing now. "Or sell 'em and keep the money instead."

Her blank face, unmoving, indecipherable, stared back. The boy stopped laughing, jocular features fading. "Sell 'em to the Army, don't you think?" his voice losing confidence. "Heard they needed …" face flushing …"good pull horses for wagons and cannon and whatnot."

Rachel was in no mood for flippancy. Disapproval bearing down, she said nothing. The boy's smirk was gone, replaced by one of humility. "Sorry, ma'am. Meant no offense. Be obliged if you just forgot what I said."

Her voice was level, the tone final. "Feed the grain in the wagon first. Replace it when I return."

"Yes, ma'am. I'll weigh it now and put it in the book."

"Do so. What do you have for forage?

"We're feeding second-cut alfalfa and orchard grass."

"Go two-to-one with alfalfa first."

"Yes, ma'am. I will."

Outside, the air was warmer. Thinking of her sons, Rachel wondered if they would have behaved like this cheeky stable boy. She doubted that Dwight, older and respectful, would be so forward. She was less sure of Watson, though, considering his truculent attitude of late. Rachel worried that one day Watson and her hired man would have a falling out, if they hadn't already come to loggerheads over something, whether real or imagined. She snapped open her husband's timepiece. It was 1:12. Retracing her steps to Jefferson Street, she crossed the river and followed the rails to the depot. There she bought a Through Fare on the Express Train to Chicago, second class, for eight dollars and twenty-five cents. She was finishing a bowl of stew at the lively café across the street when a cur, chained to the post outside, began to howl.

"Train's a-coming!" a fellow diner shouted.

The painful squeal of a braking locomotive assaulted Rachel's ears, followed by the loud clanging of an engine bell. Her eyes flared in alarm at the massive gush of black smoke ahead of the slowing line of passenger cars, and she heard the searing hiss of steam released from its coal-fired boiler. In a final puff of cotton, the 2:48 from Detroit inched closer and stopped, frightening the whimpering dog so badly it wrapped its chain around the hitching post.

"Luggage?" asked the porter, a stout, patch-bearded man about her age. "Any freight today, Mrs.?"

"Nothing." Clutching her bag of possessions, Rachel felt buoyant, pleased that her plan was coming together.

"Help you with that?"

"Thank you. No. Is this the second-class car?"

"All the way to Chicago, ma'am."

The car was half-full. Rachel chose a seat across from a young woman cradling a sleeping baby. The woman looked up and smiled, and Rachel acknowledged the gesture with a nod and a little smile. Thankful for safe travel over the past thirty-some miles, she slid into the seat and closed her eyes. An overwhelming sense of relief soon gave way to a palpable weariness, and she felt as though she could sleep all the way to Chicago.

Closing her eyes, Rachel deliberated if any passengers, like her, were taking their first-ever journey by train. The whistle blast that shattered reverie caused the baby to twitch. The car lurched, paused, and jerked again. Opening her eyes, Rachel saw a plume of black smoke and descent of fly ash swirl past the window. Thankful it was closed, she smelled the acrid odor of burning coal. Slowly, surely, the beast began to stir. As it picked up speed, she could hear and feel the click-clack of wheels rolling over rail joints. It felt good to be on the move again. Every revolution of those iron wheels would bring her closer to Dwight.

After four miles, the train slowed and the wooden platform at Fort Dowling emerged from smoke and steam. Three energetic young men, Union soldiers carrying rifles with bayonets protruding like pruning spears, entered the car. Their knapsacks were slung over woolen frock coats of dark blue. Coal-black leather boots under trousers of light blue clumped as the soldiers moved along, pushing each other and laughing. Rachel's eyes darted from one to another, and trepidation flickered through her while they brandished their rifles about like toy guns. She hoped they were unloaded. Last week John Welch had reminded Watson to unload his squirrel rifle before bringing it indoors for cleaning. These boys seemed a bit older than Watson but not older than Dwight. They tramped past Rachel and the young mother and her infant to the far end of the car where they made a pretense of stacking arms before jumping into empty seats. Rachel was surprised how the baby could sleep through this ruckus, which ceased the moment an officer, a large pistol shoved inside his leather belt with U.S. emblazoned on the brass buckle, appeared in the aisle and claimed a seat near them.

The train jolted to life again. Shutting her eyes, Rachel

recalled reading somewhere that the sound and feel of a train in motion is like the beating of a heart. She imagined that Dwight had ridden in this same passenger car last fall, with Blaze, the handsome Morgan horse Willis had given him for his fifteenth birthday, trailing behind in a freight car. Rachel remembered how ecstatic her son was on his birthday, and how pleased his father was to see him take such pride in the horse, daily currying Blaze's fine-looking coat and cleaning his stall. And then, too quickly, war intervened. For months, her husband had predicted that it was coming, that nothing could stop it, and that when blood finally did spill, why, Willis would sign up in the beat of a heart to teach Secessionists a cruel lesson. Except whenever war did arrive, Willis feared he would be too old.

Rachel remembered him saying, "What government would accept for service a man past forty?" How prescient his words seemed to her now. "There will be no bounty in it for you, my dear, even if I did try to enlist," Willis had joked.

The beat of a heart. Who knew that proud, patriot heart would cease to throb during a summer day of punishing heat spent working too hard, too long, cultivating corn in the twenty-acre field beyond the far pasture? A barefoot Watson, thirteen years old, raced home with the impossible news. Rachel was boiling a pot of new potatoes on the wood stove in her kitchen. The twins, then six years old, were setting the supper table. Panicked and out of breath, a wild-eyed Watson flung open the kitchen door and shrieked, "Mother, come quick! Poppa has fallen in the field! He can't talk. He can't get up!"

Hester dropped a porcelain platter. It struck the pine floorboards and shattered. And time stood still on this afternoon of unbearable heat.

They would not talk about it in the days and months to come. Nor would they ever forget Rachel's inhuman scream that brought bursts of wailing from the twins and skewered Watson in the doorway. "Dwight!" Rachel shouted with all her might. "Dwight! Get Blaze and go fetch Dr. Bigby! Now boy! Hurry and run! Run!"

To what end? Father never opened his eyes, dying late that night in the bed where his distraught sons and their weeping sisters, fragile and pale as the broken platter, had been born.

Rachel's mind, unhinged with grief for months, unable to recall which day of the week it was, slowly and incrementally restored itself since the terrible event with support from the church and help from her brothers, sister Margaret, and their families. Her aging father, Peter, made it his habit to drop in more often than usual. The arrival of John Welch, though, was the decisive turning point in the improvement of Rachel's health. Were it not for the hired man's cheerful, optimistic attitude, coupled with his practical experience in all matters of agriculture, she might have lost the farm that she and Willis had worked so hard to create and to keep going after Dwight went off to war.

Now, the metronome of clicking rails and swaying passenger car had a mesmerizing effect, and Rachel imagined her girls in the kitchen, their too-large, blousy aprons close to the floor. So serious were they, consumed with the task of making supper for Watson, and for John Welch.

She speculated about what the twins were preparing to eat and thought baked ham and potatoes a likely choice. She wondered what Watson was doing now that he had quit school and had no assignments to bring home. Were her reticent son and the hired man getting along, or had the friction between them grown during her two days of absence? There was no way to know. Of one outcome, however, Rachel was certain: the dilemma she had created for herself by insisting to be on this train at this moment.

There would be no solace, here or there, until she found Dwight and knew what had happened to him.

SIX MONTHS AFTER WILLIS DIED, three months before the hired man's arrival, a federal census taker had come to the Barnum farm. The month was January, the year 1860. The day was bitterly cold, and snow lay deep in the farm lane. The agent wrote: "Rachel Barnum, age 38, Hd. of Household. Occupation: Farmer." The boys were sixteen and fourteen, the girls now eight. That label, "Head of Household," stirred memories whenever Rachel peered through her kitchen window toward the knoll, a daily ritual confirming her husband's grave and parlor chair were still there. If there was sun, she might keep watch until light bathed the tombstone and it seemed to glow. Late in the day she sometimes kept vigil until a shadow from the white cedar sapling she had planted there, the day after Willis was laid to rest, touched the marker. On days of acute loneliness, she would walk over and sit for a spell in Willis' chair. Sometimes she spoke aloud to him.

Today was Thursday. Tomorrow would be one week since Marshall Dickenson had sent the telegram. While the train powered ahead to Chicago, Rachel laid a hand over her restless heart. She pressed shut her eyes and allowed her mind to fill with happy times: the bouquet of spring beauties she had gathered for her mother from a Manhattan woodlot, the slender rocking chair—a surprise from Willis—when the twins were born. Her thoughts were never far from Willis.

They met for the first time at the blacksmith shop in

Sunfield on a summer morning of stifling heat. Willis was already there with his horse to be fitted for a new bit. Rachel, who would be nineteen in October, came to pick up a scythe Peter had left for repair. Willis appeared to be older than she, four or perhaps five years older, but he didn't look familiar. She wondered who he was.

Other young men had glanced her way as she grew into womanhood, but this fellow seemed to center on her and would not look away. Rachel assumed something was awry. Had she torn her dress or dirtied it somehow on the buggy ride up Shaytown Road? He smiled and spoke first. "G'morning, Miss. If I said, 'Good morning,' you might think I meant it's good and hot."

"Indeed, it is warm today."

"Is it ever! And it's not yet ten o'clock."

Silas Rowe, the blacksmith, looked up from the forge he was tending. "Gets much hotter, I'll be working outside in the shade."

"Do you have my father's scythe ready?" Rachel asked.

"Almost. I want to put a wee more edge to the blade. How about thirty minutes?"

"Of course. I'm in no hurry. You can serve this gentleman first."

"Hah!" the blacksmith huffed. "You mean Willis? He's always in a yank!"

"That's because I'm a Yankee. New England bred and born. I'm a Yank, Silas, through and through."

Rachel took note of the young man's smile. She watched how it splayed into a face-full grin before she looked away.

"Ha, hah! Good one, there, Willis." Silas turned back to Rachel. His face betrayed smudges of soot from wiping perspiration on his leather apron. "Your father's blade's in the furnace now, Miss. It won't be long." Bellows in one hand, he opened the foundry door, and a surge of suffocating heat belched out. "Whew! No need for more air in there. It's white-hot now."

"Want to sit outside while we wait, Miss?" the young man asked. "Silas is plum-full of hot air today. He'll work faster if there's no one to talk to."

Rachel liked his playful manner. Suppressing what could have been loud laughter, she smiled and retreated to private thought: *He knows what to say and how to say it, too!*

Near the hitching rail, they sat apart on a long bench in the shadow of a leafy maple. This friendly young man, this Willis, was easy to talk to. He introduced himself, and she told him her name. When he said he knew her brother Henry, Rachel turned to face him.

"You know Henry?"

"Yes, I think we're the same age. He's twenty-four, isn't he?"

"He is. But how is it you know him?"

"Henry witnessed a land deal for me in the spring over at the bank there," Willis said and pointed. "April it was. Nice fellow your brother. Smart, too, I gather."

"Yes. He takes after our father."

"Let's see, now—that would be Peter van Houten, right? I know him, too."

"What is this? You know my father, too?"

"Well, I know who he is. And now that I've met you, Miss Rachel, I think I know your whole family. A family with an admirable reputation I might add."

This exchange flummoxed her. How could this fellow, a stranger, know so much about her family? Perceiving her confusion, Willis explained that because he brokered land transactions—selling and buying properties throughout Sunfield and adjoining townships—he knew most residents by name, if not in person.

Rachel recognized the surname Barnum from a township in neighboring Barry County and now could put a first name and actual person to it. Like her affable father, Willis was proving to be a good conversationist. Margaret had told her one measure of a man depended upon how much he talked about himself. Willis proclaimed nothing personal, least of all boastful, and it was not a woman's place to probe. He was interesting and knowledgeable. And this Willis Barnum was handsome. Those expressive brown eyes were most captivating.

Not only did Rachel enjoy talking with him, she liked looking at him but was careful not to look too hard. Glimpses were appropriate. They would do.

"Are you going to the Fletcher hoedown?" Willis blurted.

The question took her by surprise. "Hoedown?"

"The barn dance at the Fletchers. It's on the trail to Charlotte, five miles or so from your father's place."

"A hoedown?" she repeated.

"They're celebrating on account of their barn being finished. They'll be dancing to music till they can't dance no more. I'll go but only if you promise me a step or two."

"Oh, I don't know." Rachel's hesitation threatened to expose her ignorance. A pang of panic squeezed her chest. She didn't know what to say. "I'm not sure. I don't know that we're allowed to go."

Willis laughed. "Everyone's allowed to go. Nobody's waiting for an invitation to come in the mail. Or to drop out of the blue."

"Oh. Well, I don't know. When is it?"

"Saturday evening. Ask your brother Henry to take you. I'll bet he's going."

The thought of a barn dance doubled Rachel's pulse. Her face flushed from internal heat. Something exciting, something unfamiliar, was happening to her.

"Henry could be your chaperone." Willis' eyes were stuck on hers. His radiant smile was back. "I'd take you myself, but we're not married yet."

No man had ever embarrassed her like that! Rachel knew her face was as red as a ripe tomato. Surely, he saw her embarrassment. Did he also know her thrill? She looked into those alluring brown eyes and tried to stifle a laugh but failed. "Sir, your humor is too much," she spurted. "You are, are—how do they say it—'utterly too too.'"

"Then, fan my brow. They say that, too. And Lord knows it's sure hot enough for that!"

Their banter continued until the blacksmith came out of his shop. They were too engaged to notice. "Scythe's ready for field work," Silas announced. "Tell Peter to drop off a half-dollar next time he's in town."

"Oh, he gave me money. I can pay you now."

"Come back into my sweatshop and I'll give you a paid bill." Turning to Willis, Silas told him to unhitch his horse and he would see about making a bit even if was hot as the devil's den in there.

THAT SATURDAY WILLIS WAS WAITING for her at the Fletcher homestead when Henry and Rachel turned off the Charlotte Trail in their father's surrey. Rachel's stepmother, Suzanne, had loaned Rachel a tan pleated skirt with delicate floral prints and braided trim. The corseted skirt with its deep-maroon accents complemented a white blouse and matching trim. Suzanne had brought the garments, still in their packing box after three years, from their old home in New York. Rachel's dark hair, parted and fastened in the back, added to the apparel, which fit her without alteration.

A stem of cardinal flower, plucked from shade in her father's woods and plaited into her hair, was perfect. The face that looked back from the hand mirror in her bedroom pleased her. A crowned princess could not have looked better. But would it please her beau?

Oh, she was lovely and Willis knew it! He was captivated with everything about her. In their life to come, Willis joked that when he saw Rachel Barnum that evening, he was smitten so speechless he could have choked on his tongue.

Over several hours, they danced to lively jigs, paired off with other couples to a new routine called the square dance, and drew close while a waltz played through. They danced with each other except when other young men, attracted to Rachel like hummingbirds to a bright flower, interposed and asked for a turn with her.

After each number she went back to an impatient Willis, who asked no one else for dance favors because he couldn't tear his eyes from her. He was loathe to see her with anyone, and feared losing her to an interloper. Dressed in a brown, herringbone-tweed frock coat and brown trousers, Willis may have been overdressed for a barn dance; if so, no one said anything. Rumor, however, traveled throughout the township that they made for a smashing couple that night.

And no one was surprised when Willis Barnum asked Peter van Houten for his daughter's hand in marriage a scant month after the Fletcher barn dance.

CHAPTER 5

Michigan Central RR

What is more affirming of life than an infant gently roused from the deep sleep of dreams? Rachel opened her eyes a moment before the baby—arms entwined around his mother's neck—responded to a kiss, rolled over, and revealed two saucers of angelic blue. Cheeks flushed with the health that comes from tenderness and love and the unfettered sleep of innocence, the child met Rachel's gaze and smiled. Enthralled by this perfect baby, whom she guessed was about a year old, Rachel watched him until sensibility insisted she stop.

Where do the children go, when they slumber, if not into the arms of the Lord?

Had she read that passage somewhere? Or had the words manifested themselves from her own experience? It didn't matter. Rachel could not keep her thoughts to herself. "You are blessed with a beautiful baby boy."

The young woman, about half her age, beamed. "His

blond hair and blue eyes are just like his father's. We're going to see him in Chicago. He's with the First Illinois. He's got a furlough."

She told Rachel her name was Edith, Edith Wirksky. They talked into the evening while the car rocked and kept time to the music of the rails. Edith was curious about Sunfield. Rachel related the story of how a courier had ridden his horse twenty miles to the state capital in Lansing to submit the new township's name for official approval. A shower had wetted the contents of the rider's saddlebag, and no one had been able to decipher the paper petition. A government clerk had said the smeared ink looked like "some field." They had decided, then, on "Sunfield."

"I love that story!" Edith remarked. "Sunfield sounds like a wonderful place to live."

Rachel agreed that it was a beautiful place, and she could imagine home being nowhere else on earth. "The soil is rich," she added. "The fields grow good crops. Most farmers do well. It's a good place to raise a family."

"It sounds like a garden of Eden."

"Yes, I suppose it does. And in a way, it's like a beautiful garden. So peaceful. So calm there. I hope this war won't change it. Won't destroy it." And Rachel described the land, her neighbors, and the new settlements of Shaytown, Hoytville, and Sunfield while purposely withholding intimate details about Willis and their children.

Ethan, the baby, began to fuss. Excusing herself, Edith shifted in her seat, rearranged the infant's blanket to cover herself, and proceeded to feed him. Rachel closed her eyes and turned away. She was thinking about home and how Willis' passing had turned life upside down and how it had grown more stable, more normal since John Welch arrived. Her mind drifted to the consequences of choice. Had she not married Willis, had not borne Dwight and cared for him—as this young mother tended to her baby's needs—why, she would not be on this train going to her son now. That thinking led to other fundamental decisions over which she had no say and therefore no control. What if her ancestors had settled in New Orleans and not New Jersey? Would she have become a Secessionist? Would Dwight be part of a Confederate cavalry unit? Would she be on a train going north, not south, to find him?

The train stopped for coal and water. Later, it paused for a half-hour on a blackened siding and waited for an eastbound line of cars to pass. Holding Edith's baby now, Rachel pointed out the oncoming engine's headlamp, quivering as it grew larger and brighter, and she counted aloud the people going by in the weakly-lit coaches. Ethan made gurgling noises and squealed, and the women laughed, and Rachel's disquiet went away. At other stops, the train took on more passengers and, because no one got off, the second-class car began to fill.

At Niles, the conductor announced a stop of twenty minutes. In a loud voice, he reminded passengers to take their tickets with them to the toilets or food emporium and to listen for his whistle. "You'll hear it three minutes afore this train leaves," he instructed. "The engine whistle and then the bell means we're getting up a head of steam. By then you'd best be on board unless you want to stay the night in bee-ute-a-full Niles, Michigan."

At the far end of the car, the Army officer, a lieutenant as indicated by the chevrons on his coat sleeve, stood up. He adjusted the pistol in his belt and spun around to leave. The instant his back was turned, one of the soldiers made a face by shoving little fingers in his nostrils and hooking thumbs in mouth corners. With the other fingers, he tugged on his cheeks and looked down at his nose. The unexpected face was instantly grotesque, savagely piglike, and it shocked Rachel into laughter. Her wonderful reaction prompted the soldier to wag his tongue at the departing officer, who was looking at Rachel. He whipped around, but the boy's pliable face had already turned normal. Staring back at his superior, he blinked emphatically. One of his seatmates yelped; the other looked out the darkened window and smothered a giggle.

"I'll have your head for this, Huffman!" the officer glared. "I know what you're about, and when I get you—and I will get you—you're going into the stockade. Then we'll see who's laughing." The outburst over, he stormed down the aisle and left the train.

Huffman, agile as a barn cat, leaped to his feet and pretended to tiptoe after the officer. Pausing at the women's seat, he winked at Rachel. "After you, ma'am," he removed his Kepi, drew back arms, and offered an exaggerated bow.

"Upon my word!" Shaking her head, Rachel spoke directly to her new friend. "I've never seen such a performance in my life." Rachel looked up at the leering soldier. He reminded her of the oafish farm boys that always came back to school in winter, big, ignorant boys who stumbled over the words they read aloud, young men nearly as old as the teachers they taunted. "And you, sir, may move along. For shame!"

Huffman shrugged, replaced his cap, and grinned. "What's my making sport got to do with you, lady? 'Cept I got you to laugh." And he strode away with the others in tow.

Creeping into Chicago's Great Central Station, the locomotive wheezed to a stop. Its iron bell, reverberating in the cavernous building, drowned out the station clock, a towering timepiece that made a brave effort to bong out the nine o'clock hour. Rachel carried her belongings and those of Edith Wirksky, whose arms were full with a suddenly active child. Rachel sensed a sadness welling up at the certainty of losing her new friend so soon. Why, they had scarcely begun to talk, it seemed, and here they were in Chicago, the trip already over. Bending low as she walked along, Edith peered through the gritty coach windows, supposedly hoping to spot her husband. Rachel, laden with blankets and baby things, followed close.

Rachel sensed her regret was rooted in having withheld from Edith her real story, not the fabrication that she had come to Chicago to visit her cousin. Had Edith asked, Rachel might have explained why a widow would leave three children home in Michigan to come here. And to go, alone, to Missouri. Now, Rachel felt anxious over being abandoned, but she also realized there was no one to blame except herself. Had her time with the young woman consumed another hour—a simple, single hour—she could have shared her fears, her hopes, with this loyal wife and doting mother. Surely, Edith would have understood her predicament. She would have supported her decision to leave the farm.

Intuitively, but also reinforced from a lifetime of practice, Rachel knew how insularity, time spent alone, was a breeding ground for self-doubt. A niggling fear that she had chosen poorly of late swept into her thoughts. Since leaving home, she had twice forfeited the chance to open up with others, to share her plight. Over the years such behavior was familiar enough, but was it the wise thing to do with home growing farther and farther away?

HANDSOME IN HIS BLUE UNIFORM, the leather strap of an unseen knapsack crossing his heart, Joseph Wirksky stood erect along the busy platform as passengers climbed down from the train. Rachel saw how the shining buttons of his blue longcoat were fastened all the way to a clean-shaven chin. She surmised the tall, lean soldier with straw-colored hair sticking from the blue cap to half-cover his ears, was Edith's husband. He carried no rifle. A sling of white cloth suspended his left arm in a half-salute. Edith had mentioned an injury.

The crowd thickened as people disembarked to mill with those waiting. A Negro porter appeared, and then another. Pushing their wooden carts along, they yelled "Luggage?" and "Freight?" and weaved in and out to avoid bumping into anyone.

As Edith forced her way toward her husband, Joseph came alive, whooped, and tore away his cap. Smacking it along his thigh, he rushed forward and seized wife and child in a one-armed, powerful hug. Ethan shrieked in terror at this stranger who had captured him and his mother. Following close behind, Rachel instinctively accepted the infant. She half-turned so he could see his mother pressing a tearful cheek against the breast of this dangerous man in blue. Rachel cooed in Ethan's ear and stroked his blond head, even as the man was doing the same to the baby's mother.

When Rachel handed back the baby, Edith pressed her hand. "Thank you," she said. "I hope you have a wonderful time with your cousin here in Chicago. And I hope one day we can meet again."

Rachel shot Edith a quizzical look. "Oh, I'm not really going to see my cousin. I'm going to Missouri."

"Missouri?" It was Joseph's turn to be shocked. "Lot of trouble down there. Rebels thick as horseflies." A stunned Edith looked with wonder at Rachel. "Where in Missouri you got to go, ma'am?" Joseph asked.

"New Madrid."

"New Madrid? 'Taint possible! You can't get to New Madrid. They're fighting down there! Gen. Pope's there now with the whole 4th Corp."

Rachel's heart sank and she trembled. "I thought the Army drove the Rebels out of New Madrid." Her speech was imploding. "The paper said they took it a fortnight ago. I read it in the paper. It's not true?"

"Oh, it's true enough. But it ain't over yet. See, Gen. Pope can't get across the river to Tennessee where U.S. Grant wants him. Pope's stuck at New Madrid Bend." Shaking his head, as though he couldn't believe his own words, the young soldier turned to his wife. "She can't get to New Madrid. Nobody can get there."

Rachel gasped, shot through by a spasm of fear.

Private Joseph Wirksky explained how the Confederates had garrisoned Island No. 10 with a force thought to number at least three thousand men. How they had fortified the mile-long island, a short distance upstream from New Madrid, with heavy artillery, and how more batteries—including several with huge, powerful cannon—were dug in along the Tennessee shore.

Crushing despair seized Rachel as the soldier went on to say the enemy waited there to rake Pope's boat transports with shot and shell the minute the Union commander tried to cross the river with his army. Joseph was insistent. "Ain't nobody getting past Island No. 10, so long as the Rebels are there. No packets. No boats of any kind. Nothing."

Now, they were talking in the waiting hall. Rachel, sitting with Edith and the baby on a bench, was unaware of others coming and going. Dejected, slumped over with elbows on knees, Rachel gripped her head in both hands. Her head hurt; she felt nauseous. She listened, but did not want to believe what she heard, while Joseph droned on.

"The Navy's Foote got six, maybe eight gunboats, all of them covered in iron, just sitting on the river above that island. Look like black turtles out there. Might as well be turtles for all the good they're doing." Waving his good arm about, he kept at it. "Foote won't chance losing even one of his precious gunboats to the Rebels. Pope's whole army is bogged down in Missouri because of one fool-headed, stubborn Scotsman. "They say the War Department in Washington can't even get that old man to do something."

When he paused, Rachel tried to make sense of this impossible turn of events. She couldn't bear to look at the messenger of news so disturbing.

Joseph resumed his discourse. "See, it's like chess. But there's two games going on at the same time. One's between us and the Rebels. They don't want Pope in Tennessee. They got their hands full with Grant down there. The other game's between our own Army and Navy. Been in checkmate since our boys took New Madrid. Someone has to make a move. I don't see how it goes on like this forever."

Aware of Edith's hand on her shoulder, Rachel finally looked up. "How do you know all this?" she implored of the demonstrative husband.

"I just come up from Cairo on the afternoon train. Back in the winter most of the boys in the 1st Illinois went down to Tennessee with Grant. I didn't go. I got to stay in Cairo. I got chose for river duty, checking the packets and all for contraband. It's how I got hurt. Got my arm cut pretty bad in an accident."

The childhood fear of drowning in an abyss could haunt Rachel's thoughts without warning. Like now. Brothers John and Henry had pulled her back from a farm pond in New Jersey when, as a toddler, she had waded out too far. There was no one to save her now. "But I must go to New Madrid. I have to get there. Now! If I can't go by river, I'll go by shore."

"I don't see how, ma'am. It's fifty, sixty miles from Cairo."

"Well, surely, there's a rail!"

"On the Missouri side? Not anymore. Rebs, or us Yanks, tore most of it up."

"Then a road!"

"Oh, there was a road, sure enough. The King's Way. Do you know what thousands of soldiers, hundreds on horses, can do to a muddy old trail in winter? It ain't a road no more. So I been told."

"Then what am I to do?" Rachel's grief grew to wailing. Her loud cry was directed to anyone other than this young soldier, who step by shocking step, was erasing—destroying—her chance at ever seeing her son again.

"Well, if it was me, I'd wait here in Chicago, or maybe Cairo, for Island No. 10 to give up the farm. Rebs built a big trap for themselves on that island. I'm sure of that, too. I don't see how they can hold out forever."

Rachel's voice choked on her words. "I don't have forever. I don't have a day to waste. I don't have another hour to lose!" She looked at Edith and the baby. Perched on his mother's knees, Ethan was sucking a thumb. "My son is very sick. I have to go to him."

Edith sucked in a deep breath. She squeezed Rachel's arm. "My God, dear woman! Where is he?"

"He's in a hospital in New Madrid. He's dying." Her

voice trailing off, Rachel's head plunged, collapsing into her body. Her voice was a whisper. "He could already be gone."

No one said anything. The only sounds were those of shuffling footsteps and the murmur of passersby. Somewhere a clock struck half-past notes, its deep, sonorous tone a sober warning to Rachel. *Was that a premonition? Why is this happening now? What does it mean? Should I turn back and go home?*

When Joseph spoke, his commanding voice was like the final hammer blow on an anvil. "Miz Barnum, there ain't no hospital in New Madrid. I know because I spent two weeks at the one in Cairo. There ain't no hospital in New Madrid because there weren't no casualties. None to speak of anyway. Cairo is the only hospital all the way down the river to Memphis. And that one's Secesh."

CHAPTER 6

Chicago, Illinois

Rachel missed the 9:20 p.m. to Cairo by fifteen minutes. That revelation, on top of the numbing details from Joseph Wirksky, was a needle to the heart. With hope melted away, her spirit had plummeted into despair. The clerk at the ticket window told her the next train departed Great Central Station at 6:10 in the morning. While he gaped at her, a distracted Rachel reached into her dress for the leather purse, suspended between her breasts by a thin lanyard of rawhide. Counting out twelve dollars in coins, she handed them to the clerk. Later, she thought he had returned a dime and a half-dime but was too inattentive to be sure.

"You all right, ma'am?" The railway agent was talking to her through the gated window. It could have been a solid wall, such was her disorientation.

She answered with a question. "Which track?"

"That would be No. 8."

"What time does the train to Cairo arrive?" She saw his

confusion. "I mean, arrive here, in Chicago."

"Five-twelve in the morning. You can board it for the outbound any time after that. Now that you have your ticket."

Rachel looked at her fingers, surprised to find them clutching the ticket. Her thoughts were on John Welch, pinned to his words. "I could go for you. It won't be so hard if I was to go in your place."

"I can reserve a stateroom in one of the sleeper cars, ma'am, if you want me to," the clerk offered. "They're new Pullmans. Really comfortable with wash bowl and looking glass. Just six dollars more."

"No, but thank you."

"You understand the trip to Cairo is almost eighteen hours."

She was already moving away. Rachel returned to the waiting room, to the same bench, now empty, she had shared with the young couple and their baby. Slumping into the hard seat of worn oak, she fought to organize her scattered thoughts, to put back in order what had just unraveled. To rationalize her decision to do this by herself.

Yes, she could have taken John Welch's advice not to travel alone. But he could do nothing more about this setback than she could.

Yes, she might have been better prepared before leaving the farm. But how to plan for anything, let alone everything, with such little warning? There was no time to be ready!

What else could she have done? What should she do now? The answers would come if only she could think this through, slowly, clearly. There was nothing to do now except wait for the morning train. How could she have known what Joseph Wirksky knew without coming here and finding out for herself?

Rachel knew the newspapers were not always reliable. They often distorted news to fit some purpose other than reporting real facts, real truths. Joseph's report was crushing, to be sure, but was it accurate? What if his lecturing was gossip, that ugly partner to rumor? Of this much Rachel was certain: The trip had just begun, and when she got to Cairo, there would be more details, fresh information, and it could be in her favor. After all, the War was a year old already, and they say nothing changes things like war. What passes for news today can be discounted, even debunked, tomorrow.

Perhaps it was the way he said it. So confident, so certain he knew everything. Yes, that's what troubled her so. But that didn't mean the young man was right, did it? He could have mixed things up, could have gotten his facts wrong.

How could he know everything? How could he be so sure? Joseph Wirksky was a private in the Army, working from a nameless boat on the Mississippi River. He couldn't know everything. Maybe he knew nothing. Didn't he say he was in the hospital for two weeks?

He claimed there was no hospital in New Madrid. Well, he's wrong about that, isn't he? Rachel snatched the yellow paper, deftly tucked within her dress. "From: War Dept. U.S. Army regiment hosp. New Madrid, Missouri." Right there! "Hosp." means "hospital," doesn't it?

If Dwight is in a hospital, they're taking care of him. Marshall and the other boys who went into the War with her son would see to it. They knew each other. Neighbors and friends protected each other. The fact that Marshall sent the telegram was proof undeniable that he was looking out for her son!

When a food vendor strolled past, Rachel did not look

up. She wasn't hungry, only exhausted, though sleep would be impossible. Her mind was too active for sleep. The station clock sounded ten times. Retrieving the pocket watch from her bag, she advanced it a minute, two minutes, wound it a little, and put it back. She could not leave Chicago for seven hours. Seven endless hours. An eternity for someone in pain, whether someone is a mother laboring to give birth or a child suffering from a sickness. She must be patient. Must be still. Must maintain control. Returning the watch to the bag, she produced her bible. Here, among the pages with the corners turned down, she would lose herself in Psalm 121:

> *I lift up my eyes to the hills.*
> *From whence does my help come?*
> *My help comes from the Lord,*
> *who made heaven and earth…*
> *… The Lord will keep*
> *your going out and your coming in*
> *from this time forth and for*
> *evermore.*

Deep into the long night, Rachel read, and sometimes her mind slipped into a half-conscious state. Jarred awake, aware again of her surroundings, she heard anew the clock bonging and the occasional train braking into the station or thundering away. People came and went, some with purpose, some without. As long as something stirred, a city was alive whether that city was New York or Chicago. In every minute of every day, something was happening somewhere in a big city.

Rachel smelled the alcohol before she saw him. Snapping shut the book, she pulled her belongings closer and shoved the open end of the travel bag under her bottom. His ashen fingers, the nails dirty and broken, were already on the bench rail, not to steal but to steady himself. Drunk, stumbling, he could barely stand.

The child's fear of vagrant people in the Big City seared to mind like a lightning blast. Heart throbbing, throat constricting, Rachel swallowed hard and wrestled with her emotions to regain control. During the next minute or two, she realized he would take nothing, was incapable of hurting her, and her alarm dissolved to irritation at being disturbed. She saw him for the innocuous bum he was.

"Ma'am, kin you spare a half-dime?" The shabby man's voice was like a child's toy whistle. Not loud. Annoying.

He was too close. The foul breath was on her face. Rachel scrutinized him, taking in the bent shoulders, the torn and grimy coat, the matted hair streaked with gray, and thought about waving him away. Disgusted, she wondered how old he was? Much younger than her father. Her father, a proud and contented man. Approaching eighty, he still worked on the farm he and her brothers had hewn from the Michigan wilderness.

Rachel perused the intruder's wet eyes and, when they did not look away, she caught there the trace of dignity; somewhere there, the hint of independence. A former fierceness? It was not a trick of the gas lamps. Her ire over having her sleep violated was fading. "Why?" she demanded. "For whiskey? For beer? The answer is no!"

"For food." His voice was weak. "I ain't et today."

"When did you eat something last?"

"I dunno. Mebbe yestiday."

Rachel saw toes protruding from his beaten shoes. She knew what her father would do. "Wait here," she said.

With the half-dime, she bought a loaf of cold bread

and a wedge of cheese. In the dim, low-burning lamp near the vendor's stand, Rachel held the cheese to her nose and smelled Muenster. She asked for an apple. Soft like the cheese, it was a bit mealy, a winter survivor from the harvest of months ago. She thought about requesting a better candidate and remembered his teeth. The money was enough for a second purchase, a smaller piece of cheese and a handful of crackers. These she wrapped in a swatch of cloth and put in her bag.

Rachel pointed to the beggar sitting on her bench and looking at the floor. "Give that man a cup of water. When he comes for it."

Standing over him, Rachel broke the loaf and offered the larger portion. Then she presented the cheese. He took the food and began to say something, but she dismissed him with a flick of her hand. "Go and eat. That man over there will give you a drink. Water. Not whiskey."

Head bowed, he mumbled, "Thank ye. God in heaven bless ye."

She wanted to speak, but the catch in her throat wouldn't let her.

After he was gone, the picture of the frightened little girl was back in Rachel's thoughts. Shivering, she removed her blanket, pulled tight the drawstring on the carrying bag, and wrapped the rope around her wrist to discourage theft. With the blanket around legs, she lifted them onto the bench and lay on her side, legs curled. There was no pillow. The book would do.

She might have done more. Should she have done more? Such niggling doubt could spark circumspection, and that often led to a search for an apt memory from her worn bible. She recalled it without effort: *It is easier for a camel to pass through the eye of a needle than for a rich man to enter heaven.*

After Willis had passed, Rachel continued to tithe, without ceremony, increasing the amount of self-imposed sacrifice a little each year. Was it enough? How much must one have before God judges that person rich? How much must one give to earn mercy? Such questions were often in her thoughts. Rachel did not consider herself wealthy, although others might—no, would—if they knew how the Barnum bounty had kept increasing, the result of her late husband's unmatched ability to buy land at one price and sell it at another. Rachel knew that since she and Willis had married, when he was twenty-four and she nineteen, that God had blessed them abundantly.

So, was 10 percent enough? Maybe she should have given the beggar all the cheese and bread. The crackers, too. The unresolved question could lead to others. Was it not enough that she, a second-class passenger, had denied herself the luxury of the Pullman? That decision, the result of generations of denial, had been easy because it came natural to her. Rachel, and her father, and her father's father had accumulated nothing of value without the pain of sacrifice. Therefore, how could one be considered wealthy, be deemed rich if one did not spend for personal gratification? Her people had practiced the dictum, laid down long ago by the church reformists, to near perfection. It was how Rachel's grandmother, Peter's "moeder," had come to America, had married Peter's "vader," another Dutch immigrant, and had bought land. That New Jersey land, half of which became her father's inheritance, had made possible Peter and his family's move to New York City after little Helen died.

Success in the city, though, had not come without cost. Rachel knew that had it not been for the constant thrift and relentless labor, the van Houtens' achievements as farmers would never have occurred. She would not be here now, would not be waiting in Chicago for a train to take her closer to her fallen son—she did not want to dwell on that right now—had her father not left New York for Michigan, "the land of milk and honey," so they said, and where he had bought eighty heavily wooded acres, before he ever saw the parcel, and where he and his sons—Rachel's brothers— had fallen to with ax and saw and had built first a log home, and then a frame house and within three years after that had cleared the forest for cultivation. Amazing feats!

"A man who must pay interest," Peter van Houten was fond of saying, "has one foot already in the debtor's prison. 'Tis always better to collect interest, but one must remember to give God His due."

And, so, what was His exact due?

Rachel considered for a moment the plight of her neighbors, most of whom had forty acres and sometimes two forties. Cornelius owned three forties in the section next to hers, and John Dow, the township supervisor, a well-off Hollander, claimed two eighties. She and Willis Barnum, of English ancestry, had acquired three hundred and sixty acres, more than a half-section, during their seventeen years of marriage. At the time of her husband's death in 1858, he had cleared half of it through hard work and through his capacity to pay others to do so. That land, valued at $5,000 in the 1860 census two years ago, now belonged to Rachel. And one must consider the value of her personal property, $3,700 according to the government's estimate, and, now, official record.

No one, except the government, ostensibly for property tax purposes, knew what Rachel Barnum was worth. In turn, she knew little about the financial details of her relatives and neighbors. It was good that people kept such personal matters to themselves. Still, she was aware how Betsey Barnum, Willis' widowed cousin by marriage, struggled to support five children on her forty acres. Rachel knew how hard it was for the proud Betsey, who lived with her family down the road, to ask Rachel for money to buy crop seeds. Two weeks ago, or was it already three weeks now, Rachel had sent John Welch over there to teach Betsey's oldest boy, Harrison, how to help a distressed cow with the calving.

At any time, such troubles could visit any farmer, rich or poor, and among the people Rachel knew best, Betsey Barnum was the least well-off. Betsey had also lost her husband too soon but not before fathering five children, two boys and three girls, an otherwise intact family living together under the same roof. Rachel and Betsey, similar in that they were widows, different in that Rachel had means. Betsey did not.

But Betsey had her children. Gathering the blanket closer, Rachel deliberated who was richer, she or her husband's cousin? The answer vaulted to mind so forcefully that she tossed aside her blanket and sat upright. She, Rachel, was richer, and she knew why: John Welch.

CHAPTER 7

April, 1859
Sunfield, Michigan

Someone was knocking on her farmhouse door, and Rachel couldn't imagine who had come calling. Today was a school day. Watson and his sisters, Hester and Helena, had gone in the pony cart to the log schoolhouse two miles south on Shaytown Road. Dwight had not returned to school after their father passed the summer before, and was in the barn prepping implements for spring sowing. Wiping hands covered in bread flour on her apron, Rachel hurried through the parlor and opened the door.

She didn't recognize the man standing there, cap in hand, his questionable age masked by a full beard as black as an Angus steer. Rachel thought he was at least thirty, not older than forty. Probably close to thirty-five. "Yes? Are you looking for someone? Or some thing?"

"I'm here to see a Mrs. Barnum, if this is the right place, that is."

"Yes, I'm Rachel Barnum."

"I'm John Welch, Mrs. Barnum. I'm here about a posting for a farm hand. Are you still looking to hire someone?"

He told her he had heard of an opening for fulltime labor near Sunfield while at the county courthouse in Charlotte where he worked as a janitor. "I came over this morning on account of having the day off," he explained. "Otherwise, I'd be at work all day."

Rachel liked hearing that. It showed responsibility. Her question about experience with farming opened the beard to expose a grin, in turn, allowing a little laugh. "Oh, only about half my life. The first half of it anyway. I was born to farming in Vermont. Ended up here in Michigan when I was twenty."

Without equivocation, he answered her questions about sowing and harvesting and the management of livestock. Rachel regarded how when speaking he looked directly at her. He was the right age, not too young, not too old. And he had experience. She concluded the interview with, "Well, Mr. Welch, if you don't mind going down to the barn and meeting my son, Dwight, you both can come up to the house and we'll talk about an arrangement."

"That would be just fine, ma'am."

"Meanwhile, I have dough to knead and bread to bake."

An hour later, John Welch agreed to a job offer for room and board and a dollar for each day of work, with the exception of Sunday when no hard labor would occur.

April 1861

TWO YEARS LATER, ALMOST TO the day, Watson was coming in from one of Rachel's fallow fields with draft horse Sam after unloading the stone boat. It was late morning on a Tuesday. The girls were at school. Dwight and the hired man had finished mending a section of pasture fence and were sitting on the front porch waiting for Rachel's call to dinner.

Harrison Barnum, Betsey's son, raced into the yard. He was waving a newspaper and shouting. "He did it! Lincoln's finally called for an army. He wants volunteers!"

Spitting out his pipe, John Welch caught it between chore-worn fingers. "When?" He bore into the boy. "How many volunteers?"

"Now! He needs seventy-five thousand men!"

John's attention snapped to Rachel's older son. "Dwight, what will you do? You've been raring to go. Will you go now?"

The astounding news also caught Dwight unaware. Springing from his chair, he swallowed hard and cleared his throat. "Yes, I'll go. If Ma will let me, I'll sign up tomorrow."

"I'll go with you, Dwight," Harrison offered. "Wat and I will sign up, too. We'll all go in together, like the three musketeers."

The hired man broke in. "Well, that won't happen. You and Watson are too young. Got to wait a couple years."

"Then I'll lie and say I'm eighteen."

That announcement made John laugh. "Harrison, you don't even look sixteen. How could you pass for eighteen?"

The topic switched to when actual fighting would begin and where the first battle, if there was to be a real battle, would happen. As they speculated, the door opened and Rachel stepped out into a warm breeze that carried the fragrance of blooming lilacs. "Harrison," she said, "can I see your newspaper?"

Harrison handed her the broadsheet. "Dwight says he'll

join tomorrow. Aunt Rachel, will you let him go?"

The mention of family was John's cue to leave. Getting up, he offered Rachel his chair. "I'll go tell Wat dinner's ready."

Harrison had a ready answer for that, too. "He's already heard the bell. He was coming in with Sam when I came over."

"Then I'll give him a hand with Sam." Quickly walking away, John disappeared around the house.

Later, after Harrison went home and dinner was over, Dwight talked with his mother, alone. "It's only three months, Ma. Ninety days. That's all."

"No. I'm sorry. It could be over before you even got into it. Besides, I need you home for spring planting."

Her retort energized Dwight; his arms flew about as though an unseen force had taken charge of his body. "You got Mr. Welch and Watson, too! You can make do without me."

"I don't like it. I don't like you being gone at all. Three months could be six months and six months a year."

"But you know how Pa felt. He always said it was wrong for people to own other people."

"Yes, I know. Your father hated the thought of slavery. And so do I. It is wrong. It should be made illegal."

"Pa would've signed up, Ma, and you know it!"

"I know that, too, except he would have been too old. If he was still with us, he'd be forty-five now. Too old for a soldier, even in Mr. Lincoln's volunteer army."

Dwight pressed on. "I'm old enough right now. I'll go to honor Pa. I'll make you proud, Ma."

"Yes, you are. And you would. But let's wait and see what happens in the next few months."

Infuriated, Dwight stomped the porch floorboards.

He tried one last time. "Ma! I don't know if I can wait that long!"

"You must wait, Son." The serious tone of voice accentuated her anxiety. "If this becomes a real war, it could go on for a long time. We'll know more in the next few months when the crops are in and the work around here slows down."

A defeated Dwight was unable to hide his disappointment. "Well, that's just dandy, isn't it? Because the work never slows down around here."

THREE MONTHS IS AN ETERNITY for any young man with a hunger to leave home and make his mark. Confined to the grind of farm labor, time crawled for Dwight Barnum. One morning in late April, he and Watson were pruning the last tree in their mother's apple orchard, even as unfolding buds yielded perfumed white flowers that lured the black-and-yellow bumblebees. One landed on Watson's hand. Startled, he shook it off, lost balance on the ladder Dwight steadied, and crashed to the ground, bowling over his brother. Unhurt, they scrambled to their feet, and Dwight began to laugh.

"You know what Ma would say about this little accident, don't you?"

"What?" Watson brushed dead leaves from his jacket.

"You should've gone back to school after Christmas. If you had, this never would've happened."

"Yeah. You're probably right. I can hear her now."

"Wat, I am right."

In early May the brothers planted forage crops for the small flock of sheep, dozen beef cattle and dairy cows, score of feeder pigs, and several horses, including the Belgians, the cart pony, and Blaze, Dwight's Morgan. Surplus stock and grain, along with butter and eggs, always went to market for cash or barter. Their mother handled all finances—Dwight knew she would never relinquish that authority—but it was John Welch, after two years of living and working on the farm, who had become the linchpin of its management. Dwight not only admired the genial and experienced hired man, he liked working alongside him. Under John's direction, and with his willing help, he and Watson plowed and leveled and planted fields of oats, wheat, corn, and barley from five to twenty-five acres each. At the hired man's recommendation, Rachel had bought a revolutionary three-row seed drill the year before. A new hay rake called a tedder also expedited work; by early June, the first cutting of alfalfa and timothy grass was already in the mow.

Spring edged into summer—long, oozing days of torment for a would-be soldier who scoured the newspapers to learn how troops were amassing in Washington and Richmond. On June 8, Tennessee left the Union, the eleventh and last state to join the Confederacy. Now that the Rebellion had coalesced into a separate government, no one expected reunification without the spillage of blood. The only questions were how much blood and for how long.

Fieldwork over for the day, Watson and Dwight walked the tired team to Sebewa Creek, twisting through woods at the back of the farm. Their father had passed on three summers before, but his edict, to cut no timber along the fast-running stream, lived on. Much of the ninety forested acres, a haven for wildlife, remained. Over the past twenty years the property had doubled in value. Dwight had heard his mother tell the hired man how she had expected its worth to increase as the drumbeat of impending war grew louder and inflation soared.

"Money in the bank," Willis had said of the white oak,

black walnut, shagbark hickory, and soft maple that grew throughout the parcel. "We'll manage it like any crop for the good it produces, gifts that will give throughout our lifetime and beyond."

Horses watered, the boys walked them back uphill and turned them loose in the pasture. Back at the creek, they shucked sweaty overalls on the bank, stripped down, and plunged in. Along the bottom of the swimming hole, the stream coursed over smooth gravel, the water shockingly cold at first. Here they stood up to their necks, splashing each other while pebbles ticked over their toes.

One afternoon, before disturbing the tranquil stream, Dwight saw a large shadow drift from a stretch of riffles back to the darkened hole. Arriving too late to see the spectacle, Watson wondered what it was.

"I don't know. A big fish for sure. Probably a pike. It scared the bejeebers out of me. Those teeth could do a lot of damage."

"You saw its teeth?"

"No, but I'm sure it's got them. That thing was a monster."

Returning alone the next day with a pitchfork, Dwight slipped into the stream, stalked close to the swimming hole, and stood still as a park statue for several minutes before tossing a small frog upstream. Immediately, the shadow appeared, inhaled the morsal, and drifted back into darkness.

Heart thumping, mouth suddenly parched, Dwight stood still, as vigilant as the heron that hunted the shallows of the farm pond. Poised with the fork in stabbing readiness, he flipped another frog into the riffle. The instant the shape emerged, Dwight thrust his spear and then ground the tines, hard, into the gravel while the fish thrashed wildly, causing the fork handle to smack Dwight in the nose. With blood running along a cheek, he grabbed the fork with both hands and swept the heavy, throbbing load far enough onto the bank to prevent escape should his flopping catch wring itself free.

Letting go of the pitchfork with a triumphant shout, Dwight was astounded at the fish's size. More than three feet in length, it was the largest pike he had ever seen. Dispatched with a rock, it stopped thrashing, quivered, and lay still.

Arriving home with his giant trophy, Dwight's feat amazed everyone. John Welch, who said he knew a few things about fish, estimated the pike weighed twelve pounds. With a few deft flicks of a butcher knife, the hired man demonstrated the art of filleting, proving he knew more than how to run a farm. John sliced the flesh into meaty chunks, which Rachel soaked in a large pan filled with ice water. The next day was the Fourth of July. The delicious soup she made with salt pork, onions, and potatoes was enough for her family and that of Betsey Barnum's, and it made for a special holiday feast.

Most thought the fish had begun life in the Grand River into which Sebewa Creek flowed a few miles from the farm. Or maybe it had migrated upriver from Lake Michigan, the river's terminus, another sixty miles distant. Whatever the pike's origin, Dwight would remember the event as the highwater mark of a too-long summer spent waiting for war.

LATER THAT MONTH THE BATTLE of Bull Run was a week old when Dwight rode Blaze to Sunfield to pick up coffee and sugar for his mother and to trade butter for the hired man's tobacco. A newspaper on the counter of the general store revealed intriguing details about the Union defeat, an embarrassment already well-known even in remote farming villages like Sunfield. The casualty figures staggered imagination: According to this paper, more than five thousand Nationals were killed, a like number wounded.

Sharing such details with his mother would not help Dwight's cause. He thought it wise, instead, to mention something else: "The splendid Rhode Island regiments, although they lost their superb battery of artillery and many of their officers, will soon again have their ranks filled up. So will the Michigan regiments, whose gallant conduct on the field deserves the highest praise."

Dwight imagined himself as a ready-to-fight soldier in one of those regiments, maybe even a cavalry unit. Hastening Blaze through a shortcut in the woods, he needed to get home as fast as possible. His heart still raced as he shut Blaze, saddle intact, in the corral and ran to the house.

Plunking the necessities and newspaper on the kitchen table, he told his mother it was high time he joined the Army and fought for the cause. "President Lincoln is calling for five-hundred thousand volunteers. Ma, I need to go. It's time for me to enlist."

She agreed without hesitation. "I believe this War is only beginning, and you are needed. Your father would approve of your signing up. Now, so do I." Dwight stopped panting, face swathed in disbelief. Had he heard her right? "But that doesn't mean I won't worry myself to distraction every day you're away."

Dwight slapped his hands together, grinned, and presented his mother with a smart salute. "I'll be back as soon as those Rebels wave the white flag of surrender!"

September, 1861
Sunfield , Michigan

Dwight and Watson were forking sweet-smelling hay they had cut two days earlier into a wagon. Dried forage from this third cutting was ready for the barn. Like an angry yellow eye, the hot afternoon sun bore down on the shirtless brothers. Bare tongs of their pitchforks glinted as did Dwight's back and upper arms from sweat. The subject was John Welch.

"They'll depend on you a lot more after I'm gone," Dwight said, "which means you'll have to work alongside him, probably take orders from him. Except that he doesn't really order anyone around, at least not like what they'll be doing to me in the Army." He paused to rub the perspiration from his eyes. "You'll get along fine with him. He's an easy-going fellow."

Inclined to disagree whenever the subject was the hired man, Watson protested. "He'll be coming into our room when you go. He'll be taking over your bed! I don't like it one bit."

"Then tell Ma."

"I can't tell Ma."

"Why not? Stop chewing on your tongue for once and say what you think."

"Yeah. Right. You see the way Ma looks at him? She'd never listen to me. Her eyes are for him and only for him."

"Watson, listen to me. Ma depends on Mr. Welch. She trusts him. You should be glad he's here to run the farm. All of the responsibility could've fallen on you. She'll be looking to him more than ever when I'm gone."

"I don't like him coming in our room, and I don't want him telling me what to do."

"Then where's he supposed to go? Back to the granary? Stay in the parlor? You ever try to sleep on that lumpy couch in the parlor?"

Watson's mouth clamped shut. He poked at a windrow of hay, loaded his fork, and swung it with such force that he overshot the wagon. Dwight was annoyed with his brother's carelessness. "Come on, Wat. Your being mad is making more work for both of us."

"He ain't our pa. I'll do what Ma says but not what he says."

Sticking his pitchfork in the ground, Dwight leaned on it and looked thoughtfully at his brother. "You're right. He ain't Poppa. He's the hired hand. In fact, you'll likely see another hand or two around here when the corn and beans come in next month."

"He's nothing like our Pa. I don't like him." Whenever troubled or annoyed, Watson habitually flexed his jaw from side to side like a cow chewing her cud. Dinner, though, had ended an hour earlier, and there was nothing in his mouth. Dwight watched his brother chomp away. "Why don't you like him? What did he ever do to you that makes you hate him?"

"He didn't do nothing, and I don't hate him. He's just not our pa. That's all."

"For St. Peter's sake, Watson. Everybody knows that. He's here to stay, so get over it!"

"Wish I could join up with you, Dwight. Wish I didn't have to stay here alone with the womenfolk."

"Our sisters ain't womenfolk. They're ten-year-old girls. What's eating at you? Nobody understands you anymore."

When the wagon was full, they climbed aboard and sat side by side. Retreating to his customary silence, Watson turned the horses around and drove them back to the barn.

Dwight, too, had gone quiet. He was lost in events of the past few days. And he was thinking, soberly, of the days that lay ahead.

CHAPTER 8

Friday, March 28, 1862
Chicago

Rachel slept an hour and a few minutes more. She sat up on the bench in Chicago's Great Central Station and looked around for the vagrant she had benefitted. Relieved he was gone, she rubbed away what she realized was a dream from last summer's argument with Dwight and her concession to letting him join the Army. Whether she was awake or sleeping, he was always in her thoughts. Neither was her sudden hunger a surprise; she had not eaten since yesterday's stew in Battle Creek. Unwrapping the cheese, she broke off a piece and a hard fragment of bread. She ate quickly. When the simple meal was finished, Rachel returned to the food stand. Having covered the produce and cheeses and other wares, the proprietor had gone home. She helped herself to a dipper of water from the barrel behind the counter.

Walking back, Rachel heard the 5:12 enter the terminal and brake to a stop. The train was three minutes late. Fearful it might leave on time and she would miss it again, she grabbed her possessions and stepped lively through the waiting hall to Track No. 8. The engine rumbled like distant thunder, its vibration reverberating through the wood-blocked platform. Finding the second-class car, she produced her ticket but needn't have bothered. Leaning against the lamp post, arms tangled across his chest, the supervisor was immobile and apparently sleeping.

The car was empty. Rachel passed through the aisle to the end where she stowed her sack under the double seat, wound the blanket around her, and fell into an uneasy sleep. Insensitive to the subdued sounds of other travelers boarding, she awoke to whistle shrieks and bell clangs as the huge railway terminal awakened for another day of business. When the Chicago-to-Cairo line pulled away with a hiss and a bang, Rachel opened her eyes, assumed it must be ten after six in the morning, rolled over, and drifted back to sleep.

The conductor nudged her awake. "Ticket please. Ticket?"

Stirring, Rachel looked up. A hint of gray filtered through the window and into the car. She sat up, found her ticket, and handed it to the conductor. He towered over her. "Sorry to wake you, ma'am." His smile showed white teeth.

"It's fine." Hand over mouth, Rachel tried to cover a yawn. "I'm finished with sleeping."

His ticket punch made an audible click. She watched the illusory shard drift onto her seat.

Returning the ticket, he thanked her. "I believe you're bound for Cairo? We stop for thirty minutes each at Champaign, Mattoon, and Centralia. The first stop is Kankakee, but we don't leave the train for that one since the stop is so brief." He touched his cap, nodded, and turned around. The gas light above absorbed the shadow from his bulk as he moved back down the aisle.

With the gathering daylight came woodlots and farm fields. Picked clean from the harvest, the idle fields waited for seed, which Rachel knew would soon follow the plow and harrow. Sprinkled throughout one field were conical shocks of faded cornstalks like dozens of Indian teepees. Here and there, Rachel noted a fitted field that made her think of Willis, ever so eager to get a crop in the ground, a happy thought that led to a little smile. She had heard the Illinois prairie was good earth. The dark, rich soil, stovepipe black in places, looked capable of producing tremendous yields.

The train slowed and passed a white farmhouse, gleaming like bone, near the tracks, a bit too near, she thought. Rachel noticed candlelight in what looked like the kitchen and saw someone carrying a milk pail toward it from the squat barn across the yard. Her own family would be done with breakfast by now. She imagined her daughters combing each other's hair and pleading with Watson to hitch Star to the pony cart so they wouldn't be late for school. She watched John Welch clear the table while talking to himself about the work he had in mind today. Her third consecutive night away from home now over, she felt a pang of loneliness. She missed her family. She missed the hired man. Most of all, she needed to find Dwight.

Today was Friday. If the train was on time, and thus far it seemed to be, she would arrive shortly after midnight. With luck, she could get to New Madrid and Dwight as soon as tomorrow afternoon. She needed to find someone in Cairo to take her downriver, or across the river and overland, to New Madrid. If that was not to be, she would find another way. Of course. There had to be another way. Those scraps of sleep were helping her mood.

As the train wended south, Rachel hoped to calm her unease further by looking out the window at the earth coming to life, that marvelous reenactment of how spring overpowers the barren winter landscape. In a skirt of forest passing by, she saw what might be a patch of bloodroot, and then another, the flurry of white blooms looking like skiffs of snow from a winter that had stayed too long. In a wooded wetland, huge black-trunked trees were as wide as Belgian Sam's behind. These dark, gloomy sentinels—swamp oak or black maple, she thought—gave way to more cheerful clumps of willow unfurling buds of green. Closer to the railway grade, along the flooded ditch, the scarlet stems of red osier dogwood shone as though painted. An ear-piercing whistle blast shocked a pair of mallards into flushing. The drab hen exploded from the ditch first, followed in panicked flight by the male, his head a ball of polished green.

At Kankakee, one passenger left the car, and two women boarded, followed by an elderly man. The women, perhaps sisters, alighted on the seat opposite Rachel. The gentleman, maybe their father, claimed a seat next to another man across the aisle.

"Good morning," Rachel said, in response to pleasantries offered by the women, who appeared to be fortyish, near her own age. Rachel looked back to her window. Not interested in talking at the moment, she retreated to speculation. Was that a chestnut about to bloom? The women resumed an obvious earlier conversation. The shorter, younger one was speaking. "I must assume he did it out of spite."

"Well, you can't know that for certain. His behavior is odd, clearly, but that doesn't mean his intention was to hurt anybody, least of all you. I doubt he meant you any harm at all."

"I don't suppose we'll ever know, will we, my dear?"

The engine was at full throttle by the time the conductor sauntered near. Rachel wondered if he had ridden the rails for years, so adroit was the older, burly man at shifting his ample weight from leg to leg while the coach rocked left and right. Moving along, passenger seat by seat, he tottered like an enormous ten-pin about to tip over. He looked official in his woolen suit of dark blue, brass buttons on the coat fastened. Attached to his cap, also blue serge, was a silver nameplate with "Illinois Central RR" in black letters. She noted how his kind eyes peered from beneath caterpillar brows of gray.

"In one hour we'll stop for water and coal," he announced, returning pierced tickets to the sisters. "Then, at quarter-past ten, we arrive in Champaign. There, we take a thirty-minute break for breakfast, or lunch, and any personal needs."

It was after the stop for fuel and water that the sisters had tired of nattering and attempted to bring the quiet passenger into their counsel. The younger one, spying the ring on Rachel's finger, asked where she lived.

"I live in Michigan, about thirty miles north of Battle Creek."

"Oh, Battle Creek?" It was the other's turn to question. "Where's that in relation to Detroit?"

The question tripped Rachel's mind back to that youthful journey with her family. An arduous adventure, to be sure, but one also full of optimism and the joy of discovery, so unlike this mission. "Well, it's ten days by wagon team. Much faster by train, of course."

The younger one was a chatterbox. She reminded Rachel of her daughter Hester. "Oh, I so love the trains," she said. "Do you often travel by train?"

"First time."

"You'll love it. Especially if you sit far back from the engine and coal car."

"I'll remember that next time." Rachel thought about how to end this tedious dialogue without appearing rude.

"Have you heard of the new Pullmans? I'm told that's the modern way to travel."

"I have. Yes."

"We're going to Carbondale. Where are you going, Mrs. …?"

"Cairo."

"Cairo! What on earth for? That place is insane with all the hubbub of the War!"

Visibly annoyed, her grimace unmistakable, Rachel had already memorized the response, and she delivered it with emphasis as though repeating something of great importance to a child. "To visit a relative."

Startled, the younger one looked long at Rachel. "Oh," she said. Turning back to her sister, who was opening a book, she did not speak again. Rachel had already returned to looking out her window.

FOR MILE AFTER MILE, THE north-to-south rail tracks pierced the good earth of Illinois prairie, some of it having succumbed to farmland, much of it still in native grass and hardwood forest. Here and there were signs of human habitation—houses and barns, an occasional village, and small cities with their way stations and switching yards. Rachel wondered what this land would look like in fifty or a hundred years. The waves of settlers that had pushed west from the Eastern Seaboard and New England to come here would be overrun by another generation of westward-seeking pioneers, some of whom had already found new homes beyond the Mississippi in Kansas and Iowa, Nebraska and Dakota Territory. California and the expansive West seemed so much closer than it did only a quarter-century before.

As her train forged ahead, Rachel was transported back to that remarkable time of wilderness travel with her family. She was sixteen, late in the winter of 1838 when Father, his second wife, Suzanne, three sons, and two daughters packed essential belongings in a wagon and left New York for Michigan. Rachel remembered how her father's uncharacteristicly dark mood had begun to lighten once the wagon was full and the trip underway. At the time, she didn't understand why what was now known as the Panic of 1837 had forced Peter, unable to make mortgage loan payments to the bank, to sell his vegetable and fruit farm. Even now, twenty-three years later, she didn't fully comprehend why the New York City market for fresh food had all but dried up. Apparently, it had much to do with the financial policies of then-president Andrew Jackson.

Nor had she been able to grasp the unspoken reasons for her parents' anguish during those uncertain months culminating in Peter's decision to "start over" and remove his family to what he hoped was a better place. The tension Rachel had known, however, was profound; it could make her stomach quake. Her father, sometimes with the help of oldest-son Cornelius, had tried to balance sums by lantern light at the parlor table. One evening Father had grown so frustrated he cursed aloud and snapped a pencil in half. Although hard currency was scarce, the sale of the farm brought enough cash to finance the journey west and to buy land in Michigan, not with paper money but with government-mandated gold and silver, another misguided policy according to her father who said the president was to blame.

The financial turn of events that had ruined Peter's livelihood spelled upheaval for his family. As the miles from Chicago grew and those to Cairo shrank, Rachel recalled how easily uncertainty could become fear. The gnawing unease over Dwight's welfare prompted a similar pattern, and she worried if something was wrong with her stomach. Some kind of pesky ailment, not unlike the morning sickness she had known during pregnancies, caused rumbling and painful cramping. Maybe she could buy a medicine at one of the longer stopovers. For now, she could stop fretting over the future. She could turn negative thoughts to happy thoughts. Rachel had witnessed such a change in her father. She remembered how the unsettling image of him pleading with God for help became his delight at seeing the Erie Canal for the first time. It was, indeed, an engineering feat, a testament to ingenuity, he had said, as well as a dream come true. She recalled his very words: "Who would have thought that anyone could connect the Hudson River with Lake Erie? Why, that's over three hundred fifty miles!"

That journey was the adventure of a lifetime, a thrilling experience to which she shifted her thoughts now as the train rolled on. With mule power, aided at times by their own oxen lashed to a barge with thick ropes, the van Houtens had made their way down the canal to Buffalo. From there they traveled by lake steamer to Detroit where they had relied again on ox and wagon to deliver them the final hundred miles to their new home. Michigan Territory had become the State of Michigan only the year before, and Rachel had wondered if landscape had anything to do with the difference. Just outside Detroit, had the forested expanse—huge trees fusing into a green wall that seemed impenetrable and that threatened to swallow their little group—changed at all? Apparently not. Rachel concluded there was no difference in land form between territory and state.

That first night in the wilderness, Father, and each of the brothers in turn, had memorized a segment of the detailed directions from a talkative innkeeper. Their exploit was replete with cheerfulness, despite the cold and the mud trail that had braided its narrow way through the dark forest, only to break out, now and again, into openings that Father said were oak savannahs. The streams they had crossed in early spring were brim full from snowmelt and rain. It was too early for wildflowers but that meant no mosquitoes— the bane of all travelers to Michigan, or so she had heard from sojourners upon returning to New York.

On the third night, they had stayed at a way station in a place called Pontiac, while a freezing rain pelted the wood shingles of the roof. By morning the ice storm was over, and they had resumed travel with enthusiasm. Fortune smiled a second time when they found shelter in the barn of a pioneer family, Dutch settlers from Albany, they were delighted to learn. Peter had conversed with the family patriarch in English and in the old language, and Rachel recalled how proud she had been of her worldly father and how secure she had felt in his presence.

Questions interrupted this rumination, and Rachel tore her eyes from the coach window to consider answers. *Why hadn't she asked Father to go with her on this journey?* Well, that question was easily answered: His age was a liability; of late, she fussed more than ever about his health. As for the brothers and sister, they had families of their own. Rachel knew from the instant she read the telegram she would go alone. Now, niggling doubt poked at her resolve. Had she made a wise decision? She had not asked Father for advice—there was no time for that—but she had consulted her hired man. False! She had *told* John Welch she was going alone and then argued with him when he tried to change her mind. And she hadn't bothered to ask the children how they felt about their mother leaving them, alone, with the hired man. How selfish of her! Could she have been more inconsiderate? The sudden growling in her stomach was not from hunger.

Turning back to her window, Rachel's memory of the pioneer journey was clear. The rest of the way had taken them deeper into the forest where the only humans they had seen was a band of Indians who frightened them with their sudden appearance in a spot where the path was tight. Cornelius stopped the wagon while the Indians, two men and a woman with a baby, passed within arm's length. When Father smiled at them and nodded, one of the men said something no one understood until he squatted, cupped his hands, and made a motion of scooping up water and drinking it. Standing up, he pointed down the trail where Rachel and the family were going. That night they camped near a large babbling spring and slept on the ground and in the wagon.

The next day with the brothers walking ahead to clear the path of fallen timber, they made good time, even though the wagon broke down twice. Mr. van Looven, the Dutchman, had given them a pot of grease, and the brothers swabbed the axles liberally and often, and they had no more wagon trouble during several more days of travel. They found and forded the Grand River at a place called Eaton Rapids, and the next day they made Charlotte where the brother of Suzanne Beekman, Peter's second wife and

Rachel's stepmother, was postmaster. After they had rested two days, Harold Beekman led them, on foot, a dozen miles along the Indian route that wended all the way to Grand Rapids, except they had stopped forty miles short in Sunfield Township in Eaton County where Harold had claimed eighty acres in Peter van Houten's name.

Recalling that month-long expedition did have a calming effect, and Rachel was content for now to let the train take her to wherever she was going. But it also brought to surface the habitual feeling of loss upon knowing she would never again see her twin sister's grave in New Jersey nor that of their mother's in New York.

CHAPTER 9

Illinois Central RR, south of Chicago

During the train stop at Champaign, Rachel drank coffee at the food stand and nibbled most of a roasted chicken breast. The remains she wrapped in her handkerchief and added to the sack along with an apple and a handful of dried persimmons. She had never eaten persimmons but heard they were good. The one she bit into was sweet.

The slow *whoof ... whoof* of the locomotive gathering energy said it was time to reboard, followed by the conductor's sharp whistle, and "All aboard! This train leaves in three minutes."

Back in the coach, the sisters had changed seats and were now roosting like hens, their legs drawn under dresses, across from the older man that Rachel assumed was their father. She felt no offense at being left alone; in fact, she was relieved they were gone. A neatly dressed young man, perhaps a professor from the university here in Champaign or maybe a businessman, had taken their place opposite Rachel's seat. He was reading *The Champaign News-Gazette.* Lowering the broadsheet, he peered over the masthead to acknowledge his fellow rider.

"Gooday," he gestured and, without waiting for a response, went back to reading.

Returning the pleasantry, Rachel caught the headline: "Grant poised to strike in Tennessee," and part of the sub-headline, something about "Pope and Foote" and "standoff" or "stalemate." At that moment, a violent shudder, followed by a smaller tremor, passed through the car as the train pulled away, and the words began jumping on the page and she could decipher nothing.

An hour later the new passenger had stopped reading and was looking at his watch, a handsome timepiece with a silver chain attached to the vest of his suit jacket. The folded newspaper lay in his lap. He looked up and their eyes met.

"What's the news this morning?" she asked him. "With the War, I mean."

The man closed his watch and studied her. "I don't know," he shrugged in a perfunctory manner. "That's last night's paper. It's always a day behind the Chicago papers." When he paused, Rachel presumed he was weighing whether or not to engage further with her. "But there was a twister Tuesday morning down on the river."

"A twister?"

"A tornado. It came out of a bad storm somewhere south of New Madrid and worked its way north. Another twister, or maybe it was the same one, hit Cooter, Missouri."

"Cooter? Where's Cooter, pray tell?"

"I don't know. Somewhere down the river from New Madrid. The headline says, 'Three dead in Bootheel tornado; Girls thrown 300 feet.'"

"Oh, my!" Her thoughts flew to her twins, Hester and Helena. "Were they hurt?"

"Hard to believe but only one child, ten years old, got a cut on her head. The other two, about the same age, didn't get a scratch."

Her eyes flared in disbelief. "How can that be? You said it killed three people."

His hands flew up. "Well, I don't know that, Lady! They were outside playing when the twister picked them up and set them down. These storms do strange things sometimes."

In her imagination, Rachel could see the twister suck the girls into its vortex, spin away, and set them down unharmed. "That's the hand of the Almighty at work. They were saved by the grace of God, sure as we're sitting on this train."

He looked at her with curiosity. "Oh, I suppose that's true, isn't it? What's not surprising is a tornado down on the river. After all, that whole part of the Mississippi's been the stage for Hell itself. No doubt you've heard of the great earthquakes of 1811 and '12."

"Earthquakes? There? Please, do tell!"

The man leaned forward as though he had a conspiratorial secret to share. Elbows propped on knees, he tapped a finger along his cheek, licked lips, and steadied his chin with a thumb.

"Well, yes. Yes, indeed. Some of the worst earthquakes ever seen on this whole continent. More than two-thousand tremors in all. People who were there—and thank God there were no cities at the time, St. Louis being too far north and west—said the Mississippi actually changed course and ran north." He paused while the enormity of his tale incubated.

Rachel conjured up the biblical plagues; she saw people running for their lives from the earth cracking open, imagined people running from a heavenly war that rained frogs.

"It's how Reelfoot Lake was made." The man, apparently assured of his audience, went on. "Why, one of the quakes was so bad, they say it was felt by every person living in the United States at that time."

Rachel wondered if the speaker was lying or simply having fun at her expense. He certainly was lively and seemed sincere. But why hadn't her father, a young man then, ever talked about this? Why had she never heard of this calamity? Or had she heard and dismissed the tale as poppycock?

"Knocked down chimneys in Cincinnati. Why, they say it rang church bells in Boston."

"Are you a teacher? A professor perhaps?"

"No, ma'am, I'm a sales agent for a company that sells supplies to the U. S. government. And sundry other things, all legal, of course, to the troops."

He told Rachel how New Madrid was smack dab in the center of the havoc and the unbelievable destruction the earthquakes had caused. How today, fifty years later, one could still see craters, or sand boils as the locals called them, some of the boils being several acres in size. "They call it 'Earthquake Alley.' I'm not surprised at all there was a twister down there the other day." Tilting forward again, his voice lowered. "I'll tell you something else, ma'am. Another ground-buster is about to happen, somewhere down there. Any day now."

"What do you mean? Another tornado or earthquake?"

"I mean fireworks, ma'am. You can't move whole armies, like Grant and Pope are doing, onto the enemy's soil, right in his face, without a big blowup of some kind. They could be shooting at each other in Tennessee, right now. And I don't mean one of them skirmishes where a man fires his rifle and runs the other way. I'm talking about fireworks! A big hullabaloo. You should have seen the night sky light up when Foote's gunboats shelled Fort Henry and then took Donelson." Pausing, he watched her closely. "Not that I was actually there, of course."

He handed her the newspaper. "It's all in there, and it's inevitable. You wouldn't believe all the things the Army's buying to get ready for it. My company will make me a rich man by the time this War is over."

Rachel, clearly agitated, interrupted with a question. "What do you know about the fighting on the river? In New Madrid or thereabouts?"

"Ain't no fighting in New Madrid now, ma'am. Pope owns that town. Secesh abandoned it. Now, the cork in the bottle, down there on the Mississippi anyway, is Island Number 10. For all I know, that cork is about to blow, too. Any day—any hour—now."

The train was slowing for Mattoon Station. The businessman stood, tugged on his vest to straighten it, and turned to go. "There's an article on that, too. Keep the paper, ma'am. It's yesterday's news anyhow."

This information was too much to process at once. Overwhelmed, Rachel stared at the floor while the train stopped and most passengers shuttled off. She felt separated from herself. It seemed that nothing was real, was actually happening, like experiencing a mirage or falling to earth in a dream without being able to awaken. She remained seated throughout the obligatory stop, and when it was over and the passengers had reboarded, along with three or four new ones, she sat as still as Willis' parlor chair in the cemetery, as silent as his tombstone, with hands in her lap, fingers threaded together, eyes wide and downcast, frozen on the floor.

For the second time in as many days, the futility of what she had come here to do struck her with its force of undeniable reality. She knew, and now must confront the truth of what she knew, that her journey would end at Cairo, along with these train tracks. And that truth unearthed new questions. Frightening questions.

What would happen to her and the rest of the family, when she had to go home without Dwight? If Dwight died—had already died—in Missouri, a foreign country to her mind, where would they bury him?

Thoughts of little Helen, the twin sister laid to rest in a tiny casket and buried somewhere in New Jersey, sluiced her imagination. That unsettling image bled into another, the one of their mother, entombed somewhere in a New York City cemetery. Places Rachel would never see again. Gravesites she would never enshrine with flowers. For this reason, she had insisted that Willis' final resting place be on the knoll where she could see it from the farmhouse. Could walk to it. It was where any other family member belonged, were they to pass before her time came.

Now that her plan to find Dwight was all but snuffed out, Rachel was bereft of hope. Panicking, she sucked in gulps of air, sensed palpitations in her chest, and fought for composure. While the quivers subsided, she wove the blanket close and because no one had taken the rest of her seat, lay on her side, face pressed against the seat back. With legs drawn up, she held herself close until the shudders ended and normal breathing resumed.

Its firebox starved of oxygen, the train snaked into Centralia and stopped with a harrowing screech of brakes. Awakened, Rachel sat up. Knuckling away an itch in her eyes, she focused on travel mates and realized nothing had changed. The surge of panic had surrendered to hunger and with that she knew a return to reality, to common sense. It was close to eight o'clock and she needed to eat. Removing the ticket from her breast pouch, she scrutinized the tiny print.

Carbondale, the last stop before Cairo, was too brief for anyone to get off for personal needs. Rachel speculated that nothing would be open at midnight in Cairo, and she would be fortunate to find a hotel room there so late. Spending the night at the Cairo train station was a possibility, but that prospect did not mean she would have to stay hungry until morning. Someone would be selling food, here, in Centralia.

When she stood, her legs were numb, unsteady. Across the aisle, the sisters were also preparing to leave and didn't seem to notice her hesitation. Rachel waited and gestured for them to go ahead of her. The younger woman acknowledged this nicety, and Rachel returned her smile.

At the depot, other passengers must have had Rachel's plan in mind for they pressed before the display table of the sole food merchant open for business at this late hour. His scant offerings quickly disappeared. When the younger sister bought the last item, a small pie, he announced in a loud voice. "Thank you, everyone, for your patronage. I'm finished now. All sold out." The wooden sign he plunked atop the empty table shouted: "Closed until tomorrow."

Suddenly, Rachel was starving. Hours before, she had finished the chicken breast and eaten the persimmons. The young woman must have heard her gasp of disappointment. Perhaps she saw the resignation on Rachel's face. "Ma'am, would you like to have this? It looks like a prime pie, even though I dare say it was made yesterday. It's mincemeat. Do you like mincemeat? It's not my favorite."

Rachel had already turned to go. She spun around, the look of chagrin replaced by one of disbelief. "You would do that for me? After I was so rude to you?"

"You weren't rude. I was rude. I had no business snooping about your business."

"Why, I couldn't take your supper. What would you eat?"

"We have only two hours left. There's food at home in Carbondale. Please, take the pie, ma'am. I want you to have this pie."

Rachel plucked a dime from her purse, placed the coin in the palm of the young woman, and squeezed the warm fingers. Rachel then apologized. "I am truly sorry for what happened before." Her tone, her features, implied sincerity, and thankfulness. "Please forgive me, Miss."

Beaming, the smile was pure. "Of course. All is well."

Back on the train, Rachel ate the pie. The crust was tough, but the mincemeat tasted good. Later, when the Chicago-to-Cairo line paused in Carbondale and the Good Samaritan and her sister rose to go, Rachel thanked her again and bade farewell to both women.

As the train left, its forlorn whistle slicing through the night, she saw them on the landing, waiting for someone, and only then did Rachel realize she didn't know their names. A veil of remorse descended upon her like a shroud, and she resolved to do better, to be more trusting of others, to make herself more available. Even to strangers when warranted.

Night travel by train to a strange place. Rachel had known dread so recently that it had yet to uncouple itself from fear. But this demonstration of goodwill, this unforeseen act of simple human kindness from a stranger on a train, affirmed that she was not alone, could choose not to be alone. The incident made clear the importance of staying engaged with others.

Hunger satisfied, Rachel decided to read, not her holy book but another she had packed, one by Charles Dickens, a favorite novelist. Rachel and Beatrice, the Chicago cousin with whom she corresponded, sometimes exchanged books they liked. For a Christmas gift, Beatrice had sent her a copy of Dickens' book of travels in America. Although it was no novel and had been written years earlier, Beatrice said some of the destinations were where Dwight might go with the Army. Having skimmed the book earlier, Rachel expected some disappointment; opening it now, as the train bore down on Cairo, she was surprised at what she read:

"A dismal swamp, on which the half-built houses rot away; cleared here and there for the space of a few yards; and teeming, then, with rank unwholesome vegetation, in whose baleful shade the wretched wanderers who are tempted hither, droop, and die, and lay their bones …"

What on earth is this? She closed her eyes a moment and then finished the appalling sentence …"the hateful Mississippi circling and eddying before it, and turning off upon its southern course a slimy monster hideous to behold; a hotbed of disease, an ugly sepulcher, a grave uncheered by any gleam of promise; a place without one single quality, in earth or air or water, to commend it; such is this dismal Cairo."

Rachel snapped shut the book, unable to read more. Whether Charles Dickens was telling the naked truth or expounding hyperbole made no difference. Aghast, she could no more easily get off this train now than she could stop it from going to Cairo, Illinois.

THE DAY HAD BEEN LONG, and Rachel was weary. She saw the conductor, waiting outside the train station on the platform for everyone to disembark. He looked to be impatient or bored. She was the final passenger, a small woman with a large satchel, descending the steps before him. "Let me guess at your question," he sighed. "Where's the nearest hotel? The answer: They're all closed at this late hour. Sorry to be the bearer of bad news, but that's a fact."

Rachel saw a man with a tired smile, a man trying to be kind. He had also been on the train since leaving Chicago, eighteen hours ago. Rachel wondered if other new visitors to Cairo at midnight showed alarm. Having taken in Mr. Dickens' dark commentary an hour earlier, she was exhausted and wanted to sleep. "To be expected," she said, her tone flat. "I trust no one would mind if I stayed on that bench in front of the station?"

"Ha! Only a hungry rat would mind and then only if you have vittles you won't share with him." She looked at him with indifference. "Just joshing you, ma'am. You'll be safe enough here at the train depot. The bigger building all around it serves as the freight shed. There's a night watchman. I'll ask him to keep an eye out."

Rachel wished he hadn't mentioned rats. She hated rats, the reason she kept cats on her farm. "Tell the watchman, please, I'll be in this second-class coach," she said, "That is allowed, isn't it? I'll sleep on the same seat I came here on."

Adjusting the cap, he scratched the back of his head and pursed his lips. "Well, you bought a ticket to Cairo. You're here and the train's here, at least 'til morning. Seems to me that seat is yours until 8:15 when it goes back to Chicago."

Rachel asked if the coach door could be locked and was relieved when the conductor showed her how it worked, both inside and outside. "If you're staying longer in Cairo, I suggest the St. Charles. It's the best hotel in Little Egypt. If it was good enough for Ulysses S. Grant to stay there for months, why it'd be right good enough for me."

She wondered where the public privy was located and learned it was just outside the freight-door entrance, behind the depot, in back of the surrounding freight shed. She thanked him, and he wagged the back of his hand at her as he walked away. "Happy to oblige. G'night, ma'am. I can taste my beer already."

Rachel was alone. The station depot was deserted, the platform barren except for the sitting bench and a few cartons of stacked freight. A single gas lamp shed meager light over the bench. Flickering weakly, it cast jittery shadows; a sputtering sound signaled low fuel. Knowing it would soon extinguish itself, Rachel looked down the line of cars to the locomotive protruding into the inky night at the end of the freight shed. Smoke curling from its crown inched toward her. She mounted the coach steps and locked the door, found her seat, and prepared for sleep. There would be no more reading tonight, even if there was enough light, which she doubted.

THE CHILD WORE A SIMPLE brown dress. Sewn by a mother's deft hand from a dusty sack that once carried wheat to the grist mill and returned home with flour, the garment was too large for such a small body. An apron, tied behind the waist with a clumsy bow, snugged the dress and presented the semblance of respectability. The white apron matched the cap she wore to keep the dark, curly fronds from obstructing her view. The barn stall was dark, the lantern light dim. She needed to see as well as she could for the serious task at hand.

Another girl, about ten years older, held the child's tiny hand and guided it. "Touch your thumb with your first finger," she instructed, "like this." Then, she told the child to move the stool closer. "Now watch what I do."

Stretching her arm as far as possible, the child pinched the appendage between finger and thumb, just as her sister had demonstrated. The udder was warm to her little fingers, the teat soft and pliable. She must have been about four.

Her big sister told her to make a fist with her fingers and to squeeze hard, one finger at a time, from top to bottom and not to pull. Grasping the child's fingers, she showed her how to squeeze and release, to open and close her hand. She repeated Sister's words: "It's like magic when the milk comes!" Now they were laughing.

"Do you see the milk, Rachel? Do you see the magic?"

Rachel saw the magic and she smelled the warm milk and she could hear it squirting into the wooden pail. Before long the pail was full of a rich white froth, some of which slopped over the side when Sister carried it to the house with the delighted child skipping behind. "Mama!" she yelped with joy. "Mama, I milked Bella all by myself. Come see! Margaret showed me how to do magic!"

The milking dream was always a happy dream. It was when Rachel was awake and tried to make more sense of it—lying alone in bed, her mind unshackled, free from care—that it could make her uneasy. Not always, though. Just sometimes. Like this morning, if it was, indeed, morning. After all, the passenger coach was silent and black as a mining shaft. For a moment, Rachel did not know where she was. She knew, however, that she was alone, and she was frightened. A tremor of fear shot through her body. A gathering urge tugged at her bowels. She needed to find that privy.

Was desolation part of the dream, and she was still asleep? No, she was awake. Coughing aloud, she heard it. Her right hand found the left. Those were fingers, not tits, as the crude farm boys called them. Rachel felt the wedding band Willis had placed on her finger the day they married more than twenty years ago. Yes, she was awake. The pounding in her chest was real.

She stood up and shuffled along the aisle, guided by blind hands that shook while feeling seat backs. She found the coach access and released the lock, opened the door, and looked down the passenger cars to where the engine had thrust its head outside the cavernous building. Low in the night sky a slice of moon revealed the structure's outline. Morning was near, but it was still too dark to look for the toilet. She would use it by and by. With mincing steps, Rachel returned to the seat, resigned herself to a slump, and thought about the dream.

Although parts of it were always elusive, she knew the experience was true. What happened in the dream really had happened and was sealed to remembrance. She knew the other girl was Margaret, that Margaret was ten years older, and that it was Margaret who had taught her and Helen how to milk the Jersey cow named Bella.

But where was Helen? Helen appeared in other dreams but never in this one. Rachel questioned why she had no recollection, however formless but a snippet at least, of Helen helping her and Margaret with the milking. Had her twin sister already passed from this life?

They were only four years old! Why was Helen taken? Why had Rachel survived? That thought was habitual, as was the emotional slide it could bring. She must be careful now, must keep her grief at bay. The milking dream always ended in sunlight with the child triumphant and playful. Leave it there! The questions before her needed answers now. The past could wait. Time was wasting away. The telegram was already a week and a day cold. She must keep going. She had come too far to give up now.

Rachel knew from long experience how action brought distraction. She resolved to leave this passenger car the minute she could see where she was going.

CHAPTER 10

Cairo, Illinois

While waiting for daylight, Rachel collapsed in her seat and tried to stay engaged. Today was Saturday. It was Watson's day to muck the horse stalls. The girls would bake johnnycake this morning. Perhaps John Welch would bring that brittle harness from the barn to the hearth fire for warmth before softening it with neats-foot oil. The hired man always had his sights fixed on what was to come, in this instance the spring planting. He did not dwell so much on what had already happened.

A pang of longing struck, and Rachel caught her breath. She remembered John's hearty laughter though the cause escaped her. It didn't matter what it was. The thought of him pleased, and she wished he was here, now, on this train with her. His presence would be soothing. She recalled how a neighbor had referred to John Welch as "a forever optimist," which was true, but he was more than that. Much more. How had she put it to the neighbor? "A practical man." Yes, a reasonable, practical fellow who liked to be ready, who liked to plan ahead. Her father had been like that during her growing-up years. So was Willis who was wont to say, "Look ahead and only ahead. What's done is done."

Those three—the father still living, the late husband, the hired hand—were the trusted men of her life. And yet, it was John, a total stranger only three years ago, who would share the evening meal today with the family she left behind.

A sudden noise pierced her reverie. What was that sound? A rat, maybe? Was it here, inside this sealed coach with its stale air? No, it was outside, probably on the platform. The sound of scampering feet grew fainter, and Rachel knew instant relief upon letting go of her long-held breath.

Yes, here she was: alone, abandoned. How tempting to think of herself as a victim! But that would be a lie. It was her decision, her insistence, that she go alone to find Dwight and bring him home. Hester and Helena were too young to go with her into the unknown, into dangerous places where men were killing each other. Where the casualties of an unpopular war, an insurrection, were growing day by day.

John Welch? That prospect was out of the question, although it, too, was most tempting. People, of course, would think they were married, but how could she have traveled with a man she was not married to, not even related to at all? Besides, John was needed at home to manage the farm and to supervise her girls. To keep an eye on Watson, the unpredictable one. Her cousin Betsey did not need more children to supervise.

But who is supervising John Welch? Was she addled to have left her girls with a man who is not their father, not their brother? Not even their uncle? No, she was not crazy! She took a leap of faith when she hired him. She knew a leap of faith when she allowed him to live in the house. Leaving her girls in his care is not a leap of faith. It is trust. Trust that he knows no deceit. Trust that his intentions are honest. Trust in his judgment.

A soft hissing sound caught her attention. She assumed it was a dying gasp from the gas lamp although the fuel had run out hours before. She should have asked the conductor to fill it before he left for the night. Or the night watchman whose whereabouts was a mystery. Soon, day would come to Cairo, and she could leave this distressing train station.

What of Watson? Ah, yes, Watson. He's home with his sisters and John Welch. She had considered bringing her son along, but his place was also at home. Rachel didn't know how long she would be gone, and the time to plant would soon be here. What help would Watson have been to her? She could handle the team, manage the travel details, and make decisions on her own. Watson was too impressionable, as she had been at sixteen. Furthermore, he had talked about enlisting as soon as he was old enough. What if Watson came this far with her to lie about his age, join the Army here in southern Illinois, and abandon her?

Abandon! Why was that word stuck in her head? Why does it cause such dismay? She blinked away gathering moisture, swallowed the lump in her throat. Rachel needed, wanted, John Welch with her now, a vulnerability almost as frightening as being trapped in this rail car, this tomb.

The pain in her abdomen was agonizing, and she stood to leave. Hands fumbling in the dark, Rachel gathered her few possessions, secured them in the bag, and stumbled down the aisle. The station was still empty. Outside the shed entrance a brightening sky was capturing stars. The cool air brought a welcome contrast to the car's stifling still-ness as she walked along the platform past the empty depot bench, where she might have slept hours earlier, and past the line of cars. Rachel stepped outside, quickly turned the corner, and found the toilet. Holding her breath, she dis-appeared inside. When finished, she closed the door and walked back along the platform in subdued light. No one was around. The bench was still empty, a safe place to sit and wait for Cairo to reveal itself in full daylight.

There was no waiting. A shadowy movement from behind Rachel became vile hands on her breasts, instant-ly launching her like a coiled spring unwound. Shrieking, she tore fingers away and whipped around to confront, to defend. The violent action tipped over the bench, in turn knocking someone to the platform.

The assailant was a man. Surely, rape was his intent. She must fight for her life! Screaming with rage, a terrified Rachel kicked repeatedly at her prone attacker. Her boot was a powerful weapon. Grabbing his crotch, he howled in pain and scrambled to get his feet under him.

Animal fury fully aroused, Rachel allowed no such advantage and no escape. Propped against the dead lamp within quick reach was a stout pole for igniting and snuff-ing gas lights. In her hands, a stove poker would not have been a weapon more intoxicating, or lethal. Instinctively, she went for his head. Arms upraised, he tried to ward off the blows, one of which found his nose and released a tor-rent of blood.

It was his turn to scream amidst a blur of confusion punctured by an alarm rattle. Someone fired a shot outside the building. Men shouting, their boots pounding, came running along the wooden platform.

The night watchman, materializing from somewhere,

said she could have killed him. "For a little woman, you're a tiger!" he exclaimed through shocked features. "I ain't never seen a woman fight like that!"

Head in hands, chest heaving, Rachel had crashed to the restored bench and was sobbing. Rocking her body back and forth, tears streaming down, she fought for self-control. "My God, I could have been violated!" she hissed through clamped teeth. *I was violated, nearly raped! What have I done? What will they do with me?*

A few feet away, two men on their knees tended to her attacker with a rag and a small bucket of water. Legs straight out, hand cupped over his left ear, he lay beaten, his back to the station office. He did not, would not, look at her.

A freight worker offered Rachel his handkerchief. A dockhand brought a dipper of water. An hour after the attack, she was still in a daze, confused as to why whatever had happened had happened to her. The watchman said her assailant, a known thief arrested the week before for stealing a box of munitions, finally got what was coming to him. "They never should have let him out of jail," he said. "He'll be going back for a lot longer this time. Unless you don't want to press a charge."

"Oh, I *will* press a charge!" Rachel seethed with searing conviction. "A monster like that should not be on the loose."

The watchman escorted her to a small office within the station where she waited alone until a provost marshal came to take testimony. He scribbled notes, but later she could never recall what she told him. After awhile, the officer marched her attacker, hands bound, a bandage plastered over his face, past the office window. He appeared smallish, no taller than she, but slouched so badly she could not be sure.

An hour after that, the watchman, his work shift over, returned to see if she was all right. He said the man had signed an admission of guilt. "You'll probably not even have to go before a judge," he said. "You'll never see that criminal again."

He was wrong about that. For days she would see him every time she closed her eyes.

Rachel asked for a chair. Taking it outside, she sat, undisturbed, in the sunshine. Her hands had stopped shaking. The pleasant warmth helped to expel fear but did not alleviate anger. Trying to sort things out, to make sense of what had happened, she shut her eyes and was still. Her mind reached back, all the way back, to childhood, even to that day she had left a rag doll— one that had been her mother's—on the porch steps of their farmhouse in New Jersey. When she remembered the doll the next morning, the dog had shaken it to pieces. Neither she and little Helen nor older sister Margaret nor their mother could piece it together.

Pulling together her fragmented mind now was like piecing together the scattered remnants of the doll. One realization was clear: It was her fault then; it was her fault now. As a child seeing the doll murdered had made her stomach sick, and she was nauseous now. The decision to come here, alone, was the stupidest thing she had ever done. How could she have been so foolish, so dumb?

Finding someone in this wretched place, someone with a boat who would take her across the Mississippi to Missouri or down the river to New Madrid would be like stitching the doll back together. Or like finding the proverbial needle in a stack of hay. It was not going to happen. Period.

Armies were gathering in places she would never see. Dwight was there, somewhere, but she could not go to him.

Another unshakeable truth: Leaving Cairo, this pathetic town they called Little Egypt, was beyond dangerous. It was fanatical, a crazy leap into the unknown. She needed to take that train north, back to Chicago. She needed to go home immediately. There, life was certain. It was predictable.

It was safe.

But there was another problem. The 8:15 to Chicago had already left the station. Rachel was stuck in Cairo, Illinois, at least until tomorrow.

CHAPTER 11

Cairo, Illinois

Sitting alone outside the depot, a listless and defeated Rachel slipped in and out of what some might think was sleep but was an altered state of being. Time seemed to have stopped during her silent vigil that, bit by bit, helped to restore balance to body and mind. A twitch in her arm finally went away, and she could no longer feel pulsing in her throat when she swallowed. Awash in sunlight, Cairo's docks and wharves and the railway station itself beckoned with the potential warmth of good cheer. Puffballs of cotton hung suspended against a sky of brilliant blue. Somewhere a bird warbled.

The bewildering fog of terror had relaxed its grip. Withdrawing the pocket watch, Rachel was startled to see it was almost ten o'clock. Stomach complaining, she yearned for coffee, but there were other imperatives, starting with an initiation to the river itself.

It coursed nearby, just beyond the levee a few rods

away. She walked on legs unsteady at first to the high em-
bankment of earth, climbed the rough stairs of wood, and
witnessed, in disbelief, what was called a river but resembled a huge moving lake, a bay estuary absorbing the rush
of high tide. It had to be miles across, two times, three times
the Hudson River in width!

There was no bridge anywhere. How could there be
a bridge across a river as massively wide as this? "Father
of Waters" indeed! A second shock was the silence of this
Mississippi. One expected such a powerful flow to make
noise, especially at flood level when the crush of steady current threatened to breach the levee on a whim only it could
know.

And the mud-like color, a nondescript ugly brown that
permitted no gaze to penetrate. This river was full of debris:
tree limbs and root wads and what children from New York
City had called pig floats, enormous rafts of dirty white
foam from the upstate tanneries. She remembered how the
Hudson sometimes carried the stink of decay, but this river's stench was unbearable, like an overused privy in need
of lime. When an entire tree, a mature oak she thought,
went by, its intact branches waving like a drowning swim-
mer, Rachel shuddered and could not believe what she was
watching.

"Oh, my!" she cried, hand over her nose and mouth in
fear. How could anyone get across this living barrier? Her
mind sprang to the coach seat and discarded book. Rachel
had surmised that Dickens took perverse delight in describ-
ing the town and river in such a reprehensible way but now
knew there was truth to his words and was glad she had
left the book for someone else to digest. Seeing and smell-
ing this river in person was more than enough. And she
questioned why Joseph Wirksky, the wounded soldier she

had met in Chicago just two days ago, had said nothing about the river's raging condition, its horrible odor, or how it threatened to flood Cairo at any moment.

Dejected, Rachel walked back to the depot and pondered her next move. The freight stack was gone. A different locomotive, its engine grumbling, escorted a sole passenger car and appeared ready to depart. A single-file line of young men, some more boy than man, were boarding. Others, soldiers bearing rifles and dressed alike in Union blue, herded them into the car. The ones they supervised, obviously prisoners, wore mismatched clothing of predominately gray or butternut. They numbered twenty, or more, and they moved along slowly, some with heads low, a few looking about.

Rachel flinched to hear a voice beside her. "They're Rebels," someone said. "Our boys captured 'em across the river in Belmont. They are now prisoners of the United States of America."

She pivoted to face the speaker. Middle-aged, he wore a porter's cap. "Do you know where they're going?"

"Depends. If they be officers, they go to Fort Randall in Wisconsin. The conscripts go to Ohio. That's where the prison camps are."

"Where do you think these men will go?"

The question animated him. "To Hell, I hope! They can walk stiff-legged all the way to Hell for all I care! Serves 'em right for taking up arms against their own country. I got no sympathy for traitors, ma'am. Not a whit. They a shame to my mind. Look how guilty they look."

To this outburst she said nothing. The porter cleared his throat and spat. "Every day since Belmont gave up the ghost and the Rebs up and deserted Columbus, our boys been rounding up scum like these. The ones that won't repent and take the oath go to prison where they belong. I'm telling you, most won't look an honest man in the eye they be so guilty. What they done is a shame!"

They watched until the last man boarded, followed by two guards. Rachel had been silent, her neutral gaze of curiosity that of an onlooker, but now anger swept through her. These prisoners were her son's enemies. Given the chance, they would have killed him. Because of them, he was dying, could be dead by now! This realization made her blood seethe. It rekindled her resolve. Last summer Dwight had forfeited up to three years of his young life, a life of promise, of peace and freedom, to fight this blatant tyranny, to end this insurrection, to win this evil war.

There was no turning back now! She would not betray her son and go home without him. Whenever she was able to leave Cairo, the direction would be south. Not north. Not until Dwight was with her again and she knew what malevolence had come to him.

Rachel asked the porter who she might see about going down the river.

He fired back a questioning look. "Now that I *don't* know! Talk to someone over on the docks. If anyone knows, they'll know."

Rachel heard the train's departing whistle as she walked toward the docks. People swarmed the sidewalk planks and dirt streets on this Saturday morning. They clustered around an open-air market where a score of men and women, some wearing aprons, were selling produce and wares from farm carts and wagons. As she walked along the wide lane leading to what must be the docks, a whiff of saddle leather and horse manure induced a thought of Bill and Sam, and she hoped that stable boy in Battle Creek was doing right by her team.

The open door of a small café beckoned with its red-and-white checkered tablecloths and the alluring odor of fresh coffee. The prospect of breakfast eggs and flannel cakes moistened her mouth in spite of not feeling hungry. Rachel knew she should eat something, if her stomach would allow it.

A muffled sound like distant thunder threatened rain. She thought it came from somewhere down the river; here in Cairo the day was bright, the air still. At the docks, a row of packets tugged at mooring lines while the river swept along. A man with hands on hips was watching a knot of dockhands piling boxes onto one of the boats. Rachel assumed he was in charge.

"Good morning, sir, and a beautiful morning it is. Could you kindly tell me if this boat will be going downriver soon?" She stood there, waiting for his answer.

"Look, lady," he said, "take your business elsewhere. We ain't interested. We're working here." She was dumbstruck at this rude, callous remark.

The men stopped working and listened to the exchange. "I bet she's workin' too," one snickered in a voice loud enough for everyone to hear. "The real question, though, is she workin' late or workin' early?"

Rowdy laughter followed. Blood racing from her thumping heart, Rachel instantly caught the insult. It was the false condemnation that infuriated her. "What makes you think I…"

The foreman cut her off. "You oughta know better than to show up down here. I told you we ain't interested."

Making a fist, she shook it at him. "Who do you think you are? You have no right to accuse me of anything, let alone that!"

"You got no right to be down here. Got no sense either.

Go! Get out of here, right now, or I'll send someone for the marshals."

Rachel could not believe what had just happened. The very idea! Twisting away, she stomped off toward the town.

"Show me the Army," one of the workers howled, "and I'll show you the whooers!" Rachel didn't look back.

Her face was hot. She sensed a burning sensation in her nose. This censure, this unprovoked denunciation, was embittering, and her eyes watered as she walked. The deplorable incident made her more resolute than ever to leave this ugly town, this Little Egypt, with its unsavory characters, and its unprincipled people, as soon as possible.

Coffee would help to settle her nerves.

Business was brisk at the café. Rachel spied an empty table for two in a far corner, placed her bag on one chair, and sat in the other. The waitress, an older matron, smiled and took her order, but Rachel could not shake the prickly feeling that some customers, a gaggle of men at one table and a woman with a boy at another, assessed her with disapproving eyes. Cairo was a frontier town with a large transient population. Right or wrong, Rachel concluded people here were suspicious. They were mistrustful of each other. Maybe they were not accustomed to seeing a woman without a male escort. Maybe she threatened them in some way.

It was not her business. Rachel knew, now, it was her problem and demonstrably so. The face of John Welch flickered before her. Dutiful John, laying out the reasons why she should stay home and he should go. Well, neither he, nor she, had ever been to Cairo, Illinois. She, for certain, would never come here again.

She ate the breakfast without tasting it although the steaming coffee was helping to restore evenness. Amid the din of plate clatter and lively conversation, she sipped the brew and tried to concentrate on individual dialogue. A man was talking about artillery fire and Island No. 10 and how engaged the Federals must be with the enemy to be heard here, sixty miles upriver. She lost the voice for a moment in the cacophony and when it came back, she caught "mortar fire" and "gunboat cannon" and "intensity."

Was it possible the Federal Navy was overtaking the island this morning? A definitive voice snuffed out that hope: "This is Day Ten of Foote's siege. They ain't lobbing any more shells now than they did every other day this week."

Disheartened, Rachel tried to sort out what options were left. She was still fuming about the train station attack and the character assault and couldn't, wouldn't go back to the docks by herself.

The market might be a safe place to listen. To inquire. There were women in the market, and so she walked there. Loitering at each stall, each wagon, she hovered while feigning interest in purchasing something. A tinge of embarrassment goaded her into buying a couple of minor household items, small trinkets that would fit in the satchel. Hearing "packet boat," she pressed closer so as not to miss a word.

An older couple, a woman and a man, were talking. "When did he say he was going?" the woman asked. Rachel assumed he was her husband.

"He didn't say. Just that there's no river travel 'till they get those gunboats past that island."

"But he doesn't know when that will be, right?"

Irritation was in his voice. "Nobody knows, Martha! I told you before. He said whenever that Foote fellow gives in."

Rachel gambled and interrupted: "Forgive me for overhearing. Are you speaking of the island near New Madrid?"

It was the woman's turn. "Yes. The one they call No. 10."

"The one the Confederates control?"

"That's right. Y'all ain't from around here, are you?"

Was it the northern accent or her ignorance that exposed her, that revoked what Rachel had hoped was the veil of anonymity? She had noticed people in southern Illinois spoke a bit differently than they do in Michigan, just as the accent there was not the same as in New York. Or New Jersey, for that matter.

"No. I'm from up north. Michigan actually. I hope to get to New Madrid as soon as I can."

"Oh, New Madrid's safe enough," the woman said. "Long as Pope and his big blue army don't leave it with no protection when they leave."

"Well," her husband added, "when they do get across the river, he'll post some men there to hold it. That island's another story. Nothing goes past unless the Rebel says so. They say Foote's afraid to take a chance. He don't want any more of his precious gunboats shot apart. "He looked at his wife. "I say he ain't scared, he's yellow."

Were they Southern sympathizers? Rachel suspected Cairo's allegiance was not all to one side or the other. Here, the line was fuzzy, indistinct, if there was a real line anywhere at all. People north of Cairo were likely Union. Those south of Cairo probably favored secession. But unless one offered personal sentiment, it was audacious to assume and foolish to speculate. It was dangerous to ask.

Cautiously, Rachel advanced a different question. "You were talking about a packet boat? Do I dare ask what you meant?"

Again, the woman was quick to answer. "Our nephew, his brother's son," she said, nodding to her husband, "works crew on the *Arago*. It's loaded with gunpowder and other things, just waiting to go downriver. Soon as the Navy says so."

The husband must have understood Rachel's reason for intervening in their conversation. "If you're thinking of trying to go aboard, you might as well forget it. Those packets don't take passengers, least of all women. You'd have to be a working man to get on one."

"How about getting across the river? Instead of going down the river."

"Now, why would you do that? Ain't nothing over there but swamp and flooded timber."

"Isn't there a road over there? To New Madrid, I mean."

"If there's a road, it's underwater. Ma'am, you got to understand. This river's the highest it's been in years. It's flooded for miles over there."

Rachel's pitched response announced stress. "Is there any way to get to New Madrid at all except by going downriver?"

"Well, you could go up the river to St. Louis and take the King's Highway."

"Yes, I heard about the King's Highway. The Army all but ruined it though, didn't they?"

"I suppose they did. Probably a 'low way' now. Some of it anyway. I mean, it's near two hundred miles from St. Louis to New Madrid."

"Two hundred miles! How could it be that far by road? That's three times more than by river!"

"I would wager it is."

As Rachel walked away, crestfallen, she heard the woman say to her husband. "Poor dear. She seemed so desperate to get down there to New Madrid."

CHAPTER 12

Cairo, Illinois

Rachel walked without purpose throughout the town. Because she did not know what next to do, she paced up one street and down the next. It didn't matter where she went because she was going nowhere at the moment. Without prospect, there was no hope.

Had she stayed on the farm, instead of wandering about this dreadful city with its scurrilous people, she would be rocking back and forth in her favorite chair while knitting mittens or making a shawl. Invariably, the repetitive push/wrap/pull/pick/drop of knowing fingers helped to appease a troubled spirit. Knitting, producing, relaxed the mind, in turn opening the door to fresh thinking, to new possibilities. In a strange way, going over and over the mundane knitting regimen merged with her walking cadence and stirred an uplift of her mood.

It also brought weariness. Rachel wondered how far she had walked. Two miles? Three miles? It made no difference. She wanted to sit down. Her route had taken her through Cairo's threadbare neighborhoods, by its taverns with their shoddy facades, and past several churches. She stopped before one. Finding the entrance door unlocked, Rachel walked inside and sat in the last pew.

The hymnal she picked up was Presbyterian. Although Rachel had never been in a Presbyterian church, the wooden altar with IHS emblazoned below the ubiquitous cross was a near copy of the one in her Methodist Episcopal church. Steeped in the doctrine of Dutch Reform while growing up in the East, she was familiar enough with Protestant dogma and ritual to be comfortable here. A large stained-glass window, a colorful circle depicting The Last Supper, guarded the sanctuary like a multi-colored eye. Sunlight streaming through several clear panes of glass was adequate for reading. She found her treasured Psalms, long favored for their poetry, commenced to read, and found the respite she needed.

It was well into afternoon when Rachel suspected she was not alone. Closing the book, she looked around. Someone, an elderly man she thought, was arranging papers on the pulpit. He must have entered without notice from another door. She spoke first. "Good afternoon. I hope I'm not unwelcome here." Her voice was loud in the emptiness.

Obviously alarmed, he looked out at her, and it seemed that he was trying to match a name to the face that peered back. "Oh, no. Not at all. We're happy to have you here. You are most welcome in this church."

He had a pleasant voice and a captivating smile. "I just wanted a quiet spot to sit and read."

"Well, First Presbyterian is the right place for that. I'm Robert Whitlowe, one of the deacons here."

She matched his smile and said, "How do you do, Mr.

Whitlowe? The pleasure is mine."

Stepping down from the chancel, he approached, paused at a respectable distance, and asked if he might sit for a moment in the pew across from hers. For a half-hour, perhaps longer, they discussed the gospel and shared thoughts on the effects of the War here and elsewhere. They talked about the president's handling of the unprecedented crisis that had torn apart the nation. She found him to be an affable man, interesting and easy to talk with. He listened well and asked no personal questions.

Rachel told him her name, and he invited her to attend tomorrow's worship service.

"I would like that very much. Thank you. I rarely miss the Sunday service."

"Tomorrow is rather special," he confided. "Commodore Foote has agreed to give the sermon again."

"Commodore Foote? You mean the Navy's Foote?" She was taken aback. "How did you ever arrange for that?"

"Well, he's in Cairo again, right now." Deacon Whitlowe's laughter was gentle. Rachel leaned forward to hear. "He wants to get the *Carondelet* back in his fleet. She was badly damaged at Fort Donelson. Then, during last week's tornado, a tree crushed her smokestack while she was moored along the bank over in Missouri."

Curiosity was all over her face. "But how did it happen that he will be here?"

"Yes, it's a gift, isn't it? Well, he came to the service even though he had injured his foot. Walked in out of the blue on crutches. When he saw we had no pastor, he asked us deacons if someone would be leading the service. We told him no, so he went up into the pulpit and did it himself.

"How about that?" He grinned and laughed again. "Mrs. Barnum, he's his own man. A very devout man and a faithful Presbyterian. Gives Sunday sermons on his flagship for any of the sailors willing to attend. I have no doubt tomorrow's message will be inspirational. The one he gave before was completely impromptu. No notes at all."

She was flabbergasted. "He just walked in out of the blue?"

His smile was radiant. "Yes, he most certainly did. Just like you."

Taking in his words, Rachel thought for a moment of their implications. "Oh, I so look forward to hearing him tomorrow. Mr. Whitlowe, again, I thank you."

When she rose to go, he walked her to the door and opened it. Outside, she embraced the bright, warm afternoon. The visit encouraged Rachel to question her harsh appraisal of Cairo's citizenry. A familiar bible verse popped to mind: *"Do not judge or you too will be judged."*

A brief walk and she was back in the city's business center. Knowing she could not go to New Madrid or Chicago, not today anyway, she was aware of the need for lodging. The thought of a third straight night in a train station brought an involuntary shudder. She wanted a real bed in a room with a light she could extinguish on her own. She needed private space to tend to personal matters. Recalling the words "St. Charles Hotel," she couldn't recall who had said them.

However, it couldn't be far; Cairo was not *that* big. She slowed her pace along the sidewalk to study passing buildings for signs of a hotel. Three Negroes walking abreast toward her might know. As they approached, the man stepped into the street first, followed by an older woman and a younger one. The last time she had known such deference from colored people was in New York City a long time ago. Seeing a Negro in Eaton County, Michigan, was a rarity, so uncommon she couldn't recall if she had ever seen one.

Rachel nodded acknowledgment, bade the trio good afternoon, and asked for the whereabouts of the St. Charles. The way they paused and looked at each other made her wonder if they were freed or indentured. The man looked away and gestured. "Oh, it be over there, ma'am." He seemed suspicious. Or nervous.

"Over where, sir?" The women wouldn't meet her gaze either.

The awkward exchange caused Rachel to realize that talking to a white woman made them uncomfortable. The man appeared to be thirty or thirty-five. She wondered if anyone had ever addressed him as sir.

He said, "End of this here walk, ma'am." Go left a little bit. It's at the corner there."

"Thank you," she said. "Thank you much, sir." Walking on, still in the street, they didn't see her grateful smile.

Two third-floor rooms remained unrented at the St. Charles Hotel. An attendant showed her both chambers; she chose the smaller one for a half-dollar less. The bed was decent, the covers clean. Perching on the vanity below a small mirror on the wall were a large porcelain bowl and matching water pitcher. Placing her bag on the only chair, Rachel noted the empty chamber pot beneath. A single gas lamp mounted over the bed would brighten the little room. She had everything she needed.

Downstairs in the dining room, she ate a good supper, the wave of utter fatigue arriving just as she finished her meal of baked fish with potatoes and gravy. Satisfied with the present state of affairs, knowing she had done all she could do today, she retired to her room. Enough daylight stole through the west window to allow reading without the lamp. Crawling under covers, she lay on her back and fell asleep before prayers were finished. Her hands still pressed together, the open book lay across her torso when she awoke in the morning.

Mississippi River, below Cairo

COMMODORE ANDREW HULL FOOTE WAS in captain's quarters on the *USS Benton*, his flagship, when the day's third telegram arrived. The instant he read "St. Louis" on the envelope, his scalp prickled with irritation. He knew it was from the headquarters of Maj. Gen. Henry Halleck, Supreme Commander for the Army of the Mississippi. Flag Officer Foote expected the missive was yet another plea to move his gunboats past Island No. 10, "as expeditiously as possible," lest Gen. John Pope and his army remain stranded at New Madrid when they were "desperately needed elsewhere."

Foote knew the Union plan and the integral part his fleet of eight gunboats, chains of mortar rafts, and support vessels were expected to play. Once the enemy's shoreline artillery was destroyed or spiked to silence, troop transports would shuttle Pope's 4th Corps across the river. They would then attack the island, demolish the Rebel batteries, and rout, capture, or kill the occupying enemy force. Then, Foote would take his armada downriver to its next target, Fort Pillow, and on to the city of Memphis. Meanwhile, Gen. Pope would march his men to the Tennessee/Mississippi border where they would more than double the size of Grant's command awaiting their arrival.

Such was the Union strategy to overpower the river towns one by one, all the way to and including New Orleans, and to break the Confederate strength in two. Mastery of the river was the means to controlling the Western War Theater, but absent the Naval fleet, it would not happen. The annoyed flag officer tore open the envelope and quickly scanned its contents. His instincts were correct; parts of Halleck's plea were word for word.

Foote wanted to do the Supreme Commander's bidding but not at the cost of losing any of his ironclads, or wooden vessels for that matter. The Navy fleet was too important to trust to military men whose war experience was Army and not Navy. He had already telegraphed Gideon Welles, Secretary of the Navy, that he would not move any warships past heavily fortified Island No. 10 "unless absolutely ordered to do so."

Therefore, he would also rebuff Halleck's newest entreaty. Recalling how only a month ago two gunboats had sustained damage during the capture of Fort Henry, and how plunging cannon fire at Fort Donelson had disabled three more, was still embittering to him. Those Pyrrhic victories had forced him to send the damaged ironclads back to the Naval yard in Cairo for extensive refitting and repair.

Biting a lip, he tossed aside Halleck's telegram.

Foote's skilled pilots balked at facing another close encounter with enemy artillery and needed no encouragement to anchor upriver and wait. Rebel shells sometimes hit vulnerable pilot houses. At Fort Henry, one had found the engine room of the *Essex* and exploded its boiler, scalding to death a wheelman and burning several sailors. The Commodore himself had narrowly missed being killed aboard the *Cincinnati* when a shell crashed through the pilot house, missing him by a foot and ruining the ship's steering controls.

Pacing within the small confines of his quarters, hands behind his back, Foote took a deep breath and released it slowly. Other worries were eating away at him. His prized ironclad, the *Carondelet*, was also back at the Naval yard, the victim of a recent tornado that had unearthed riverbank cottonwoods, one of which crushed her smokestack and killed a sailor.

Continuing a siege and bombarding the island from a distance was better than running the gantlet at No. 10. It bought the Flag Officer time, perhaps enough time for a controversial scenario to play out. There was talk that Gen. Pope, trained as a military engineer, might authorize his 25th Missouri engineering regiment to dig a canal through the flooded woods above the island. One of Pope's officers had explained the idea during a recent meeting on the *Benton*. Foote's eyebrows sprouted a new shape when he learned the canal would have to be nine miles long and deep enough for gunboats to navigate. The preposterous idea that caused him to shake his head in disbelief was one more excuse to sit idly by on the river like the fleet of turtles he commanded.

Further, the Flag Officer had experienced trouble sleeping but not from the vibrating rumble of the Benton's engine room. The cause was unease. At fifty-six years old and four decades into a naval career, he feared he was losing the verve he had known as a younger leader. Having sailed the world, Commodore Foote had protected American interests and enhanced her reputation while battling Caribbean pirates, seizing slave ships packed with illegal human cargo off the African coast, and destroying barrier forts on the Canton River in China.

Self-doubt, not the lack of bravery, was the reason for inertia. The Commodore had been a blue-water sailor, never the commander of a brown-water arsenal. His experience was with sail, not steam, and he was unhappy when

Washington sent him to the Western rivers. Thus far, the highlight of this newest assignment was overseeing the construction and outfitting of his promising gunboat fleet.

But after learning the iconic warships were not invincible but vulnerable, Flag Officer Foote was reluctant to commit them to combat. From his platform atop the flagship, he saw how slowly they moved. "They're not only turtles," he had told a junior officer. "They're sitting ducks."

With so much on his mind, Foote found it hard to sleep undisturbed. The long absence from home was a constant reminder of how tentative military life had been and would always be as long as he served. That near miss on the *Cincinnati* was no dream to try and shake off. And his foot still throbbed with pain from an injury suffered a few days later during the bombardment of Fort Donelson. He had been in the wheelhouse of the *St. Louis* when a Rebel shell exploded, sending shards of wood flying everywhere. Now, weeks later, he still hobbled on crutches.

The confidence, therefore, of the man some newspapers called "Stonewall of the West" waned, and he wanted to go home to New Haven, Connecticut, to be with his second wife, their two daughters, and two sons.

On March 19, two days after leaving Cairo with the fleet, Foote's ironclads and mortar boats had begun the three-week siege of Island No. 10 with the firing of ordnance at the entrenched Rebels. An aide had handed him several telegrams in the presence of two civilian guests. Sorting through them, the commodore opened one and learned that his thirteen-year-old son had died after a brief illness. Excusing himself, Foote repaired to his cabin. Fifteen minutes later he was topside again, perfectly composed, the staunch military man accustomed to putting duty ahead of personal needs.

Sick at heart all day, he was too ill to eat supper. After rereading a recent letter from his son, he could not sleep at all. The next morning a longer letter he wrote home to express his deep sorrow and to soothe his wife only served to deepen depression.

CHAPTER 13

When Rachel stepped into the wide street before the St. Charles Hotel, sunlight was winning a morning battle with shade. She crossed to the warm, bright side and walked the mile or so to First Presbyterian Church. Arriving early, she could have sat anywhere but chose the same rear pew as yesterday. The maxim of Methodists never failing to claim a seat farthest from the pulpit could be more than jest or self-deprecating humor. It could be true!

She had slept without disturbance and felt much better than when she had gone to bed. Yesterday's raw events still perturbed her, but the danger itself was long over. Rachel had survived a horrendous choice to travel here alone, but this church with head deacon Mr. Whitlowe promised respite. Maybe here misfortune would turn into good luck. She fantasized that her decision to sit in the same place was the right one.

Rachel considered a third possibility: That she was not here by coincidence but that an unseen hand had guided her on this same Sabbath morning as the Naval Commander for Western Waters. If so, how could she know how it was that she was here until she knew why she was here? That answer depended on the consequence, if there was to be a consequence.

Without announcement, Commodore Andrew Hull Foote strode into the church. Gingerly mounting three steps to the chancel, he lay down his crutches and limped to the pulpit. He bore no clue that he was a faithful man of God. He had no blousy black robe about him. He wore no white collar. Rather, his attire was Federal blue, and he wore his uniform with pride. An expert tailor had cut and sewn the pressed trousers. His dress jacket, buttoned to the bearded chin, showed no imperfection. With its handsome epaulets of rank and gilded sleeves, he appeared the epitome of an American military officer.

But was he a preacher? The first words suggested he was not. He said he knew military school, not seminary. He opined that he would prefer to hear an ordained pastor or an Army chaplain this beautiful morning, and he paused, waiting for such a volunteer. When no one came forward, he admitted he was simply a layman believer willing to share the good news to any heart prepared to hear.

The voice was gruff, the delivery clipped and strident, as one might expect with military speech. But it was what he had to say, not how he said it, that fused Rachel to her seat. His invocation was a stirring call to worship, followed by the Affirmation of Faith printed in the hymnal. Along with the seventy or so others, Rachel stood and read the words aloud and joined in singing "How Great Thou Art." Afterward, when the people were again seated, the church fell silent, the parishioners engaged with anticipation. Mr. Foote opened his bible and said:

"From Exodus, Chapter 21, Verse 16: *Whoever steals a man and sells him, and anyone found in possession of him, shall be put to death.*

"And from Galatians, Chapter 3, Verse 28: *There is neither Jew nor Greek, there is neither slave nor free, there is no male and female, for you are all one in Christ Jesus.*"

Then the Commodore looked up, paused to evaluate his audience, and said, in his own words, "Brothers and Sisters, I submit to you that slavery is not only a sin …"

A handful of worshippers stirred and briskly rose to their feet.

"… it is an abomination to God the Father and to his only Son, our living Lord and Savior!"

The offended made their hasty way to the aisles and left the church. The door closed with a bang, and for a long moment, there was no sound.

Stiffened from shock, Rachel gripped the top of the pew before her with both hands. Having never witnessed such a rebuke, she shivered from excitement. To walk out on a speaker was rude, but to reject what a preacher, ordained or not, had to say was the height of vulgarity. She was further stunned when the commodore watched the deserters file through the door and said nothing about it. Acting as if nothing at all had happened, he continued his message. With eyes transfixed on Mr. Foote, Rachel leaned back into the pew.

"We are told in Philippians 2, verses 1-8, that the feeling of superiority in general to anyone is a sin because all humans, men and women alike, are made in the image of God.

"That said, to truly understand God's Word, we must understand why there are so many references to slavery in both the Old and New Testaments. We must refute why some insist the bible justifies slavery. Consider, for example, Deuteronomy 23, verses 15-16: *You shall not give up to his master a slave who has escaped from his master to you.* And Ephesians 6, verse 5: *Bondservants, obey your earthly masters with fear and trembling, with a sincere heart, as you would Christ.*"

Next, he said these passages, as well as many others, did not justify slavery. That all of God's children—rich and poor, young and old, black and white—were equal in His eyes. He explained that "servant" and "slave" meant the same thing and that it was common practice for the Israelites to sell themselves into servitude, for an agreed-upon period of time, as "willing debt-servants" to those who loaned them money or something else of value.

He shared and interpreted more passages, concluding with James 2:1-9 and James 5:1-6, and said, "Slavery is the world's worst expression of economic discrimination and favoritism. The Lord does not abide slavery. It is among the most grievous of all sins and an abomination to Him."

Foote then interpreted how the insurrection was more than an assault on America's constitution, "that all men are indeed created equal," that it is a rebellion against God and, therefore, must be defeated.

And he sat down.

Those who remained had listened with rapt attention. Rachel expected a long sermon, the endless kind she was used to, but this man's message lasted less than a quarter-hour. When Commodore Foote had settled into a chair beside the pulpit, Deacon Whitlowe led the singing of "Stand Up, Stand Up for Jesus" and gave the closing prayer during which he thanked the good Flag Officer for "gracing First Presbyterian with your presence and for sharing your illuminating insights to the Holy Word."

Following the offering, members sang the Doxology, and the service was over.

Several parishioners wanted to greet Commodore Foote and talk with him. By the time Rachel reached the chancel, the line was long but that didn't matter. She would patiently await her turn, preferring, hoping, to address him alone. From a front-row seat, she reflected on the brief sermon's impact.

Her husband would have been moved by Mr. Foote's interpretation of those bible verses, how his words were unequivocal and so very true. No rampant abolitionist, Willis Barnum was nevertheless opposed to human bondage of any kind and, in particular, he deplored the practice of slavery. From the day she first met her future husband, at the blacksmith shop in Sunfield, he had assured her that he held slavery to be illegal and that the South would one day be made accountable for practicing it and protecting it.

It was easy to recall his justification because he declared it from time to time. "Ever since breaking away to forge our own nation," he would say, "we have retained the best of British practices in language, law, custom, and, to some extent, religion. Slavery is the sole exception. The British abolished that wicked practice a generation ago, and it is high time America followed their example."

Raised in Massachusetts by parents of English descent, Willis Barnum's veneration for all things English was natural to him and, by his influence, to Rachel. So, too, was the expectation that both Watson and Dwight would share their father's sentiments. As did she.

WHILE SHE WAITED, IT WAS Willis who occupied her deepest thoughts. One morning a couple of months ago, the sun had come out from behind rolls of wet, gray clouds that looked like a rumpled rug made from sewn-together rags. It was late in January and the winter thaw had finally come. The bright sun was a welcome change. Rachel walked to the cemetery, wiped dry her late husband's chair—she had come to call it Contemplation Chair—and began a monologue with her first and only love. So much had happened over the three and one-half years since the heart attack that ended their life together. Sitting before his grave, she told Willis how Dwight had grown to be the man he had aspired him to be, a brave soldier who went to war to honor his father, a young man willing to forfeit his life to wipe clean a nation's shame. Rachel told Willis how Watson had lasted a year longer in school than Dwight, was almost a man himself now, and was sure to follow his brother into the fight if the Rebellion went on. She shared with Willis how Hester and Helena were almost as tall as their mother and would be young women before long.

The long wait in the church pew was uncomfortable, and Rachel stood for a moment and stretched. Seated again, her thoughts drifted to how Willis had led their family in prayer before evening meals and how he always had asked each member, from left to right around the table, what they had been most thankful for that day. Swift as a card trick, the image of Willis morphed into that of John Welch and his habitual place at meal time. The unexpected transition rattled Rachel. A hand flew to forehead, fingers squeezed her temples to make sense of it. There was no immediate answer. She needed to think about this.

Appearing from nowhere at age thirty-three, John Welch had grown so crucial to her that Rachel knew she could not manage the farm without him. With Dwight gone, she depended on her hired man more than ever. She knew that inviting John into her home to live was providing the stability she needed and that he seemed to want, too. A form of life insurance, it was proving to be of mutual benefit. These glimmers of reality were helping to explain how thoughts of Willis had melded to thoughts of John.

Based upon what she knew of John Welch's past, dribbles and drabs that he shared from time to time, he had stayed longer on this job than any other since leaving home in Vermont as a young man.

Rachel was certain Willis would have approved of her practical arrangement with the hired man. John Welch was an easy man to like, and he was trustworthy. His attention to work details, as well as his ability to organize tasks, was more than admirable. It was inspiring. Mr. Welch was a worthy model for her sons to emulate.

Those were the facts, the realities Rachel knew to be true. But there was more. She knew there was more. The Christmas season, only three months ago, had been hard. The good will, the communal cheer that always came with the period of the Savior's birth, had had an opposite effect on her. The holiday festivities reminded Rachel of happy times now gone. A sadness would come over her, at times without warning, an unmistakable gloominess as undefinable as the soft, marly creek bottom where she had swum as a child. There was no point in talking about it to anyone because, if she couldn't fathom why she felt the way she did, how could anyone explain it to her? Only Willis could help. She always felt a little better when she talked with Willis. In winter, during such bouts of despondency, the bare fingers of the maple near his resting place seemed to call her to him.

One morning as the new year loomed, Rachel sat at her

kitchen table, head in hands, and wept. The graveside session with Willis had failed to make her feel better, nor had reading her bible brought relief. The coffee, what was left of it, bubbled away on the wood stove and was too acidic to drink. Rachel's one glad thought was that she was alone. The girls had gone to a neighbor's. Watson and John Welch were outside chopping wood. No one was around to see tears trailing each other down her somber face.

The door suddenly pitched open, and the hired man was standing there, looking at her, a blubbering mess. How humiliating!

"Mrs. Barnum, what on earth is wrong? Are you ill?"

Snuffling, she tried to finger away the tears. "Nothing. Nothing is wrong."

"Did you hurt yourself? How can I help you?"

"I don't think you can. I'm sorry, John. I'm just not myself this morning."

"Well, you're still Rachel Barnum, and I don't want you hurting about nothing. You know I'm here for you." She sniffled and looked up at him. "Mrs. Barnum, Rachel, tell me how to help you." Handing her a clean dish cloth, he sat down beside her.

"I don't know what's wrong." She wiped her face. "I'm out of sorts today. Just a little sad, I suppose."

His hand had found her shoulder. The taut fingers that patted it became a gentle clasp. Rachel heard the crack of Watson's ax splitting wood. John's soft voice was empathetic. "I'm sorry things aren't well for you right now. If you want to be alone, I'll go out. In fact, I'll tell Wat not to come in for awhile."

"No. Whatever it is, it's going away. Thank you, John."

As the queue for Flag Officer Foote shrank, Rachel wondered about these and other things that were changing her life. Always, her thoughts returned to Dwight and whether she would ever see him again.

TWO OR THREE STILL WAITED. Rachel evaluated what to say to Mr. Foote and how to say it. What to include, what to leave out. She watched with intense interest to the exchange he was having with one of the deacons.

Commodore Foote seemed to be a considerate man. Sitting there, crutches at his side, he listened to each person, offering short shrift to none, while allowing no one to dominate their conversation. But was he compassionate? Would he approve her petition, short of her having to beg for it? Realizing how hard it was for her to ask anyone for anything, her heart began to accelerate. A spark of fear ignited.

If need be, she would plead. She would not beg. Above all else, she would maintain her composure, her dignity. When her turn came, Rachel realized the first wish had already occurred: They were alone in the church now except for a junior officer, attendant on his superior. The young man, watching from some distance, Foote's crutches in hand, would not intrude.

After introducing herself and thanking him for such a moving sermon, she moved right to the point. "Sir, can you tell me how long before river travel to New Madrid will be allowed?"

He stared back as though studying her. His answer was guarded. "I don't know the day. If I knew, I would not tell you. I would tell no one." It was his turn to ask questions, and they were ripe with suspicion. "Why do you want to know? Is your loyalty Union or Confederate?"

Rachel stammered out a response. "Sir, my boy is a cavalry soldier with the 2nd Michigan ... he took sick with a fever … he's dying … he just turned nineteen … he may already have gone to the Father!"

Voice choking, she cleared her throat and turned away, squeezing shut her eyes to force back gathering tears. When composed, she looked back and he seemed smaller, withdrawn, his face drained of color. What happened here? Why does he look so distraught? Did she upset him?

Rachel grew nervous. She began to tremble. Her disjointed answer must have unsettled him. Solemn, unresponsive, he seemed to have gone somewhere. She watched him look down, engrossed with his hands. Fingers entwined, his thumbs chased each other. The uncomfortable moment passed, and he looked up at her. "How do you know this?"

"By the telegraph," she said. "Ten days ago, tomorrow. I must get to New Madrid now. Is this somehow possible?"

The steady gaze was penetrating. His dark eyes were nearly black. "No, Mrs. Barnum. It is not possible. Not yet. I'm sorry."

"Then when, sir? When?"

"Soon. We've been shelling that island for two weeks. The enemy can't hold out much longer. That's all I can tell you, Mrs. Barnum. I'm sorry. I'm truly sorry for your son."

"Then will you pray for him?"

He must not have expected that. His little smile said it pleased him. "Yes. Of course, I will pray for him. And for you."

"His name is Dwight Barnum."

And with that Commodore Foote went to his knees, invoked the Almighty, and asked for mercy for mother and son. The brief prayer finished, he had one more question. "When the river is cleared and the enemy defeated, how do you expect to get there?"

"To be honest, sir, I do not know."

"Then I would advise the Western Sanitary Commission. They're preparing a hospital ship now for aid downriver wherever it's needed most. Look for *The City of Memphis* in the East Wharf area. They always need nurses and maybe more volunteers."

Rachel could scarcely believe what he had said. What she had heard. Giddy with excitement, she felt like skipping out of the church. After Commodore Foote and the aide were gone and she was by herself in this wonderful church on this ideal Sabbath morning, she prayed for Dwight, for those at home, and for personal strength. Rachel thanked Him for bringing her and the good Navy officer here, and she prayed that this unforeseen turn of events, this gift of fortune, might, indeed, be a miracle.

Upon stepping outside, though, Rachel wondered where the sun had gone. Hiding behind a sheet of gray nothingness, it was now a diffused lens of light. Her legs felt a little heavy, such was her disappointment with this change in weather, but she vowed not to let dismay steal her optimism. Despite yesterday's savage and painful incidents, she decided to revisit the levee in search of the hospital boat. She would avoid moored packets with crews aboard and any solitary men. An hour later, she climbed atop the levee again and was relieved that others were out and about. Couples young and old and families with children had come to see how high the river was and to enjoy a stroll on a warm Sunday afternoon.

If anyone thought it odd to see a lone woman walking here, they kept it to themselves. She said "Good day" to anyone who acknowledged her first. One couple holding hands appeared to be approachable. "I beg your pardon," Rachel began, "but could you point out the East Wharf?"

"Of course," the man said. Dressed in Sunday finery, it

appeared that he and his wife had been to a church service. He released his wife's hand to point up the river. "It's down the line there, past that tug. You looking for a certain boat?"

"Yes, I am. *The City of Memphis.*"

"The hospital ship? Yes, she stays over there. But she's not there now."

"Do you know where she is? Where she went?"

The woman had been looking at Rachel. She glanced at her husband for the answer.

"Well, I don't rightly know," he admitted. "Think she pulled out yesterday. Probably went up the river to St. Louis, or maybe up the Ohio to Paducah. They were loading her to go somewhere."

"Would you know when she'll return?"

"No. She comes and goes. My guess is she'll be back before long to go downriver."

"Downriver?"

"Oh, to be sure," he added. "They'll need her for the sick and hurt down there."

"Down there?"

"Why, down in Tennessee or Mississippi. They're building big armies down there. Both sides are. Sooner or later, they got to fight."

Rachel asked about Island No. 10 and how *The City of Memphis* could get past it and when.

"See that black boat out there? The one that looks like she's half-sunk? That's a gunboat, ma'am. The Navy's got a bunch of them. Rebels on the island have no chance once the Navy puts them to serious use."

"I sorely wonder when that will be."

The woman nudged her husband and spoke for the first time. "So do we."

The man changed the subject. "Lot of cloud cover today." He was looking at the river. "Hope it don't rain. It won't take much more for the old boy to top his levee."

"Good day to you, ma'am," the woman offered by way of parting.

Still buoyant from her discussion with Commodore Foote, Rachel decided to walk back to the St. Charles. If she tired along the way, she planned to pay one of the dray or coach drivers that plied the hotel routes to take her there. Walking would help to organize her thoughts. What John Welch was doing at the moment and how he was getting along with Watson and her daughters was foremost in her mind.

CHAPTER 14

Sunfield, Michigan

Woodstove warmth and the tantalizing smell of fresh coffee pervaded the kitchen the instant John Welch opened the door and stepped inside. Morning chores over, Rachel's hired man returned his lantern to the small table where he and Rachel sat at breakfast and planned the day's work. Removing his jacket, he hung it on its customary peg alongside the others, found his favorite cup, the porcelain one—the tin ones were too hot when filled with steaming coffee—and poured away. That first cup was always the best, a just reward for daily ritual that insisted a hired man forsake his warm bed before daybreak for the drafty bowels of the cold barn, abandoned by the Belgians that had taken their body heat with them.

Chapped fingers caressing his mug, John laughed to himself. At least the milk cows' nipples were warm. He enjoyed the solitude that followed a task completed. To be sure, it hadn't been that way in the lumber camp where work began at first light and ended when the light was gone. Where quiet time was impossible in a shanty overflowing with boisterous, unruly men who swore and farted and snored in their sleep. His thoughts coasted to Dwight and how he was managing life in an Army barracks, how six months of absence could seem so long and so short at once.

The hired man had no soldierly experience. Too young to enlist for the War with Mexico, perhaps too old for this War of the Rebellion, he could nevertheless imagine how Army life was like the lumber camp: loud, competitive, chaotic. How the absence of women dictated the disorderly ways of men.

John liked Rachel's older son. More than twenty years ago, he had been like Dwight, full of promise and hope, an idealistic youth who needed to test himself to find himself. John would have signed up for Union service at eighteen, just as Dwight had done. The difference, inconsequential now, was that John Welch had left home at eighteen because the home where he was born had disappeared.

The Welch ancestors were Yankee to their marrow. Emigrating from England more than a century before John was born, they had settled in southern Vermont where the soil was suitable for farming once they cleared the land of trees and glacial debris. Boulders that could be moved had seen new life as walls built to define properties. The smaller rocks became stone cemeteries, mounds of gray that grew larger each spring on every settler's farm.

An only son, young John had helped to harvest those stones upheaved by frost action and had learned the farmer's trade from his father. Mere weeks after John entered his first schoolroom, his mother died during a late-in-life childbirth, a tragedy that also claimed the boy's infant brother. John then doted on Lillian, his older, only sister who assumed the role of surrogate mother and shepherded him through the primary school years. When Lillian left home at twenty-one to marry an ill-mannered blacksmith apprentice, John was heartsick but still had the father he loved. Now fourteen and with no interest in further education, John and his father worked the farm, and their toil was rewarded with abundance.

But it was not the monotonous, unending labor that sprang him loose. A devastating fire drove him away. He had gone to help a neighbor with barn repair and was spending the night away from home when flames broke out from loose stones in the Welch chimney to engulf the clapboard house in flames. John's father, who had not remarried, died trying to save family keepsakes when a plastered wall gave way, pinning him to the floor.

Returning home the next morning, John could not believe the smoking remains of what had been home. Finding Father's charred body was so abhorrent that John screamed at the top of his voice, but no one was around to hear. Lillian lived in the next town over, miles away.

There was nothing to hold young Welch after that. He and Lillian saw each other infrequently because John's skin prickled in the company of his uncouth brother-in-law, and his sister's attention had turned to the lout and a growing family of her own. When spring arrived, John sold the property, for too little he came to realize, and gave half the money to Lillian. Packing a rucksack, he heeded the cliché advice of Horace Greeley's and lit out for the West and whatever adventures it held for him.

He stopped long enough in Buffalo to work for a few months at a shipyard. On a whim, John then boarded a steamer to Cleveland where he found work making steel at a foundry before going with the axles he forged to Detroit and a fledgling carriage shop. Driven by a nagging aimlessness, he wandered alone, not understanding what he was looking for, knowing he did not find it in place after place.

Years later, while in Bay City, Michigan, working as a common laborer with others building a ponderous home for a lumber baron, John learned that lucrative work was about to open up on the upper reaches of the Muskegon River farther west and north. The rich owner-baron was starting a timber-cutting camp near Evart to take out white pine that blanketed the region. John jumped aboard a coach to Midland and walked the rest of the way, arriving in camp a few days later. At twenty-six years old, with work experience in the woods limited to chopping and splitting firewood, John signed on as a lumberjack for bed and board and seventy-five cents a day. The year was 1851, the War a decade into the future.

He hadn't spent enough time anywhere to build a lasting relationship with anybody, man or woman. An almost-exception was Miranda, the dark, foreign lady from Canada whose English was hesitant. On Saturday afternoons Miranda would venture across the Detroit River by ferry from Windsor to visit John in Detroit where he lived. By now he had quit the carriage factory and worked as a commercial fisherman on the river. John grew fond of Miranda over the few weeks they had known each other. The problem was that Miranda liked her whiskey, and John liked his whiskey too much when he was with her. And Miranda, he came to realize, was not about to relinquish a prostitute's lucrative life in Canada to be his permanent lover in America. The evening she arrived at his boarding house with a vial of special laudanum was the day John Welch decided to end his drugging ways and any more couplings with Miranda.

Nursing his coffee in Rachel Barnum's kitchen, he relived those vagabond days. Pausing at the escapades with Miranda, he felt like slapping himself. To think he had considered asking her to marry him! Only a sucker could have been so easily duped.

He chuckled and shook his head. How could he have been so stupid? Hadn't the years proved he was unfit for domestic life? Having saved no money, he had no home and owned no land. Others might think of him as a drifter, a vagrant; he preferred "temporary traveler," a label that held out hope, though improbable, that one day he might find roots. After sending Miranda back across the river to stay, he migrated to Bay City, Michigan, where he learned how to lay brick and frame walls for the lumber baron. The house finished, John turned to the lumberjack trade.

Later, when the pine ran out along the Muskegon River, he decided he didn't want to cut timber anymore. So, he abandoned life in the woods for life in the city, rambling southward to Grand Rapids where he labored two years for a company that made furniture; and when he tired of that, found janitorial work at the Eaton County courthouse in Charlotte. It was there that he learned of a farm woman near Sunfield who was looking for a hired hand. John Welch was thirty-five years old.

One boring morning, hanging onto his broom for support, he read the posted notice a second time and noted how a spark of interest spread so quickly to the flame of possibility. How odd! Was it those years of absence from planting and harvesting that triggered this sudden appeal? Perhaps. Was it is his habit of shucking jobs when tedium set in, which it always did, even at this moment with another floor to clean? Probably that, too.

His imagination drifted to a third idea. The thought

of a woman—a widow, maybe—in need of help, intrigued. Thinking the mundane task of sweeping could help to sort out the matter, John went back to work, thrusting his broom back and forth as though it was a crosscut saw. Or a cattle prod.

A stirring beyond the wall told John that Watson was out of bed. The morning routine of Dwight's younger brother was to hitch pony to cart and drive his sisters the two miles to school. John closed his eyes and thought anew how life's vagaries had brought him to the farm of Rachel Barnum and how rapidly things changed, were still changing, since moving inside with his employer and her family.

Willis Barnum had died the summer before John's arrival. Thinking back to the spring morning when he stood on Mrs. Barnum's porch and said he was available for hire, John recalled seeing the signs of a neglected farm: a half-field of still-standing corn, a heaping manure pile waiting to be spread. Lot of work here, he remembered, and cracked a little smile. Still a lot of work here.

The day after Rachel hired him, he started with the corn harvest. He met her stairstep family—Dwight, sixteen; Watson, fourteen; the seven-year-old girls Hester and Helena. He liked her family, and they in turn seemed to like him. Life in the granary was comfortable enough though spartan. All he needed was a bed, and Mrs. Barnum had seen to that. She gave him an extra blanket although the season of frigid cold and heavy snows was over, and the warming nights hinted at spring. If he was still here come fall, he would ask her for a small stove. After two weeks, she had said she was happy with the work he did and how he went about doing it.

As the weeks and months passed, the threat of domestic

war fumed like an angry black cloud. No one denied that War was coming and coming soon. It was common knowledge that when Dwight came of age, he expected to sign up and go to the fight, leaving Watson to help their mother and the hired man run the farm.

Thinking about Watson, waiting for him to come out from the bedroom, spurred a facial tic, a sign that John was vexed. Early on he had decided that Watson was a troubled lad. Whenever the hired man looked into his eyes, the boy would turn away. If spoken to, he sometimes walked away. Watson's unwillingness to engage suggested that Rachel's unhappy son would resist help if any help was offered. The mouth that spoke few words was always active, chewing on something no one could see, no one could understand without some effort to talk about it. Or so it seemed to the hired man.

Knowing what it was like to lose a father, John Welch felt sorry for the boy. He remembered how hard it had been for him to shake the grief that went with him to many jobs in many places and that still could bring a flicker of sadness. Something besides grief, though, held Watson in its grip. John grimaced and clenched his jaw, thinking that anger was the reason. Resentment over losing a loving parent John could comprehend. What baffled him so was the boy's aloofness, his seeming determination to stay apart from others, especially people he lived with and who loved him. Watson's obstinance more than confused the hired man; it frustrated him, and added to the gulf between them.

Tapping his fingers on the kitchen table like a trumpeter brought no answer to this enigma. The thought of either of Rachel's sons relating to him as a substitute father was so preposterous it made him chuckle. Why would anyone think of him as a Pa? He was a father to no one and had no inkling of how to be a father. On the other hand, a friend he could be and would be, except for Watson. How could anyone be a friend to someone if they thought of you as an enemy?

Muttering, John shook his head and got up for more coffee. Parked again at the table, hands wrapped around the mug, he thought of his own mother, gone for so many years, and his long-absent sister Lillian whose favorite saying, "Kindness conquers all," still lingered. Well, the Barnums' gentle and gentlemanly hired hand had been kind to all, including their farm animals. Dwight had said as much before taking Blaze with him to Grand Rapids and Army training camp. Rachel's daughters treated John Welch as though he was a favorite uncle. But Watson? What could be done with Watson, except wait for the day that might never come?

As though summoned, a ghostlike Watson floated into the kitchen. The hired man decided to say nothing, to see if the boy would talk first this time. When he didn't, John broke the silence. "Good morning there. Coffee?"

"No. Maybe later." With those three words hanging in the air, Watson slipped into his coat and vanished outside. John went back to thinking about his gypsy life before coming to alight at the Barnum farm. After three years, he still liked it here and had no thought of leaving. Rachel would have to fire him first. Having become indispensable to her, he couldn't imagine that happening. Besides, there was their mutual attraction to consider. The longer John Welch lived on the Barnum farm, the more he wanted to stay here. The flush of desire that spread to his chest and tingled there told him so.

CHAPTER 15

Cairo, Illinois

Rachel walked an hour back to the St. Charles Hotel. There was no need for hurry. The fact that *The City of Memphis* was gone was a disappointment, not necessarily a reversal of fortune. She would pin her hopes on the hospital ship's return. There were things she could do to prepare, to be ready when the ship did come back. A wonderful opportunity had presented itself, and she must take full advantage. Having a good plan was necessary, if for no reason other than it kept hope alive.

First, though, she must educate herself. Rachel had learned many things since leaving home but needed to know much more. Details like *The City of Memphis'* itinerary. Would it stop at New Madrid or pass on by? Had it departed Cairo to go up the Mississippi or up the Ohio? How does one offer to serve on her and in what capacity? Who was in charge of operations on that vessel of mercy? Would she be welcomed aboard or turned away?

Trumping those important questions were the ones that marinated in her mind: What was Dwight's immediate condition? What caused that fever, and what were Army doctors doing to help him? Rachel refused to believe her son was no longer alive but wanted proof, needed proof. Could she find out through the telegraph? Was the railway office the only station in Cairo? Surely someone in Cairo could help her!

Her mind spooled with other unknowns. Prices were frightful here, all because of this senseless war. A fifty-cent restaurant meal in Charlotte was a dollar and a half here. Had she brought enough money? No, she was certain to need more. The number of gold and silver coins her daughters had counted out on the kitchen table back at the farm was limited to the capacity of the change purse tucked away within her clothing. Of this much Rachel was confident: She was no fool when it came to money. Willis had insisted she keep up with his land transactions, over time convincing her to take charge of matters financial, both household and business. She became so efficient he jested that she could "squeeze a half-dime from an Indian-head penny." But when he wanted to buy something that she thought was extravagant, Rachel was "Mrs. Scrooge."

What had annoyed her then, whenever he said that, was applicable now. Rachel was familiar enough with promissory notes and other paper issuance in use these days to know that none of it was legal tender outside the locale of issue. That sole banknote, folded and sequestered in her leather purse, was good as gold, but only if another bank agreed to honor it. Today was Sunday. She would inquire first thing tomorrow morning when the banks would be open.

And, then, what of the children left behind on the farm with Mr. Welch? There had been no contact for close to a week. She must write to them this afternoon and get those letters in the mail, yet another task for tomorrow.

Since the hospital ship was not here, Rachel would take advantage of its absence. She would "use the time wisely," as her mother had reminded Rachel, her brothers, and sister enough times to become "Mother's Mantra." Ascending the hotel steps, Rachel noted a wet quilt of gray had snuffed out the gauze of morning light. The first raindrops were falling before she left the front desk, two newspapers in hand, and climbed the stairs to her room.

That afternoon when Rachel opened her door, the delightful odor of fresh-baked bread sharply reminded her she had not eaten today. Seeking the source of the aroma, she came down the stairs and saw the dining room full of boarders and guests. Despite her hunger, or perhaps because of it, Rachel experienced giddiness, a little rush of satisfaction that she had chosen the ideal place to eat.

A Negro waiter, standing at attention between the reception and dining rooms, waited for her to descend before stepping forward like a statue come to life. He was a tall, lean man with a face the color of coffee-with-cream, evidence that his amalgamated blood was Anglo-Saxon and African. His trousers were dark, his jacket white as the Dutchman's breeches that bloomed before other wildflowers in her woods at home. Rachel needed to look up to speak to him.

"Do you have available a place for one diner?"

"No, ma'am, but I got one for two."

Rachel's sense of gaiety merged with one of magnanimity. Smiling, she said, "If another guest will be dining alone and have to wait, I would be pleased to share it."

"Oh, yes, ma'am. I will remember that, ma'am," he acknowledged with a bow.

He led her to a dainty table next to a fireplace with glowing embers, arranged her chair, and ensured she was comfortable. She couldn't resist sniffing the single daffodil in a tiny vase she would be careful not to upend. The waiter announced today's supper: roasted chicken with sweet potatoes, green beans, and cornbread, and "the best apple pie in Illinois."

The meal he brought to her was the best Rachel had known since leaving the farm. She ate with solicitude, savoring each bite. Upstairs she had written the girls separate letters, taking care the words of affection were different, the sentiments the same. The letter to Watson would assume a different import. She would write it later.

She was waiting for dessert when the waiter returned, not with pie but with a man. Younger than she, he wore a white shirt with an open collar beneath a brown jacket. The matching pants and darker boots betrayed no blemish. A hat with stiffened brim was in his hand. Rachel assumed he was a businessman, like so many others in Cairo.

"Good day," he greeted with a smile. "William here says you might accept a table guest. My name is Charles Duncan. I stay at the hotel. That is, whenever I'm in town."

"If it pleases you, sit down, sir," Rachel said. "The hotel is certainly busy this afternoon. I suppose the rain has something to do with that."

"It's pouring down now. Ma'am, I don't mean to impose. I realize this is, shall I say, rather unprecedented."

"We are living in unprecedented times," she said and smiled back. "It's perfectly acceptable that strangers share a table."

"Yes, unprecedented. It's the right word, indeed it is. Thank you for allowing the pleasure of your company." Passing his hat to the waiter, he sat down. The table was so small that Rachel adjusted her chair so their knees wouldn't touch. She steadied the shaking vase.

"Not at all," she said. "I'm finished, waiting for dessert and coffee. The food was wonderful."

He agreed. "Meals at the Delta Hotel are good, too, but better ones are here at the St. Charles, especially on Sundays. After the breakfast I had, or should I say didn't have, I could hardly wait to get back here."

He was proving to be quite a talker, and she listened with interest. Mr. Duncan said he had been across the river in Paducah this very morning with Sherman's troops. "What was left of them at any rate," as the general had taken his army south to join Gen. Grant. "I now understand why the soldiers tire of hardtack and sowbelly," he laughed. "Two or three meals of that questionable fare will last a man a lifetime."

"A bit ago," she volunteered, "I read about General Sherman leaving Kentucky."

"Oh? What paper was that, may I ask?" He leaned forward.

"I think it was the Louisville paper. They gave it to me at the desk."

"Yes, the *Courier*. You can take that one to the bank. It's accurate, most of the time anyway. Some of these papers—'rags' I call them—report rumor, not fact. But I shouldn't tell tales out of school."

"What do you mean?"

"Ma'am, I'm a correspondent. I follow the War for the *Boston Globe*. I know I don't get it right every time either, but I always cite my sources. If they lie, it's on them. I don't mean to boast, ma'am, but—far as I know—no one has ever pinned an untruth on this news hound."

Rachel found her loquacious guest, whose accent she

recognized as Eastern, to be more than interesting. Mr. Duncan was intriguing, and he had information. Not only did he talk fast, but he displayed a healthy appetite, and the way he raced through supper reminded her of Watson. Her son also gobbled food like a hungry hen. She wondered if the frenetic newspaper business with its constant pressure to be first with the story, first with the printed page, contributed to his eating behavior.

His words came back to her. He did admit, however, to being quite hungry. A bite of pie remained before her when the reporter plunked down his knife and fork. "I do apologize for my table manners," he said as though he knew her mind. "Or rather the lack of them. I hope I didn't offend you."

The comment made her chuckle. "No. Not at all. I have a boy at home who eats fast, too. I like to think it's his mother's superior kitchen skills."

"Ha! That's one for the books. You said 'home.' May I ask where home is?"

He was easy to talk with. Rachel was surprised at how much she had to say, and to a perfect stranger. His manner was not obtrusive in the least. Listening with patience, he did not interrupt her commentary, now a monologue, and seemed engrossed with everything she had to say. When Rachel mentioned her earlier life in New Jersey and how she had been familiar with New York City, the correspondent nearly left his chair. "You know the city?" Amazement blanketed his face. "I began my career at the *Tribune*. I live in Boston now, but I don't get home like I should. The *Globe* has me chasing this War, east and west."

She told him her husband's family hailed from Massachusetts.

"Hah! Irish stock I'll bet."

"English, but likely Irish, too. The surname is Barnum."

"Barnum? Ha! Any relation to the Barnum of Tom Thumb fame? What a huckster that P. T. Barnum. Why, he could sell a snake a pair of suspenders."

Rachel laughed aloud. "No. No connection, at least none that I know."

"I would have been surprised if he was related. You're far more sincere than P.T. Barnum and his ridiculous sideshows." Charles Duncan's tone grew more serious. "How did you come to live in Michigan, Mrs. Barnum, and what, for mercy's sake, are you doing in Cairo, Illinois?"

"Well, that's a long story," she replied in a lower voice.

"I want to hear it," he said in a collusive whisper. "Would you be willing to tell me?"

"Well, I suppose, Mr. Duncan. But not here. They are waiting for this table."

He gestured for the waiter. "William," he said. "Have the front desk put Mrs. Barnum's meal on my account."

"Please," Rachel protested. "That's not necessary at all, sir. I cannot accept your generosity."

"Pshaw! My paper pays reasonable expenses in the pursuit of a story. I think I'm about to hear a fascinating one."

MEANWHILE, THE STORM HAD GROWN more intense. Bursts of wind and violent sheets of rainfall pummeled the hotel windows. In the reception hall, Rachel and Charles Duncan sat in cushioned, high-backed chairs away from the doors and a flurry of people coming and going, talking and laughing. The blending of so many voices in a crowded antechamber with lofty ceiling created an ongoing background murmur advantageous to a private conversation. Confident the reporter, notebook balanced on his lap and pencil in hand, was the only person listening, and because he listened with concentrated attention, Rachel poured out her story.

The gist of what she shared was the purpose of her journey, but he had a way of coaxing details—ages of the children at home, how long she had been widowed—which she surprised herself by sharing without hesitation. Over the course of ninety minutes, Rachel told Mr. Charles Duncan, War correspondent for the *Boston Globe*, more about herself than she had told any one person at one time in her entire life. Raised within an insular family whose members kept personal matters to themselves, she was aware that her present behavior was out of character.

That old maxim "the Dutch won't tell you much" was far from the truth. Regardless, Rachel felt no shame and no guilt. What she knew was relief, the sense of freedom that comes with burden's release. And perhaps that was because what she could not tell to those who knew her, she could impart to a perfect stranger. He was "perfect" because he did not judge. As far as Rachel knew, those were facts, not opinions, he scribbled in his compact gray notebook.

But it was unreal. bizarre was more accurate, how she felt detached from herself by talking without constraint about herself. Stopping a moment for him to finish writing whatever he was writing, Rachel imagined herself suspended in the airy expanse above the scene. There she was, small in the spacious chair, her face earnest, lips moving without sound, hands gesticulating what she could neither speak nor hear. And there he sat, a larger form bending toward her, his forearms on knees, the pencil clutched between fingers of his right hand as it fed the notebook words she could not read.

Deep into her story, Rachel paused again and deliberated whether to ask what she was thinking. She decided to be blunt. "What are your intentions, Mr. Duncan? What will you do with what I am telling you?"

He answered without hesitation. "It will make a wonderful article, Mrs. Barnum, a human-interest feature. My editor likes to balance the War news with stories that have little or nothing to do with troop movements, with battlefield casualties, and the like. That merely cite statistics. He encourages me to submit stories like yours."

"You mean there are others?"

"Well, no. At least not yet. Yours is the first I've heard. But if this war goes on as long as many expect it to, I believe tales like yours will become commonplace. Think about it, Mrs. Barnum. For every soldier that fights and dies in battle a mother, a sister, a father, or a brother waits at home, hungry for news of their loved one.

It was Rachel's turn to listen. She hung on every word. "Hearing nothing, knowing nothing," he went on, "how many will have the courage, as you do, to go looking for them?"

He stopped talking to write something, and Rachel considered his words. Courage? She had no courage. She was determined, yes, but what did that have to do with courage? Some would say she was foolish; others that she was daft, out of her mind.

Looking up, he examined her face as though to memorize it and said, "Your story will be an inspiration to many. I'm indebted to you, Mrs. Barnum, for sharing it so forthrightly, so honestly."

"But I had no choice, you see! I had to go. I *have* to do this, Mr. Duncan. Don't you understand?"

"Yes, I do understand, but I also disagree. You *had* a choice, Mrs. Barnum. You chose. And that is the story I intend to write."

"But it's not finished. It won't be over until I find my son."

"Yes, I understand that, too. You said you received a telegram. Do you have it? May I read it?"

"Certainly. Will you allow a moment?" He turned his head while she retrieved the letter. "Here," she offered. "It's rather brief, I'm afraid."

His eyes devoured the words. "Do you know this Second Lieutenant? This M. J. Dickenson?"

She explained how her late husband had sold land to Marshall Dickenson before the War. At thirty-four, Marshall was the oldest volunteer to enlist last summer along with Dwight and the other boys and men from Sunfield and surrounding villages.

"Marshall and his brother Willard were mustered into the Army with my son in Grand Rapids. Dwight said in a letter they were made officers because of their age. Willard is four or five years younger than Marshall. Willard's the quartermaster sergeant for Company B. All the Eaton County boys are in Company B."

The reporter had been writing something but heard every word. Wetting his lips, he said, "Mrs. Barnum, I may be able to learn if your son is still alive."

Rachel gasped. Her hand sprang to her mouth. Hoping no one heard or saw her disbelief, she leaned forward and dropped her voice. "What? How? How can you do that?"

"Through the telegraph. As a correspondent, I have access to the wire. It's how I send my dispatches to the paper."

"Is it really possible?" She was amazed. "Someone on the train said the Government banned civilian use of the telegraph. It was being reserved for the military."

"That is true, Mrs. Barnum. "But I, and certain other established correspondents, have letters of authorization signed by the War Department. Some of our generals, unfortunately not all, support our efforts to keep the public informed. They know an informed public is a supportive public."

He explained that senior officers had access to the wire. Second lieutenants barely qualified. That was how Marshall Dickenson could send her the telegram. That was the reason her answer back to him made it through the wire.

"But I don't know if he ever received it."

He stood up and stretched his arms. "I'll find that out, too," he said. "In fact, I'll try to send a telegram now. If I get through and receive an answer, I'll leave it at the front desk with instructions to deliver it to your room at once." A huge grin had overtaken his face. "Mrs. Barnum, I must say, you are not the only person who needs to know if Dwight is still alive."

She was speechless. She wanted to thank him, to ask if she would ever see him again. But he was already out the door, his hat pulled low for protection from the rain that continued to drench the city.

CHAPTER 16

Sunfield, Michigan

John Welch added wood to the stove and refilled his coffee cup. Voices from their bedroom told him Rachel's daughters were up and getting dressed. He could hear their chatter about goings on at school: how sick the McMaster girl had been, what story Miss Amble would read today. In the kitchen they offered unsolicited greetings. How different from their glum brother. John wondered who was making breakfast this morning.

"It's my turn to do the eggs," Hester announced. "Mr. Welch, you want them turned over and the yolks broken?"

"Yes, Missy Hester. Just like always. Thank you."

Helena asked if he wanted three pancakes or four.

"You make them so good, Missy Helena, I'll have four hundred this morning."

She knew the game. She took the bait. "Then who gets to eat the three hundred ninety-six left over?"

"Still smart as your mother," John said. "Always knew

it. Now, where'd you girls put that syrup?"

Helena's cue. "Same place where I hid it yesterday. In the cupboard."

Pretending surprise, the hired man smacked his forehead. "Warms up enough today, your brother and I will set the taps and buckets and get our fair share of this spring's run."

"Can we have maple sugar candy?" Their excited voices overran each other.

"Of course! Where's the reward for all that hard work if we don't make candy?"

The twins had finished breakfast and were clearing the table when the door sprang open. Watson stuck his head into the kitchen. "Pony's ready. You girls coming?"

John looked up. "Wat, don't you want breakfast first?"

"Maybe later." The door closed.

After they left, John shoved aside his plate. Tamping tobacco into his pipe, he decided to smoke inside, something he never did with Rachel home. He lifted the stove lid and held a sliver of wood to the flames. When the shard caught fire, he touched his pipe bowl and sucked on the stem, his thoughts ephemeral, like the blue smoke he exhaled.

What had brought him here? What caused him to linger so? Was it happiness? No, not that exactly. Contentedness? Closer. A sense of belonging had started after moving inside from the granary when Dwight left, and the sentiment had deepened since. The connection he felt to Rachel Barnum and her children was real, and for the first time in memory he knew he feared losing something tangible were he to move on. Yes, the old wanderlust was still there, but its hold had softened.

There was no reason to leave; in truth, it would be wrong to leave them. She depended on him now. She, who had lost a husband and watched a son ride off to war, needed him. The corral in which he now found himself was one he had helped to build. Being confined like this, though, made him a little nervous. Fingers rubbing, he set down his cup and allowed the conundrum to shape itself. Was this a problem or an opportunity?

No one had ever needed him, like this need. Until now employers had relied on his long hours of labor, and sometimes his experience, as he learned new trades. Once work expectations and wages were agreed to, the *quid pro quo* ruled until the project was finished or he grew bored, quit, and moved on. Honest to a fault, he had never been fired, had lost no job due to laziness or ineptitude. For these reasons, as well as his constitutional cheerfulness, agreeability, and *esprit de corps*, the bosses had been reluctant to see him go.

John Welch credited his family for who he was. A fiddle-footed nature notwithstanding, his character was a testament to a mother's early love, a sister's nurturing, a father's guidance. Always, though, he had moved on, always on his own terms except when the lumber baron's new home was finished, and all the workers were out of a job and left for greener pastures. Several times while working elsewhere he had rejected offers of more money or advancement to management if only he would stay. He never did. The itch to gather his few belongings and go to the next best thing, whatever and wherever that was, was too strong to keep him in place.

It was different here, and Rachel had a lot to do with it being different.

Rachel's letter was three days old when it had arrived at the farm. Tearing open the envelope from the St. Charles Hotel, John hungrily read the words. Her hand was clear;

Hester would not need to decipher. He understood every word.

His face fell upon learning she was still in Cairo, unable to pass some big island held by Rebels and keeping her from New Madrid and Dwight.

Mention of the cat triggered a grunt and a smile. She had, indeed, given birth to five kittens and now nursed them in the nesting box John had made and arranged in the granary. What caught and held his eye was the greeting. "Dear John," so much more familiar than the sterile "Mr. John Welch" on the envelope. And the ending: "All my love, to each of you. Rachel and Mother." The words announced that he had attained family stature. Why else would she extend her love to a hired man? He habitually referred to her as "Mrs. Barnum" and always called her that in the presence of her children, more often by her first name if they were alone. The one time he gambled and called her "Mother," she gave him a questioning look and said nothing. But what did she mean by signing the letter "Rachel?" Was this a signal that he meant more to her, perhaps much more, than hired help? He felt his blood move.

Later that morning, her daughters at school and Watson having yet to return, he washed the wild leeks the girls had found in the woods and was peeling them in the kitchen when he thought about how the contents of her letter were like the onion's layers. Each one he peeled away, his imagination took him to another layer of meaning. He was sure he meant more to her than paid labor. Gone was her depressive state when he had first arrived. After Dwight left, her anxiety returned, and he had helped with that, too, by being cheerful and optimistic, careful not to interfere in family matters unless someone asked his opinion or advice. By engaging her withdrawn son as much as Watson would allow. By checking his manly instincts to protect her daughters and her.

John inferred that because Rachel respected him, trusted him, she had begun to defer to him, at least when the subject was farm management. He knew, and, surely, she knew as well, that he was dependable, consistent, and loyal. But was there more to their relationship?

Speculation of this sort could quicken a heart. He believed that he belonged here on this farm at this time in his life. But the thought of belonging to someone else and the prospect of someone else belonging to him made for a tricky association of need to want and want to need. Trying to sort through it all was appealing, exciting, but it made him uneasy, too.

Peeling away at the leek bulbs, his thoughts became words, spoken to himself alone in her kitchen. "It ain't fear, exactly, so what is it? New ground to turn over and see what grows? Yeah, there you go. Seeds sprout only when planted in soil that's ready for them. There's seeds here. They're in the ground. They're growing."

The metaphor made John smile. He wondered if she was of a like mind. It would be presumptuous to ask, of course, but not wrong, not premature, to ponder. Daily labor on the farm with her gone was giving him time to think about such things. About what could be. This much he knew: After ten days' absence, he missed her. And he was sure he would be lonesome for her, maybe even miserable, were he to leave for a life somewhere else.

Taking in a deep breath, he let it go, slowly. The time had come to call her by her Christian name. Always. Even in front of the children.

JOHN HEARD THE CART AND pony turn off Shaytown Road and enter the barnyard. He figured Watson to be hungry now, hungry enough to stay in the kitchen awhile and eat. John got up, opened the stove, and tapped the pipe ashes into it. It was high time for a talk with Watson. Returning to his seat, the hired man waited for Rachel's uncooperative son to come in. The door opened, and the boy entered with an armful of stove wood. He plopped it into the fuel box, hung up his coat and hat, and looked around. "Any cakes left?"

"We saved you some. Between the tin plates there. Might still be warm."

"Warm enough." Watson doused his stack of pancakes with syrup. He started for the bedroom to eat alone.

"Have a seat, Wat. Need to ask your advice."

"About what?" His voice lacked enthusiasm.

"About tapping time. Think it will be warm enough to-day?"

"Maybe. It's warmer out now than when I left."

Sensing an opening, John pressed on. "We could take turns with the brace and bit. Those maples ain't getting any easier to bore. I can use your help."

The boy sat across from him. Famished, Watson wolfed the pancakes, washing them down with swigs of coffee. "I'll help," he said. "When do you want to start?"

"How about when you're done eating?"

"Sure."

John interpreted this agreeable exchange as a right time to introduce the subject no one talked about. "Did I ever tell you about my father?"

Watson looked up, his mouth full. He shook his head.

"He died in a house fire, in Vermont where I grew up."

Watson looked straight at him. He didn't turn away. "When was that?"

"When I was eighteen. A bit older than you are now." Watson's mouth moved as though chewing. The pancakes were gone. John thought it was best to let him speak next. If he would speak.

"What'd you do?"

"I ran away. Been on the go ever since. Close to twenty years now."

"Hmmm." Watson, chewing, stared at his empty plate. "That's a long time."

"It takes a long time. A man's only got one father to lose. One mother, too."

The boy shot him a look. "She died in that fire, too?"

"No. She passed earlier. When I was five."

Watson studied the hired man's face. "You were five?"

"You might say I was an orphan. At least I was the day my pa died. No brothers. An older sister was married. Had her own family." Weight grew in the ensuing silence. When John coughed and swallowed, his voice was close to a whisper, the tone soft, but the words were clear. "I tell you this because I know what's eating at you. It ate at me. It still hurts a little. You can't get past something that makes no sense."

Watson's hands clenched to fists. Eyes jammed shut, he struck the table and swore, "It ain't fair!" He pounded the table, again, shouting, "Ain't fair! Why? Why?"

John waited for the fury to ease. He hoped the boy wouldn't bolt for his room. Or run outside. "You're right, Watson. It ain't fair." John's sober voice was even, without emotion. "But you ain't alone. What happened to you happened to me."

Hands behind his head, lips trembling, Watson leaned

back and stared at the far wall. Probing his cup with a spoon, John extracted a coffee ground and then another. After a long moment, Watson stood up and said, "Time to go drill us some trees, Mr. Welch."

CHAPTER 17

Monday, March 31
Cairo, Illinois

Rachel had never written to Watson. Until a few hours ago, when she'd finished her letters to the twins, there had been no need to write to any of her children because she had never been away. Nor had they. The exception, of course, was her elder son. Since October she had mailed letters to Dwight every two or three days because he was always in her thoughts, and because she feared he would not receive them all. The messages might not be forwarded to new places the 2nd Michigan had gone or would go. The rationalization: It was better to write too much than too little.

The long day that began with worship service at First Presbyterian Church and ended with the intensive newspaper interview was replete with possibilities. Her mind, overwrought, was too stimulated, and she was unable to stay asleep. Standing barefoot before the dresser in her room at the St. Charles Hotel, the water pitcher and wash-basin removed to make space, Rachel thought about what to say to Watson. The words she had penned to her daughters came easily enough. These words were harder. Much harder.

> *Dear Watson,*
> *It is after midnight in Cairo, Illinois, and rain is falling hard. I cannot sleep in my hotel room. I am thinking of you because …*

Unsure what to say next, she stopped writing, laid down the pen, and pressed fingers against her brow, hoping to force the right words. Preoccupied with so many thoughts at once, she struggled to make sense of any, most of all why this task was so difficult. Maybe she should wait for morning. No, her mind was too active for sleep. Rachel would not say a word about the train station attack or the incident at the docks. She would hold to what was necessary to say now and leave unsettling details for another time. Or never.

The night clerk at the front desk had been generous with paper and ink. Discarding the first draft, she began anew:

> *Dearest Watson,*
> *I ask you to read this letter aloud to your sisters and to Mr. Welch. Perhaps at supper when you are together? I am well, in Cairo, Illinois, and staying at the St. Charles Hotel. I hope to have news of your brother very soon, maybe before this day (Mon. March 31) is over. I will write again as soon as I know anything.*
> *I do not yet know when I can leave here, or how I will get to New Madrid across the flooded Mississippi River. New Madrid is 60 miles or more down the river from Cairo. Cairo is protect-ed by levees, by dikes like the ones in the picture book from the*

Old Country. The land across the river is underwater for miles. Rain is pouring down now. People here are worried the river will breach the levees and flood Cairo as this has happened before.

Our soldiers now occupy New Madrid, but the Rebels control a large island upstream and won't let any of our boats go by. Everyone here thinks the Rebels can't hold out much longer. But until they are whipped or driven away, I must stay here.

There is nothing else to share except that I love you all and pray you are safe at home. God bless each of you.

Watson, be assured you are forever in my thoughts and prayers. Thank the Lord for His watchful care over you and your sisters. Allow Mr. Welch to direct the farm work and be ever helpful to him.

Your loving Mother

Satisfied, Rachel folded and inserted the letter in an envelope, which she left unsealed in the hope there would be more news before the day's mail went out. She addressed the envelope to "Mr. Watson Barnum, Shaytown Road, Sunfield Michigan," extinguished the lamp at 2:15, and returned to bed.

RACHEL AWOKE TO A FILM of weak, gray light infiltrating the lacelike curtain of her hotel-room window. The rain had stopped. By 6:30 she was washed, dressed, and downstairs before the front desk to ask questions of the daytime clerk, a narrow-faced man whose eyeglasses threatened to slide off his nose. He surveyed her from gray-green eyes above the frame.

Were there any messages for her this morning?

"None. Sorry, Mrs. Barnum."

Was Charles Duncan still registered?

"Can't say. Haven't seen him."

Did the clerk know where the telegraph office was located?

"At the post office."

And what time did the post office open?

"Eight o'clock."

And the bank?

"Nine o'clock."

Rachel thanked this man of few words, who restored his spectacles to their proper place and replied with a dismissive, "Good day, ma'am."

She thought it prudent to have her coffee in the reception hall. There she could keep watch over this standoffish clerk, who might not alert her to any messages. When a courier boy brought a bundle of letters, she watched the officious clerk sort and pigeonhole them according to their respective owners. Disappointed to see her slot remained empty, Rachel realized with a start that no one, except Charles Duncan, knew she was here. Those at home could not know until they received her letters.

Checking Willis' pocket watch, she saw it was 7:30. The day would be long, insufferable without some news of Dwight. While waiting, she thought about this peculiar town, this so-called "Little Egypt." Without a doubt, Cairo was host to a troupe of characters. The confluence of the two major rivers surely had attracted a range of humanity from soldiers to speculators, from preachers to peddlers. Aware as a youngster that New York City's immigrants came from the world over, she concluded that many people in Cairo were also foreign but in ways well beyond language and custom.

Visitors here were not seeking a new home. They were looking for a bargain, a deal, or a hustle. It was no secret the region beckoned to newcomers because it represented the frontier's edge with all its promise of adventure, its prospect of unlimited opportunity. She could relate to this appeal; after all, the untamed wilds of Michigan had lured her family west not that long ago. She paused in her thoughts to again visit that time in her life and to consider how quickly twenty-five years can pass when one looks back, as opposed to imagining the next quarter century.

Time spent thus far in Cairo convinced Rachel that it was not like Detroit or Chicago and perhaps other cities of the burgeoning Midwest. Cairo was a beehive for the uncivilized and their foul-mouthed behavior. Lawless types lived in this anarchic city where most people ignored each other and lacked goodwill. Life here was frenetic when compared to the isolated, rural existence she knew. Rachel's Sunfield neighbors went out of their way to care for each other. She thought of Cairo's citizens, some of them anyway, as anonymous profiteers looking out for themselves and avoiding others.

Rachel was not alone in this sentiment. Charles Duncan had mentioned that listening to her story was an absolute delight because it was free of cursing. He avowed that most soldiers couldn't speak a sentence without uttering an oath and that the sailors were far worse. "When the tars come ashore," she remembered him saying, "Cairo's women need to lock their doors."

He had cautioned Rachel about leaving the safety of the hotel at night. The city's population used to be two thousand citizens. Now it was three or four times that number with soldiers, contractors, and salesmen coming and going. Little Egypt was rife with sharpers, scalawags, drunks, and painted ladies. Mr. Duncan said there were more grog shops than churches, and it was all because of the War.

"The Army depot is less than a mile away at Camp Defiance," he had said. "The Navy has its boatyard here, and, of course, there's the railway and the docks."

"Oh, yes, I know all about the depot and the docks," she had told him through a reflexive shudder and refrained from detail.

"Not safe. Not safe at all. Do be careful, Mrs. Barnum."

Tasting her coffee, Rachel wondered where Charles, whom she deemed a cosmopolitan man, a *bon vivant*, was now. Was he in his room, still sleeping? She doubted that; he had too much energy to stay in bed. Was he out and about running errands? Doing interviews? Had he been called away on a new assignment? If that taciturn clerk at the front desk knew, he was not about to tell her.

At 7:50 she walked to the post office, arriving as the postmaster was unlocking the door. Fifteen or twenty people were already in line, most likely because it was Monday morning and the post office was closed yesterday. The reporter was not among them. Rachel joined the column and when her turn came, bought stamps for the letters and learned there was no news for her. Was there mail, however, for Mr. Charles Duncan, mail she might deliver to him at the St. Charles?

"No. No, there is not," the suspicious postmaster snapped. Mildly irritated, Rachel left hastily while he was reading the destination of her letters.

Earlier, she had passed the Planters Bank of Cairo and, retracing her steps, noticed another, the City Bank of Cairo. Rachel knew that competition among financial houses could be favorable for depositors, borrowers, and anyone else needing banking services. She waited in front of the larger, ornate Planters Bank building and when the door opened precisely at nine o'clock, stepped inside. A young man escorted her to a barred opening behind which an older gentleman was removing his jacket. He wore a white shirt with a pale blue bowtie, the color of a faded robin's egg.

"Good morning." He smiled through handsome teeth that belied a man who looked to be sixty. "May I help you?"

He was not a tall man. They regarded each other with level eyes. Rachel began with a question of her own. "Are you the bank manager, sir? I wish to speak to the person in charge."

"I am. My name is Winston Hunt. How can I be of service, Mrs …?" The smile was still there.

"Barnum. Rachel Barnum. I'm from out of town and in need of a transaction." Rachel handed him her promissory note from the Eaton County Bank in Charlotte, Michigan. The note was a loan guarantee for up to five hundred dollars. Clearing his throat, he swallowed the smile and asked if she needed some, or all, of the money today.

"I would like $200. That should be enough until I go back home."

"Certainly, Mrs. Barnum." The smile was back. "I can forward you any amount to four hundred fifty. Two hundred is fine today, but if you need more later, Planters can provide that, too. Our interest is now 10 percent, because of inflation, which, as you might expect, is because of the War."

"Ten percent is acceptable," she agreed. "My bank said to expect eight to ten." Mr. Winston Hunt seemed to be trustworthy. He said he would prepare the papers, provided she understood the transaction: two hundred in cash to her, for which her bank would send $220 to Planters. The note would then be guaranteed for the remaining $280.

Rachel nodded in agreement. "I understand, Mr. Hunt, but will need something larger than my leather purse to carry so many coins. Do you have a sturdy pouch?"

His smile blossomed into a grin, revealing a cheek dimple. He began to chortle. "Oh, no, Mrs. Barnum, we no longer deal in specie for large transactions such as this one. Now we do business in the new paper."

"New paper?" Unease was in her voice. "Mr. Hunt, whatever do you mean by 'new paper'?"

"New greenbacks. They are so new you may not have seen one. The original greenbacks the Government began circulating last summer were demand notes, not legal tender. The new greenbacks are legal tender, as of this month."

Her eyebrows shot up. "May I see one?"

"Of course. You can see them all. Look. I have them in five-, ten- and twenty-dollar bills."

She scrutinized each note. There it was on the back: "This note is a legal tender for all debts public and private."

"This is quite wonderful!" she exclaimed.

"Yes, it is, isn't it?" He broke into a hearty laugh. "No more heavy coins to lug around. Unless you want to, that is."

"The gold and silver I brought with me is still acceptable, though, isn't it?"

"By all means, Mrs. Barnum. If you have gold specie and wish to sell, our bank is offering a premium of 8 percent."

"Let me understand you, Mr. Hunt. If I gave you a gold dollar, you would give me a paper dollar, a greenback that is, and eight cents. Do I have that right?"

"That is correct. I'll make you an offer, Mrs. Barnum. I'll increase the premium to 10 percent for you. If you happen to have $200 in gold coin, why you could negate the twenty dollars in interest you are about to pay for your new greenbacks."

Rachel had already decided this gentleman banker

could be trusted; now, as figures danced through her mind, she knew his math was correct. But she would never part with her coins, gold or silver. Besides, she had less than twenty dollars of it left in her purse.

She signed the documents above his signature. After he counted out her crisp, new greenbacks, Rachel offered her hand to further seal the transaction. She could not believe so much money could weigh so little.

Taking a different route back to the St. Charles, Rachel came upon an intersection congested with blue-uniformed men atop loaded wagons pulled by mule teams. It appeared the Nationals were taking a supply train somewhere. She wondered if their destination was Camp Defiance, the docks, or the railway station. In the town of Cairo, where nothing stood still, freight via Army wagon or business dray was either coming or going all day long.

On the corner before her, a newsagent was shouting something and waving today's edition of the *Chicago Tribune* over his head. She took one and plucked two other newspapers from his display rack. Charles Duncan said many of the nation's major dailies had embedded a reporter with the Army or Navy and often with both forces. Each gunboat was a temporary home to at least one correspondent and sometimes two or three.

The main reason, he said, was because Commodore Foote was so accommodating to the journalists. Foote was much like Gen. Grant. Not only was he willing to share information, he made himself available for interviews. Charles said it was the nature of certain military leaders to be cooperative because reporters often knew things the superior officers didn't know. He liked to think of it as one hand scratching away an itch on the other.

Walking along, Rachel recalled Charles' story about

meeting Grant for the first time. The general's headquarters was on the second floor of the St. Charles Hotel, and the correspondent hoped to show him the letter of authorization from the War Department, the prerequisite for securing a pass. Entering the room, he asked the clerk at the front desk to give the letter to Gen. Grant. The clerk, wearing a blue shirt without sign of rank, laid aside the pipe he was smoking, opened the envelope, and began reading.

"He then welcomed me and shook my hand. I had no idea I was speaking to Gen. Grant himself," Charles had said, "a most unpretentious man."

Rachel had no doubt the connected and cavalier Mr. Duncan was her best hope for news about Dwight. The morning would be complete if he had anything at all to tell her. However, back at the hotel, she learned Charles Duncan had not returned. Rachel refused to let disappointment sink into disconsolation. Instead, her thoughts swung to the realization that two of the needs she identified yesterday had already been met. The letters home? Written and mailed. The concern about money? Resolved. Oh, that she would learn something, anything, about her son.

But the day was young. If she saw Mr. Duncan again so soon, he might have no information. So, if need be, she would wait in the reception hall all day long. She could think of no alternative. At least she had her newspapers and all the time necessary to read them. With luck, one of those papers would contain details regarding *The City of Memphis.* She was good at sums in school; a three-out-of-four success rate was the same as 75 percent. Rachel would try, as much as she could, to keep that notable equation in mind.

She wished, however, she had not bought a copy of *The Cairo City Gazette.* The unsettling article about a shooting that erupted when a local man tried to stop bounty hunters from forcing a runaway back to his slavemaster triggered a spate of fear upon learning the incident occurred only two blocks from her hotel. The rest of the day Rachel remained on constant alert so as not to miss Mr. Duncan.

When he did not return, her intemperate stomach complained throughout the night.

CHAPTER 18

Tuesday, April 1
Sunfield, Michigan

Invariably in springtime, Shaytown Road turned into a mud-drenched corridor, a caramel-colored mess known to suck wagon wheels to their axles. The freezing nights of late March tightened the road until morning thaws undid its tentative resolve, and the cycle began anew. By the time Watson left school to return home on this warm morning in early April, the road was a disaster, and he hoped the pony Star was strong enough to keep her cart from bogging down. Otherwise, Watson must get out and walk the little filly, adding more gobs of clay-like mud to his leather boots already caked from yesterday's neglect. Watson suspected this day would be a long one. But it was not without reward, a handsome reward at that.

Had his mother not taken the Belgians to Battle Creek, Watson might have helped the hired hand to firm this sorry trail with the grader Rachel had bought a couple of years before. The law obligated Sunfield Township landowners to maintain their share of the passageway, but Shaytown Road was so abysmal Watson questioned whether even the new blade could save it. The solution he decided upon was not laziness but deference: Wait for Nature to repair herself. Enough sunshine and he wouldn't have to do a darn thing.

What could not wait was a close inspection of Star's leg. Watson noticed how the animal wouldn't put full weight on her right rear foot. He reasoned a stone had been caught in the pony's shoe; when he got home, he would look into it.

Adding to the morning's catalog of annoyance could have been another issue, one that he resolved an hour ago. An altercation with the schoolyard bully. Watson knew Tobias Sanford from the days they'd shared a classroom and remembered how they had vowed to quit school together, but Tobias stayed on after Watson left for good last winter. Among the dozen boys Miss Amble taught in her single-room schoolhouse, he and Tobias were the oldest. Neither was a scholar. But Watson knew Tobias to be a tough nut, a boy hard to like or to befriend because Tobias was aggressive and got into trouble with their teacher. The older and larger Tobias had grown, the harder it was for Miss Amble to manage him, an issue that gave Tobias license to escalate his pranks. With Watson gone, the unruly boy dominated both classroom and playground without fear of punishment or regard for those he taunted.

"He said my face looked like a cowpie," Helena had wailed on the ride home yesterday afternoon.

Watson shrugged. He had said similar things to others. "What's so terrible about that?" he said, his tone indifferent.

Hester answered for her sister. "He dragged Helena

over to the pasture fence and showed her!"

"What do you mean, he 'showed her'?" Watson asked with sudden interest.

"He used the pencil he stole from her to make a face in the cowpie."

Watson turned around to look at Helena, downcast, hands folded in her lap. "Tobias did that? That's pretty rotten."

Helena spoke up. "He took my hair tie, too, the pretty red one Ma gave me for Christmas. Stuck it right in the fresh poop and laughed. Said if I wanted it back, to climb over the fence and see what I looked like. And get it myself."

"That idiot," Watson hissed to himself.

"Told me to wipe it off on my dress!" Helena howled. Watson flushed from heat rushing to his face.

"That was Tuesday," Hester added. "This morning he grabbed a cinnamon bun out of our lunch pail."

"He did that? Then what happened?"

"He said I could have it back in eight hours! But if I lifted my dress, for his eyes only, I could have it back right now." Helena sniffled and began to blubber.

"Ma would be really mad," Hester said, "if she knew."

"Well, *I* know!" Watson shouted. "*I* know and I'm mad as hell!"

The pony had entered an impassable stretch and was straining to pull the full cart along. Enraged, Watson glanced down at his mud-drenched boots. Vacating the seat, he handed the reins to Hester and climbed down. Grasping Star's bridle, they trudged along for awhile. Watson was thinking about his brother, weighing what Dwight would have done were he home. That evening, over supper, Watson decided not to tell John Welch. He warned his sisters to keep the incident to themselves. He didn't want the hired man's help or his advice. He would settle this on his own in the morning.

He did settle it, as of an hour ago.

Waiting for his sisters to disappear into the schoolhouse, Watson got down and tied off Star to the hitching rail. It wasn't long before he heard the slosh of hooves advancing along the sloppy road. It was Tobias Sanford, and he was riding the same mule he always rode to school. Mule and rider sidled up next to the cart and pony. Neither boy spoke but the way Tobias sized up Watson, standing there straight as the rail post, fists at his side, intimated he knew why his old classmate had come back.

Tobias swung a long leg over the mule's rear, tied him off with a half-hitch, and stared at Watson through eyes of ice. Tobias was bigger, half a head taller, and he lorded his height superiority by stiffening his neck. "What do you want, Barnum?" he sneered. "Never mind. I know why you're here."

"You can't treat my sisters like that. No more, Tobias."

"Says you and what army? I'll treat 'em how I want." Tobias' hands went up, fists ready to strike or defend.

Dwight had shown his brother a trick before leaving home, and Watson used the move to advantage against this opponent who outweighed him by forty pounds. Seizing Tobias' wrists, Watson maneuvered a foot behind the boy's leg and pushed hard against his upper body. A surprised Tobias fell backward to the ground and banged his head against the wooden post. Cursing, he vaulted to his feet and came up swinging. "That'll cost you!" he roared and flailed away in a mighty effort to pummel Watson into capitulation. It didn't work.

Watson delivered a knee to his assailant's privates, a

quick and devastating strike. Yelping in pain, Tobias doubled over and dropped his hands. The motions put his face at the perfect level for Watson to dispense a crippling blow. One swift punch put Tobias on the ground again to writhe and swear between groans. The battle was over in seconds. Miss Amble and a few students who heard the fracas and rushed to the door were too late to witness anything.

One of the spectators was Hester. She smiled upon seeing Tobias flat on his back. Watson sent her a brief, two-finger salute before Miss Amble herded everyone inside. Turning to look back, the teacher hollered out, "Tobias looks hurt!" Her voice was loud above the din of student chatter. "Watson, how bad is it?"

Watson was already untying Star. "I don't know," he retorted. "Ask him."

On the slow, tedious return home, Watson felt no remorse. Dwight would have approved of how he overpowered the bully, how Watson had avenged their sisters' mistreatment. He also hoped he hadn't hurt Tobias too much. The prospect of Mr. Sanford coming to the house to confront him was possible but of no real concern. Watson would slip away and wait in the barn until Tobias' father left. Watson laughed without shame when he imagined John Welch trying to defuse a situation about which he knew nothing and could do nothing about.

Back home he escorted Star into the barn, discovered a small stone that had worked its way under the shoe, and dislodged it with a pick. Being right about the stone further improved his mood, and he didn't mind having to clean his boots after all. He was feeling so fine he scraped each of the pony's hooves and gave her a carrot from the root cellar.

Cairo, Illinois

THROUGHOUT MONDAY NIGHT, RACHEL'S SLEEP was interrupted by dreams of confusion and doubt, which did nothing for peace of mind. Besides being exhausted this morning, her stomach still hurt, and she wondered if she had fallen ill. Her throat was sore, arms ached, and temples throbbed. There was no sense of fever—she was free from chills or sweats—nor was there a cough. Rachel tried to remember when she last felt so poorly, but her mind refused to align itself with a single cogent thought. She could be anywhere but here, in a small room in a large hotel in a wretched town. The only certainty was her wish to leave as quickly as possible. There was only one way to be rid of this depression and that was to hear news, any news, of Dwight. She could manage what she knew if only she could know something. This morning's illness was because she knew nothing.

Was he dead? Was he alive? If alive, did he suffer? Is he afraid? Whatever on earth was physically wrong could be healed, could be made whole again. He was young. He was strong. If he was still in the hospital, even a basic field hospital with limited medical supplies and instruments, a doctor would relieve his pain, a nurse would alleviate his discomfort. But no one except a mother could console a frightened child. Rachel tried to recall the times she had fretted over her firstborn, this baby who had come too early, how she had attended to his every need, rocking late into the night until sleep overcame them both. But there were too many times, her current state of mind too fractured. Trying to dwell on any one incident was like unraveling a ball of yarn to figure out where it began.

Dwight would always be a child, her first child; until

she knew what had happened and how he was faring, there was no peace. And even though she knew it was wrong to blame Charles Duncan for her predicament, she struggled to hold him faultless. Why has he not come back to the hotel? Why has he left no news?

Sitting on the bed edge, head in her hands, eyes staring at a knot in the wood floor, Rachel tried to dredge back his words. "I'll send a telegram now." Or was it, "I'll *try* to send a telegram now?" Did he not say, "I will leave the answer at the front desk?" No, that's wrong. He said *if* he received an answer, he would leave it at the front desk.

He was a kind man, a gentleman. He would not trifle with something so important to her. Then why did he smile when he said she wasn't the only person who needed to know Dwight's circumstances? Was that huge grin he flashed one of empathy, or did it disguise a game he was playing, a cruel stunt of some kind?

Her head would not stop pounding. Was she losing her mind? Apprehensive, unwholesome thoughts only worsened her melancholy. She must be patient. He will return. Hadn't that desk clerk, the approachable one who worked evenings, said last night that Charles Duncan was in and out of the St. Charles so often that management did its level best to leave his room unrented between visits?

The clerk confided that Charles had not checked out and was likely to return before long.

Why couldn't she be so positive? She could and she would. The alternative was to admit failure and return home without Dwight.

Rachel decided to wash, comb her hair, part it to either side, and tie it back. She would wear a different dress today, the light green one with the white collar. She would eat something downstairs, drink more water than usual, and ask for the strongest coffee available. Perhaps a waiter would indulge her by adding honey to the coffee as her mother sometimes did to hours-old brew to lessen its bitter taste.

Reading today's newspapers, if the news was favorable, might also ease her disquiet. Yesterday's editions had not been helpful at all. The papers she bought and the one someone left in the reception hall made no mention of the vaunted hospital ship. The news was all about the War and there was much to report. A growing army of Confederates under a general named Albert Johnston was marching from Corinth, Mississippi, to a port on the Tennessee River called Pittsburgh Landing. Grant and his army were already in the area. That dispatch reminded her of the sales agent on the train and his prediction of fireworks there before long.

A St. Louis paper, the *Missouri Republican*, had reported the siege of Island No. 10 was now in its third week, and pressure was growing on Flag Officer Foote to commit his ironclad armada to an all-out assault.

Major troop movements in the East by the Rebel and Federal armies motivated an editorial writer to predict this second year of the Rebellion would prove far more contentious than the first, that this was "no 12-month war," and the nation should prepare for devastating consequences.

Those articles, along with local events and other happenings of no interest to her, were the summation of yesterday's news. The lone exception was a report from the Associated Press that greenbacks were now legal tender throughout the United States. The piece predicted the Secessionists would find them most desirable, and counterfeit printers would now have something to do.

Lifting her dress with one hand, Rachel held the rail with the other and descended the steep stairway with slow, careful steps. Downstairs, she was pleased to note the brusque attendant of yesterday had gotten out of bed on the better side today. He greeted her with a complimentary copy of Tuesday's *Tribune*, "fresh off the midnight train from Chicago." She thought perhaps he didn't recognize her because of the dress. However, without solicitation, the clerk reported that Charles Duncan was still away.

What caused this reversal? Was her mind still playing tricks? In the dining hall, she asked for strong coffee with honey, if available, and was surprised when the waiter returned with both. For breakfast, she would try flannel cakes and warm hominy.

"Oh, y'all will like those grits, ma'am," the congenial waiter promised, "especially if you douse 'em with some of that honey. That's the way the missus serves 'em at home."

Rachel nodded and thanked him. The morning was turning out better than expected. The coffee was more stout than usual but not at all bitter because of the dollop of honey she added but also because someone in the kitchen must have blended it with chicory. Or so she assumed. Whatever the reason, she found no fault with taste or efficacy, for the pulsing in her temples was already subsiding. Breakfast over, Rachel strolled out to the hall to see what was in today's paper.

Half of the front page was devoted to military maneuvers in the East and to various bills moving through Congress. She read an editorial supporting the Army's demand that newspaper correspondents refrain from reporting military plans until after their execution "lest they provide advance notice to the enemy." Citations included a report from one Southern paper that the Federals were digging a canal through flooded timber to New Madrid with the purpose of bypassing Island No. 10. The editorial concluded with, "How was this information obtained if not from press leaks or the infiltration of Rebel spies into our ranks?"

A dispatch from Cairo mentioned that the siege of Island No. 10 continued with the firing of sixty-one cannon shots by the Federal gunboats on Sunday and fifty-three shots yesterday.

She had finished scanning the *Tribune's* inside pages and was perusing the advertisements when a gentleman sitting near her asked if the paper she read was Tuesday's edition. Assured that it was, he offered to trade newspapers. "I have the *Cairo Times*," he said, "and the *Evanston.* Have you seen them?"

"I have not," she answered. "And, yes, I thank you for the offer." The Indiana newspaper included an unsettling brief about one of the hospitals in Cairo: "A soldier was taken sick and sent for his family, consisting of his wife and one child. On the night after their arrival the mother died and the next night the child died. Before their bodies were consigned to the earth, the grief-stricken husband and father also breathed his last. This is but a single episode in this terribly wicked rebellion."

The story brought a stab of new pain to her temples. Folding the newspaper with haste, she tossed it onto an empty chair and commenced to read the *Cairo Times*. The weekly listed city council proceedings, the next meeting date of the Ladies' Guild, and the like, but what drew her eye were freight shipping details and local military activities. Among anticipated dock arrivals and departures along the city's wharves was joyful news that *The City of Memphis* would return to East Wharf from St. Louis with new Sanitary Commission supplies. Rachel vowed to be at the dock when the hospital ship arrived sometime tomorrow afternoon.

Buried deeper in the paper was a brief article about how Soldiers Hospital, with accommodations for fourteen hundred patients, was preparing for an influx of casualties from "an imminent battle" either down the Mississippi or up the Tennessee. The Sanitary Commission would provide oversight and coordination for the sick and wounded.

She deliberated whether the hospital itself would accept a volunteer worker in exchange for passage downriver whenever safe travel resumed. She decided to inquire, and the transformed attendant at the front desk provided directions to the hospital. The headache was gone, supplanted by this new ray of hope.

CHAPTER 19

Cairo, Illinois

Arriving at the dominant red-brick building called Soldiers Hospital, Rachel walked inside and immediately a peculiar odor overwhelmed her senses. For the rest of her life, the smell of ether would be a moving reminder of this day. The anesthetic's inescapable presence brooks no trace, such is its power. Wherever, whenever Rachel was exposed to the odor of ether, memory would swirl her back to Soldiers Hospital in Cairo, Illinois.

The source was impossible to trace to a single room or hallway. Unseen, unfelt, it hung on the air in the receptionist's office where Rachel coughed, cleared her throat, and introduced herself to an older woman pouring over a large book wrapped in black leather.

The woman glanced up and said "Good morning" to Rachel, who dabbed at smarting eyes with a handkerchief. Nonplussed, the receptionist continued. "Mrs. Barnum, you said? I'm Angelina Cordray. I apologize for the ether.

We've had two operations already this morning." Running a finger over ledger entries, she added, "And I see we're not finished."

"I've never smelled anything so sharp," Rachel said. "My word, it's stronger than Limburger."

"Oh, we're accustomed to it. Breathe through the cloth and within a short while it seems to go away. What brings you to the hospital, Mrs. Barnum? Are you here to visit?"

"I'm here to volunteer," Rachel grimaced. "At least I think so."

"Hmmmm," the receptionist murmured through a tight, knowing smile. "That's wonderful. We always need help. Do come with me, Mrs. Barnum, and you can talk with our administrator."

Rachel held back nothing during the meeting with Dr. Delbert Anson, retired surgeon now hospital administrator, who assisted with complicated operations as an advisor because his aging hands had lost much of their precision, the fingers no longer deliberate and steady. Fitting them together, perhaps to mitigate trembling, he placed his hands on the desk and listened to Rachel. "You wish to volunteer as a hospital aide in exchange for passage to New Madrid? Do I have that right, Mrs. Barnum?"

"Yes. I can prepare meals, wash bedding, and change bandages. I have a lifetime of farm experience. Whatever is needed I will do. Wherever I can be helpful, I will help."

Nodding approval, he said, "Well, I sympathize with the need to get to your son. And you are aware of the situation down there?"

"I know there's no travel down the river from Island Number 10. Not until the Confederates leave."

"Yes, that's the nub of it. The island's been in a state of siege for some time now." He looked into her eyes as though they held the answer to the question not asked.

Rachel's voice reached a higher pitch, the words spilling forth. "Two weeks! Some days I hear the cannon fire. I've been reading the papers every day since coming to Cairo, waiting for something to happen."

She appreciated his attempt to console her. "Waiting is the hardest part, Mrs. Barnum. I have no illusion about that."

"Oh my, yes!"

Dr. Anson drew a large breath, releasing it bit by bit. His pained expression told her to expect something she didn't know. "Whenever that island falls," he began, "there is no assurance that either of the Commission's two ships will go to New Madrid." Her eyes flared. He hesitated and continued. "You know the Union Army is stuck there, for the time being anyway, but what you may not know is that most of the few casualties from the New Madrid fighting were removed to St. Louis some time ago."

She tensed again and said, "You said *most*. Have any soldiers been brought here?" Enlivened by the possibility, Rachel left her chair. "Dr. Anson, could he be here? Do you think my son is here?"

"Is the last name also Barnum?"

"Yes, Barnum! Dwight Barnum."

The doctor stood up. "What unit? Infantry?"

"No. Cavalry. He's with the 2nd Michigan Cavalry, Company B."

"Excuse me a moment," he said. "Mrs. Cordray has the patient records."

The few minutes he left her alone crept by like an excursion ship inching its slow, torturous way to berth while impatient passengers crowded the rail, waiting for the gangplank to drop.

When Dr. Anson returned, his face telegraphed disappointment. "I'm sorry, Mrs. Barnum. He is not here, has never been here. I did, however, send a runner to the post office with authorization to wire an inquiry directly to Gen. Pope's headquarters."

"You did that? Already?" Amazement was all over her face.

"The surgeon for the regiment should know where your son is. What his condition might be."

"Bless you, Dr. Anson!"

The doctor responded with a grin and a slight shrug. "It's one of the important things the Sanitary Commission does for the families of soldiers," he explained. "Sometimes our requests are answered quickly. Sometimes we wait hours, sometimes days even."

"I have nothing to do in Cairo *but* wait."

"Well, the post office closes at five o'clock. That's a little more than seven hours from now. The hospital courier goes back and forth all day with messages. If he brings back any news about your son, Mrs. Cordray will tell you. You can wait in the lobby if you like."

"If it please you, sir, put me to work. I simply cannot sit by and helplessly wait."

A supervisor assigned Rachel to the second-floor ward. The hours ticked on while she helped to empty chamber pots and change the bed sheets of fourteen patients, most of whom had come to Soldiers Hospital from Paducah or Columbus, Kentucky. One soldier had fought in Belmont across the river in Missouri late in the fall and still suffered from pneumonia. As a farm wife and mother, Rachel had tended to minor injuries and had grown accustomed to seeing blood but was unprepared for the wounds of war. Carefully removing the bandages on a soldier's leg, she gasped at the mangled flesh. The infection on another's arm was so bad she called for assistance. The nurse that came to help her wash and redress the wound said she dealt with such ghastly sights by imagining doing something else.

"I feel so helpless," Rachel said. "Is there nothing more we can do for him? For any of these poor men?"

"Being with them is the most important," the nurse said. "The doctors do what they can and then move on to the next patient. Our job is to give them as much comfort, as much care as possible."

Watching the nurse gently spread a cool cloth over the soldier's fevered brow, Rachel retreated to private thought. After a long pause, she said, "You're doing the Lord's work here."

The nurse stopped dabbing, turned, and looked up at her. "Yes," she said, "we're on sacred ground here. No one deserves to die alone."

Two inmates were Confederate soldiers assigned to beds at the far end of the ward. When Rachel came to them, she saw one was a boy. He could not have been a day older than fifteen. Images of her own sons flickered through her mind. *He looks younger than Watson! Why is he even here? Who made him come here?* Watching her stare, the soldier in the next bed spoke up.

"That's Chauncey. He ain't doing too good. Talks a lot and makes no sense. Now he don't even wake up."

"What's wrong with him? Is he sick? Is he hurt?"

"I don't know. They say his fever's gotten real bad."

She saw Dwight lying there. The boy's lips moved when Rachel touched his face. It was hot. Her voice announced distress. "He's burning up! Where is Chauncey from?"

"Oh, he's a Alabama boy, ma'am. Lost his brother at

Fort Henry and was took prisoner. He was here when I got here from Donelson."

The soldier asked if he could have some water. When Rachel returned with a pitcher and dipper, she helped the man, whose arm was heavily bandaged and supported by a sling, to sit up and drink. Then she wiped the boy's face with a damp cloth.

"I been praying for him," the man said. "He's a good Baptist boy. He just wants to go home and help his mother and sister plant their crop 'fore it's too late."

The boy mumbled something, but neither Rachel nor the soldier could understand what he said. "When was the last time Chauncey talked to you?"

"Lessee now. Since two days ago he ain't made no sense at all."

Their conversation prompted the boy to mutter something. She caught one word. When Rachel heard "Mama" the second time, she leaned over, her mouth close to his ear. She spoke in a whisper. "Mama is here. Chauncey, your mama is here. Mama is with you, now." She ran her fingers over his heated face before turning back to the boy's wardmate. "Would you like to pray with me?"

"Yes, ma'am," he said. "I truly would."

Regardless of the various duties Rachel performed that day, her thoughts did not stray far from the plight of her son. Some tasks increased her anguish. She saw Dwight in the suffering of each patient but none more so than the Rebel boy named Chauncey. Injury and illness, the naked proof of war's consequences, made her angry. She wondered why differences must lead to conflict, to incite men to take up arms and kill each other. War was unnatural to a modern society. And civil war was heinous for how it ruptured families. For pitting fathers against their sons, brothers against each other. The torment it caused for women and children was indefensible. It was not right for sons to die before their mothers and fathers.

During a rest break, she leaned back in a lobby chair, far enough for her head to press against the wall, and closed her eyes. The nurse's words returned: "We're on sacred ground here. No one deserves to die alone." Unable to get Chauncey out of her mind, Rachel pledged to keep doing whatever she could to relieve suffering wherever she found it.

Deeper in reverie, she saw herself at the farm on a morning in May, her favorite month. Birds were singing, and the sky was a sapphire blue. Sunshine flooded the barnyard. She saw John Welch and the team coming back from a newly turned field, the steel curve from the plow blade gleaming in the sun. The twins, laughing with joy, held kittens in their laps. Watson curried the pony Star.

She saw her church and identified fellow congregants, pew by pew, as everyone rose to sing. She imagined Cousin Betsey Barnum and her fatherless, stairstep children: three girls wedged between a brother to either side, the taller Harrison, proud as a rooster guarding his flock, towering above them. Moving on to other neighbors, one by one, she could picture them and their homes. These images transformed into other happy thoughts. Fishing for chubs in Sebewa Creek. A morning buggy ride to the Grand River for a family picnic. The Fourth of July gathering last summer when Dwight thrilled onlookers, young and old, by lighting the firecrackers he got from bartering his pocketknife.

Why had War come to turn the peaceful world she loved on its head? Because no one owned anyone in Sunfield, slavery had no direct, personal impact upon anyone

Rachel knew. What few Negroes lived in the county were free, as far as she was aware. She knew no Negro people by name but had made a moderate contribution to a church in Charlotte that was collecting funds to support a Negro family from Jackson. Court costs, accrued while fighting extradition proceedings brought on by a slavemaster who sent bounty hunters to reclaim what he insisted was private property, had saddled the Negro family with debt.

The court declared the petition illegal, and the slave-catchers returned to Kentucky without reparation. Rachel heard the family moved on through an "underground railroad" to Detroit and was now farming their own land in southern Ontario.

The sale of people as though they were animals was beyond abhorrent because it destroyed families. It brought a war. Notwithstanding, that evil War had come to Eaton County in insidious ways, none more so than the sons and fathers who left their homes and mothers and wives to fight in it.

A profound sense of regret was displacing her morning depression. Setting aside the chair, Rachel rose and stood erect, her back against the lobby wall. Standing there, her shoulders pinned to the wall, she vowed to forego any further self-pity, regardless of what obstructions lay ahead. She must try harder to think about the plight of others and to help if she could. She needed to do this, and not only because she had the means or because others might be less fortunate. It was the right thing to do.

IT WAS A QUARTER PAST four when the receptionist located Rachel. She nearly spilled a pail of soapy water when Angelina Cordray strode into the ward and announced that Dr. Anson wanted to see Mrs. Barnum right away. "Did he get a message?" Rachel's breath came so fast she began to pant. "Is there any news?"

"I don't know but I expect Dr. Anson does. He said to come now."

Heart racing, Rachel rushed downstairs to the administrator's office. A waiting Dr. Anson ushered her inside, closed the door, and invited her to sit down. She trembled with anticipation. He spoke the facts without emotion, his voice sober, serious. "Your son is still alive. He has smallpox. He's in quarantine in a tent in New Madrid."

It was the news Rachel craved. It was the news she dreaded. Relief arced through her like an electric current, followed immediately by a schism of dread. Such were the all-consuming emotions that quaked through her, and she lost self-control. Chest heaving with sobs, she plummeted into the chair and huffed for air.

During the next half-hour, Dr. Anson brought her water, then tea. He sat with her on the visitor bench next to his desk. His voice was quiet, reassuring, as though addressing an inconsolable youngster. "All is not lost. Your son is alive. Mrs. Barnum, that is what you must hold onto."

Rachel had soaked her handkerchief with tears of joy, tears of apprehension. Dr. Anson gave her his, neatly folded, from a pocket inside his white physician's coat. He patted her shoulder with empathy, and when she leaned into him, he extended his arm and hugged her for a long moment.

Relaxing the tight hold, he withdrew his arm. Sniffling, Rachel thanked him and whispered in a reedy voice, "I'm all right now, Doctor. That helped more than anything."

When she had regained composure, he asked her to clarify when the telegram she had mentioned was written and when she had received it. Penciling details on a scrap of paper, Dr. Anson deliberated a moment and announced that Dwight had in all likelihood survived the disease's early stages, its most virulent period, and was on the way to recovery. "Contracting smallpox is not always a sentence of death."

He went on to speculate. "My concern has to do with the possibility of an epidemic. Your son caught this from someone and may have passed it on to others. It's rather odd the Sanitary Commission has heard nothing of a smallpox problem over there, in that area. But that could be because a plague is just beginning."

Her thoughts were elsewhere. "You really believe Dwight is recovering?"

"The answer to that is when he was infected. The fever referenced in your telegram was eleven days ago. Adding a minimum of ten days from contraction to first symptoms suggests he was exposed at least three weeks ago. Maybe earlier. At any rate, lesions could be forming by now. At a minimum, he would be in the pustule stage."

Rachel heard the words as hammer blows. "Dr. Anson, I'm not sure I understand."

"He's past the intense pain and the high fever. The rash stage should be over, too. I'm sure he still itches terribly, worse than a bad case of poison ivy. No doubt they're doing all they can to make him comfortable. They'll be insisting he not scratch any lesions. Those must scab over, harden, and fall off before he can see others without fear of infecting them." He stopped to let her take in this clipped assessment. "The point, Mrs. Barnum, is that your son is alive. I don't believe he will die from smallpox."

Rachel let go an immense sigh of relief. "The Lord has answered my prayers!"

"Let's not get ahead of ourselves," the doctor cautioned.

"Anything can happen. Of course, you can't see him until the last scab is gone. Or he could infect you. For that matter, so could anyone else with smallpox in quarantine with him."

"But, Dr. Anson, I can't get the smallpox."

"Why is that? What do you mean?"

Pulling back the dress sleeve, Rachel pointed to faint spots. "Those are from cowpox. My twin sister and I got it as children from milking our Jersey cow. I'm still immune, aren't I?"

Dr. Anson broke into a huge smile, shook his head in wonder, and said, "The Lord has, indeed, answered your prayers."

It was his hearty laughter that brought a smile to her face, the first time she felt hope this mighty since leaving home.

CHAPTER 20

Cairo, Illinois

Dr. Anson found someone making a delivery to the St. Charles Hotel and arranged for Rachel to ride along. She forgot his name, maybe she never knew his name, such was the euphoria that had swept over her. The abstraction she had known that morning was back, but this mood was so different. It was not dark and defeating, and she did not feel ill. What she felt was surety that her ordeal was almost over, that soon she would be with her son. Dwight was still sick, but he was *alive*.

Rachel did remember, with clarity, that Dr. Anson had said *The City of Memphis* with its cargo of medicine and supplies faced delay and would now arrive in Cairo by noon tomorrow. Convinced the hospital ship was her best hope at getting to New Madrid, apart from the vessel's haphazard schedule, Rachel would go to East Wharf tomorrow and ask for a Dr. Schmidt, show him her letter of recommendation from Dr. Anson, and volunteer for service. Beyond that, she had no plan and no power to direct future affairs.

Or so she thought.

Back at the hotel, Rachel was halfway through supper when Charles Duncan stunned her by showing up at her table. His unkempt appearance was shocking. The correspondent wore no hat, and his hair was wild. His jacket, unbuttoned, revealed a filthy shirt, and his trousers were rumpled and stained. Rachel looked askance at mud-speckled boots, at a face that was haggard. His eyes said he was exhausted.

"Mr. Duncan!" she said, "are you not well? What's wrong? Where have you been?"

"Come to the hall," he pleaded in a low voice. "I shouldn't be here in this condition. I apologize for my appearance, Mrs. Barnum, and for this rash intrusion." His tone dropped. "I came because they said you were here."

Rachel, bewildered, spread the linen napkin over the remains of her supper and followed him to the reception hall. Choosing the same chairs, they duplicated the arrangement of two nights earlier. "What has happened to you?" she repeated. "Have you taken ill?"

"More about me in a moment. First, I have news about your son. The telegraph line from New Madrid to Sikeston to Birds Point was down all day yesterday. It worked for a little while this morning, then stopped again until this afternoon. A message came through barely an hour ago."

Rachel cut into this monologue. "You went to New Madrid? How?"

"No, not New Madrid! I was just across the river in Missouri at Birds Point. I was on my way to Sikeston." His words were rapid-fire. "Anyway, by the time I got back to the Point, the wire was back up ... I am so sorry to tell you this … I learned your son has smallpox. But he's alive. Mrs. Barnum, Dwight is still alive!"

Rachel took no pleasure in telling him she already knew. "The Sanitary Commission here in Cairo told me, also late this afternoon."

He was astounded. "Then you must know Dwight was wounded in the New Madrid fighting."

"Wounded?" her face contorted. "You mean shot? How can this be?"

"I don't know all the details. Just that he took a piece of shrapnel in the upper arm. The shell that exploded also killed his horse."

Tremors of nausea swept through her. Her mind raced to the telegram. "SICK WITH FEVER." *Sick with fever from what? Injury? Smallpox? From both?* She was sinking, getting smaller. The sudden defeat was like tumbling down a steep hill after trying so hard to reach the top. Mumbling, she refused to believe. "Blaze is dead? This cannot be! Dwight could never abide losing his horse."

"I'm very sorry, Mrs. Barnum … Rachel. But now you know as much as I know."

Rachel bent low to keep private the tears spilling down her cheeks. Clamping her head between tense fingers, she barely registered Charles' consoling hand on her shoulder. "I wish I could help," he pleaded. "Is there any way to make this better for you?"

"Just be with me awhile," Rachel whimpered between convulsive sobs. "I'll be all right in a bit."

They talked until nightfall cloaked the town. Having no notebook, Charles wrote nothing of their discussion. The waiter came into the hall and asked if Rachel would like the rest of her supper warmed. She thanked him and declined. Soon after, the dining room went dark, and someone closed the door. Rain began to spatter the hotel windows. They talked on. She was quiet, her thoughts jumbled, as he unwound the day's trial.

Much later, whenever trying to recall what happened, she would forget certain details. Had they reversed roles, she could have filled a journal that evening. She would try, without success, to find published articles he must have written about his harrowing experience. She never saw the story he planned to write about her. After a year, she would cancel her subscription to the *Boston Globe*, but that was also because the news was already stale when the mailed papers arrived in bundles at her farm.

THE INCIDENT HAD TO DO with Charles Duncan's capture by a band of Rebels who answered to a guerrilla leader called the Swamp Fox. The correspondent had been riding with a patrol of Union cavalrymen with orders to protect engineers dispatched to ensure the telegraph lines worked and to repair wires sabotaged by the enemy or damaged by storms.

For some reason, possibly to finish notes or sketch a scene, Charles loitered after the engineers had restrung a broken wire. When they rode off, along with the cavalry detail, he found himself alone. Sometime later, not longer than an hour, perhaps half that time, a cadre of horsemen, a dozen or more rough-looking men, burst from the woods and bore down on the unarmed reporter. Surrounded, he offered no resistance.

They demanded to know where the repair patrol had gone. Charles insisted he didn't know, pointed, and said "Somewhere down the line."

"I see where they fixed the wire," a man with drawn pistol said.

"Romayne, git yer skinny self up that tree and unfix it," another insurgent ordered.

When Mr. Duncan divulged that he wrote for a newspaper, the *Boston Globe*, they became abusive in language and deed. One rogue liked his hat and stole it, telling the reporter to go back north and fetch a new one. Someone else took his notebook so he could "tell no more hateful lies." The probable leader, a bearded ruffian wearing a bowler hat, unsheathed a Bowie knife, spat a foul stream of tobacco juice on him, and demanded to know who owned his horse.

"The United States Cavalry," Charles responded in a voice that didn't sound brave at all.

Another man laughed. "He ain't tellin' no lie, Mose. Can't y'all read? Says so right there on the saddle."

"Then we'll take his nag, too," Mose said. "And you'll lead 'em."

The man flaunting the pistol bore a ruthless expression. Still mounted, he looked down at the hapless reporter. "Lessee what's in them Yankee pockets. Turn 'em out!" Fearing for his life, Charles handed over silver coin and some paper money. "Greenbacks!" the robber yelped. "Now we all know you're the devil himself!"

A brief argument about whether to kill the captive, tie him to a tree, or leave him along the trail was settled when Mose said, "Let him go. He can walk ten miles back to the river."

This is what Charles Duncan did, arriving back at Birds Point during a thunderstorm. While waiting in the telegraph office for the rain to end, a message from New Madrid came through. An hour later he was back in Cairo, looking for Rachel Barnum.

WHEN CHARLES LEFT FOR HIS room, Rachel departed for

her own, ascending each flight of stairs and stopping at the landings between floors. Knowing Dwight was still alive, was a reasonable night's sleep possible for the first time since coming to Cairo? It didn't sound as though the wound from a fortnight ago was life-threatening. If only she could know more.

She recalled the time Dwight had cut his hand while sharpening a double-bit ax, and how he tried to convince her it was nothing to get excited over. Rachel insisted he accompany her to the Sunfield doctor's office, a three-mile trip in the wagon. The doctor agreed the cut was serious although the bleeding had almost stopped. Rachel washed and dressed the wound every day for a week in spite of her son's persistence she was being fussy as a mother hen and since he was almost a man now could take care of himself. When the accident happened, Dwight was fifteen, halfway to sixteen, and had attained his adult height of five feet, ten inches. Rachel knew then the day would come when she must let him go. But not yet. Not yet.

Dr. Anson had said *The City of Memphis* was scheduled to dock before noon and would not leave Cairo before her cargo was unloaded, but Rachel also feared how the War upset plans and changed timetables. Therefore, she would leave nothing to chance. She would be at East Wharf by the dinner hour and, if the assigned berth was empty, simply wait there until the ship arrived.

Before extinguishing her lamp, she began a second letter to John Welch, paused after a few sentences, and questioned why she was writing to him and not the children. When no explanation came, she resumed writing. Had she more time, she would have written separate letters to the others. Such was the immediate justification for writing to the hired man, but another reason had seeped into conscious thought. She missed John deeply. Had that supportive embrace by Dr. Anson or the comforting hand of Charles Duncan on her shoulder belonged to John Welch, she would not have hesitated to respond in kind.

The awareness of her affection for John, what it really meant, demanded introspection. But not now. Consumed by the day's events, she needed to clear her mind and rest. As soon as she finished the letter, she would go to bed.

She wrote with haste in a hand as clear as possible. She expected Mr. Welch would have a problem with some of the words, but Hester was a good reader and could read it to him if need be. Rachel explained the latest developments regarding Dwight, mentioning twice that she could be gone another week or longer. She said to remind Helena to give the cat extra milk and wondered anew if she had become a mother and how many kittens there were. She told John she prayed for him, the girls, and Watson and asked him to remember Dwight and her in his prayers. She thanked John for assuming the extra burden her absence had caused, sent her love to all, and signed the letter "Rachel and Mother."

Affixing a three-cent stamp, she descended the stairs to give the letter to the desk clerk. However, no one was there. While waiting, she browsed through what remained of the day's papers on the service counter. Several men, apparently sitting around a table or standing before the bar in an adjacent room, were having a lively discussion. She overheard much of what was said.

"I told you it was true," someone declared in a loud voice, "and now it's in the local paper. Here's what it says: 'An atrocious murder was yesterday committed in a drunken brawl on the levee in a drinking saloon, which flourishes here in spite of provost marshals and martial law.'

"See? I *told* you it was true. Why did you doubt it?"

Someone else broke in with, "Who got killed?"

"The saloon owner! Man named Joeb. Got into a fight with a drunk patron who stabbed him."

A new voice chimed in. "They banned all liquor sales." Rachel thought she recognized this voice, perhaps from breakfast or supper. "But that don't stop some from drinking."

"True enough, Hiram. Present company included."

Others joined the conversation while cigar smoke drifted through the open door. She heard the thud of a drinking vessel on wood.

"Where'd he get the hooch?"

"Probably from the saloon itself. Or maybe from one of the gambling joints."

"How about a house of shame?" someone guffawed.

"Why not? Look how easy it was for us!"

Following loud laughter, another man changed the subject. "Those provost guards are mighty quick on the trigger. Look how they shot that marine from the *Louisville* a couple weeks back at one of those joints."

"They could come in here, Jonas, and arrest you before you could drain the evidence in that glass."

"Here? At the St. Charles? Naw! They won't bother nobody here."

"I wouldn't be so sure of that."

"This town is going to Hell."

"This town has gone to Hell, thanks to the military."

Stepping into the lobby, one of the patrons noticed Rachel waiting at the counter. Pretending to address her envelope, she did not look up. The man hesitated before slipping back into the room and closing the door behind him.

When the attendant returned, he informed Rachel that a horse and dray traveled each morning to and from the wharves for fifty cents, a nominal fee for the five-mile ride. She pledged to hire the service, which would save her two hours of walking.

After all, the spirited talk of a recent murder down at the docks was all the more reason not to walk there alone.

CHAPTER 21

Tuesday, April 8
New Madrid, Missouri

Day after day of confinement to a sick bed affords a stricken soldier all the time in his insular world to contemplate what could have happened, what did happen, and what may happen if his condition won't improve. Eight days in a field hospital near New Madrid, Missouri, is an eternity for nineteen-year-old Pvt. Dwight Barnum of Company B, 2nd Michigan Cavalry. Wracked with pain, confused with fever, Dwight does not know the hour of day or night, nor is he aware of the days that come and go. Fleeting moments of lucidity lead to incomprehension until dulled by a morphine shot. A sudden attack of shivers or sweats, and the cycle begins anew.

The intolerable thirst he suffers this morning had not occurred during the first week of internment when Dwight could replay the chronology of his brief soldierly career. The forming of the volunteer regiment, twelve hundred strong, at the Grand Rapids fairgrounds in early October, was a heady time of camaraderie. He knew several of the loyal Eaton County boys and made friends with others who also had brought their fine horses to training camp. A month of marching and drilling did not dampen their enthusiasm; on the contrary, it boosted expectation and strengthened resolve.

Leaving Grand Rapids by train on November 14, the 2nd Michigan met a cheering crowd in Detroit where the troopers enjoyed a bounteous meal before boarding cars on the Alton and St. Louis for southern Illinois. At the larger towns they traveled through, throngs of citizens had rallied to wave and send them on with cheers of gratitude. Injured, lying prone in bed with nothing to do, Dwight thinks of the pretty girl in Decatur who offered a cookie through the car window and blew kiss after kiss at him until disappearing when the troop train moved away. Imagining her helped to lift his mood, if only for a short while, during those early days of confinement.

At Alton, the troops boarded transports and crossed the Big Muddy to St. Louis where they bivouacked at Benton Barracks on the city's outskirts. Thousands were already there; thousands more were on the way. The cavalrymen received sabers and Colt revolvers for sidearms and Colt 5 shooting-revolving carbines for their saddle scabbards. After three more months of intensive training, the 2nd Michigan was as well drilled and well equipped as any mounted unit in the Army of the West. And they were spoiling for a fight.

Company B's first casualty was Joseph Boyer, a young man Dwight knew from neighboring Roxand Township. Joey's passing from dysentery at the training camp in mid-January was sobering proof that enemy bullets were not the sole agent of death in this crazy war.

Ordered south to Commerce, Missouri, on February 21, the regiment joined others to amass a fighting force of twenty-five thousand men under the command of Maj. Gen. John Pope. Dwight and his fellow soldiers knew the Army's strategy was to take New Madrid from Confederate hands and then cross the Mississippi and drive the Secessionists from Island No. 10. The grand plan would require support from Naval Commodore Foote's gunboat fleet, back on the big river after recent victories at Fort Henry on the Tennessee River and Fort Donelson on the Cumberland. If the strategy was successful, the Mississippi would then be open to Memphis, and Pope's forces could march south to join Grant and his Army of Tennessee.

Schooled by Col. Gordon Granger, a West Point graduate and friend of Gen. Pope, Dwight counted himself among the fortunate to belong to the 2nd Michigan attachment. A strict disciplinarian, Granger and his officers had whipped the recruits into such ready condition that the colonel earned the rank of brigadier general and achieved added responsibility for the 3rd Michigan Cavalry. This combination formed an independent division numbering more than two thousand. Riding six abreast in dashing formation, the waves of horse soldiers in their dark-blue jackets and lighter trousers made for an intrepid Federal force.

In spite of feeling miserable while the hours and days drone on in his sick tent, Dwight's heart swells with pride whenever images of those cavalry units dance through his mind.

Blaze, the buckskin gelding Dwight's father had given him on his fifteenth birthday, was intelligent, affectionate, and loyal. Dwight is assured that Willis Barnum, who knew horses as well as anyone in Sunfield Township, would have been proud to see his son on this handsome, immaculately groomed animal, a testament to good breeding, dedicated training, and exceptional care. Dwight knows his father would have agreed that no son treated his horse better or loved it more.

So Dwight thought as he lay on his back while recuperating from illness and injury. But the youthful mind is an active mind, and happy memories can flip to those of bitter trial as quickly as luck changes with the next hand of playing cards.

ON MARCH 2, FICKLE WEATHER greeted Pope's army as the men rode and marched southwest from Commerce for twenty miles before turning due south for thirty more miles to New Madrid. Here, forested lowland dominated much of southern Missouri along the west side of the Mississippi, which suffered record flooding in the spring of 1862. What had been a dry road became a mud bog that demanded a Herculean effort to negotiate. The passageway, which crossed the railroad coming from Birds Point on the Mississippi, was called the King's Highway. To Dwight and his fellow troopers, it was neither a highway, nor was it fit for a king. The final leg to New Madrid was the worst, and they had been in the thick of it.

Fanning out before the miles-long column of blue were teams of engineers that scoured the countryside for timber to stiffen a corduroy road of sponge. Dwight found himself in a crawling crusade of thousands on foot and horseback advancing on a path half-buried in boot-sucking slosh. Behind him came the cannons and their limbers with 500-pound chests of ammunition and the horse teams straining to keep them moving and the two-wheeled caissons with more weight yet from ammo boxes full of spherical case shot and other projectiles. Wheels sank to their hubs. Trudging along behind the artillery and support vehicles was an endless string of mules dragging more than two hundred supply wagons through the perilous mire.

Tedious progress under such taxing conditions was reason enough for celebration that night around hundreds of sputtering campfires. And there were campfires, provided there was fuel to find and wood to burn if it was not saturated from rain turned to sleet.

Given the wet and cold conditions, Dwight was among the many who coughed themselves to sleep that night. Awakening to an ice-coated world, he hoped the nagging cough would not worsen to catarrh or pneumonia?

Cavalry form the vanguard of an army on the move, and the Confederates must have been expecting this blue swarm. They greeted the Federals with artillery fire from two forts along the river and from gunboats at anchor to protect them. Because the small town of New Madrid stood between the invading force and the river, apparently the Secessionists had burned a dozen houses to the ground to improve the accuracy of their cannon.

A brief skirmish with Rebel cavalry ensued, and Dwight was disappointed his company was not involved. That night Pope's army camped close to town where it awaited the arrival of huge siege guns already ordered from Cairo. An engineer by training, Pope had proved to be an expert in logistics. His objective was to sweep the river clean of gunboats, silence enemy batteries on the Tennessee shore, and bombard the entrenched Rebels—thought to number at least five thousand—into surrendering or abandoning New Madrid. The siege guns, if they arrived on time, could prevent the need for an all-out assault and save many lives.

Tugging at anchor, shackled to the Missouri riverbank

ten miles upriver, lay Commodore Foote's restrained and useless flotilla. Pope needed those ironclads to fulfill his grand design, but Foote refused to commit a single one to a risky run past the island. It was no secret that recent damage some of his boats had endured from enemy artillery on the Tennessee and Cumberland rivers was the alleged excuse for inaction.

March 4 brought a dusting of snow, and that evening the Federals endured three casualties. The next day Col. Plummer, commander of Pope's 2nd Brigade, moved three-thousand soldiers, including Dwight's company and other units of the 2nd Michigan, ten miles downriver to Point Pleasant, a small settlement with a river landing. Hoping to entice an attack from at least some of the Rebel force at New Madrid, Plummer's men dug trenches for defense and made preparations for placing artillery.

The work continued for three days while under fire from Rebel gunboats that had moved downriver to harass them. Company B was assigned to protect Plummer's work crews and to repel local militia loyal to a guerrilla leader named Jeff Thompson. Known as the Swamp Fox for his skill at leading raids and escaping capture, the mythical Thompson and his band of two hundred mounted followers were a constant threat. If they were not skirmishing with Union cavalry patrols, they blocked roads by felling trees across them, cut telegraph wires, and destroyed sections of railway.

Although he had yet to fire his pistol or rifle at the enemy, Dwight was excited to be a part of any action. The diversion to Point Pleasant, though, was an unsuccessful feint, and the hoped-for Rebel attack didn't happen. On March 12, when Pope's heavy guns arrived via rail to Sikeston, and mules hauled them to New Madrid on large-wheeled carts,

Pope recalled Col. Plummer's troops from Point Pleasant to assist with the siege. A disappointed Dwight now understood the Army's twin maxims: hurry and wait. Pope ordered another regiment to ready gun emplacements and to build breastworks above newly dug trenches. The men worked all night while a third regiment stood guard.

By morning the siege batteries were in place, and commanders assigned two regiments of Illinois infantry to the trenches on either side to protect them. Gen. Pope placed another ten thousand troops on both sides of the King's Highway where they awaited orders to attack, defend, or provide backup if needed. Company B and other companies of the 2nd Michigan were eager to hold the far right just beyond the protective breastworks.

Captain Henry Shaw had chosen Dwight as Company B's guidon bearer. Ahead of his fellow horsemen, sitting tall in his lightweight McClellan saddle with open seat, Dwight clutched the short staff of the red-and-white-striped swallowtail banner with its letter B in blue in his left hand. He wrapped Blaze's reins around the fingers of his right hand. Dwight was the one mounted soldier in the company; the others stood by their horses and also waited for orders. Before moving up the line into this lead position, Dwight checked to ensure his pistol and carbine were loaded.

Upon reaching the front, however, a tremor of fear raced across his scalp. Seated above the standing soldiers, knowing he was an obvious target, was unnerving. His breath quickened.

With dawn came fog from the river a mile away. A roar of Union artillery signaling the battle was on shocked the Confederates, their backs to the river. As the morning brightened, through the smoke and fog the Rebels discovered Pope's army laid out before them, in position and ready to attack. Idle gunboats were easy targets: Union artillerymen trained their pieces accordingly. The pilothouse of the *CSS Mohawk* took the first round. Other guns aimed at the forts blew apart two cannons at Fort Bankhead and one at Fort Thompson. These explosions killed two Rebels and wounded three others.

Once they settled down, enemy gunners proved equal to the task. Returning fire, they scored a direct hit on a 24-pound gun, killing one Federal artilleryman and wounding a half-dozen others. A series of shots silenced two field guns, shutting down the battery. Withering fire from the Rebel gunboats repulsed an assault by Brig. Gen. Paine's division of Illinois infantry, a half mile from Fort Bankhead. The action resulted in the loss of eight Federals with twelve others injured.

Dwight saw the increasing mayhem. He heard the unearthly shriek from the Confederates following each successful artillery strike. Fellow soldiers had talked about this so-called Rebel Yell; now that Dwight has heard it, fear tugged at his loose bowels.

All morning long as the smoke thickened, he witnessed the deafening war of artillery and smelled and tasted the acrid tang of gunpowder hanging in the air. In a determined effort to quash the siege batteries, Rebel gunners sent a torrent of shots, many of which burst close to the cavalrymen waiting for orders. The 10th Illinois manning the siege guns next to the Michigan cavalry lost ten men killed and twenty wounded. High up on his mount, Dwight watched destruction spread while his heart pounded and his dry throat pinched like a rope knot around it.

When a Rebel shell tore through a line of Indiana infantrymen stationed near the road, he was horrified to see several soldiers fall to the ground, legs shot off from under

them, like a row of cordwood falling apart.
And then war happened to him.

CHAPTER 22

Cairo, Illinois

Sometime during the night, a blinding lightning flash and immediate crack of thunder awakened Rachel to war. Another burst of light and a deafening crash revealed shaking curtains despite her hotel window being closed. Torrential rainfall beat upon the pane, followed by hailstones and a rising wind that began to howl like an animal possessed. Paralyzed with fear, Rachel thought of retreating downstairs; instead, she sat upright in bed, while grotesque blasts of lightning illuminated the room. The wind grew stronger, louder, screaming like a locomotive bearing down. The building trembled before the storm's fury, and Rachel saw chunks of material fly past the window.

Tornado! She tore from bed and crawled under it. Just then the window burst, sending shards of glass throughout the chamber.

The violence ended as fast as it had begun. Panting, shaking with fright, Rachel remained under the bed and listened to the moaning wind subside. Glimmers of lightning told her the storm was moving, chased away by rumbling peals of thunder that grew faint. A moment or two of eerie quiet succumbed to the soft patter of rain on her window-sill. Rachel thought of lighting her lamp if it was still on the vanity. Instead, she lay hidden and waited for measured breathing to return.

A while later, someone rapped at her door. A male voice inquired if she was all right. Was she injured? In an unsteady voice, she responded that she was not hurt, but petrified. The rattle of a key in the door followed and then the comforting glow of lantern light when the night clerk swung it open. Assured she was not harmed, he told her to wait in the room until he could gather the other third-floor tenants. A few minutes more and a dozen guests followed the man and his lantern, like single-filed sheep, down the long, twisting stairwell. Safe on the first floor, Rachel claimed the reception hall chair that Charles Duncan had occupied a few hours earlier.

She thought Charles' room was on the first floor, and hoped he, too, had escaped injury. Trying to collect her thoughts, to stop shaking, she sat in the semi-darkness until dawn and spoke to no one.

All morning long, the St. Charles Hotel lobby buzzed with talk about the tornado. Couriers, uniformed soldiers, businessmen, and townsfolk came and went to seek and dispense information, to speculate, and to investigate. If the correspondent was among the crush of curious citizens or those with official interests, Rachel didn't see him. She stayed off to the side of the frenzy at the front desk and throughout the lobby.

Due to the shortage of kitchen help and waitstaff, the dining room opened late to registered hotel guests. The concierge turned others away. Rachel ordered a simple breakfast of warm oatmeal and coffee. Returning to her room, she was gratified to see that nothing was missing and there was no damage other than the broken window. Someone had already swept the floor clean of glass fragments.

Downstairs again, she learned the hotel's heavy slate roof had blown away and now lay scattered throughout the town. Someone said the roof weighed thirty tons, an astounding testament to the storm's strength. Hearing that, Rachel shuddered. The roof was mere feet above the ceiling of her room.

Tornado updates came in all morning long. The storm had roared upriver from somewhere below Cairo. The steamship *Philadelphia*, loaded with corn and towing several ice boats, sank with all hands lost. The tornado leveled several unoccupied Fort Defiance soldiers' barracks.

Upon learning that one or more levee breaks had flooded much of Cairo, Rachel wondered how badly this terrible storm would upset her plans. She also knew there was little if anything she could do except press on and try to stay resolute. Throughout her life, whenever she struggled with threatening issues or unresolved problems, Rachel thought of her father and what he would do if faced with a similar circumstance. Thinking about him now and the sobering fact that she could have been killed had an organizing effect, and she decided to wait outside for the ride she hoped would still come.

She grew doubtful after sitting for an hour on the front porch while watching evidence of the storm's aftermath. Sections of wooden boardwalk floated by the hotel. A Negro man wading across flooded Ohio Street led a milk cow on a rope. The water above his knees wet the animal's balloon-like udder. While waiting, she found some solace during this warm morning of bright sun. A pair of mourning doves had built a nest in an evergreen bush beside the porch, their peaceful cooing an antidote to last night's ferocity. The gentle doves made Rachel think of her farm, and she knew a gentle wave of wistfulness. She watched the birds fluttering in and out of the bush while people passed in and out of the hotel, their boots reverberating loudly along the porch boards.

The horse and wagon arrived at half-past ten. The driver, a mulatto man about forty with graying hair at the temples, stopped his dray next to the hotel steps and offered a friendly greeting. Standing on the drowned lower step, he lifted her with great care into the wagon. Reboarding, he held the reins and clicked his tongue, and the horse, a handsome roan with ebony mane, splashed along the street. Ignoring his soaked boots, the man drove the dray at a slow pace to prevent his passenger from getting wet.

The hour-long ride included two delivery stops but no additional riders. Along the way, she could see considerable storm damage. Some houses were missing roofs and a couple had collapsed into the inundated streets. She wondered if Cairo had been flooded before. Her talkative driver assured her it had.

"Oh, yes ma'am. I was here for the June rise of '58. It was bad, too, but I think this one is worse. It sure smells worse."

The stench was, indeed, overpowering. She needed no further incentive to leave this miserable town, made uglier as the tornado's after-effect unfolded before her.

Rachel had been hearing the steady throb of an engine since leaving the hotel. As they neared the levees, the pulsing sound grew louder. She wondered what it was. "That's a steam pump you hear," the driver said. "The city bought them after the last flood to keep water out of town. The one you hear is pumping water back to the Mississippi. The pump over on the Ohio River will be running this morning, too."

Rachel admitted she had never seen, nor had she heard, a water pump so powerful it could drain an entire town. She questioned how it worked.

"They run on steam power, just like the trains."

"That's amazing. Modern marvels, both of them."

"Yes, they are. Steam power runs the country now. Someday it might be something else. Did you hear about the observation balloon the Navy sent up last week?"

"The what kind of a balloon?"

"A balloon big enough to carry three men. The Army thought the idea was crazy, but the Navy found out it actually worked." He explained how Commodore Foote had authorized two artillery officers to go aloft with the balloon's inventor, a German man, to help them see why their gunboat shots kept missing its targets.

"You mean the shells they're using to drive away the Rebels? I've heard the explosions all the way to here in Cairo."

"Yes, ma'am, from Island No. 10. They found their guns were set too high to hit what they were aiming for."

"How did they tell this to the soldiers on the ground?"

"They used signal flags. But they could have strung a wire for the mobile telegraph. The balloon was tethered to the ground, you see."

"That really is unbelievable!" she exclaimed. "What do they put in such a balloon?"

He said he didn't know but probably hot air. "They got it up more than 500 feet. Too high for the Rebels to hit it with their muskets."

Rachel was eager to alleviate her recent panic by conversing about such matters with this gabby driver. His mother was a freedwoman born in Indiana, and his father was a cooper from Kentucky who made barrels for the whiskey distillers. A single child, the driver grew up in Indianapolis and had gone to school there. He still thought about enlisting in Mr. Lincoln's army, but, because of his age and color, he would be rejected or given a menial job.

She asked what he meant by that, and he said the Negro wanted to do his part in the fight for emancipation. "This War is about us folks," he said. "We want to help if they would let us."

In the silence that followed, she thought about what the driver had said. She knew Willis would have approved of this man and his allegiance to the country. She wondered if other Negroes felt this way.

At the docks, Rachel saw more evidence of storm destruction. Overturned boxes lay scattered about, and some had blown into the river and were caught by pilings. Boats of all sizes used the busy river. A few berths were missing vessels that had probably broken free and could be somewhere downstream. The docks they passed were lively with many hands loading some vessels with freight and offloading others. The flurry of activity made her think of threshing time on the farm when all hands came together for a shared purpose.

The driver had told her to look for a steamer flying a yellow flag, the sign of a hospital ship, and there she was, an enormous vessel moored to pilings, a boat three stories high and all of ten rods long. Rachel saw *Memphis* painted across the upper deck brow and a yellow flag flapping high above. She was elated *The City of Memphis* had escaped the tornado and found her berth at last.

The driver asked if she wanted him to wait and when she declined the offer, he mentioned he had a late-afternoon dock delivery and would look for her upon his return. Rachel paid the fare and thanked him.

A dockhand put down a crate he was shouldering and advised her to walk with care along the wide gangway as it might be slippery after last night's deluge and there was no guardrail. Other men, perhaps volunteers as she hoped to be, stacked boxes along the boat's narrow prow while others whisked them inside. Two men bearing a third on a stretcher disappeared, along with the cargo, somewhere in the darkened interior.

Rachel learned Dr. Schmidt was in his office on the second floor; if she cared to climb the stairs, she would find him aft.

Sitting at a desk, quill in hand, he looked up from delivery bills of lading and asked in an officious tone how he might be of service. He did not offer a seat. An elderly man, though probably not as old as Dr. Anson, the Soldiers Hospital administrator, Dr. Schmidt's face offered no welcoming smile. Rather, it wore the demeanor of a serious man preoccupied with matters of importance, at least to him. Rachel repeated the introduction of yesterday and waited for a response. He answered with a question. "Why do you wish to go to New Madrid?" When told, he said, "Ah, I see. And then you'll abandon your responsibilities and leave us?"

His sarcasm was off-putting to her. Rachel fixed her eyes on his. "What would you do, sir, were you me?"

He seemed surprised at her boldness. Putting aside the quill, he leaned back, presumably to evaluate this plaintiff, not to decide what the little woman could do for the Sanitary Commission but to determine who she was. "You said something about a referral from Soldiers?" Rachel handed him the letter, which he opened tersely and read with darting eyes. "Why didn't you say it was from Dr. Anson?"

"You led me to believe it would not matter."

She could tell Dr. Bartholemew Schmidt had grown uncomfortable. Perhaps he was unaccustomed to being challenged, questioned by a woman. Resettling in the chair, he flicked his tongue and swallowed. He regarded her, standing there before the untidy desk. Gone was the frown, replaced by a look of kindliness. "Oh, but it does matter, Miss Barnum. Coming from Dr. Anson, it matters greatly. Please forgive my clumsiness."

"It's Mrs. Barnum," Rachel said with grace. "Dr. Schmidt, do you require help on this boat? I am more than willing to serve if there is a need."

"Oh, I'm certain there is. If you'll go up one flight and ask for Miss Dawes, I and the Commission would be most grateful. Tell her what you can do to help us, and she will have an assignment for you."

The brief interview ended without a word spoken about the tornado.

Upstairs she found an amiable Miss Dawes, nurse supervisor for *The City of Memphis*, talking about the storm with two other women volunteers. When they returned to work, Rachel introduced herself and described what she could do. After the brusque encounter with Dr. Schmidt, Rachel enjoyed the easy familiarity with her.

"Do you have nursing skills, Mrs. Barnum? We have a critical need for nurses."

Rachel smiled. "Well, I have four children, and I'm still raising three of them at home. Does that qualify?"

The nurse supervisor laughed aloud. "Mrs. Barnum, Rachel, if you don't mind, you may be overly qualified!

And do please call me Jane. There is no need for formalities among our volunteers."

Over tea and a light lunch of biscuits with marmalade, they discovered mutual interests in horses, gardening, cooking, and reading. Although Nurse Jane Dawes was at least ten years younger, had no children, and had not married, Rachel found much to like about this knowledgeable, practical woman. When the conversation shifted to Rachel's purpose for coming to Cairo, she told her story and felt affinity when Jane admitted she would have done nothing different had she been Rachel.

With only a dozen invalids on the ship, the patient roster was light, a stark contrast, according to Jane, from the more than two hundred wounded that had received treatment here after the fighting at Fort Donelson. Jane led a tour of the ship, pointing out several recent improvements.

"The Commission is not a year old, yet we have learned many things," she explained. "Donelson taught us we needed to do better, beginning with preparations." She said facilities on ships like this one needed fitting up, and there was a demand for transports to take the seriously wounded to established hospitals.

"We needed more medical supplies and abundant stores of wholesome food and more volunteers including doctors and nurses. The public has been most responsive, and we've made many changes," she said with obvious pride. "In some respects, we are just beginning."

Nurse Dawes told Rachel that volunteers received room and board at no cost, showed her a small but adequate berth, and gave her an agnew, an open-collar nurse's shirt to drape over her skirt and with long sleeves she could roll up. The nurse supervisor advised her to check out of the St. Charles tomorrow morning and return to *The City of Memphis* as soon thereafter as possible. She could remain onboard until the river opened up to New Madrid.

"I hope that will be soon," Rachel said, amidst a little stab of guilt. "But I also want you to know it is an honor to serve here, and I thank you for your kindness. I appreciate your understanding my predicament."

"Not at all, Rachel. Welcome aboard."

CHAPTER 23

April 8
New Madrid, Missouri

During the early days of confinement Dwight could recall shreds of what had happened to him but now, wracked with fever, he knew nothing except a blinding headache and a knot of throbbing pain in his back.

Blast shrapnel from an errant round had struck him and his horse at the same time. Legs buckling, Blaze collapsed with Dwight still atop. The hand flying to his left shoulder came back red. Shocked senseless, Dwight was staring at his bloodied hand when fellow troopers pulled him from the saddle. Two others ran to him with a hand litter and carried him to safety behind column after blue column of soldiers being held in reserve.

An assistant surgeon with the 2nd Michigan saw him coming, ducked into a supply wagon, and emerged with scissors in one hand and bandages in the other. Cutting away Dwight's tunic where the red stain was spreading into blue cloth, he exposed the wound, muttered a curse, and began probing with forceps to evaluate the damage. A fragment of iron had entered Dwight's upper arm just below his shoulder. Discovering the shard had passed through and was not embedded, the doctor, mere college years older than Dwight, set aside forceps and felt with fingers to see if any bones were broken. Reality overcoming shock, Dwight lurched and yelped from the pain.

"Easy, soldier. You'll be all right. Nothing's broken. Good, good. That's good."

With great care, an attendant lifted Dwight's head and pressed a small glass of whiskey to his lips. Swallowing as ordered, Dwight's throat burned and he began to cough. "Lie still!" the doctor demanded, "so I can stop the bleeding. Lord Almighty, it's too high up for a tourniquet."

After cleaning the wound with alcohol, he said he could see coagulation beginning. The doctor packed the torn flesh with gauze and wrapped a linen bandage over it. The orderly helped him raise Dwight to a sitting position. Working together, they wound long strips of linen around his chest, under the right arm, over the left arm, and tied the ends with a surgeon's knot. Apparently satisfied his patient would live, the doctor left to see about another injury. His parting words: "You're a lucky fellow. No severed artery."

Dwight heard the attendant, who followed the doctor out of the tent, speak for the first time. "He kept saying 'Blaze.' What was that about?"

That afternoon, soldiers transported Dwight in a wagon that bounced along a shoddy trail for a mile from the battle, now reduced to sporadic gunfire. Arriving at a hospital tent, they carried Dwight inside and placed him on a cot. The shelter, and others like it, were on the grounds of the Newsome-Phillips house being held in reserve for injured officers.

Two regulars already occupied the six-man tent. Both were Wisconsin artillerymen wounded when the piece they operated blew up from a direct Rebel hit. One soldier had lost his left hand; the other suffered a severe leg wound requiring amputation that evening in the surgical tent next to where Dwight lay immobile. The surgeon operated with the aid of lamplight but without ether for fear of explosion, instead relying on chloroform. The doctor saturated a sponge with the anesthetic, held it over the writhing patient's nose until he passed out, removed the shattered leg above the knee, applied a tourniquet to the thigh, and bound the stump with bandages. The entire operation lasted twenty minutes while Dwight drifted in and out of consciousness.

Deep into the night, after the young man two beds away either had died or slept in a coma, Dwight heard what soldiers call phantom screams. Trapped in a web of delirium, he was certain the screeching came from the boy with one hand who coughed throughout the endless night and whose middle bed was close enough to touch.

Dwight knew real, excruciating pain that came and went in swells. If he slept at all, it was only for a few minutes between jerking awake. Unlike his tentmates, he hadn't lost body parts, and he thanked God for that and for the morphine jabs that someone wearing a white jacket—whether man, woman, or ghost he wasn't sure—administered between rounds of pain. Shattering light from lanterns that came and went threw unreal patterns on the tent walls, adding to his confusion and fear.

As the new day began, a heavenly war with real lightning, earsplitting cracks of thunder, and volleys of rain came to New Madrid. Despite his misery, Dwight knew he was fortunate to be warm and dry in a good tent. After the storm moved on came a moment of stillness, and his thoughts rambled back to a time on the farm when another spring storm shook him and his brother awake and how Watson had counted the seconds between lightning strikes and resounding thunderclaps, insisting that each second was equal to one mile until blinding light and sound were one terrifying blast and how the next morning they discovered the ancient and massive oak behind the house had split in two and, by pure luck or the grace of God, the half that crashed to earth had fallen away from the house and the half still standing required an hour of sweaty labor with the two-man saw to topple, such was its girth.

Memory flees before reality. Unable to sustain the past, Dwight returned to the present. He knew he was lucky to be alive. Upon hearing the far-off roll of a morning bugle, he could neither restrain tears nor stifle groans at the thought of his horse. He wondered if fellow soldiers would tend to the beloved partner he feared was dead. Dwight wanted to believe heaven held a special place for faithful animals; if so, he knew Blaze was there, and he might see him again. The tent mercifully silent, Dwight slept for an hour, until someone pulled aside the stiff door flap, and the light of day poured in.

Hours later in the warmth of a spring afternoon, a medical aide allowed Dwight to sit outside, provided he kept his arm in the sling and was careful not to aggravate the wound lest it start bleeding again. Rufus Lisco and Peter Dow, Company B messmates and friends from Sunfield, paid a visit. They squatted before their injured comrade, whom they had known from school days together. A pensive Dwight sat in a chair, the injured arm on his thigh.

"I heard the Rebels hightailed it last night," he said by

way of greeting. "I haven't heard shooting all day."

"Yessir, they're long gone," Rufus confirmed. "Lit out for that island is what Capt. Shaw figured."

"Or ran off downriver," Peter said. "They left most everything behind. Wagons, horses, tents, even their fort guns. New Madrid's a ghost town."

Rufus threw up his arms and shook his head. "They didn't even bury their dead. Those Rebel boys are pure heathens. That yell they make sounds like Satan himself." Leaning sideways in his chair, Dwight was not paying attention. His thoughts were on his horse. No one said anything.

Rufus broke the silence. "So, how you doing, Dwight? Anything we can do for you?"

"Yeah, bring my horse back. What happened to him? Where is he?"

"We buried him, with plenty of help from the Vermontville boys."

"I didn't know there were so many shovels in this Army," added Peter.

A low moaning gave way to a breaking voice. "Oh, Lordy, that's what I was afraid of." Lifting his head, Dwight looked at Peter and then Rufus. "I owe you fellows, both of you. I owe everybody who helped."

"Captain gave us leave to do it," Rufus said. "He said a horse that beautiful shouldn't lie above ground."

"You don't owe us nothing," Peter added, "except to get better and back in the saddle."

Dwight was thinking about the September morning, six months earlier, when Henry Shaw had recruited him. "Captain's a good man," Dwight said. "He knew my pa."

"Only a horse man like Capt. Shaw could know what Blaze meant to you."

"That's true enough. But he also knew Blaze. He raised

and broke him before selling him to my father." They talked a little longer and stood to go. Dwight was feeling better.

"Well, you saw the elephant," Peter said.

"So did you," Dwight grunted, a thin smile coming. "We all saw the elephant. I just didn't get out of his way."

A FORTNIGHT AFTER THE BATTLE for New Madrid, the countryside was coming into the full bloom of spring. As the river receded and swamp waters shrank, wildflowers appeared. Migrating birds Dwight had never seen and could not identify returned from wintering places, also mysteries. He noticed these changes on brief walks throughout the sprawling Yankee camp and on visits to where his friends had buried Blaze. The Eaton County boys had chosen a slight ground swell a stone's throw from where horse and rider had fallen. Thankful, sad, Dwight sat beside the mound of fresh earth and thought about how his life had changed forever.

No one challenged his silent and solitary vigil. Each visit ended with the grave accepting a wildflower plucked from the greening land by a one-armed soldier who replanted it here. The ritual, three days running, reminded Dwight of strolling with Blaze in the pasture at home. He would come back with cowslips or violets, a never-failing delight to his mother and sisters who arranged them in a vase to brighten the supper table.

Passing soldiers nodded and left him to private contemplation. Walking back to tent quarters, whenever Dwight neared the campfires of others, they would look up from their dice games of chuck-a-luck or craps, note the sling of white, and offer tacit approval with a nod, a smile, or a sitting salute.

Although there was talk of sending Dwight to Cairo or

St. Louis for general hospital care, before a likely discharge for disability and a train ride home, he asked for and was granted a temporary stay with his regiment. At first, he tried to convince a doubtful 2nd Lt. Marshall Dickenson that he could heal here as well as somewhere else where he wouldn't know anyone, but it was the appeal with reference to Willis Barnum that worked.

"You know how my father felt about this War coming," Dwight had said, "and you know I signed up to honor him."

"Yes, I know. Your dad was a good man."

"If you send me away now, you know I'll be back before long. I'm on the mend. Look, I can already move my bad arm."

"I'll talk to the captain."

And Capt. Shaw approved the reprieve, provided Dwight could manage a horse whenever the army of Gen. John Pope "gets across this blasted river." No one knew when that would occur. Those willing to speculate wagered on which would happen first: Either Commodore Foote decided to run his gunboats past Island No. 10, or Gen. Pope's engineers completed the bypass canal through the flooded woods to Wilson's Bayou and from there to New Madrid.

Either way, Dwight hoped his wound would have at least another week to improve.

But Dwight took ill the day after his plea to stay was granted. On Wednesday, his head and back began to hurt, and he felt weak. On Thursday, the pain was unbearable, as intense as the shoulder wound had been, and there was a fever. Summoned to the shared tent with Rufus Lisco, which Dwight had reclaimed after four days in the field hospital, the regiment's assistant surgeon determined the wounded soldier's body temperature was high. Alarmed, he ordered Dwight back to the hospital tent for observation.

That evening Dwight's temperature spiked, and he was unable to eat, drink, or speak sensibly. By Friday morning, March 23, his face and lower arms had erupted in a rash. Swallowing was limited to little sips of water. When a second doctor confirmed the probability of variola, they removed the sick young man to an isolation tent. Rufus relayed the disturbing news to Marshall Dickenson, and that's when the 2nd Lieutenant used the wire for a terse note to Dwight's mother.

By Tuesday, the fever was gone, but a severe rash had spread to chest and legs and was morphing into blisters. Positive that Dwight had contracted smallpox, Charles Henderson, the 2nd Michigan's surgeon-in-chief, mandated that no one except former victims of smallpox or those that had been vaccinated, could enter the patient's tent or go anywhere near it.

When Dr. Henderson told Dwight why he was so sick, he also explained there was no cure and that whether he would recover was up to the young man's health, his brave soldier spirit, and the will of God. "My first concern is the wound you sustained," he said. "It must heal properly. You've got an infection with this disease. You don't need another from the wound."

The doctor charged a volunteer, a retired Missouri farmer who claimed he had smallpox as a boy and the pitted scars to prove it, to keep the wound as clean as possible. "Change the dressing each day and make this brave fellow as comfortable as possible," were the doctor's final orders.

"I will do that and more," volunteer Clement Stafford said. "I have a fair hand if Dwight will tell me what to write and where to send his letters."

Whenever Dwight felt like speaking, and was able to drink and eat a bit, he would tell Clem what to write. "The one letter I need to send right now," Dwight insisted, "is to my mother."

Dwight knew about the telegram 2nd Lt. Dickenson had sent to Rachel. What Dwight did not know was that she would not receive any letters he dictated. That was because his mother had already left the Sunfield farm for New Madrid, Missouri.

CHAPTER 24

Cairo, Illinois

Rachel's return to the St. Charles Hotel took longer due to extra deliveries and added riders who came and went. A bit harried, the mulatto driver from the morning run was less talkative but still his courteous self. Rearranging cargo items to make more room for Rachel and a peddler from St. Louis, the driver apologized for delay. Rachel didn't mind. Lost in thought, she said little beyond customary niceties. Arriving at the hotel as the gas lights were coming on, she noticed the floodwater had retreated. The bottom stairstep was now visible.

Inside, she couldn't throw off the feeling that things had changed forever. It was hard to believe there had been a tornado last night because there was no discernible damage and life was normal, at least by the dubious standards of Cairo. The fantastic events from the time she went to bed until now belonged to another time and place.

Was it all a dream? No, it was real and still was real.

There was the waiter William, dressed in his immaculate white jacket and standing at attention before the dining room entrance. There was the staircase with its fourteen steps between floors, steps she always counted going up and coming down from her room. And there was the front desk with the same night attendant who had led her and others down the stairs to safety only hours ago. Maybe coffee with her supper would help make real what seemed fantasy.

Her room key in hand, the clerk greeted Rachel with a smile, asked if she was all right, and hoped she had enjoyed the day's excellent weather. Thinking of Charles Duncan, she asked the clerk if anyone had been killed or injured.

"No," he assured her, "not from the hotel at any rate. I don't know about the whole city though. News is still pouring in."

"Is Mr. Duncan still registered?"

"I'll check," he said and turned away. "No, Mrs. Barnum. He left before the noon hour." She then asked about the status of her room. The attendant told her he thought the window had been repaired but probably had not yet been replaced.

She asked him to move her to another room. "For one night only. I don't think I can sleep even a little in that same room. Or on that same third floor, for that matter."

Opening the registration book, he ran a finger over the pages. "How about 218 on the second floor? It's down the hall from General Grant's old quarters."

"Is there a higher rate?"

"Well, yes, there is, but pay no nevermind to that, Mrs. Barnum. You've had enough inconvenience for one day. There will be no extra charge."

She accepted the new key, thanked him, and went upstairs to move her belongings. After supper, she retired to her new chamber and went to bed.

Thursday, April 3

ROOM 218 WAS A DECIDED improvement over Rachel's former accommodations on the third floor. Knowing she had more space may have helped her to sleep well. Perhaps she slept too well for when she awoke, bright sunlight washed the room. At peace, swabbed with warmth, she lingered in bed and then washed, dressed, and went downstairs. The lobby timepiece confirmed it was after nine. Waiting before the front desk, she again sensed unreality. It defied reason that a tornado had wreaked havoc upon Cairo when this hotel continued to function normally. Activity in the lobby was ordinary. Businessmen and others, their voices subdued, came and went at a leisurely pace.

One would have thought nothing extraordinary had happened. But Rachel had seen some of the devastation with her own eyes. And now further proof lay on the counter in the bold headline of the *Chicago Tribune*: "TORNADO AT CAIRO." Below it were smaller headlines detailing the damage: "Boats, Buildings and Barracks Destroyed," "Fearful Loss of Life,"and "The Town Flooded with Water."

Bowing low to remove an extra paper from under the counter, the attendant told her to keep the one she read. Reassured she had three hours until checkout, Rachel took the paper into the dining room. After breakfast, she carried her coffee and the newspaper into the reception hall.

Spreading the broadsheet on a table, she read THE LATEST NEWS BY TELEGRAPH and focused on the dateline "Cairo, April 2, 1862." Eyes snapping back and forth, she sped through the reports: "A tremendous gale from the northwest passed over Cairo about 3 o'clock and for a time the destruction of everything movable seemed inevitable. Barracks and homes were leveled to the ground. Shipping in the port was badly injured.

"The loss of life is supposed to be fearful but not ascertained as of yet. A large number of transports were in the river between this point and the Tennessee River below and it is feared they have suffered considerably, but it is now too early to understand the full extent of the gale and the destruction.

"The steamer *Philadelphia* is reported to have sunk with all on board."

In addition to local damage reports, Rachel learned that steamers and transports involved in the blockade of Island No. 10 might have suffered, but there was "Nothing of interest from New Madrid and below."

A second dispatch from 10 p.m. reported gunboats and mortar boats had escaped injury but two transports, the *Pike* and *Swallow*, sustained heavy blows. "The damage done to steamers and property along the river is immense. The Evansville packet *Courier* barely escaped destruction." A few lines later, "At Paducah the storm was very severe, unroofing thirty houses, including the Marine Hospital and a large warehouse adjoining the wharf boat."

Recalling windstorm damage in Sunfield, Rachel knew it had never been this bad. Small tornadoes, the likes of which were rare summer events, might lift the roofs from a couple of neighborhood barns or topple a few trees, mostly dead snags at that, but the destruction of this scale was an "end of days" scenario.

As she prepared to leave, a young man, face flushed from running, dropped off a fresh dispatch at the front desk. Rachel sauntered over and, seeing the clerk was preoccupied, picked it up. Scanning for downriver news, she found a brief mention: "The gunboats and mortars are firing semi-occasionally, and the Rebels reply just when they please."

Rachel was not surprised that "Water soaking through the levee in Cairo went up another five inches last night and was still rising. Both the steam pumps are working however." She already knew, "The stench in Cairo is intolerable and much sickness must follow this flood."

She learned, though, how the storm's intensity created mayhem far and wide. "The wooden barracks at Birds Point caught the gale about midships and had to cave in largely. So also at Fort Holt … . The storm was exceedingly violent in the vicinity of the Cumberland River … . The hospital boat *John Ivers* was severely injured at Mound City and several buildings destroyed."

What if that ship had been The City of Memphis?

Knowing the river was still falling was good news until Rachel read that a small boat tied to the levee and occupied by a poor man and a family of five persons "parted from her moorings during the gale and all were drowned."

A reflexive sob caught in Rachel's throat, and she gulped a huge breath. *I survived and this entire family is gone forever?* Oblivious to who might be watching, she clasped hands together, dropped her head, and said a brief and silent prayer. She thought of returning to the Presbyterian Church to commiserate before the altar but rejected the urge because of flooded streets. Furthermore, time was crucial; Jane Dawes expected her at the hospital boat. The nurse supervisor could be looking for her this very moment.

Told the dray came by every couple of hours, Rachel paid her bill and went outside where two men, a salesman and his assistant she assumed, awaited a ride to the train depot. Within a quarter-hour, the new driver, a serious, self-important lad about the age of her sons, pulled in and loaded up, and they were on their way.

Reaching *The City of Memphis* in early afternoon, Rachel stowed belongings in her room and reported for duty downstairs. Assignments entailed scrubbing the floor of an empty ward, inventorying stocks of medical supplies, and bringing the evening meal to patients, two of whom she fed their soup by hand. The work helped to pass what remained of the day but could not drive away unending concern for Dwight. On the contrary, as the hours elapsed, she worried about her son all the more because of news to which she was privy.

Twice that afternoon Nurse Dawes sought her out to share developments. Two or three nights before, on Monday Jane thought, Commodore Foote had approved a bold plan for fifty soldiers from an Illinois infantry unit to invade the island. Under cover of darkness, they hoped to surprise enemy guards and disable as many artillery pieces as possible. Fifty sailors, ten from each gunboat, comprised the raiding party. According to a news dispatch, the raid succeeded in spiking six large cannons.

A little later the nurse supervisor said another paper reported the Army expected to complete its diversion canal before the falling river would prevent heavy ironclads with their eight feet of draft from navigating the bypass channel. "I expect you won't be with us long," she told Rachel, who was on her knees scrubbing. "As soon as we receive our itinerary, I'll inform you."

Rachel looked up from her work.

"I pray there's a stop at New Madrid," she sighed, a trace of doubt in her voice.

Jane agreed. "I do, too, but if a battle in Tennessee starts before one for that island, we could be going up the Tennessee, not down the Mississippi."

One of the patients had offered Rachel yesterday's Cincinnati paper. In it was a story about a tornado that had struck the New Madrid area early Tuesday before roaring upriver to Cairo. Thinking this had to be the same twister that hit the St. Charles, she hoped its beginning had been less severe than its ending. Reading on, she learned that three men from the 7th Illinois Cavalry were killed and others injured when a tree fell on their tent.

Clearly, the storm had not spared its fury from wherever Dwight lay wounded and sick. The New Madrid tornado claimed some horses, flooded the road to Commerce, and drowned a large portion of the Sikeston railway. Favoring neither North nor South, it then uprooted trees on its way to Island No. 10 where it took the lives of a Confederate private and two officers before sinking a Rebel transport. Havoc continued when the tornado whirled back across the river and tore down the smokestacks of two Union transports.

The report made sleep impossible. Twitching, lying prone in bed, Rachel fought to control panic. Surely, Dwight had suffered this storm. Had he survived it? Was he still alive? Rolling to her side, she ransacked the bag of belongings and found her bible. While reading by candlelight in her berth at Cairo's East Wharf, she wondered if God sent such destruction as a prequel to the storms of war. Was that tornado a herald from the dark and bloody battlelines forming a little farther to the south?

CHAPTER 25

Sunfield, Michigan

Hester and Helena were practicing the waltz, and Helena was having difficulty following her sister's lead. "You have to step back," Hester directed, "and *then* you slide left. It's the opposite for me. I step forward and slide right."

Helena protested. "It would be easier if I could lead and *you* followed."

"You will lead, silly. We'll take turns. Now, step back, left, and forward. One-two-three. Come on, Helena! Count with me, one-two-three."

John Welch came into the parlor. His grin flashed white teeth nestled within his coal-black beard. Clapping approval, he said, "You ladies are quite fetching this morning. The beaus would pine for a chance to dance with either of you. Both of you."

Helena stepped from the imaginary square. "You really think so? I feel *so* clumsy!"

"Nonsense! Why I'd have to fight 'em off. With the biggest stick I could find."

Hester was giggling. "We need music. I *wish* we had music."

The hired man laughed with them. "Why, even if I had a fiddle and knew how to use it, it'd be too fast for waltzin'." Raising and lowering hands like a music conductor, he began to hum in time: "Dum-dum, da-da. Da-da, dum da-da, da-da. Dum-dum …" Resuming their dance steps, the twins picked up the tempo.

John Welch had grown fond of Rachel Barnum's daughters. Sweet girls both, he saw a bit of resemblance, more so in Helena, to his sister Lillian when she was around ten or twelve. Memories of her were those of a quiet, serious girl who doted on him as their mother had. After their mother passed, Lillian taught young John how to tie his shoes. She helped him learn his numbers and letters. Because their father didn't court and did not remarry, Lillian was the matriarch during what John had come to realize was a happy and secure childhood. He was more man than boy when Lillian left to marry the derelict who took her away, out of their lives. Her departure left them like a milking stool with only two legs. Lillian was the missing support, and to John's young mind, the leg most available and therefore most crucial.

Now, twenty years on, it had taken John Welch a few weeks to recognize Helena from Hester and Hester from Helena. Side by side, Helena was a smidge taller; otherwise, their features were indistinguishable. Hester had the higher voice and was much more demonstrative, what Rachel said was a mouth of pure brass. Whereas Helena's demeanor was submissive, Hester tended to question the way things were and was not above challenging authority. If anyone asked John Welch to describe Rachel's daughters, which no one ever had, he would say Helena was reserved, much like their brother Watson, and Hester was engaging. Helena quiet, Hester garrulous. Helena always dutiful, Hester at times disobedient.

John imagined Hester becoming a schoolteacher of note. He saw Helena as a nurse and a good one. Having no experience raising children, the hired man often wondered how Rachel did it, and did it so well, on her own. He observed it was not an easy task. For that reason, he concluded that children needed two parents, that one was not enough. He also wondered if his hesitation at becoming too involved with any of Rachel's four children was a good choice or a poor one.

However, the more time he spent around them, in the home with them, the more he questioned if he should have married and had a family of his own. This much he knew: Had he fathered anyone, he would have wanted daughters like Rachel's and a son like Dwight. As for Rachel's second son, John was not so sure. Oh, he wouldn't be sorry to have sired a Watson—the boy was difficult, to be sure—but John thought he knew the seed within the shell. How could it ever be easy to lose a father? he reasoned. It sure wasn't easy for him.

How different were daughters than sons! Watson had been so standoffish that John Welch thought it best to leave him alone, to let him sort things out for himself. On the other hand, they had worked well together when tapping maples the other day. It was wishful thinking, a fantasy no less, to imagine the thaw that had coaxed sap to open up in a dormant tree had a similar effect on Rachel's frozen son. For sure, her girls were never upside-down like Watson. They liked being teased; it was easy to joke with them.

What was fun for them was fun for him, too. What was really important was Rachel's approval of his easygoing manner with her girls.

Life on her farm centered on the kitchen. Untrained as a cook, John had learned some basic kitchen skills while a timberman. When Cookie, the preparer of everything a working man ate, took to a sickbed, John volunteered, along with a couple others, to provide meals for the whole camp of two dozen lumberjacks. What had been sawdust on his woolen clothing became flour, and he mastered how to tie apron strings behind his back. Three weeks away from the woods taught him how to bake bread and make stew. After that first week, the men's grumblings stopped, and the chow line for second helpings grew. At the Barnum farm, he had just gained a new reputation—an accomplished baker of heavenly cinnamon rolls.

With Rachel gone, making the buns for her children pleased him as much as it did them. Tucking a pair of oven-fresh cinnamon buns in the girls' school lunch pail, John included a personal note: "Made in the kitchen of Rachel Barnum by John Welch, world-famous baker." Another: "Prepared with perfection for two of Sunfield's spring beauties."

Helena saved the creative notes to share with their mother when she came home.

During Rachel's absence, it was too early for field work, freeing the hired man to test his culinary skills between morning and evening chores. One day Watson came home for dinner with two cleaned cottontails he had shot while out hunting that morning. John bled out the rabbits in salt water before quartering them on the butcher block with Rachel's meat cleaver.

Recollecting how one of Cookie's volunteers made

stew, John began by rolling the pieces in flour and browning them with lard in a deep-sided iron skillet. As the meat sizzled, he added salt and pepper and crumbles of dried marjoram from the herb garden, donated a slug of hard apple cider, and turned the heavy skillet into a Dutch oven by adding a lid. Opening the stove door, John pushed aside glowing red embers with a stoker and positioned the Dutch oven in the new cavity.

"I can taste supper already," he laughed and clapped his hands. And he told his "assistant chefs," to keep watch lest the meat burn, slid into his coat, and went outside to help Watson with chores. Back an hour later with Watson in tow, John inhaled the tantalizing smell of meat stew. His prayer thanked Watson for starting supper and the twins for finishing it. He concluded by admitting it was the best-looking rabbit he had ever smelled and soon would be the best-tasting rabbit he ever ate. Forking a leg onto his plate, he cut a tender piece and popped it into his mouth.

The others waited expectantly. "Can't be wrong when you're right," he said and stole a wink at Helena.

"You're just saying that," she said. "You don't really mean it. Do you, Mr. Welch?"

"I say what I means and I means what I say. Best dadgum bunny this side of Sebewa Creek. Not sure of the other side though." The hired man winked at Hester. "Never ate a rabbit over there."

Even Watson agreed it was good.

Two evenings later, after supper, they were in the parlor talking about local happenings. No one brought up Dwight's condition or mentioned Rachel's absence because there were no details to share, no recent letters to discuss. Talking about those missing would serve to expose fears about which they could do nothing except worry all the more. Rachel taught her children as she had been taught: "What's done is done because no good comes from crying over spilt milk."

They knew the proverb well, having heard it again last fall when Max, a favored border collie that herded Rachel's sheep and was the children's pet, had died and they held an ad hoc funeral service over the grave her boys helped the hired man to dig.

John Welch used different words to explain why private thoughts are sometimes best kept private: "Personal feelings are like the poison ivy. If you scratch the itch, it'll itch even worse. Best to let it lie."

That evening in the parlor, Helena asked Mr. Welch if he thought there were any wolves left around Sunfield, and he allowed he would not be surprised at all if there were. "Bears, too. Lucas Kesten shot a bear over by Vermontville a couple weeks ago. A big hungry boar came out from winter sleep with lamb on his mind. Lucas tracked him back to the den and shot him inside. Took three men and a horse to drag him out of there. Well, three men anyway. That horse was near scared to death and wasn't much help." The hired man's grin grew to hearty laughter that spread around the hearth where they warmed themselves.

Watson said he had heard about that bear and asked if anyone had put him on the scale.

"Not that I know of," John said, "but they figured he was all of five hundred pounds. The meat was tougher'n a hog's hide."

Hester jumped up from the sitting couch. She was ready with a taunt. "Yuck! When did you ever eat the hide off a hog, Mr. Welch?"

"Well, not today. But the one I ate yesterday was plenty tough." Chuckling, John proposed they remember the story as the bear that ate before it got eaten before it got spit out. The girls looked at each other and laughed. Watson shook his head and mumbled something.

Hester asked when John was a lumberjack if he had ever seen a bear that big and if he had ever killed a wolf. He said he had not, that if you believed the Indians, killing a wolf brought bad luck. He admitted he didn't know if the saying was pure superstition or if there was any truth to it. He told the story from years ago of a Vermont neighbor who poisoned two wolves from a pack that had come down from Canada and were taking his sheep, one by one, all winter long.

"The killings stopped after those two wolves bit the dust. But about the time the new grass came, the rest of the farmer's flock were wiped out from some disease. The local Indians said it was punishment from Manitou, their god."

He paused to let the story take hold in their imaginations and said, "But, no. I never killed a wolf or even a bear for that matter. Shot a wolverine once, though," he offered as an afterthought.

"Tell us that story," Helena pleaded.

"Well, there's a reason Michigan's called the Wolverine State. They're here, all right, but few people have ever seen one. They are one *shy* animal, that is until you run into one. Then they're nasty as a shrew with his tail on fire." He went on to tell the story. "In the lumberjack camp one day I went down the Muskegon River with Cookie to check on the beanhole supper he put in the day before ..."

"Beanhole?" Watson broke in. "What's a beanhole?"

John explained how lumber camp cooks needed to stay ahead of the log drive by at least a day. Finding a sandy bank along the river, they would dig a big hole and build a fire in it. When the wood burned down to a bed of coals, the cook would take a large Dutch oven, "big around as an old snapping turtle's shell," and fill it with fixings—raw beans, chunks of salt pork or bacon, molasses, salt and pepper, maybe a cup of maple syrup, and enough water to drown the beans so they wouldn't dry out—drop a few coals atop the lid, and bury the pot in the sand like some pirate treasure.

"That's called a 'beanhole,' Wat. Then, they marked the spot—Cookie liked to use a strip of red flannel tied to a stick—so the log drivers could find it the next day. They would uncover the pot of beans, cooked and still warm, and have a supper made and ready to eat."

Hester interrupted. "But you said you killed a wolverine. How? What happened?

"Well, I was just coming around to that, Missy. I don't know if Cookie had a forewarning or maybe it was just a hunch, but I went along with him the next day to check on those beans. When we got there, we found out a wolverine had got to it first. It was like a bomb had exploded. The fire was dead. The pot upside down, lid in the river. Beans everywhere, the salt pork gone."

"How did you know a wolverine did it?"

"On account he was still there, protecting it like he owned it! He growled like a bear and charged right at us. I didn't know an animal could be so mean. We backed away and ran off a bit. I have no doubt those teeth could tear a man to pieces."

"How big is a wolverine?"

"Oh, about like a cub bear. Maybe fifty pounds. Got claws like a bear, too. It took three shots from my rifle to kill that nasty critter. Stunk worse than the county-fair outhouse!"

That comment prompted Watson to ask how a lumber

camp smelled after a big supper of baked beans.

"Oh, you wouldn't want to know firsthand. It gets pretty rank in the bunkhouse."

Dramatically pinching her nose, Hester pretended to swoon and said she was going to bed. Helena got up to follow her sister, and John stayed up to regale Watson with another story, this one about working in a Grand Rapids furniture factory and watching a man lose his thumb and two fingers to a mill saw.

A little later John sat alone, poking the fire and thinking he might have found a family of his own. He reminisced about all the menial jobs he had signed on to over the years. Farming would always be the most satisfying, but he also liked making things from wood. Those basic carpentry skills he had learned in Bay City had adapted nicely into crafting furniture in Grand Rapids. Maybe after morning chores he would see about making Rachel a surprise when she came home.

Meanwhile, he could hear Rachel's daughters talking in their bedroom. Helena was complaining that Hester's feet were cold. "Get them off me," she grumbled.

"Then give me back my share of the quilt!"

When the subject switched to the hired man, Hester had a question for her sister. "Think they'll ever marry?"

"Who?"

"Ma and Mr. Welch! Who do you think?"

Helena hesitated. "I don't know. If it happened, I guess it'd be okay."

"Well, I like him. The truth is, Helena, I could see him as our pa."

"I like him, too, but I don't know about *that*!"

"Well, think about it, Helena, because I sure do."

CHAPTER 26

Friday, April 4
Cairo, Illinois

Rachel awoke to sunshine pouring through the small porthole in her room. Her husband's watch, gleaming as she turned it over, declared 7:20, enough time for devotions on *The City of Memphis*, lashed to the wharf while time and the river flowed on. Rachel's plea was the same as every day since leaving home: that Dwight was alive, that she would find him in time. She prayed that today would bring an end to waiting and to suffering for both mother and son. If that was not to be, she asked for mercy and for patience to endure yet another day of bleak anticipation.

Rachel took breakfast with the ship's staff of surgeons, assistant doctors, nurses, and general aides like herself but merely pecked at the plate of bacon and eggs and potatoes set before her. Beyond civilities, she did not engage with the other dozen volunteers at her table this morning.

She was content to be unnoticed, not discounted but

rather overlooked, anonymous. Her attention was not on any of the speculative conversations around her: Which army was stronger and would strike the first blow? How many tornadoes had been recorded? When would the ship leave, and where would it go? Through the din of voices and clash of dishware, she felt a tap on her shoulder. Aware that someone asked if she was finished eating, Rachel nodded a response and surrendered her half-eaten plate of food.

When she rose to go, Nurse Dawes asked if she was unwell. Rachel said, "Not at all, Jane, just distracted. Please give me plenty to do today."

As the tedious hours passed, she grew more enlivened and initiated conversations with two other aides, also new volunteers. By late afternoon, she felt better about being aboard *The City of Memphis*, the right place to be because, in reality, there was no place else to go. Except home, which was unthinkable without him. Without ever seeing him again.

But that night Rachel again experienced insomnia. Between needing to go on and wanting to go home, she felt torn apart. When reading could not calm her anxiety, she revisited fond memories. If she could avoid dwelling on loss and affix her thoughts on good things, she might get a few hours of sleep. What better way than how the family had managed to tame the wild land that was now home?

WITHIN THREE YEARS AFTER COMING to Michigan, Peter van Houten claimed land, found temporary shelter in the form of a primitive log home that he and his sons built, and turned the forest into a farm. The arduous task of clearing mature, virgin timber demanded superhuman effort. Rachel, sister Margaret, and their stepmother Suzanne brought noon meals to the woods where the men labored all day. Rachel remembered how hard they worked, alongside occasional others eager to earn a per diem wage from her father.

Clear cutting began with small openings, trees that had died from disease, lightning strike, fire, or age. Toppled by windstorms, the once-majestic trees with girths to four feet each were chained and removed by yoked oxen. The men expanded these natural openings by taking out live timber with heavy axes and sharp, crosscut saws six feet in length. An axman chopped a notch on the side where he wanted the tree to fall and then stepped back so a tandem of sawyers could slice deep enough through the growth rings of history—for some trees were seedlings when Columbus discovered the New World—for the tree to totter, crack, and crash to earth. Before shouting "TIMBER!" the axman made certain all men and animals were out of harm's way. Once the giant spire was down, they lopped off limbs, sawed the trunk into logs of desired length, and hauled what they didn't want to the burn pile.

A three-man team could have a three-hundred-year-old white oak on the ground within an hour of the first ax blow, although removing it from the forest required more time.

Hickory, oak, and hard maple were among the hardwood species laborious to cut but that burned well when dead and dried. On the contrary, white pine cut faster but was harder to burn because it oozed resin that smelled like turpentine and stuck to hands. The slash fires burned for weeks, filling the woods with the piquant odor of blue smoke. Because dead trees burn faster than live ones, that first winter the van Houtens girdled the larger ones to kill them before leveling with the axe and saw later.

Peter ordered the best trees, those straight-grain pines

and oaks free of boles, to be set aside for the portable saw-mill owned by a neighbor on Sebewa Creek. When dried, the eight-, ten-, and sixteen-foot-long boards, each up to two inches thick, became frame houses and barns. Rachel felt pride whenever passing by a big, sturdy barn built with lumber made from her family's woods. The largest barn, owned by a Shaytown Road farmer, boasted twelve-inch-thick, white oak beams thirty-six feet long. The heavy beams required a team of Percherons and the aid of a massive pulley and strong ropes to raise into position. When finished, the hip-roof barn was thirty-six feet wide, seventy-two feet long, and thirty-seven feet from peak to ground.

Rachel knew the feeling of awe upon looking up into the barn's vaulted expanse. The builders had made roof rafters by bending long, four-inch wide, inch-thick planks of pine and stacking them atop each other. Now four inches square, each rafter attached to the ridge pole with round wooden pegs. Inside this barn, she always felt puny. Standing there in the blasting light from an east-wall window, Rachel fantasized about being back in one of New York City's towering churches or being swallowed in some soaring European cathedral. Staring up at the huge, ribbed rafters, it was easy to imagine the biblical ark turned upside down.

Like other money-strapped settlers, Peter van Houten bartered for much of his needs. Offering trimmed logs in exchange for a saw blade turned by a water wheel, Peter was able to build his home and farm structures at reduced costs. His sons packed wooden barrels with ashes from the massive fires that burned from spring into fall and delivered them by wagon to Charlotte. There they sold or traded the potash for crop seed, flour, and other commodities.

A low rumbling noise interrupted Rachel's musing. Sitting up, she wiggled to the bed's edge, hugged her pillow, and listened. Was this thunder from a gathering storm? Cannon fire from downriver? She heard it again, still far off, and then it stopped. Failing to identify the sound or its source after a few minutes, she lay down. The pillow behind her head, sleep still far off, she slipped back to the past.

Cutting timber and burning trash was half the battle to clear land. The other half, which some argued was worse, was removing tree stumps. Favoring sand and sand-loam soils, the roots of mature white pine had grown deep. Rich in resin, these root wads defied a hot fire or the slow-burning cycle of decay. During that first year, the van Houtens planted corn and oats between the stumps, a haphazard practice that returned meager yields.

There had to be a better way. They found it after announcing a work bee in the county newspaper. Rachel, Margaret, and Suzanne spent days baking bread, making pies, and preparing Dutch hachee stew. Women from their church contributed plates, silverware, cider, German knefla, sausage and sauerkraut, pickles, and carrot casserole.

A score of neighbors and friends arrived one Saturday morning in April when the snow was gone and the mosquitos had yet to come. The overcast day was not cold enough for heavy coats nor warm enough to remove woolen shirts. Workers cleared five acres of stumps by the dinner hour and four more acres by the supper bell. A joyous Peter declared the logging bee a huge success even though "that heavy German fare cost at least an acre this afternoon."

Exposing the stubborn root tangles with shovel and ax, the men cut through tentacles, attached chains, and used oxen power to wrench away the stumps. An innovative contraption called the stump machine helped. Positioned directly over a stump, the tripod-shaped device relied on a large screw suspended by heavy chain to the tripod apex. Embedded in the stump's top and harnessed to an oxen yoke, the screw turned as the animals walked around the tripod. The clever fulcrum design allowed vertical extraction of the stump. Lying in bed, Rachel remembered thinking how it was like pulling a giant impacted tooth.

Ever the frugal farmer, Peter then found a second life for his pine stumps by using them to fence a pasture. The idea worked so well Rachel and Willis adopted it when the time came to build their own farm.

Rachel awoke clear-minded. Although her room on the hospital ship was much smaller than either of the pair she had occupied at the St. Charles, she did not feel confined. To the contrary, she felt secure, knowing that people needed her here. Purpose fueled hope. But it was Dr. Schmidt's staff meeting after lunch that contributed the most to her improved outlook.

As operations director for *The City of Memphis*, Dr. Bartholomew Schmidt was a veteran at organization, a precise man who liked to share his knowledge. He began the meeting by explaining its purpose, "to apprise staff of current developments in the Western War Theater" and how outcomes would dictate the hospital ship's next move.

"An hour ago," he told the eager audience, "I learned the *Carondelet*, from our Navy flotilla, ran the enemy gantlet of artillery at Island No. 10. This risky maneuver occurred last night. By the grace of God, there were no casualties."

He went on to say that Gen. Pope's army was, thanks to the brave *Carondelet*, at least somewhat protected from enemy firepower on the Tennessee shore and could be crossing the river at this very moment. When all soldiers were on the other side, they would regroup and drive the Confederates with their inferior numbers from the island.

"You will remember there was much sickness at New Madrid, but few were wounded in the fighting there," he said. "There will be many more casualties in the battle for that island, if the Rebels are determined to keep it. We may be going there next. And very soon."

Rachel hung on his every word.

One of the doctors raised a hand. "Dr. Schmidt," he asked, "after the island, then what? Will we go on to Memphis?"

"If we are told to follow the gunboat fleet, which as you know has no medical support, then I would say yes. Fort Pillow, of course, would be the next encounter. Followed by Memphis." The administrator then sounded a contradictory note. "Unless Chicago sends us up the Tennessee to Pittsburgh Landing. The enemy under a Gen. Johnston has as many as forty thousand men marching there to confront Grant who commands a like number."

A murmur from the audience grew louder as listeners took in these staggering numbers. Dr. Schmidt listened for a moment before adding in a loud voice that pierced the cacophony, "One of our sister ships, *Louisiana,* is already on her way to Pittsburgh Landing and may very well need our help. That is if casualties are many. You can imagine how many casualties if eighty thousand men start killing each other."

"Good grief!" someone shouted. "Unbelievable! Island Number 10 or Pittsburgh Landing? What a dilemma!"

Dr. Schmidt agreed. "A dilemma for Chicago, yes. Remember, our directives always come from Chicago." He told staff to be ready to leave "at a moment's notice" and ended the meeting.

Rachel's heart sank, knowing the outcome could create

another quandary. If the hospital ship was sent up the Tennessee River, how would she ever get to New Madrid? An hour later she posed the question to Nurse Dawes, who delivered the answer with cool logic.

"Rachel, you *must* stop this destructive thinking. When that island is under control, the river will be safe all the way to Fort Pillow. Fort Pillow is miles below New Madrid. You should have no problem finding a packet or some such to take you as far as New Madrid."

Miss Dawes' mild rebuke stayed with Rachel the rest of the day as she went about her duties with renewed enthusiasm. The work over, she volunteered to help clear supper tables and wash dishes. Retiring to her berth without a daily paper, she had no disturbing news to read. So, she wrote new letters to her girls, pledging to write Watson and John Welch tomorrow. Tired from the day's activities, she slept untroubled by fearsome storms or wild dreams and awoke ready to face the new day.

Sunday, April 6

THE TELEGRAPH WIRES IN CAIRO hummed all day. Some news reported speculation, some faded to hearsay with the next dispatch. A crowd assembled at the post office, which opened in late morning and closed an hour later when provost marshals removed the curious, along with the unauthorized, and locked the door. Eagerly awaiting any news, a larger gathering clustered outside the railway office.

Meanwhile, rumor ran amok on *The City of Memphis*.

In Tennessee, the Rebel army under Gen. Albert Johnston, after a forced march delayed by poor weather and bad roads, attacked Grant's troops, which some reports said were unaware of the massive force bearing down on them. Because his soldiers had never faced combat, parts of the Union lines collapsed, were overrun in places, and were driven back two miles to the Tennessee River. Casualty numbers were running frightfully high near a small country church called Shiloh. Someone in the crowd shouted, "Shiloh? That's supposed to mean 'place of peace!'"

"The Battle of Shiloh" as incoming messages now referred to the bloody encounter, prompted the Chicago headquarters of the Western Sanitary Commission to order *The City of Memphis* to depart Cairo at once and ascend the Tennessee River with as much speed as possible. The ship, having taken on a full load of coal the day before, cast hawsers and steamed up the Ohio with twin stacks chuffing black clouds of smoke on its hasty way to the Tennessee River mouth.

Standing alone on the wharf next to the vacated berth, her bag of belongings at her feet, Rachel fought to contain an upwelling of fear that came with not knowing what to do next. Should she return to the hotel in hope of finding a vacant room? Charles Duncan might have returned by now. Or maybe he was still downriver with the other embedded journalists. Charles had said his paper wanted him to remain in Cairo and monitor the gunboat fleet, his primary assignment. The chances of him being at the St. Charles, therefore, were no better than the odds he would be downriver. Rachel concluded there was nothing he could do to help her, no matter where he was.

Should she revisit the docks in hope of securing passage on a delivery boat, a loaded packet waiting to leave Cairo for a place somewhere down the Mississippi? That option was the most appealing, but she knew it was too dangerous to wander unescorted about the docks.

Should she go back to the Presbyterian church, pray to

God, and leave everything in His hands? No. She could, and would, pray here as well as there.

The answer came in a rush. Return to Soldiers Hospital and ask Dr. Anson for help! He would know what to do and would help her do it. Why had she not thought of that first? Another unanswered question for parsing later, when her mind might be settled.

She found Dr. Anson at the hospital, not in his office but in a patient's ward talking to the floor nurse in charge. Upon seeing Rachel, he broke into a grin. "I knew you'd be back. Knew it an hour ago when I learned *The City of Memphis* pulled out for Tennessee."

Rachel was so happy to see him, she felt dizzy. "If riverboats could only travel as fast as the news does!"

"Speaking of which, I have some for you. And it's good news at that."

Returning to his office with Rachel, Dr. Anson made known his plan. A directive from Chicago called for the delivery of medicine and other Commission supplies to the gunboat flotilla. "Every one of those ironclads has one hundred-eighty sailors aboard. Adding the men on the support vessels—the mortar rafts, tugs, coalers, and transports—there have to be more than fifteen hundred of our boys fighting a war without any medical care." He went on to explain that many sailors, as well as some reporters on board, had become ill with dysentery and other ailments and needed the Commission's help.

He told Rachel how the Government had contracted with various packet companies to deliver food and mail, along with tons of munitions to the fleet. "Never mind the irony of sending bullets with bedsheets. One of those boats, the *Arago*, has space for basic medical supplies. Chicago wants them delivered as soon as they can be loaded.

"You could go downriver with the *Arago*."

"I could go? Women are allowed on a supply boat?"

"It's more a question of authorization than an official ban. You'll go for the Sanitary Commission. As our agent of record. You will ensure the supplies are delivered and sign some papers. That's all, Mrs. Barnum. I can make it official."

She shook her head in disbelief. "I could go? When would I leave?"

"The minute that island is ours. Maybe as early as tomorrow. Maybe as late as Tuesday." His smile was broad. "How's that for good news, Mrs. Barnum? Rachel?"

"It is truly wonderful!" Dr. Anson, you are an angel of mercy."

With a laugh, he waved away the compliment, even as she rubbed away tears. He told her she needed to stay at the hospital, not at the hotel, to be available without delay. "If you don't object, you can choose any one of more than a thousand hospital beds." The smile lines on his elderly face fell, his tone suddenly sober. "I assure you they won't be empty for long."

CHAPTER 27

Monday, April 7
Cairo, Illinois

Throughout Sunday, conversation in Cairo centered on Tennessee and the fate of Gen. Grant's force, renamed the Army of the Mississippi. A flurry of newspaper dispatches reported horrendous fighting at descriptive places besides Shiloh Church—the Peach Orchard, Water Oaks Pond, the Hornet's Nest, and an unnamed thicket of oaks—all retreating, defensive positions Grant held as long as possible with his untested troops. The day mercifully ended with his army neither beaten nor demoralized. Artillery shelling from two Union gunboats and reinforcements from Gen. Don Carlos Buell had arrived in time after marching on the double-quick to save the day. Both Union and Confederate armies, however, suffered heavy losses, actual numbers of which could not be verified. Reports from the field said the Rebels lost Gen. Johnston.

Civilian nurses and doctors marshaling upon Cairo to

　　　

help where needed packed the train from Chicago, arriving Sunday night. Hoping for word of the *Arago*, Rachel discreetly followed a beleaguered Dr. Anson throughout Monday. Breaking away from time to time, she tended to patients and aided Angelina Cordray, receptionist, who made a valiant effort to accommodate the crowd of visitors drawn to Soldiers Hospital. All day the lobby doors opened and closed to couriers delivering messages and packages.

The lobby clock had struck five notes when Dr. Anson, unavailable in his office all afternoon, opened the door and looked out at her. Wearing a frown, he gave a negative shake, mouthed "tomorrow," and disappeared inside.

"He's been with so many people today," Angelina told Rachel and four or five others over supper in the staff dining quarters.

"Everything is happening at once," a nurse said. "I'm worried sick by all this fighting in Tennessee. I know we'll be deluged with casualties, starting at any time."

When talk drifted to developments on the Mississippi, including the news that a second ironclad had slipped past the island, Rachel took it to mean an omen that her time had come. Turning to the receptionist, she said, "If I must leave early tomorrow before seeing you, would you please see my letters are mailed?"

"Of course. Leave them on my desk, and I'll see to it."

Midnight was minutes away when Rachel sealed the last envelopes containing her letters to John Welch and Watson, extinguished the lamp, and turned expectantly to sleep.

Tuesday, April 8

Rachel boarded the *Arago* at 4:35 after being roused

from sleep in an empty patient's ward at Soldiers Hospital by Dr. Delbert Anson, facility administrator. For the third time in less than a week, the doctor had made her cry, not from sadness but from joy at receiving fantastic news. An hour earlier, at 3:25 a.m., the Confederates surrendered Island No. 10 to Commodore Foote. Rachel's harrowing delay in Cairo was over.

The weather was cold, and drizzle fell from a smothered sky so dark no starlight peeked through. With the last boxes of medical supplies aboard, the *Arago* shucked mooring lines and, her roaring boilers full of steam, turned downriver. Ahead, over the forest, red dawn broke through wrinkled clouds like a skin eruption, and the new day began. Wrapping her new slicker of India rubber close, Rachel realized she was on the Mississippi the instant the clear water of the Ohio changed to a dirty brown. Moving along on a waterway so immense, she was surprised at how a ship as large as the *Arago* could seem so small, so paltry. Ten days earlier while standing on the levee, rooted to earth and looking out over the Father of Waters, the perspective had been different. She hadn't felt so ... how would she explain to those at home? *Insignificant?* Yes, that was the perfect word.

An overpowering sense of liberation moved her while leaning over a guardrail. It was wonderful to be traveling again, but now, closer than ever to her goal, the feeling was more than relief. She could have admitted rapture but didn't. That would be wrong because it was premature. She must see him first, a revelation she hoped was a few hours, a few miles, away.

Rumbling from the *Arago's* engines sent a steady throb to the forward deck where Rachel stood and watched the far shore unfold. The shuddering tickled her feet until she grew accustomed to it. It also had a hypnotic effect and that induced daydreaming. The memory of that other travel experience by boat, when her father and brothers offloaded their belongings from canal barge to lake steamer at Buffalo, emerged. That vessel had chugged its relaxed way along Lake Erie to Detroit, not benefitting from the advantage of downstream current like the *Arago*, and the lake steamer's short journey up the sweeping Detroit River was much slower.

Her thoughts rambled to loved ones at home. Today was Tuesday, and the girls would be up and readying for school. Oh, how she missed her girls! And moody Watson and even-tempered John Welch, too. More than longing, however, characterized her mood. She imagined how worried they were, how frantic they would have grown after two full weeks of her absence.

An eternity to her. An eternity to them, too.

Have they gotten the first letter yet? Is Hester helping her sister with the arithmetic problems that Helena finds so troublesome? Is Watson getting on with John, or are they bickering over something so trifling neither will remember it by milking time?

Questions without answers were unsettling because they could lead to what Rachel knew was one of her biggest faults, thinking in terms of *What if?* There were never immediate answers to what if questions. Experience said that resolution came from tamping down her anxiety, from having patience. Fretfulness had been a personal flaw, and therefore a weakness, for as long as she had been aware of it. Rachel could not remember how or when such dithering began, but she suspected it was related to the need to control outcomes, another disparaging truth. She would never forget how alone she had been after losing her sister and then her mother, dreadful events that time had melded into one. How bereft she had been for months after Willis died. As Rachel stared at the murky current below, the old habit came creeping back. What if she couldn't find Dwight after all? What if she found him too late?

Close at hand, the aroma of coffee overruled her negative thoughts. One of the deckhands, a man with sympathetic eyes, offered her a steaming mug with a warning to hold the handle or risk burning fingers. Gingerly he passed the battered mug. "Just made it," he grinned. "Someone on a riverboat will always drink my coffee. If they're desperate, that is."

She laughed and thanked him.

"Been on the big river before, ma'am?"

"First time. It seems bigger when you're actually on it, not just looking at it from shore."

"I've been told more water passes Cairo, Illinois, than any other place in the country."

"Oh my, yes. I can believe it."

"I never tire of it." Turning his gaze upriver, a hint of nostalgia was in his voice. "I never get bored when I'm on Old Man River. Something new every time. Up or down."

"I can believe that, too." He looked to be forty-five, maybe fifty.

"Like today, you know? Twenty-four seasons and you're the first woman I ever seen on the Arago."

The attack at the railway station tore into her mind and her hand shook. Rachel assessed his face for clues. Was this a carefree conversation? Or purposeful? She could think of only one thing to say. "That must seem strange to you."

"Not really, ma'am. Just different."

He told her his name was Sidney. She concluded his

smile was sincere, and he was devoid of intent.

"It's a pleasure you're aboard, ma'am."

"Thank you. And your coffee is delicious."

"If Captain didn't drink it all, I'll get you another cup."

To Rachel, the river varied in width between a half-mile and a mile. Drifting along with the current, her engines running at idle, the *Arago* moved at the speed of a trotting horse and buggy. The captain, a veteran Mississippi River pilot, according to Sidney, was adept at negotiating the channel, which twisted like a pig's tail. Sometimes he steered toward the Missouri shore before veering toward the Tennessee bank. When the densely forested shores came close, Rachel noticed previous high-water marks on individual trees, some dead, others with green leaves unfurling.

It was clear the river had fallen at least a foot.

After some time, she began to realize the skills needed to read this perverse river, how the pilot must study the mutable current and pay attention to shoreline features. On outside bends, the *Arago* hugged the opposite shore where constant flow had carved a deep channel. Safely through the turn, the captain then followed the shifting, unseen channel back to where it snaked closer to the other shore. A leadsman to each side of the packet's narrow prow dropped heavy plumb lines over the side to gauge the river's depth. Sometimes these men, the pilot's eyes, alerted him with hand signals to steer left or right. In addition, to avoid being grounded on hidden sandbars, their careful watch prevented a collision with logs, branches, and half-drowned trees the *Arago* passed.

When Sidney returned with more coffee, Rachel asked him if he knew anything about the *Arago*. He told her that wooden river packets were notorious for having short lives with many falling victim to groundings, snags, flood debris, ice jams, or fires from boiler explosions. He said the *Arago* was a wooden hull sternwheeler built in Brownsville, Pennsylvania, and had never been, as far as he knew, in a serious accident. One hundred seventy-six feet long by thirty-three feet wide, she claimed six feet of freeboard when empty. She was equipped with three coal-fired boilers to power a like number of engines boasting twenty-inch, inside-diameter cylinders with five-foot-long piston strokes.

"You know a great deal about this boat," Rachel marveled. "How can you remember such detail?"

"Oh, I'm just a curious fellow, I suppose," Sidney chuckled. "Besides, numbers have a way of hanging around in my head. I've been on the *Arago* many times, usually on her freight runs between St. Louis and Pittsburg. She docks at Cairo a lot."

Pointing to the piles of artillery shells stacked throughout the *Arago's* deck in large, conical stacks, Rachel wondered what they weighed.

"That I don't know, but they're heavy enough to draw down this old packet deeper than usual in the river. Those leadsmen have to keep their eyes peeled today."

Several times the spotters signaled imminent contact with floating obstacles and, once, an entire uprooted sycamore. Rachel wondered if the tornado, which did so much damage a week ago, had ripped it from shore and thrown it into the river.

Entranced by such spectacle, she stood and watched until a sudden snow squall sent her to the pilothouse for a quarter-hour. The first mate and a couple of laborers already there for shelter nodded acknowledgment at seeing a woman aboard while others expressed diffidence.

As the morning wore on, vessel traffic increased, and the *Arago* was caught up in a pattern of following the leader behind other downbound packets and a tugboat herding a pair of coal barges. About five miles below Island No. 8, the column passed two plantation farms on the Missouri shore. She spotted an opening in the heavy forest, a breach out of place within a wall of green. Sidney explained it was the diversion canal cut by Federal engineers for the gunboat fleet to connect with Wilson's Bayou.

"They say they cut those flooded trees a full eight feet underwater with huge saws and brute force. By the time they finished the job, though, the water was too shallow for the Navy's turtles, but the Army transports got through to New Madrid." He told her by then one ironclad had already gotten past the island. "A couple nights ago, another one made it by."

"It's amazing how they did that," she marveled.

"The canal? Yeah, but it's a waste of time and work, if you ask me. Typical government boondoggle." He pointed downstream. "That there is Island No. 9."

Rachel was astonished. "It's huge!"

"No bigger than No. 10. She'll be coming up, 'bout halfway through the New Madrid Bend."

A little later she saw it. Assuming Island No. 10 would be timbered like the river's banks, she was surprised it was barren of trees except for patchy scrub willows. Created over the years, according to Sidney, the island was an enormous sandbar, a mile long and several hundred yards wide. The ironclads *St. Louis* and *Mound City*, their twin stacks belching ebony clouds of smoke, lay beached along the expanse, and they saw long threads of people walking up gangplanks to board transports.

"Those must be the prisoners," Sidney said. "Looks like they took a bunch of them."

"There certainly is a lot. I wonder how many."

"Thousands, ma'am! Look at all the tents they left behind."

Rachel saw the tents, strung along the shore like white specks of flotsam. She saw the artillery emplacements and the huge guns themselves, both on the island and higher up on the riverbank. She began to understand why Commodore Foote was so adamant about not losing any of his turtles to such prodigious enemy firepower.

"See that monster cannon?" Sidney pointed out. "I believe that's the Lady Polk Jr. They say she can throw a 128-pound shell across the river and then some. The shells she fires are so big they call them iron gateposts."

"The Lady Polk Jr.? Wherever did that name come from?"

"In honor of the Rebel Gen. Polk's wife. The Rebs put the first Lady Polk into action at Belmont last fall, but somehow a charge got left in her barrel. When the general himself came up to Belmont to see her shoot, she blew up. Killed ten crew members and some spectators."

Rachel was shocked. "How do you know any of this?"

"Oh, a man with ears hears everything on this river. The explosion knocked Gen. Polk off his mount. Killed the horse, too."

That made her think of Blaze and wonder how Dwight was managing the loss.

Two miles past the island, Rachel noticed several half-sunk vessels. She asked Sidney what had happened. "Were they sunk by our Navy?"

"I imagine the Rebs scuttled 'em. Looks like they tried to plug the channel so our boats couldn't get by."

Rachel could read *Ohio Belle*, *Desoto*, and what appeared to be *Mears* on upper decks above the waterline.

"Oh, there's the *Red Rover*." Sidney pointed to a large

three-story vessel with a sunken stern. "I know that one real good, too."

At that moment, they heard a loud crack! Lurching to port, the *Arago* pivoted and now faced upstream.

CHAPTER 28

Mississippi River near New Madrid, Missouri

Had Rachel and the boatman not been holding onto a guardrail, they would have been thrown off their feet. The powerful impact caused one of the ordnance stacks to fall apart, spilling heavy shells to roll across the *Arago's* deck.

"Stay back!" Sidney shouted. "Don't let go that rail!" Stopping one spinning shell with his foot, he picked up the missile. Other men ran out from the pilothouse to secure more loose rounds and to ensure the other artillery piles remained intact.

Rachel heard loud profanity coming from the pilothouse. The Rebel Navy was successful in sinking at least one vessel in the river channel. There could be others. The immediate concern was whether the *Arago* had sustained damage and was taking on water.

While minutes passed, the stricken ship lay pinned with current breaking around her hull and sluicing her sides. Rachel heard a muffled holler from below: "She's sprung a leak! Send help to man the bilge! A smaller packet passed on the vessel's starboard side. Someone aboard bellowed he had no towlines but would see about sending a tug to help.

Grumbling, cursing, the first mate shouted back that a tow was no help. "We're a sternwheeler for God's sake! Tell Foote to shove us off this wreck or come get his precious shells!"

Twice the *Arago's* captain ordered the engines reversed in an attempt to dislodge the vessel. Each time the effort failed. An hour passed while the deckhands worked in two-man teams to operate the force pump below deck. Deep into the second hour, a Navy tugboat appeared from down-river, drew alongside the stranded packet, and signaled he would make contact with the bow in an attempt to push her off the obstruction.

Sidney told Rachel to go inside for her safety. Retreating to the pilothouse, she sat on the floor and covered her ears from the painful roar of the reversed engines. Violent throbbing shook her body until the tug bumped the *Arago's* bow. The trapped boat shuddered and wrenched free, the deckhands whooped approval, and the captain turned the *Arago* back downstream.

"All in a day's travel," Sidney concluded. "Every morning brings a new day on Old Man River."

Coming out of New Madrid Bend, Rachel could see what remained of the town. As the *Arago* neared, she observed the aftermath of war: houses burned to their foundations, trees toppled, artillery pieces unlimbered, wagons upended—some missing wheels—a fort wall with gaping holes from cannonading.

The landing itself bore evidence of an army that had

come and disappeared: deep wagon ruts littered by count-less horse prints, beaten paths trodden by thousands of boots from soldier units five hundred strong crowding onto waiting transports. And still, the army had come here and left. She imagined how mules and horses, some bearing loaded panniers, others drawing supply wagons, boarded the overcrowded transports that had returned empty to take another load across the river.

Rachel took in the entire scene while the *Arago* tread-ed water a few hundred yards offshore and waited for a dock vacancy. Glancing downstream, she saw an ironclad low to the water, its stacks spewing smoke from engines at idle, and wondered if Commodore Foote or Charles Dun-can was aboard. Or were they on other turtles that Sidney said had already gone downriver to hunt Secessionists. A quarter mile upstream from the ironclad, she noted a line of floating, square-shaped objects with large projections cen-tered on each.

Sidney told her they were mortar rafts. "They can throw some of these shells here a mile or more. The bigger ones are for the turtle boats to fire on Fort Pillow. Memphis, too, if need be."

When a loaded transport pulled away from the dock, the *Arago* crept forward to take its place. Various Army offi-cials were waiting to receive her cargo, and Rachel hurried to countersign the hospital bills of lading after an obligato-ry inventory alongside an official from the Sanitary Com-mission. She wondered if the Navy Commodore himself would note the signature and remember her.

It was after four o'clock when Rachel stepped off the walkway onto Missouri soil. The Commission agent said her son was probably at the Newsome-Phillips farm, the closest field hospital to where the Michigan cavalry had formed on the morning of the New Madrid battle three weeks ago.

She asked if there was a quarantine in effect there. He assured her that, indeed, there was. "It's in a tent near the farmhouse. Last I knew four or five of our boys were isolated there with the smallpox. I'll be taking some of these necessities there if you want to ride with me."

During the ten-minute buggy ride, the agent tried to engage her with news from the second day of fighting at Shiloh, how Grant's reinforced army had whipped the Rebels yesterday but at bitter cost. He said those killed, wounded, or captured in the appalling battle would number in the thousands on both sides.

Preoccupied, Rachel spoke few words, responding with a perfunctory "yes" or "really." She would remember little of anything he told her.

After such a cold spring morning, the day had warmed, but a chill was descending with the fading light when they arrived at the Newsome-Phillips farm. All day she had been troubled, her anxiety wavering between eagerness to see him and fear of discovery.

Halting his team of mules at a safe distance, the agent pointed to a white tent glowing like a lighthouse beacon. "That's the hospital fly, Mrs. Barnum, the quarantine shelter. I don't know names but am guessing your boy's in there. Would you mind taking this box with you?"

Stepping down from the wagon, she took the container of supplies and asked if he would wait for her.

"I'll be back after delivering to the house," he said. "Last I knew two officers are recuperating there. If your son's not there, we'll go on to the next camp and look for him there."

Thanking him, she repeated that, yes, she was immune, inoculated.

Seeing a woman approach, an impassive fellow lounging in a chair before the tent entrance came to life. Getting up, he spoke with a southern drawl to ask who she was. Hearing "Barnum," his sober expression instantly changed into one of delight. "I knew it!" Clement Stafford gushed, whacking his leg. "Dwight swore y'all would come! We been writin' you letters near every day for two weeks."

Despite Clem's warning, Rachel was not prepared for this moment. Ecstatic that Dwight was alive, she fought for self-control the instant she saw him. His face was covered with circular spots the size of schoolboy marbles. Most of the skin lesions bore scabs that had crusted and fallen off to reveal pitted scarring. Below the wound, his bared arms, thin as kitchen-stove kindling, were folded over his chest. His eyes were closed. Dwight was sleeping.

His arms were pocked like his face. Rachel throttled a bawl. She knew her son would be marked for the rest of his life.

There was more to horrify. Pulling back the blanket with great care, she gasped. The tall, lean boy who, at best, weighed one-forty, had lost a frightening amount of weight from eating poorly, she inferred, if he had eaten at all since being confined to the sick tent. Rachel could see rib bones protruding like the carcass of some large animal that had died years ago out in the pasture and lay abandoned.

Hand over mouth, she smothered a shriek and stepped outside where Clement Stafford waited out of respect. "I know it's bad," he said, subdued. "Believe me, Mrs. Barnum, the doctors and the Commission are doing everything we can."

Chest heaving, blubbering now, Rachel stifled a moan and burst out, "For Heaven's sake at least move him into the house!"

"That's for officers."

"Heavens to mercy!" she roared. "I don't care one whit who's allowed there and who isn't!" The outburst startled her. Hearing a groan from inside the tent, Rachel tried to collect herself before speaking again. This time her voice was hushed, and it was insistent.

"That big house has only two patients? He'll go there first thing tomorrow morning if I must carry him myself!"

"I don't mean to challenge you, ma'am." Clem Stafford chose his words carefully, "Beg your pardon for saying it, but he's got the pox. So do those other boys with him."

"He's way past infecting anyone! Don't the fool doctors know that? Where are they? I'll tell them myself!" She stood there, irate, hands on hips, demanding an answer. She saw Stafford's face turn red. He, too, was close to losing composure.

His voice, however, was gentle. It was calming. "Mrs. Barnum, most surgeons and assistants, and most every nurse, went with the Army across the river. A couple took the really bad fellas to St. Louis." Rachel tried to concentrate on his words, on what he was trying to tell her. "They left this morning. Mrs. Barnum, I've gotten quite fond of Dwight and couldn't leave him and the other boys alone in this tent. I thought it best to stay on and do what I could for them. Maybe that was a lame idea." Pausing, he added, "I know it ain't much, ma'am. I figured it's better than leaving them to chance."

Rachel's voice fell to a whisper. "Of course," she said, sniveling. "Oh, Mr. Stafford, you must forgive my insensitivity. I had no right to say those things, to talk to you like that."

"It's fine. Nobody would blame you."

"Bless you, sir, for what you've done here for Dwight and those other poor men."

"No need to feel bad about it. I'll ask the powers that be over there at the house if they can move Dwight in the morning."

Relieved, she sighed and nodded.

"Someone bigger than me will have to decide, though. To be honest, Mrs. Barnum, I don't know if he can be moved."

"Why? What do you mean? It's not far. You and I could carry him."

Flummoxed, Clem shot her a penetrating stare. "You didn't see the wound he's got?" Rachel's eyes flared. "Go see for yourself, ma'am."

Parting the entrance covers, he followed her inside. She saw the three other patients for the first time. No one looked older than her son.

"If you lift that dressing," Clem advised, "careful as you can, you'll see it ain't healing up proper."

He held the lantern while she tenderly pulled back Dwight's tunic, exposing his injured shoulder. Most of the wrap remained stuck to the wound. Seeing it, Rachel gulped, held a deep breath, and whimpered. "Oh, my. You are right, Mr. Stafford. I don't think it's healing at all. It's all discolored."

"It's full of pus, I know. But the doctors look for that. They say the more pus, the faster the healing."

"Then why *isn't* he healing? Why *isn't* he better?"

"I don't know," Clem said and left the tent. Returning a few moments later, he brought warm water so she could soak the bandage for easier removal and replacement. Dwight winced, opened his eyes, and stared into hers while trying to identify who she was.

"Ma?" The voice was thin, barely audible. "You're here?" His eyes fluttered and closed.

"I'm here, Son. I came for you. Mother is here now. Everything's going to be fine."

The flicker of a smile told Rachel all she needed to know. She wiped his face with a fresh cloth and let him go back to sleep.

After Clem left for his bed at the house, she carried his chair into the tent and sat next to Dwight the entire night without the benefit of sleep or anything to eat. Neither tired nor hungry, Rachel was thankful to be with her son at last, as she repeated often in prayer during those long hours.

Wednesday, April 9

THE NEXT MORNING CLEMENT STAFFORD brought Rachel a big bowl of warm oatmeal with brown sugar, and a large mug of hot coffee. He said his supervisor, a medical student also staying at the house, promised to examine Dwight and anyone else in quarantine for potential transfer to the house, seeing as there were extra beds now. The Commission cook visited with breakfast for the invalids. While Clem tended to them, Rachel dwelt on her son.

Passing a strip of bacon under Dwight's nose, she succeeded in waking him and, after some coaxing, got him to take a few bites of pancake and to sip some tepid coffee. Encouraged by his appetite, though sparse, Rachel tried to get him to talk. Mumbling, he seemed disoriented and slept in fits throughout the day. In a moment of clarity, he asked about Blaze and if anyone had put flowers on the horse's grave today. Rachel said she would. While he slept, she bathed him as well as she could. The medical student paid a brief visit to look at Dwight's wound and to check on the smallpox status. He cleared one soldier for transfer but advised Rachel to keep her son in the tent because he was so weak and the wound was not improving.

When she asked why, he said he didn't know. "Your son might have contracted erysipelas. He has a fever, which makes me wonder, but with so many eruptions on his face, I can't tell for sure."

"What can be done?" Rachel asked.

Ignoring her, he continued. "I'm more worried about blood poisoning. That happens when the blood gets contaminated. That brings on a fever, too. It's possible that's why he's so sick, besides having the variola."

Again, Rachel asked what could be done for him.

"Nothing." The young man's answer was conclusive, ending further inquiry. "Keep him comfortable. Get him to eat if you can. And pray like the dickens."

That night Rachel slept on one of the empty beds. And the next night and the one after that. Throughout those days and nights, she stayed by Dwight's side, spoon-feeding whatever he would eat, keeping him hydrated, and changing and washing soiled bedding.

Sometimes she read her bible aloud for Dwight's benefit and hers but also for Clem Stafford and the two remaining soldiers in isolation. Rachel hummed familiar songs, mostly hymns, and sometimes when she sang—for she was known to have good range and a soothing voice—one or both of the patients joined.

During this protracted time, she watched Dwight slip away, a little each day. Despite his constant fever and sporadic sleep, she was able to comfort him in the same ways as when he was a sickly child. She had nursed him through the measles, but she was not able to stem whatever sickness was taking him now, hour by excruciating hour.

The long vigil afforded an inordinate amount of time to think, to reflect, to remember. At home her days were always filled with activity, forever propelled by the responsibilities of a mother, a manager, and a work partner on an active, productive farm. Church obligations each week sapped time and energy as did her efforts to be a helpful, dutiful neighbor. Here, however, there was nothing to do but wait and hope.

The southern latitude heralded spring a full two weeks ahead of advances at home. The War had been here. Now it was gone, replaced by bird songs and wildflower blooms, a tentative and welcome lull. Her thoughts had coalesced, and they were resolute: I found my son. I will not leave without him. The rest is not up to me.

CHAPTER 29

Friday, April 11
Army field hospital, New Madrid, Missouri

The days in Missouri had taken on a timeless quality. Rachel could not recall another period in her life with nothing to do but wait. Gone was the habitual burden of responsibility, the constant expectations of others, the forever need to decide outcomes. She had thought that by coming here, alone, she could direct what happened next. How odd, then, that the people she had met, the incidents she had experienced—mile by mile, hour by hour—were outside her control.

The irony was profound! Sitting in Clement Stafford's chair outside the tent entrance, Rachel sorted through events of the past two weeks and concluded she must relinquish the urge to manage outcomes. Was there a compensation to such resignation?

Perhaps. From those hours of reflection emerged thoughts she had denied, feelings deferred. As hope faded that Dwight would somehow shake off this pestilence, Rachel grew aware of how lonely she was. And could become. Oh, her longing for Willis would never go away, she was sure of that, but the intense grief and sheer numbness were long over. Agony had surrendered to a muted aching. Moments of melancholy were infrequent.

A creeping glacier, its movement imperceptible, is a powerful phenomenon. In that invisible way, a new longing had permeated old feelings. Wanting a connection, Rachel knew a growing desire for intimacy with another. She missed being held. She coveted a loving touch. She yearned to be loved. And here in greening Missouri just as the land experienced rebirth, she knew changes in her life were coming. That those changes had much to do with John Welch were undeniable.

He was no longer the wanderer who had landed at her farm like a lost ship looking for harbor. Her first impression, that he could be a questionable drifter with a sketchy past, was not accurate. As she came to know him, he was not a dubious character at all but rather a man of integrity. A hard worker, the man she had hired was charitable and kind.

She recognized how moral upbringing as a boy had secured his stature as a man. Why, if John Welch ever uttered an oath, it was under his breath and to himself, never directed to others. Why, since moving into the house, he had grown accustomed to attending church with the family, choosing the other end of the Barnum pew from her. She knew this to be right and proper.

Because everything that selfless John Welch did was in consideration of her, in deference to her, her admiration for him had blossomed into an indisputable attraction to him. Being away for so long told Rachel how much she missed him.

A groaning from the tent startled her. Springing from her chair, she drew aside the tent flap and peered inside. Dwight hadn't moved; the disturbance came from Samuel, the Ohio boy whose cot was along the back wall. Quietly going to him, careful not to wake her son, Rachel saw fever in Samuel's glazed eyes. Seeing the water dipper in her hand, he rolled to his side, and drank sparingly. She wiped his face on her apron and patted his head until the eyes closed, and he slipped into sleep.

Outside again, Rachel was thankful for the afternoon warmth. She smelled apple blossoms and listened to a mule braying from a stable beyond the farmhouse. Hearing the trill of an oriole, she fantasized the bird sang because it was going home to her farm, a happy prospect that brought John Welch back into her thoughts. How well did she really know him? Well enough to trust her daughters to him. Well enough to trust his judgment on most farming matters. He had become like a partner. Did she trust him enough to become a partner in marriage? Well now, she smiled, that depends on love, doesn't it?

Do I love this man? Like I loved Willis? No! How could I love anyone like I loved Willis? Willis was Willis, my one and only.

Would Willis have approved of John Welch? Yes. Would Willis have wanted me to be happy? Yes. Of course he would.

The thought of loving John Welch as a husband and lover sparked an old but familiar feeling: palpable pleasure mixed with fear, of certainty with uncertainty. It tingled through, and it led to a mind game she had played with Alice, a primary-grade friend and schoolmate in Miss van Royken's class in New York City. Pretending to read each other's minds, they would take turns questioning and answering.

"How would you feel if he walked out of your life?"

"Oh. Not good. Not good at all."

"What would you do?"

"I might cry."

"That's it?"

"No. There's more. I would ask him not to go."

"And why is that?"

"I don't know."

"That's not true! You do know. Don't you?"

"I think so."

"You think, or you know?"

"I don't know. I'm not sure!"

"Liar, liar! Dress on fire. You *do* know!"

"Yes, I know."

Say it then."

"All right, all right, I love him"

"I knew it! Knew it all along."

"Yes, I did, too."

Recalling that game from thirty years ago brought a little laugh. The last time she had laughed aloud was something Charles Duncan had said the evening she met him at the St. Charles Hotel.

Sunday, April 13

EARLY IN AFTERNOON TWO DAYS later, Rachel had a surprise visitor. Charles Duncan, securing a ride on an empty coaler returning to Cairo, had bribed the pilot into docking at New Madrid for two hours so he could look for her. He said a dockhand thought she might be at the Newsome-Phillips farm. Charles was elated to find her there.

They talked away from the tent, and the correspondent made her laugh over something silly he shared, a simple joy she had missed. He said he told Commodore Foote he was sure she had made it to New Madrid and now could prove it. He mentioned the good Flag Officer had prayed for her safety, and she liked hearing that, too.

When Charles asked about Dwight, Rachel fought to admit she was losing him, and the prospect of taking him home alive dimmed with each passing hour. This news upset Charles and threatened to defeat the joy of their reunion. Perhaps the reference to home prompted him to announce that today was the anniversary of the Fort Sumter attack. In a serious voice he said Fort Sumter was the kindling that had set the insurrection on fire. His tone turned sad upon telling her he had not seen his wife and family for months. "Rachel, it's time for both of us to go home."

She hugged him then and held him close. Charles' arms encircled her small body. Rachel buried her face in his chest and in a muffled voice said, "Charles, you have been a life-saver to me."

His voice fell to a whisper. "I wanted to help you. Wanted to do what I could for you, Rachel." He then apologized for not having had time to write her story for the newspaper.

Looking up, she saw Willis in those handsome eyes of hazel. "Oh, Charles. That's not important to me. You have done so much for me that really matters."

He bent down and kissed her lips. A spark of joy flushed through her. She captured a deep breath and hesitated before gently breaking away. Hands on his shoulders, she looked into those lovely brown eyes once more. "I hope to see you again, Charles. You are a true friend. I shall never forget you."

Seeing him was like a long-awaited rendezvous of life-long admirers. The stir she felt swelled to a rousing uplift when he said goodbye, mounted the cavalry horse on loan from some trooper, and rode off toward the river.

He looked back once, and Rachel returned his wave. She watched him until horse and rider vaporized with a turn in the road. The eruption of tears that followed was a potent fusion of joy and sorrow. Rachel sat on what remained of a tree felled by storm or shell, wiped dry her eyes, and tried to make sense of the warring feelings that had consumed her all over again.

Returning to the quarantine shelter sometime later, she learned another man had come calling.

RACHEL WONDERED HOW THEY ALWAYS knew. Why they always drove a black coach.

Walking back to where her son lay stricken, she noted this solicitor had tied his pair of sable horses to a plum tree bearing purple flowers. Stenciled gold letters on the hearse were large enough for her to read "R. L. Peabody, Embalmer." He favored a stovepipe hat. His trousers, evening jacket, and bowtie were also black as tar. The blouse was a single white garment. Rachel watched him approach with confident, manly strides.

The year of war had already afforded a bad reputation for "vultures who preyed upon the dead," as one daily had described them. Rachel's brief meeting with him was all business. He would embalm any soldier who died on the battlefield or from disease, including smallpox, for a hundred dollars. A client could buy a pine coffin he himself had made for another five dollars.

He dealt in gold, silver, and greenbacks, and his service tent was near the King's Highway about a hundred rods, a bit more than a quarter mile, from the Mississippi. He was available on short notice until April 15 when he would leave.

Rachel knew it was a robbery. She also knew there was no option. Ice would melt. An untreated body would spoil. It was a long way here; it is a long way home. Her stomach grew queasy thinking about any part of the inevitable scenario.

One question remained: When?

Dwight answered it when he passed sometime during the following night, either Monday, April fourteenth, or Tuesday, the fifteenth. Sleeping in a bed next to him, Rachel never knew the exact time he slipped away. She awoke knowing he was in the Lord's arms, and in a prayer wracked with crying, gave thanks for sparing her son any more suffering.

Samuel, the remaining patient, had improved and prayed with her. Clement Stafford came from the house with breakfast and paid his respects.

Clem helped to arrange her travel home. She would not go back on the river, nor would she return to Cairo. A half-company of horsemen had orders to escort the Federal paymaster to New Madrid when he arrived by rail at Sikeston. For protection, Rachel went to Sikeston with them, riding next to a soldier-driver on a wagon bearing a coffin destined for Dubuque, Iowa, and another for Battle Creek, Michigan.

In St. Louis, she transferred to a ferry, crossed the Mississippi, and boarded the Alton and Chicago train, the same one that had brought Dwight from Grand Rapids to Missouri five months earlier.

Relief tempered the overwhelming sadness Rachel felt. Numb, exhausted, she had done what she came to do and no longer needed to brood over endless outcomes. She had lived through his leaving her so many times, in conscious thought and in dream, that Dwight's final going away was no more real than it was some grand design she could not understand.

CHAPTER 30

Wednesday, April 16
Alton & St. Louis RR

Sometimes on the long train ride to Chicago, while the passenger car click-clacked and rocked in that singular rhythm endemic to travel by rail, Rachel closed her eyes and thought about the people she had met since leaving her farm. She remembered the mother and child in the seat across from her when she boarded the outbound train in Battle Creek. Edith Wirksky was rocking her baby Ethan, asleep in his mother's arms. The image of the beautiful child with the innocent smile and heavenly blue eyes carried Rachel back to that happy time when Dwight was a baby, and she was a young mother. In those first years of marriage to Willis, thoughts of war were as far away as heat lightning on the horizon.

And sometimes Rachel's mind wandered from the timely way her family grew after Dwight was born, to the scorching summer day her husband passed, to the winter morning John Welch came to her farm.

The thought of John reawakened her feelings for him, feelings that had grown in proportion to the days of absence. Rachel pondered whether he missed her and could love her. Did love her. Her heart said John did love her, but he was not the demonstrative type. How would she know for sure? She had little doubt it would be up to her to take the initiative. To say the words first. He was … she searched for the right word. Passive? At times, yes, but he could be assertive when the subject was land or livestock matters. Unconfident? Perhaps. Sometimes he acted unsure, apprehensive even.

She ransacked memory for examples. There was that time the twins were arguing on the front porch about something so trivial she couldn't recall now just what it was. John was trying to mediate, listening to one's explanation and then the other's. Their loud bickering brought Rachel outside. Separating them, she ordered Hester to the garden to pick tomatoes for supper and sent Helena to the washing line to retrieve dried clothing.

He could have done something to put out the fire between them. Why didn't he?

"Fire" uncorked another event, this one only a month ago when John caught Watson smoking in the barn. Watson had pilfered some of John's tobacco to try out a crude pipe the boy had whittled from a corncob. She knew nothing of the incident until Hester tattled. Hester said John had explained to all three children how fire was a barn's worst enemy because of hay in the mow and animals confined to their stalls.

Hearing this story an hour after it happened had made Rachel's blood boil. Angry all afternoon, she confronted Watson at supper, demanding to know what her son was thinking. When John said that was the problem right there, that Watson wasn't thinking, she had shot the hired hand a look that he might have taken to mean she thought of him as a co-conspirator. Recalling the incident now, Rachel realized that, to John's mind, the look was probably one of accusation: Why didn't you come down harder on the boy? Why did you keep this serious infraction from me?

She remembered those were her exact thoughts at the time. Now, she considered the issue from John's perspective. Maybe he would have told her but was waiting for her to calm down. He was not her children's father and had no authority to mete out discipline. Although Rachel sometimes wished he would seize the initiative, she had never relinquished control, had never asked him to help manage her children. The behavior she thought was indifference at best, unwillingness or inability at worst, could have been simply discretion. Out of respect for her, he would not usurp her authority unless she permitted it.

Rachel knew all too well she had never delegated such authority to him. Or to anyone else, except Miss Amble at school and perhaps Willis' cousin, Betsey Barnum.

During this protracted time of return travel, she also realized with greater clarity that her life would never be the same again. With Dwight's passing, Watson was her only son. If the Rebellion went on another year, or more, Watson would follow his brother to war. The thought of losing Watson, too, wrenched Rachel's heart and filled her with dread. She resolved to make life better for Watson. To try to draw him out, to get him to talk instead of bottling up his feelings, to find less fault in the boy, to treat him more like the man he was becoming.

While the train bore on, Rachel wondered what would become of her daughters. Dwight's passing would impact their lives, too, but how? Already ten years old, they would soon be young women with minds of their own. Their future also weighed on her mind.

Watching villages and farms and woods appear and disappear through the train window, Rachel questioned what she had gained from her journey. Yes, she had succeeded in finding her son, but at what cost to those left behind? Yes, she was bringing Dwight home, but Dwight was gone, was consigned to what was, not to what will be. It was when she thought about the people who had helped her, and those she had borne witness to, that the answers began to jell, to make sense to a racing mind now slowing to a wobble, like a child's spinning toy.

She had fed a hungry man at a train depot without knowing his name. Because a boy soldier, a supposed enemy, did not die alone far from home, she had gifted a mother she would never know. No mother could ever be an enemy to her! In spite of her own insufferable loss, Rachel's breast stirred with the power of recompense. She had God to thank for that, and thank Him she did in a long, silent prayer while the passenger coach rocked along.

She must have been sleeping for when she looked out the window, night had come and there was nothing to see. Except her own face, weary and withdrawn. The image that stared back seemed old, and it led to a deeper reflection: What would make her happy with whatever amount of time was left of her life? Somewhere inside—whether it came from Rachel's heart or head was unclear—something had budged. A sense of self-awareness was growing. She could learn to be more giving, to share more of herself, to not hold everything inside as Watson did. Oh, she had modeled insularity so well for Watson! She could open up more, be more trusting of others. The ability was already there. It had been so easy to tell Charles Duncan, a stranger then, her life story. And there had been others, also strangers until she shared her plight and purpose with them. Jane Dawes, nurse supervisor on the hospital ship, was suddenly in her thoughts, followed by Dr. Anson and Clem Stafford. They had helped her, too, because she had trusted them first.

But she would never see them again. Who would she see? Who could she count upon when this ordeal, this solo journey into the unknown, was finally over, and she was back home? Connection with Beatrice, the Chicago cousin, was limited to letters. Rachel's aged father was not well, and her brothers and sister were consumed with their own lives. Of the friends and neighbors who attended her church, Betsey was a promising confidant. She and Betsey shared similar circumstances, and their children often played together. Rachel vowed to reach out to Betsey more as a friend, not just as a neighbor.

John Welch darting into her thoughts had a galvanizing effect. It was so obvious her mind whirled. Why hadn't she thought first of the person she trusted the most? Rachel knew that answer: She had taken for granted John and his steadiness, his loyalty, and—what she felt with a quiver that raced through her—his love.

No more.

During a protracted stop at Decatur, rail workers broke apart the freight cars to assemble new lines. The delay gave passengers more time than usual to deboard and walk about the town. Rachel was returning amidst the loud coupling and shunting of box cars when she noticed the one containing Dwight's casket was gone. In a panic, she hurried over to the conductor to ask what had happened.

Holding the passenger car railing with one hand, he had mounted the bottom step and was about to sound the boarding alarm.

"No need to run," he said to the woman who had rushed up and was panting before him. "You got three whole minutes."

"What happened to the soldier car?"

"The coffin car? It's over there." He pointed to a track spur. "It's waiting on a different line to Chicago."

"Why not this line? I paid for delivery on this train."

"This train, that train. They're all going to Chicago. It'll get there a couple hours after you do."

"Oh, no! My son is in that boxcar. I won't leave him to chance."

"This line is now passenger-only. That one's freight-only."

"Then I'll go with him as freight."

The surprised conductor gave her a piercing look. "Still have your ticket to Chicago?"

"Yes."

"Well, then show it to the yard foreman. Tell him I said to open the door. Soon as that freight engine hooks up, you're going to Chicago with the patriots."

"What is your name, sir? What do I tell him?"

"You tell him P. J. Boswell said so. See? Right there on the lapel." The shriek his whistle made forced Rachel to cover her ears.

During the cargo run to Chicago, solitude and sensory deprivation caused old thoughts to bubble through her mind. She saw Helen and herself as the little girls they were, playing on a farm and picking daisies for their mother, so pretty, her unburdened hair the color of ripe chestnuts. As that image faded, along with others, sometimes she would see a young girl, alone, searching for headstones in a rural cemetery somewhere in New Jersey. She imagined an older girl wandering among crowded monuments in a New York City graveyard. And she saw herself, sitting in Willis' crumbling chair before his granite marker on her isolated Sunfield farm.

As THE QUEUE OF BOXCARS inched into the Chicago railyard, a screaming whistle shattered Rachel's vigil. When the door to the coffin car rolled open with a bang, daylight exposed someone sitting on a casket, hands splayed on the pine boards, daring anyone to touch it. A yard worker was shocked at seeing a woman alive among so many dead. In a frightened voice he asked where she thought she was going.

"Home. Going home now."

The fear in his eyes insisted he dared not look away. "And where might home be?"

"Michigan. I'll need the train to Battle Creek. This is Chicago, isn't it?"

"Oh, I see. That would be the Michigan Central line." His weak voice lacked agency. "It's over in the north bay." Jerking a thumb backward, the yard worker knocked off his cap. Stooping to pick it up, he remained fixated on her. "Tracks 10 and 11."

Rachel asked for a porter. The worker's immediate whistle was a jolt; her hands flew to ears.

"Sorry for that," he apologized and offered a sheepish look, the kind one makes when caught executing a prank. His snicker did not release the tension between them. "If you want to just walk on over there, ma'am, I'll have your cargo delivered."

Rachel catapulted to her feet, hands on hips. "This is

not cargo! This is my son! Second Michigan Cavalry, I'll have you know that. Sir!"

Her reprimand shredded any façade of self-assurance, and he removed his cap. "I am so sorry. My ignorance is no excuse. Please forgive me."

Unstiffening, Rachel sat down again and crossed her arms. "I'll wait for the porter. I won't leave him in some freight yard. He's going nowhere but home. With me."

Later that day she rode in a passenger car bound for Battle Creek, the last one before the boxcar containing her son's casket. When Rachel arrived home, she would bury Dwight next to his father, the only place on earth he belonged now; a second reason to go there, to visit more often, to stay longer. Having John Welch repair Willis' chair was more important than getting seeds in the ground.

CHAPTER 31

Friday, April 17
The Road Home

Arriving in Battle Creek the following afternoon, Rachel paid a trackside courier to bring her wagon and team. The two men loading the coffin onto the buckboard refused compensation. "I hope he got some of those stinking Rebels first," one of them said, a comment she did not appreciate and pretended not to hear.

At the stable Rachel paid the boy attendant and thanked him for the good care he had given Sam and Bill. She noted the boy's improved behavior, and when she knew he would not ask who was in the box, added a small gratuity. The token surprised him.

Rachel then left Battle Creek without more words, steered the horses onto the Lansing-to-Battle Creek trail, and kept her eyes on the road, acknowledging no fellow sojourners she overtook or passed going the other way. It was a good day to go home, with sunshine and the lack of wind making for balmy travel. Another time Rachel would have observed how much things had changed since coming down to the city. She would have seen bright patches of flowers flourishing in woodlots, the occasional farmer plowing with mule and horse teams. Such was her focus on getting home at last.

In Bellevue, Rachel checked into the same room at the Eagle Hotel. In the dining room, Gen. Grant's staggering losses at Shiloh was the main topic of conversation. Keeping to herself, she did not contribute, ate a small supper, and went to bed without reading.

Back on the road soon after it was light enough to travel, Rachel drove the horses all day, stopping every two or three miles for them to rest after being stabled so long. She knew they were making good time when passing through Kalamo in mid-afternoon. The plan was to make the McConnel's before dark, ask to pay them for supper and bed, and leave at dawn tomorrow. If the road remained passable, she could arrive home in time for supper with John Welch and the children. Her mood was buoyant. How precious that will be. She felt like she had been gone forever.

Sunlight depleted, dusk pulled the land closer. Rachel knew her chickens were scratching their way to the roost. The temptation to press on was strong; she knew she couldn't. Wouldn't. She was mere hours from home when the *clop-clop* of shod hooves drew Lucy McConnel and her husband to the road. Knowing that Rachel was safe, her journey to somewhere nearly over, Lucy brushed away a welcoming tear. Angus McConnel, her husband, took Rachel's hand as she stepped from the wagon seat. Her boots scarcely touched the ground before Lucy had her in a broad embrace.

"Mrs. Barnum! Rachel. You've come back! I have prayed for you morning and night since you went away from here."

"You must be famished," Angus said. "We were just sitting down. Come. Eat. Emerson will do right by your team after supper."

The boy Emerson and his sisters clustered around the wagon. Tiptoeing, hands on the board frame, the McConnel girls pulled themselves up to peer inside. "What's in that big box?" the older one asked. "Is someone in there?"

Lucy gave them a threatening look. "Mary," she began, "don't …"

"Come, children," Angus interrupted. "Time to finish supper. Mary, set a plate out for Mrs. Barnum."

Turning to obey, Mary began to whisper to her little sister. Rachel heard their words. "I bet it's the relative, that sick person she talked about."

"What sick person?"

"The one she went away to see. Bet that's who's in that box!"

After supper Lucy sent the girls out with Emerson to feed and water the horses. A weary Rachel did not resist their offer to stay the night. She needed sleep. She did not want to appear ungrateful to these kindly folks whom, she knew, hoped to learn whatever she was willing to share. She decided to cancel the burden of inquiry, to let the expectant air out of the room.

"It's Dwight," she began. "My boy. I had to go some miles downriver, down the Mississippi River, to find him. I got to him when he was still alive." She would not say that repulsive word.

"I couldn't bring him home the same way."

Gasping, Lucy covered her mouth with one hand and held tight to the chair with the other. Angus, head in hand, sagged in his chair. "Oh, no! We wondered as much. Hoped it would not be so."

They did not, would not probe. Rachel broke the stillness by adding minimal details of where, when, and how. She divulged without color, staying within the boundary of fact. When she stopped talking, Lucy, eyes brimming, managed to say, "So sad. Rachel, I could not have done what you did."

"Yes, you could, Lucy. I believe you could, and you would."

"War is tearing the country apart," Angus said. "It's turned what's normal on its head …"

Rachel's thoughts shot to the casket. *A child dying before his mother dies is not normal. It's abhorrent. An abomination!*

"… going to take a lifetime to put things right again, if that's ever even possible." Angus droned on.

Thoughts swarmed through her. *Yes. A lifetime. The rest of my life!* Staring at her half-eaten supper, an overwhelmed Rachel fell silent. Incapable of explaining sensations too raw, of further discussion at all, she asked to repair to bed. Angus' sincere condolences were appropriate. When Lucy held her close, Rachel's dam came close to bursting, but she held back, knowing that once started, the tears would not stop. Collapsing into bed, she did not wake until morning, not even when the active McConnel girls churned in their sleep to either side of her.

Over breakfast, she apologized for being a poor guest, but her hosts dismissed any concern. When she insisted on paying something for their kindness and care, Angus was adamant that she abandon any such thought. "Your son already paid," he said with conviction. "Your son paid for all of us, Mrs. Barnum. God bless you, and Dwight."

On the Ionia Trail later that morning, Rachel was thinking about Willis and how her life had changed after meeting him. Margaret was the first of Peter van Houten's children to marry. Asked for by a widowed farmer with two children from neighboring Vermontville, Peter consented, and Margaret had moved away. Cornelius found a young Sunfield woman to his liking. Buying forty acres from his father and stepmother, Cornelius and his wife built a home and farm there. Brothers John and Henry stayed home another three and five years respectively to work on their parents' land. Rachel was the youngest of Peter's six children and the last one to marry.

While passing through Vermontville with only a few miles left to reach home, Rachel recounted the personality traits of her late husband. His baritone voice when he sang aloud in church. His high-pitched laughter so easy to identify in a noisy room. The way he could put people at ease, even strangers, with that infectious smile, and his innate ability to draw others out from shells of shyness. She would never forget Willis' carefree manner. His voice would be in her head for as long as she lived.

Rachel would never love anyone in the way she loved Willis, but that did not mean she would never love again. It would be different, of course. Why would it be the same? There is but one first in everything we experience. First love. First child. A second attachment has to be different because it cannot be the first. The rational mind says so.

But the heart speaks a different language. Yes, it is hard to let go, but there can be no restitution without, first, a relinquishment. Rachel has a chance at another love in her life. And she has another son and two daughters waiting for her to come home.

A PLUME OF HARDWOOD SMOKE laced with the sweet odor of maple pervaded her neighborhood as Rachel's mud-streaked wagon turned off Shaytown Road and into the barnyard. A team that pulled in harness knew, were expected to know, the next step whether the end of a furrow or the end of a journey. Since passing through Vermontville, Sam and Bill surely knew they were coming home. They needed no words of encouragement or direction from her.

Most of the fields they had passed lay fallow, too sodden to plow, and Rachel smiled to see they were still making syrup this deep into April. She fancied John Welch was in the sugarhouse and hoped Watson was helping him. When one of the Belgians whinnied, figures spilled from the shack. Hands held high in victory, a beaming John Welch fast-stepped toward her. Watson followed with Harrison, neighbor Betsey's son, close behind. Rachel's daughters were nowhere to be seen.

John Welch was shouting. "Thank God, you are home!" He took the hand she offered and after the first step down seized her by the shoulders and lifted her high. Holding him close a moment, she buried her face in his smoke-perfumed shirt before pulling back and turning to Watson.

"I missed you, Son. Oh, how I missed you. All of you!"

Watson accepted her embrace. "We got your letters, Ma, both of them. Hester and Helena are out looking for lilies to give you when you got home."

"They're in the woods by our house," Harrison announced. "I saw them when my ma sent me over here to see if Mr. Welch needed help. I'll go tell them you're home now."

"Thank you, Harrison," Rachel said. "Tell your mother there will be a funeral on Sunday, after the church service."

When Harrison left, Watson asked to see his brother, and when Rachel said that couldn't happen, Watson was instantly agitated. "He's my brother. I want to see him! Why can't I see him?"

She explained that Dwight didn't look the same now, that it was better to remember him the way he was. "The man I paid for preservation did a poor job, on account of his being in a hurry. Or maybe being lazy."

Watson kicked at the ground.

Rachel went on. "I don't want the casket opened. Lt. Dickenson gave me a little picture, what the soldiers call a *carte de visite*, of Dwight in his uniform. That's what is good to remember him by."

Grumbling, Watson walked off in a huff. John was nuzzling the team. "He was starting to come around. Truth is we were getting along pretty good." He patted Bill's nose. "This ain't much of a homecoming for you, Rachel. I'm so sorry."

"I came as soon as I could. Already, Dwight's been gone almost a week."

"And you've been gone three weeks or more. So long. Too long, Rachel."

She told him it was important to her that Dwight be buried on the Lord's Day.

"Tomorrow *is* Sunday, April 20," John said. "Hope it doesn't rain." Studying her worn face, seeing her exhaustion, his soft heart turned to putty. "So happy you're back home, Rachel. They missed you so. More than I missed you ain't possible, I hope you know."

A smile fought through her weariness. "I missed you, too, John Welch. I thought of you often." Pressing fingers over his rough hand, she squeezed it for emphasis.

IT DID NOT RAIN. SUNDAY afternoon was warm, the sun at times breaking through fleecy clouds that followed each other like a parade of sheep heading to pasture. The funeral service concluded with Pastor Towner's reading of the 23rd Psalm. The girls held hands and cried while John gripped Rachel's fingers and blinked back sorrow. The levee breached for Rachel when Hester, and then Helena, laid bouquets of trilliums on the casket; and Watson, tears spilling with the others, contributed the first shovelful of earth. When it was over, they walked back to the house and sat in the parlor with relatives and church congregants.

The sun slipped below horizon-hugging clouds, an orange fireball that shed swirls of magenta and indigo until fading away. As the day grew dark, John excused himself before the others, to look over a late-born lamb he said, and to close the barn door.

The next morning Rachel discovered a new chair before the two graves.

EPILOGUE

A front-yard maple blazed green-gold the day they married in Rachel's parlor. Many of the same folks at the funeral heard them exchange vows that Sunday afternoon in October, six months on. Helena and Hester were overjoyed to have a father again after half of their young lives had gone by without one. They had begun addressing John Welch as Pa weeks before the wedding. He wanted that and Rachel had approved. It was different with Watson, though, as it had been since John's arrival. His brother gone, Watson withdrew deeper into himself and appeared more restless than ever. He stopped attending church; sometimes his chair at the supper table was empty. Considerate enough to his sisters, Watson often ignored his stepfather and tended to avoid his mother. He initiated few conversations. When spoken to, he responded with few words or didn't talk at all. As the months passed, Rachel's anxieties grew with the increase of tension in the home and the rising rate of War casualties.

Fearing the unknown consequence, Rachel did not ask

John to intercede with her sullen son. Pressuring the man to do something, anything, about Watson now might drive the boy out of her life forever, and so Rachel resolved to live with the outcome she blamed herself for creating. But why should gaining a husband mean having to lose a son? She had no answer to this conundrum. Of this, however, she was certain: Nothing would lessen her remorse for having favored Dwight at Watson's expense. Her nightly prayers for guidance and forgiveness grew more fervent as winter became spring and summer turned to fall.

A year after she and John married, Rachel conceived. John Welch's constitution as a kind and gentle man—a helpful partner who had cared for her and now loved her without condition—had drawn her to him during a tumultuous time of her life. Knowing she had miscarried years earlier when married to Willis, John was protective of their joy together, but she suspected his peaceful disposition had limits. Always there are limits.

Rachel fretted over what could happen if John's steadfast nature ruptured.

The day the moldboard plow broke and an ill Silas Rowe, the Sunfield blacksmith, was unable to rebuild it for days, was the climax to a ragged spring of unstable weather. It seemed as though everything that could go wrong on a farm—a lame horse, a milk cow that hadn't freshened, a weasel that got into the coop and killed half of their laying hens—went wrong that spring. When John didn't come to supper one evening, the twins went looking for him. Finding their stepfather sprawled out on the granary floor, they feared he had died. The whiskey bottle Rachel didn't know about lay shattered, slivers of glass everywhere, the air ripe with alcohol.

The incident terrified them and alarmed her, and she

worried it could happen again, or something worse could occur if the men in her life did not make right what was wrong between them. Rachel recalled a story John had told from his timbering days when he broke a man's nose for calling him a cheat after John won at cards and claimed what was left of the man's pay. Beneath that calm demeanor lay a temper though she had not witnessed it unbridled.

Watson's penchant for being in a strop much of the time was one trigger. She knew that, too.

It happened in May when Rachel was seven months with child. Of all the possible catalysts, it was the shovel, a simple tool Watson had forgotten to return to the shed after spading the garden and was now rusted. Watson exploded when John mentioned it to him.

"If it's so important to you, put the stupid thing away yourself!"

The day had not gone well for John Welch. Returning home from Sunfield without his plow had lit a fuse. Watson's obstinacy was the powder keg. "Watson, you got it out and used it last. Be responsible for once, and put it away." The boy when John first came to the farm was now a man. Glaring in defiance, Watson swore at his stepfather.

"If you was my son," John said as evenly as he could, "I'd kick your ass all the way to Sunfield for cussin' at me like that."

"If you was my real Pa, I wouldn't kick yours!"

Ire welling, John stepped back, planted his feet, and anchored hands to hips. "You'll never accept me, will you? I know your problem ain't me. Never was me. Your being mad at the world's got nothing to do with me."

"You're wrong, old man. Got everything to do with you.

You're the one who married Ma! You're the one who made her pregnant."

Rage engulfed John Welch. "You ungrateful little squirt!" he roared and swung a fist.

Ducking, Watson seized the shovel. Wagging it before his stepfather, he threatened. "Do that again, old man, and I'll crack your skull!"

John was no coward. He was no fool. Rachel flashed before him. He unclenched his fist. "Go ahead, Wat," he said, his voice trailing off, "feel sorry for yourself. The Army'll know what to do with you. I know I don't."

"I'll be gone the day I'm eighteen. One week from today."

"All I know is you're stupid as stupid can be. Running off to the War ain't no different than me running away when I was your age. Took me a long time to figure out I was a dumbass, too." He glowered at Watson. "Had to find a life worth living for first. I found it here."

Watson thrust the shovel blade into the garden. His hands dove into his pants pockets, and he rocked back on his heels. "My running off to war's got nothing to do with you, John Welch. I'm going because my poppa couldn't. Dwight never got to fight and came home in a box. I'm signing up before they make me go."

John shrugged and sighed. "You'll find your way," he said, his voice steeped in resignation. "I hope you don't get killed looking for it." Glancing up he saw Rachel watching them from the kitchen window.

He stopped walking to glance back at Watson, still standing in the garden, and said, "Your mother couldn't abide another death in her family."

Rachel and John Welch, c. 1863

Willis H. Barnum, c. 1855

Helena and Hester Welch, c. 1863

Watson Barnum, c. 1863

Dwight Barnum, c. 1861

AUTHOR'S NOTES

The making of a historical fiction

Many years ago I met Lindsay Welch, Rachel's great-great grandson, at his family's hardware store in Sunfield, Michigan. Like many small-town retailers, Lindsay was struggling to stay solvent. Retiring early, he donated the building and property to the Sunfield Historical Society, a nonprofit group of volunteers that are keeping area history alive through the Welch Historical Museum.

Knowing of my interest in history, Lindsay shared a journal written in 1984 by his grandmother, who was also Rachel's granddaughter-in-law. *Myrtie's Memories*, the 136-page, typewritten memoir, contains references to Grandma Rachel. This entry, in particular, intrigued:

"She and Mr. Barnum had four children. Dwight, born Feb. 16, 1844, a Union soldier in the War of the Rebellion, died while in service, Apr. 20, 1862. Grandma Rachel drove an ox team hitched to a buckboard and brought Dwight's body home to be buried. I believe it was in Tennessee. I'm not sure. Made the trip all by herself."

Was this true? Why would a forty-year-old woman, widowed on the eve of the Civil War, risk her life by searching through a war zone for her fallen son? How did she do it? First, I had to know if the story was true or a family tall tale.

I began research by securing Dwight's military records from the National Archives Trust Fund in Washington, DC. I learned he died from a fever in a regimental hospital in New Madrid, Missouri, on either April 13 or 14, 1862 (the records list both dates). However, his tombstone in the Welch family cemetery in Sunfield Township states the date of death was April 20, which was a Sunday in 1862. This discrepancy was another mystery.

Forty-year-old Rachel was mother to three other children: another son age sixteen and twin daughters eight years old. Who would have taken care of her family while she was away? By what means did she travel, and how long was she gone? I researched timetables and fares for both the Michigan Central and Illinois Central railways and dove into the historical records for military maneuvers in the Western War Theater. I dug through Mississippi River packet logs and searched for business establishments in the towns through which Rachel would have traveled. Research involved the names of local banks, period currencies, costs of goods and services, and the weather in Michigan, Indiana, Illinois, and Missouri on the dates Rachel could have traveled through these states. I looked for anything that shed light on the customs, practices, regulations, and policies in vogue and in place during the spring of 1862.

Local land-ownership records and the U.S. Census for 1850 and 1860 answered questions about Rachel's means, and *Myrtie's Memories* offered scant but nevertheless insightful tidbits about her personality and character. For example, when the first death occurred in Sunfield Township, there was no designated cemetery. Donating a plot of land within site of her homestead farm, Rachel reserved a spot for her own family. Sixty-six years after Rachel died, Myrtie wrote, "After she and Grandpa John were married, she had quite a large plot put aside for the Welches."

Rachel's May 29, 1918, death certificate cited "jaundice" as the cause of death. Her obituary offered intriguing details about her Christian faith, such as this passage: "On entering her home, one rarely found her sitting without her bible, which she gained as a prize for faithful attendance at Sunday school when but a small child in New York City." But it was Myrtie's words that spoke the truth about her generosity. Rachel furnished most of the money to build the Dow church and never told anyone of her largess: "Grandma Rachel did so much for people who needed help but never wanted it mentioned.

"A grand old lady!" Myrtie concluded. "I was proud to be a granddaughter, even though I was just an in-law!"

During the more than twenty years I worked on Rachel's story, these and other sources helped me to understand what kind of woman she was. They don't, however, explain why she left her family to find Dwight, her nineteen-year-old son, or what it was like to travel alone to dangerous places during the Rebellion's first year. To find out, more than one-hundred forty years later, I would need to walk in her footsteps.

So I did. What follows are excerpts from the journal I kept in spring and fall of 2004.

Saturday, April 10

IF I WERE A CROW and decided to fly south from my home
in southcentral Michigan, in about six miles I would be
winging over the farm that Rachel and Willis Barnum
hewed from the wilderness in the early 1840s. What did the
land look like then? What is it like now? Does it hold clues
to help me understand the challenges of pioneer travel, of
what it was like to plow ground behind a horse team?

Kerry Haynor is a neighbor and friend who lives on a
one-hundred-five-acre farm between my place and what
was Rachel's property. His grandfather broke ground and
homesteaded here in 1875. Surely the grandfather knew
Rachel van Houten Barnum Welch, his neighbor only three
miles away. Kerry maintains a grass landing strip and owns
a 1939 Aeronca Stick Chief. He has offered to take me on an
aerial tour of the neighborhood and beyond, including the
rutted trail—now a paved highway—that Rachel took on
her way to Battle Creek, Michigan, in the spring of 1862 to
catch the train to Chicago.

Haynor's preflight routine involves twanging the
plane's wires and cables to check for tightness. While he
pumps air into a soft tire, I wonder about the safety of this
pre-WWII aircraft, which resembles a Piper Cub and can
accommodate a pilot and one passenger who must share a
single seat and safety belt. Noting my interest in a patch of
duct tape on the left wing, Kerry mentions that it's there to
help hold a root seal in place.

"That's the gasket where the wing bolts to the airplane,
he explains. "The duct tape keeps it from flopping in the
wind. It's nothing to worry about."

Um, okay. Squeezing aboard, I observe the instrument
panel is as simple as a small plane's dashboard could be:

An altimeter, airspeed indicator, compass, and flip indicator are the only dials. The fuel gauge is a wire on a cork, perched atop the fuel tank in front of us. As long as the wire moves, the cork is floating in gasoline. If it stops moving, it's time to land. There is not enough space for a parachute. That's fine because I have no experience with, and zero interest in, skydiving.

"Put your left foot next to your right foot," my pilot advises, "and don't bump the throttle with your knee. That's the throttle. The kill switch is over there, in case the plane takes off."

Takes off?

Kerry reads the puzzle on my face. "I'll be outside," he smiles, "starting the engine."

And with that, my neighbor walks to the front of the Chief, raises his arms as though in supplication, grasps the wooden propeller, and yanks hard. On the second pull, the sixty-five horsepower engine catches, and the prop springs to life in a counterclockwise blur. Vibrating madly, the Chief threatens to move but doesn't. Ducking under the wing, Kerry presses himself into the seat and takes the safety belt I offer. While the motor warms, he checks the elevator and ailerons. Satisfied, he opens the throttle and taxies down the mown runway. A brief sprint and we are aloft.

Maximum speed on the Chief is only eighty-five, ideal for cruising. The single fixed wing attaches to the fuselage above the windows, which are made of Plexiglas. The window slides open, and I'm glad I brought my camera.

I have snapped pictures from small aircraft many times: a Super Cub in Alaska, a Bell Ranger helicopter in Labrador, Beaver and Otter bush planes elsewhere in Canada. I have photographed Great Lakes harbors, moose in Alaska, and musk ox and caribou in Canada's Far North. Like the novelist James Michener, I love the aerial exploration of landscapes, whether sculpted by glaciers or arranged in puzzle-like patterns by man. What could be more interesting than discovering local environs from five hundred feet? And what better time than early spring when naked trees allow one to see the oak-forest floor?

Soon we are flying over Rachel's old farm, and I see the Welch family cemetery where she, her children, and both husbands are buried. A drainage creek slicing through a lowland seep is a series of pretzel bends. Crisscrossing the seep and hardwoods are deer trails that look like wandering cow paths. When Kerry banks the Chief, the earth opens up to the camera. In my mind's eye, I imagine Rachel and her family planting corn, harvesting wheat, and collecting maple sap.

We follow Shaytown Road, which remains graveled to this day, south to Allegan Road and fly over Vermontville. An Amish farmer plowing behind his team of draft horses could have been John Welch long ago. Nude maples, their dark trunks in stark relief to pale-yellow detritus, declare that Vermontville, a village of seven hundred people, is aptly named.

Sheets of ice that advanced and then retreated thousands of years ago gave this region its gentle rolling nature. The glaciers were kind, leaving morainic ridges of sand and gravel that cut across the land in a southeasterly direction to create streams that flow into small lakes. The loam soils of Eaton County grow good crops. Barry County lies a mile to the west of Ionia Road, which we trace to Kalamo and Bellevue before banking southwest to Battle Creek. I imagine Rachel in her buckboard, holding the reins of her team, making torturously slow progress along a mud-drenched path.

Returning to the airstrip an hour later, Kerry's landing is flawless. He cuts the throttle, and we coast to the barn. "Let me pay you for some gas," I offer, as we pry ourselves from the cockpit.

"Why?" he asked. "We only burned three gallons of fuel. The tank holds twelve gallons."

"So, you have about four hours of flying time between fuel stops?"

"Four hours is all a person can take in this little plane," Kerry says and stretches his arms again.

Wednesday, October 13

I'VE ARRANGED FOR A BUGGY ride with an Amishman named John Miller, who will take me along the Ionia Trail (now Ionia Road) through Vermontville to Kalamo. I want to know what it is like to travel by horse and carriage although when Rachel Barnum came this way, the clip-clop of shod hooves on pavement would have sounded foreign to her.

It is a cool evening in the low forties and light rain is falling when John hitches Commanche, his twelve-year-old gelding, to the covered buggy and we start out south toward Kalamo, seven miles away. Although the season is wrong, I suspect the weather was about the same when Rachel left her farm and family in March, 1862.

With the horse pulling at a steady trot, we pass through Vermontville and its maple-lined streets ablaze with fall fire. Red, green, gold, and orange glow on this turn-down day of gray sky and fading light. John switches on his yellow flashing lights to warn motorists. I'm glad to have noticed a triangle safety sign on the buggy's rear.

John Miller is three months older than I am, and he, too,

has a beard. Typical of Amish men, he has no moustache. His beard is a half-ring of gray-white around a full face, which blushes a little, perhaps from high blood pressure or the cool air that shows our breath here in the coach.

Miller is dressed in insulated denim—faded blue pants and a newer jacket. I can't tell if his clothing fasteners are hook and eye or snaps and buttons. His black work boots feature eyelets and lacing studs. He wears brown jersey-cotton gloves and a black hat of felt. The Millers are traditional Amish folk. Mrs. Miller bakes pies and cookies in her work kitchen, inside a building unattached from their modest ranch-style home. She sells the baked goods on Saturdays, parking her rig at a corner service station a few miles from home.

Candidate signs in the yards we pass are a reminder that the presidential election is only a month away. "Do the Amish vote?" I ask my host.

"We see ourselves as pilgrims passing through this life," John explains. "We do not vote. We get down on our knees and ask God to give us the best candidate."

Conscientious objectors, the Amish refuse to serve in the military. In exchange for not enrolling in the Army during the Vietnam War, John worked for two years in a state mental hospital. "My brother didn't have that opportunity," he says, "and was sentenced to jail for three years. He served one year and was released on probation for the other two years." The judge who sentenced his brother told the prosecutor not to send him any more C.O. cases. "It's the only time in my career that I ever sentenced an innocent man," the judge is reported to have said. "I won't do it again."

Commanche plods along, walking up hills and trotting on the downslopes. The standard-size, dark-brown horse weighs about twelve hundred pounds and was culled as a trotter on the racing circuit. A soft-leather collar protects Commanche from injury. Hames go over the collar and accept the buggy's long wooden handles. Commanche wears blinders; Rachel's horses most likely never wore them as there was no traffic in 1862. Next are the bit and reins. Britchings are loose straps around the horse's thighs that keep the coach from running into the animal. A crupper strap goes under the tail.

Miller says Commanche pulls at seven or eight miles an hour and trots two or three times faster. Because Rachel was driving a wagon and had to contend with poor roads, her horses (or oxen, according to *Myrtie's Memories*) would have walked slowly. "I doubt if she could have gone more than fifteen miles in a day," John tells me.

In Vermontville, I note a building with 1862 written on it and wonder if it was here when Rachel passed through. In Kalamo, the United Methodist Church dates from 1868; however, the Lutheran cemetery boasts a sign that says 1812. I find this hard to believe. Was anyone here in 1812, a quarter century before Michigan attained statehood? There are more people dead than alive in present-day Kalamo.

We pass tranquil farms, Canada geese grazing in winter wheat fields, and maples and other hardwoods blazing in autumnal glory. Pokeweed, its blood-red stems and clusters of dark berries that resemble grape gobs, appears here and there in the ditches. John waves to most oncoming drivers and greets people by name as we pass them sitting on their porches or raking leaves.

He studies his rearview mirror for a long moment, and when a bicyclist pedals by, hollers out, "Hello, Nelson!" Nelson Yoder, about twenty, wearing suspenders and brown work pants, is hurrying to a basketball game. He rides his bicycle ten miles from home and somehow has the energy to play the game before pedaling home and milking the cows. When Rachel passed this way, James Naismith was a year old, the game of basketball would not be invented for another thirty years.

Miller and I talk about farming, house building, hunting, conservation, and religion. He tells a story of a non-believer named Jesse from Missouri. "I simply couldn't understand why he thought God didn't exist," John relates. "I was so surprised that I never asked him, and I'm sorry now that I didn't do my Christian duty to try to get him to change his mind. He died a few months after I met him. I feel guilty and regret it to this day."

I suggest that John probably did witness in his own way, and he thinks about that and says nothing.

At Kalamo, he turns Commanche around and we start back. Two miles north, we stop again for traffic on M-79. It is dark when we return to the Miller home, and I remember to retrieve the sack of cookies Mrs. Miller had offered when we rode out.

One never turns down a homemade Amish cookie.

Monday, October 18

FIVE DAYS AFTER THE HORSE-AND-BUGGY ride, I board Amtrak No. 351, *The Wolverine*, in Battle Creek on a cloudy morning of thirty-five degrees for the three and one-half hour run to Chicago. The train, inbound from Pontiac, leaves on time at 9:49. The fare of eighteen dollars is a bargain compared to the eight dollars and twenty-five cents that Rachel paid for the same trip.

Bob Conroy, a retired school teacher from Cairo, Illinois, has agreed to take me downriver in his boat to New Madrid, Missouri. A phone call to him brings news of good weather expected for tomorrow afternoon on the Mississippi. "The river is not too high," Bob reports, and it's not too cold. The rain we're getting now is supposed to stop, and there is no threat of driftwood and other debris on the river."

I hope to gain an appreciation for the obstacles Rachel had to overcome, only the war going on now is in Iraq, not an insurrection in America. As the Western focal point of the Civil War, by some accounts I will learn the city of Cairo in 1862 was busier than Washington, DC.

Today is one of those cold-to-the-bone mornings when heavy, wet air sucks up a train's whistle blasts as we pass through a landscape on fire. Maples blaze yellow and red from backyards in Kalamazoo and woodlots outside Niles. Along the tracks, crimson sumac rages. When Rachel came this way, she would have seen the green leaves of spring unfolding along with blooms of Dutchman's breeches, trilliums, marsh marigolds, and other wildflowers.

The industrial belt that begins at Michigan City, Indiana, is also the end of autumn beauty. Here, along the southern Lake Michigan shore, the leaves are a tired green from summer drought. At Porter, the sun pops briefly to reveal slick pavement from a morning rainstorm. Under the Gary smokestacks, loaded coal cars wait to be relieved of their burden. A burly railway official, bobbing with the swaying coach, strolls along the train's uncrowded aisle, making one think of a bowling pin about to fall over. His dark blue suit, black shoes, and white shirt suggest he is the conductor. The trainman's cap confirms it.

We enter the south terminal of Chicago's Union Station four minutes early. I spend an hour of the four-hour wait in the Great Hall Waiting Room, rebuilt, along with the rest of Union Station, in 1991. I wonder what the station looked like when Rachel was here. Likely smaller in size, it was also newer because the Illinois Central had begun operations only nine years earlier, in 1853.

Recalling a popular diner off Clinton Street within walking distance, I don my backpack, grab my laptop computer case, and head out into the brisk wind of downtown Chicago. I would have left my luggage in a rental locker except authorities removed them after 9/11, three years ago. It is forty-seven degrees this afternoon. Thinking of my sweater, bulging the backpack like a dromedary's hump, I secure the top button of my field jacket and press on to 565 W. Jackson Street, home of Lou Mitchell's Restaurant.

Known around the world, the diner has served U.S. presidents, actors, sporting heroes, and other luminaries. It's located at the beginning of Old Route 66 in the city's West Loop. "A Chicago Institution," the sign says. "Open Monday-Friday 5:00 a.m. to 3:00 p.m." A matronly hostess offers each patron a donut hole. Ladies also receive a small box of Milk Duds, a time-honored tradition dating from 1958. I order a bowl of bean soup and a chicken-salad sandwich, and both are excellent. "Tell the cook," I mention to the waitress.

"Tell him yourself," she replies, pointing with a pencil withdrawn from her apron. "He's right there."

And so I do. The cook, a small, thick Black man wearing a baseball cap, appreciates the compliment. "My job depends on it," he smiles through flashing teeth, one of which is gold.

The wind has increased its bluster and building shadows have lengthened on my stroll back to Union Station. I wonder if the homeless people I see this afternoon—a young man huddled under a dirty blanket, a toothless old man holding up an "I'm hungry" sign of corrugated cardboard—are descendants of the scary old bums and winos that surely were here when Rachel passed through Chicago. Did that generous, faithful woman offer alms to the chronically poor in this City of the Big Shoulders? Should I?

Back at the station, I board Train No. 391, *The Illini*, for the five-hour run to Carbondale. In Rachel's day, the Illinois Central ended at Cairo. Ironically, it was easier for her to get to the riverboat town of Cairo than it is for me in this era of the cell phone internet. I must wait at the Carbondale Greyhound station for five hours, from ten o'clock at night until three in the morning. The bus will then whisk me twenty miles east to Marion where I'll wait another three hours for the transfer to Cairo—nearly ten hours to travel eighty miles in total. On the other hand, given the recent termination of several hundred Greyhound stations in small towns across America, I am lucky to secure public transportation at all.

On the train to Carbondale, the fellow across the aisle, a man in his early thirties, is a nonstop talker. His target, fortunately, is not I, but the young black man, in maroon sweat pants and parka, sitting next to him. I could have made the same mistake by choosing a seat next to this boor. His voice is the resonating type that permeates earplugs. He talks about nothing and everything in a verbal pummeling of his seatmate, trapped there in the upholstery, unable to escape. Indifference and ignoring on the part of the young man seem to spur the loudmouth on to more claptrap about his apartment, his job, his opinions, and his experiences. "Really," the young man keeps repeating until succumbing to "Uh-huhs" and, finally, silent stares.

The drone of the bore is so overwhelming that I leave for a long visit to the dining car to see what's on the menu.

Upon returning I say nothing for fear of diverting his attention to me.

We roll through Homewood, population of about twenty thousand, and by the time we reach Kankakee, a city with thirty thousand people, night is falling hard. For three hundred thirty-two miles we parallel Hwy. 57, which also cuts across the black earth of the Great Illinois Prairie. The Carbondale coach is half full; the Champaign car, which I pass through enroute to the dining car, is one-quarter full.

A driving rain sheets along the windows and pours into the brief space between cars. In the instant required for the door in the next coach to open, I absorb a mild shower while standing there, waiting. When I return to my seat, the bore is reading a book; the young man in maroon sweats next to him is either sleeping or feigning sleep. It doesn't matter. The bore has succeeded in talking him to death.

"Which way to the restroom, sir," the man asks, peering over his book and sizing me up. Shrugging, I shake my head and say nothing.

Several times the train slows to enter a siding and then shudders to a halt while freight trains whoosh by. Federal rules mandate that freight trains have priority over passenger trains. The delays put us behind by twenty minutes when we enter Carbondale at 9:55. The Amtrak station here is small with enough plastic scoop seats for perhaps two dozen people. Behind a gated window sits a clerk, an older woman who is not happy to see the score of us disembark. The first sign I read is a warning: "We have no information about Greyhound. Please don't ask." When I made my Amtrak reservation earlier on the phone, I inquired about the bus station location. I look across the street and, sure enough, there's the familiar red-and-blue sign with the white greyhound. The sign appears above the entrance to a small courtyard leading to a darkened business of some kind. Freak's Place Tattoos anchors one side of the courtyard. A submarine sandwich shop is on the other.

The entrance is locked. I walk around the block, past an unnamed bar with a Stroh's Beer sign over the door and the loud "chock" of struck pool balls coming through the open door. On the back street is another parlor, Hard Times Tattoos. Completing the walk-around, I pass the Varsity Theater with its blank marquee and recross Illinois Street. The Amtrak station is already empty, except for the scowling woman behind the security counter. Signage indicates the station is open until 4:20 a.m.

That is nearly five hours from now. I decide to sleep awhile at Motel 6, which a phone call assures has rooms available and is less than a mile away. I call Yellow Cab and am told that a taxi will pick me up soon. While standing outside I watch two empty cabs streak by.

Realizing no one wants to pick up a three-dollar fare, I begin walking on deserted streets to the motel. A block from the train station, I pass the Yellow Cab Company dispatcher, seated at a desk behind a lighted window, and wave to him. He smiles and waves back, knowing I'm the guy who made the call. It's not his fault if the cabbies don't want to bother with a cheap fare.

A little farther, I notice a young couple walking out of a building that could be a nightclub. Holding hands, they stop for an embrace and kiss and then head for opposite sides of an aging black Chevy S-10. "Want to make a quick five bucks and take me down to the motel?" I wonder aloud.

"Sure, why not?" the young man answers. His girlfriend looks at me, then at him, and back to me. It's okay, she seems to signal.

They are Corey and Erin, both in their early twenties.

Erin pushes aside a small mountain of clothes, a case of empty soda bottles, a battered Coleman lantern, and other articles to one side of the back seat. I replace the stack with my own stuff and squeeze past the torn fabric of the passenger seat, which Erin holds forward. The ride is short, and I secure my thirty-three-dollar room by shoving a credit card under the thick security glass of the after-hours window.

The attendant, a young Indian man with a bright smile, agrees to awaken me at two o'clock. Roused on schedule, I shower, shoulder the pack, and walk back to the station. It has rained while I slept; I hope distant lightning flashes are from the retreating storm, not from an advancing one. "Poured like hell," reports the attendant at the Shell station on Walnut Street, where I stop for coffee. The station is just up from Walgreens, across from the Army/Navy recruiting station. "A funnel was reported seen at Murphysboro," he adds. Murphysboro, a town of about ten thousand people, is ten miles northwest of Carbondale.

Outside, street lights resemble opaque yellow moons in the pools of rainwater. The Amtrak station parking lot is flooded. But the trains will run. I can hear the throb of diesel engines before crossing the tracks of what many still call—and the stenciled sign insists—the Illinois Central Railroad.

Arriving fifteen minutes early, I wait outside in the warm night air. If it was springtime, I might hear tree frogs singing. Rachel did not hear frogs singing, at least not here, because I doubt she left the train with such a short run remaining to Cairo. The only sign of life is a woman sitting on the station steps out of the streetlight glare, her head between her knees. She senses my presence, stirs awake, and asks if she can buy a cigarette, for a quarter. "Sorry, ma'am. I quit when they went to forty-five cents a pack."

Later, she informs me I can go to Los Angeles for a hundred sixty bucks on the train. "That's a bargain," she says.

"You going to L.A.?" I inquire.

"I don't know. I'm thinking about it."

People wander into the station: an old man with a suitcase, a blind man hanging onto the harness of a yellow Labrador retriever, a young man with a duffle bag, and a middle-aged couple. Exactly on time, my bus swings around a corner, tires hissing on the wet pavement. The rubber-hinged doors part and I hear the driver yell "Break stop!" before he emerges. Seven or eight people follow him out the door; several light cigarettes, and the others, most toting luggage, wander into the Amtrak station.

The driver, a powerful-looking Black man of about forty-five, wears leather gloves without fingers. "You're just going to Marion," he announces in a polite voice while perusing my ticket. "I'll put my things under here in the luggage bin. You can carry your stuff aboard and ride in the seat behind me."

A passenger, hands in pockets, mumbles something to the driver. The passenger appears to be a young man of twenty or twenty-five, but I can't see his face in the dark. "I told you, you can't sit behind me," the driver says, wagging a finger. His voice has switched to one of authority, like that of a no-nonsense P.E. instructor barking orders to his students. "You have to do what I tell you." Perturbed, the young man grinds out his cigarette under a tennis shoe and climbs onto the bus. When I enter, I notice the seat behind the driver is empty. Otherwise, the darkened bus appears to be full of slumped-over sleepers.

As we pull away, the *City of New Orleans*, Amtrak train No. 59, is just entering the station. Marion is asleep when we arrive twenty-five minutes later. As I'm getting off, someone stands up to follow. "This ain't no break stop," the driver announces in a loud voice. "Sit down!"

"Can't I have a smoke?" The voice belongs to the young man who wanted my seat.

"You get off this bus, you ain't getting back on," the driver warns. He watches the young man through the rearview mirror. Satisfied, he nods to me, closes the door, and drives off into the night.

Marion, Illinois. The town is dead at 3:30 this morning. The bus station is a lighted sign next to Marion Cab Company. The "station" is a bolt-secured park bench atop two cement steps and is sandwiched between vending machines for Royal Crown Cola and 7 Up. I sit with my back to the window of the squat, cement-block building, headquarters of the cab company. Three feet on the other side of the glass is a bored blond woman, leaning back in her chair, filing her nails. Looking up at me, she does not smile and seems tired. Cigarette smoke curls from a plastic ashtray; a Pepsi can roosts precariously close to the edge of her desk. If she was chewing gum, she would be the quintessential overpaid and underworked secretary bored to tears.

She and I are the only people alive, and we might as well be a continent apart. It's okay. Unable to hear the television flickering before her, I appreciate the silence. Someone pulls up to the Family Video store across the street and drops off a tape. An American flag next to the store begins to flutter about the same time I feel a chill. I pull my sweater from the backpack, slip it on, and button the jacket over it. A while later, still shivering, I secure my belongings under the park bench and walk into Marion's historic-town district.

The former train depot is now home to the Marion Lions Club. I walk past the Harvest Kingdom Worship Center to Tower Square in the city center where the United Way thermometer stands at 40 percent on its march to a record goal of $240,000. Marion seems to host too many banks and financial institutions, if you count the pawn shop, and not enough restaurants. In fact, there are no restaurants, no cafes, no diners, and no coffee shops, at least in this part of town. A venerable Methodist church and a newer Baptist church are dimly lit. Nothing stirs, although I fancy the sun-faded deer heads in the basement barbershop across from the police station follow my progress.

Back at my park-bench post, I wait for something to happen during the two hours left before the 6:25 transfer. Suddenly, the phone rings behind me, and I hear the muted voice of the blond dispatcher. Turning around, I notice a blanket move on a couch along the far wall. Business, at last! Roused from sleep, the driver rubs eyes, laces tennis shoes, slips on a jacket, and wanders out the door. He doesn't see me sitting there less than ten feet away. The engine of his Buick Century, the color of a faded plum, turns and catches and he flies off into the dark.

Slowly, the town comes to life. A stray cat tiptoes from the shadows, lingers a moment, and then does double-time across the street. Two more patrons drop off videos. The Wonder Bread truck glides past. A police cruiser follows and then a garbage truck. A crease of daylight in the east brings a shift change at the cab company. The driver I saw earlier greets his replacement. "How'd it go?" the new man wonders.

"Yeah. Made a dollar."

I am aware of one claim to fame for Marion, Illinois. The federal penitentiary, which opened here in 1963, housed Leonard Peletier, the Native American who, along with Albert Garza, launched a forty-two-day hunger strike in 1984 to protest prison conditions and prisoner treatment. I don't remember the outcome.

My bus finally arrives, again on time, and I board for the final leg to Cairo an hour away. I'm beginning to understand the slow pace of travel, something of great concern to Rachel who raced against time. But the cost is cheap: twenty-two and a half dollars for the two tickets on Greyhound. Rachel paid almost that much for the pair of train tickets that brought her from Battle Creek to Cairo.

Tuesday, October 19

Mickey Blackburn, executive secretary of the Cairo Chamber of Commerce, is waiting for me at the bus station, which doubles as the town's sole gas station. I know it is Mickey because the license plate on her black Mercury Marquis says MICKEY 59. Her husband, whom I will meet later today, is 75 and has worked two years for the chamber, which dates from the Rebellion's end in 1865. A pleasant woman with short-cropped, silvery hair, Mickey whisks me off to breakfast at Nonny's Diner. There, we meet George Pomeroy, who works for the Army Corps of Engineers. George wears a baseball cap that says "Bass Maintenance Corp. General Contractor." He thinks the distance from Cairo to New Madrid is about thirty miles but will check and get back to us.

Cairo is a shadow of its former self. After WWII, the city boasted a population of more than eighteen thousand. Racial strife in the 1960s sent many people elsewhere, and the same economic problems that subsequently battered the industrialized Midwest sent shock waves here. In the year 2000, the population was forty-eight hundred; today, four years later, it has slid to thirty-two hundred. Bunge Corporation is the key employer with one hundred twenty-five workers processing soybeans to make meal and extract oil. Gutterman Chrysler, Plymouth, Dodge & Jeep is the sole auto dealer.

"We're mostly service workers now," Mickey explains. "People earn a living working in community health, at the nursing home, and for the city."

Opinions on the distance from Cairo to New Madrid range from nine miles to sixty-two miles. Pomeroy, a tall, thin man with a deep southern accent, informs us the mile marker at Cairo is 963. It is 895 at New Madrid. Therefore, the distance is sixty-eight miles. That sounds right because references from the Civil War peg the distance at sixty miles or so.

George explains that Cairo is a delta surrounded by levees to keep out rising waters from both the Ohio and Mississippi rivers. The last serious flood occurred in 1937 when women and children were bused out of town. That year Mound City, just upriver on the Ohio, was flooded. "Our problems come when both rivers are high," George says. "Then we get sinkholes from the seeping process." Flooding in the spring of 1862, according to newspaper accounts at the time, was as severe and possibly worse.

After breakfast, Mickey takes me to the Mound City National Cemetery, which lies in the Y between Mounds and Mound City, small towns a few miles north of Cairo. The cemetery was dedicated in 1864. Contained within are exhumed graves from casualties at the Battle of Shiloh, April 6 and 7, 1862, and other clashes, perhaps including those at New Madrid and Island No. 10. A total of 2,637 soldiers and sailors from all northern states who "lost their lives in defence (sic) of their country" are buried here, along with a few Confederate soldiers. Their names are enshrined on a huge monument in the cemetery center. Of the many epithets at the heads of several rows, one I scribble into my notebook:

> *On Fame's eternal camping-ground,*
> *Their silent tents are spread,*
> *And Glory guards with solemn round,*
> *The bivouac of the dead.*

Mound City is a beautiful cemetery, reminding me of an earlier visit to St. Laurent with its white crosses in Normandy. Simple white tombstones at Mound City mark the fallen, many of whom are unknown soldiers. Magnolias line the highway leading to the cemetery, and surrounding fields hold acres of soybeans awaiting harvest.

Back in Cairo, Mickey shows me the Historic District, a neighborhood of cobblestone streets, magnolias, ginkgoes with their fan-shaped leaves, and towering old homes called Magnolia Manor and Riverlore. At the old Customs House, now serving as a museum, I meet Russell Ogg, a local historian and volunteer. About seventy-five, Russell is friendly and knowledgeable. He tells me he retired from three jobs: a grain buyer for a big corporation, a postmaster, and a supervisor of weights and measures for the Illinois Department of Agriculture. I wonder but don't ask which job caused the loss of two fingers on Russell's left hand. His wife Louise is the museum curator.

Ogg tells me that during the Civil War, all boats had to stop at the confluence of the rivers to be inspected for contraband. At the war's outbreak, the U.S. Army controlled this "key to the West." Later, the Navy took over.

The museum, with its three stories of artifacts and exhibits, is a fascinating place. I see a 1/32 scale model of the

USS Cairo, the sole ironclad of Commodore Andrew Foote's fleet not to see action during the siege of Island No. 10. The black, turtle-shaped, 13-gun ironclads rode low in the water and carried incredible firepower for those days: two guns aft, four to each side, and three on the prow. The rear guns were unprotected—the rest of the boat was wrapped in iron plating that could withstand heavy bombardment.

Russell shows me Gen. Grant's desk and his actual eating utensils—a small fork, a spoon, and a skewer for stabbing meat. At first glance, they appear to be made of plastic but are bone that is somewhat transparent. The tools fold together, remindful of a crude Swiss Army knife. It's amazing to look at these artifacts and to know the famous general lived in Cairo for several months. I wonder if Rachel met him, or at least saw him, unlikely because he had already taken his troops to Tennessee by the time Rachel arrived here.

An 1860 Cairo map shows Levee Street on the Ohio River. The Illinois Central came down from the northeast between this street and Commercial Avenue. Wharf boats tied up on the Ohio River between Fourth and Seventh streets. Vessels leaving Cairo for the south, therefore, had to go downriver around the point where the Mississippi enters. The Ohio was blue and clear; the Mississippi was turbid and muddy. Maps and photos show the wharves and the Delta and St. Charles hotels, the latter of which was a major player because the Illinois Central terminated on its north end. The New York Central and the Mobile & Ohio also ended at this hotel on the west side, and packets tied up here, too. Because most commercial trade passed through the St. Charles, it was a beehive of activity during the Civil War.

On the second floor, Russell shows me a packet boat journal dating from the spring of 1864. I must decide on a boat that Rachel could have hired for those final miles to New Madrid. We consider several from the hundreds of possibilities. The key question is whether the craft saw service in the spring of 1862. Wooden packets had notoriously short lives due to fires, ice jams, and river snags. Later, while perusing a copy of *Way's Packet Directory* at the Cairo Public Library, I discard all candidates except one: the *Arago*. Ogg photocopies the sternwheeler's statistics, which I will include in my yet-unnamed novel.

More good news: According to *Island No. 10: Struggle for the Mississippi Valley*, by Larry J. Daniel and Lynn N. Bock, the *Arago* delivered nineteen hundred artillery shells to the Federal fleet under Commodore Foote, who had laid siege to Island No. 10. This delivery occurred in March or April of 1862, proof that the packet was in service. Apparently, the U.S. Navy had contracted the vessel's services. I now have the name of an authentic packet and evidence that Rachel could have been a passenger.

The question is, When? Major General John's Pope's army drove the Rebels from New Madrid on March 14. The next step was to overtake the island and destroy the enemy's artillery batteries there and along the Tennessee shore through the New Madrid Bend, a huge S curve upriver from the town. Pope could then march south to Tiptonville on his way to bolster Grant's army.

But Pope needed the protection from Foote's gunboat fleet, anchored upriver from Island No. 10. The problem, which became a three-week-long standoff between the Army and Navy, was Foote's refusal to risk his valuable ironclads to an all-out assault, or to run the gantlet, even in the cloak of night, past the heavily armed island.

This first siege of the Civil War thus began during the fight for New Madrid and ended with the surrender of Island No. 10 in the early morning of April 8. Because Dwight died on April 13 or 14, Rachel had a narrow window of five or six days to find passage to New Madrid from Cairo, locate her son, and do what she could for him before he passed. That scenario, of course, assumes that he was still alive whenever she reached him.

According to his official military records, Dwight was present for Company B Muster Roll in January and February, 1862. The Roll for March and April (apparently the troops were paid every other month) includes this remark: "Died at New Madrid April 13, 1862." Four other references, however, indicate death occurred on April 14.

In the Company Descriptive Book, Dwight is listed as 19 years old, about 5 feet 10 inches with a light complexion, blue eyes, and sorrel-colored hair. Born in Eaton County Michigan, his occupation was farmer. He enlisted in the Army on September 9, 1861, in Sunfield, and was mustered into service on October 2 in Grand Rapids by Capt. Henry R. Mizner for a period of three years. The Casualty Sheet lists death as caused by "Fever, April 14/62." It was certified by Lt. M. J. Dickenson.

Those are the known facts.

Assuming Rachel knew of Dwight's illness and tried to come to his rescue, she could not have passed Island No. 10 until April 8, at the earliest. Did she wait in Cairo, for news that the island was safely in Union hands? And then, did she journey downriver to see her son in the regimental hospital (a field medical tent) before he died?

Or did Rachel learn of Dwight's passing and then, through letter and telegram, ask that his body be held for her to take possession? Did Union authorities ship the body by rail, wagon, and boat to Cairo for Rachel to accept responsibility for it there?

Either way, was his body embalmed? According to author Lynn Bock, sick or injured officers were placed in homes turned into hospitals, and regular recruits were consigned to field tents. Only officers were routinely embalmed. On the other hand, given the light Union casualties in the New Madrid/Island No. 10 campaign, it is reasonable to assume that an Army surgeon or professional undertaker could have embalmed the body, especially if Dwight's commanding officer requested it after being petitioned, in person, by his mother. How else could she return home over several days without the body spoiling?

It is also likely that Rachel knew 2nd Lt. Matthew Dickenson, who grew up in Vermontville, Michigan, about five miles from her farm.

Following in Rachel's footsteps helped to answer such niggling questions and to shape the kind of narrative I wanted to write. I considered both a documentary and a novel and settled on the modern genre known as biographical fiction or "biofic." The story would unfold within the realm of what really happened and what could have happened.

For lunch at Shemwell's Bar-Be-Que, I order a shredded pork sandwich for three dollars and coleslaw for thirty cents more. Eyeing the pie choices, I choose pecan over coconut. Shemwell's dark-paneled walls and Naugahyde booth seats, scattered tables and chairs, and lunch counter are reminiscent of a 1950s diner. A sign on the wall behind the cash register warns that a half-dozen patrons are not to be trusted and must pay with cash. It's not easy for a café in small-town America to be profitable.

The sun finally appears on this day that promises to reach the high seventies. Fans turn lazily in the restaurant. I eat from a Styrofoam plate and bowl and ask for a knife and fork. In the tiny public restroom, I must bend over to see myself in the small mirror on the linen-roll dispenser. Returning to my seat, I bump my head on the low-hanging door frame. A lack of competition means that Cairo eateries don't have to impress beyond a basic standard. But the food is good, one of the two waitresses smiles a lot, and the prices are attractive to local patrons and visitors alike.

I am ready to meet Bob Conroy for the trip downriver. A physical education teacher and coach, Conroy, age sixty, retired ten years earlier. We meet at the Chamber of Commerce office on Eighth Street, next to the vacant Gem Theater and across from a boarded-up building and the Elks Club. On the five-block walk from Shemwell's to the boat launch, I pass The Hewer, a statue of a Greeklike god striking something with a hand tool, a 1906 tribute to steamboat Capt. William P. Halliday, the former mayor of Cairo and original owner of the St. Charles Hotel.

The mystery of the river distance is now solved. Bob Conroy has confirmed it with three experts: a riverboat captain, an official with the American Federation Barge Line, and a dispatcher for Cairo Waterfront Services. All agree the distance is sixty-two miles. Cruising along, our trip takes three hours, including engine-idle time to accommodate waves created by barges and to talk with catfish anglers.

Don Turner, a friend of Conroy, has agreed to drive the boat trailer to New Madrid so Bob won't have to run his seventeen-foot Rinker back upriver. Joining us for the journey is David Barkett, owner of a local funeral home and the coroner for Alexander County. David, in his early fifties, is a history buff. "Illinois is a northern state in southern territory," he tells me. "Did you know Cairo is below Mason-Dixon?" Another interesting fact to consider for my novel.

Kentucky Bridge, which links Illinois to Kentucky, is the first bridge we encounter, followed by Missouri Bridge. A railroad span, linking Illinois to Kentucky, lies a mile upstream from Cairo on the Ohio River. None of these bridges, all of which can be seen at the same time, was here in 1862. According to the National Historical Railway Association, the bridge for trains was built in 1889.

Except for the occasional fleet of barges, the river looks like it did when Rachel was here. There are no power lines, no bridges, no development, no Coast Guard vessels, and no evidence of the Army Corps of Engineers. A small auto ferry connects Hickman, Kentucky, with Dorena, Missouri. The Missouri shore is wild and barren, except for an occasional boat ramp high and dry above the water. The Kentucky side hosts the communities of Belmont and Hickman, both of which are barely discernible from the river. Besides the barges, the difference from Civil War days is the buoys that mark the twisting channel. My host and pilot steers to the right of red buoys and to the left of green ones.

The current is five to seven mph, just like it was in Rachel's time. The current creates huge sandbars in places that change the river's shape. Island No. 10, which was a mile long and several hundred yards wide, disappeared around 1900. The Mississippi, both today and then, ranges in width from one-half mile to one mile. The flat-calm current, gurgling around the buoys and swirling here and there, has the same nuances as it did a hundred and forty years ago. Conroy, an avid boater, says the river is ideal for water-skiing.

It is a peaceful, pleasant afternoon with temperatures crowding eighty degrees and a sunny sky that sends shafts of light through fleecy clouds. David wears shorts; Bob has donned a polo shirt, boating slacks, and sandals. Monarch butterflies drift their way southwest from Kentucky to Missouri, flaring orange when washing up and over the boat windshield.

The enormous barge fleets create such powerful wakes that we must slow down or be slapped silly by the waves. A single tugboat pushes up to twenty-four lashed barges—four vessels wide and six vessels long. The shallow transports, each appearing to be one hundred to two hundred feet long, are heaped with coal or sealed with fuel and chemicals. One is hauling pulp logs for the Mead-Westvaco mill at Wickliffe, Kentucky. By the time we enter the New Madrid Bend, we have encountered three barge fleets upbound and one downbound.

We pause to talk to a pair of commercial fishermen working trap nets in the shallows near the ferry line. They pull a pair of twenty-pound catfish from their livewell. One is a blue catfish, the other a channel cat. "We really want to catch flathead catfish," one of the fishermen who wears chest waders, tells us. "They're bigger, you know."

At four o'clock we pull into the boat launch site at New Madrid where Don Turner is already backed up and ready to load the Rinker. The gas gauge is below one-quarter full. We have burned perhaps a dozen gallons of the fifteen gallons the tank holds. Turner says the road trip from Cairo was forty-eight miles.

From the boat launch, I call Margaret Palmer, executive secretary of the New Madrid Area Chamber of Commerce. By the time Margaret arrives, Bob and his friends have the boat loaded, and we shake hands all around. He refuses any money for gas for either his boat or pickup. "Pass it on to someone in need," he says. "Besides, I enjoyed this little adventure. If you weren't here, I probably never would have gone this far downriver."

Margaret informs me the area experienced eleven tornadoes during last night's storm. A twister in Cooter, Missouri killed three people. "Where is Cooter?" I wonder.

"I don't know," Margaret admits. "Somewhere south of us, I think. The whole region is a target for tornadoes."

In her white sedan, Margaret gives me a quick tour of the town of thirty-three hundred people. Key employers are Miranda Aluminum with eleven hundred workers, Associated Electric, a coal-fired power plant with two-hundred fifty employees, a milling company called Riceland with eighty people; and Contact Industries, a building contractor for telecommunications. I note an idled sawmill, which Margaret explains closed in April. "But the town seems to be growing," she says. New Madrid is the New Madrid County seat for the nineteen thousand people who live here. In 1860, the population was fifty-six hundred. By 1870, it had grown to sixty-six hundred.

I am exhausted from thirty-six hours on the road with little sleep. Margaret drives me to Marston, a crossroads on I-55 about eight miles away, where I have a reservation at the Super 8 Motel. I walk a quarter-mile over the bustling Interstate to Jerry's Café, a hole-in-the-wall eatery connected to a gas station/party store. At Jerry's, I order fried pork chops for five dollars and ninety-nine cents. They are good, even though the mashed potatoes started life as flakes in a box, and the green beans and corn are from a can. In bed at the motel, I replay the incidents of the past two days, and, somewhere between Marion and Cairo, Illinois, fall into a sound sleep.

Wednesday, October 20

MARGARET PALMER PICKS ME UP this morning at 9:30. Our first stop is the New Madrid Museum where curator Harriet Porter proves to be a wealth of information. In addition to files containing soldiers' letters and diaries, the museum houses local Civil War artifacts and memorabilia. For instance, I study an accountant's ledger stipulating CSA payments to locals for services rendered that include blacksmithing, building of wagons, and selling of horses. A Mr. J.H. Howard was paid $327.73 for coffins and lumber delivered to the secessionist government on January 10, 1862. I wonder who went into those coffins and where were they buried? Did Dwight Barnum end up in one of them?

Another paper trail refers to Confederate soldiers being disinterred after the war and reburied elsewhere. There are no cemeteries in the New Madrid area although there are a few graves, the tombstones unreadable, near the old Bloomfield home a couple of miles from town. The home served as a hospital for officers, because most residences in the town proper were burned or destroyed by the Rebels or from Union shelling.

From a letter by G. Wellington, an Indiana infantryman, written home on March 25, 1862: "The small pox is raging here for 8 men died yesterday and there is some that died every day."

Did Dwight die from smallpox fever? Other causes could have been dysentery, typhoid or cholera, mumps, or measles. These latter two diseases were running rampant through the Rebel camps at this time. Most soldiers who fought here on either side had not been vaccinated and were exposed to the elements that—in the winter of 1861-62—included snow, sleet, rain, lots of mud, and cold temperatures. Being crowded in tents, taking forced marches over long distance, and eating irregular diets lacking in both quantity and quality could take a toll on the body of a healthy young man.

I learn that Maj. Gen. John Pope was born in Louisville, Kentucky, on March 16, 1822, making him six months older than Rachel. I wonder if she met him and what such an exchange would have entailed.

From the museum, Margaret and I wander to the nearby observation deck that offers a clear view of the Mississippi for four miles both upstream and downstream. Across the river is Tennessee. An interpretive exhibit explains the battles for New Madrid and Island No. 10.

Our next stop is the Hunter-Dawson Historical Site to meet Mike Comer, site administrator for the Missouri Department of Natural Resources. Comer, a professorial-looking man in his early forties, sports a trim beard and mustache. His office is in a trailer next to a small parking lot across from the Hunter-Dawson home. According to Comer, who has excellent historical knowledge of local military matters, Pope used the mansion for his headquarters. "Bodies were often sent home early in the War," Comer explains, "and it seems feasible that Dwight might have died from smallpox."

He says during the Rebellion's first year there was considerable freedom of movement between the lines, and armies were not on the move like they were later. Casualties, including those in this area, were light, but Shiloh changed all that. "After Shiloh," he says, "people on both sides came to know the War as a killing machine."

For lunch, Margaret and I weigh the options at two family restaurants: Johnson's, which serves a buffet, or The Grill. Assured The Grill might have a little more atmosphere, we go there, and I order the daily special—meatloaf, purple-hull peas, mashed potatoes, cornbread. For dessert, there is coconut cream pie, peanut butter pie, and lemonade pie. We share one of each, and they are delicious.

Then it's off to the New Madrid library where I meet Martha Hunter and Jerrie Ruth Palmer. The librarians are most helpful in my quest for accuracy and detail. Martha tells me her husband's aunt owned the Bloomfield home, which burned about fifteen years ago. Martha remembers seeing the carved names of soldiers on the windowsills while they recuperated in upstairs bedrooms on blood-stained cots.

Jerrie Ruth shares a book containing a photograph of a Civil War doctor embalming a man covered in a sheet and lying on a wooden door resting on two barrels in front of a tent. Another photo shows an embalming tent with a sign over it: "Embalming the Dead. Free from odor and infection. Dr. Bunnell."

I can now deduce that Dwight's body could have been embalmed. As mentioned, few soldiers were buried in the New Madrid vicinity because there were few deaths from the fighting and the low, swampy ground was not conducive for burial. There is a reference in the book by Lynn Bock and Larry Daniel to gravediggers (other soldiers) having to stand on coffins and cover them with mud to keep the caskets from floating away, a grisly reminder that jeopardized morale of the living troops.

For a day-by-day account of the weather in the spring of 1862, I make photocopies of *My Diary by Ed Farley, Civil War Fighting Man*. I also gain information from Jeffery Karl Smart's master's degree thesis—*The Key to the Mississippi Valley: The Island Number Ten Campaign Feb-March 1862*. Authors Bock and Daniel relied heavily on this source.

Our final stop is at the law office of Lynn N. Bock. Unfortunately, he has just left for the day. Luckily, he agrees to return. During my interview, Lynn shares the kinds of details that can make a historical novel compelling. One suggestion is that the Cape Giradeau newspaper may have packet boat schedules from 1862. Another tidbit is that the Federals operated a telegraph road from New Madrid to Charleston, Missouri, across the river from Cairo. Messages were then hand-carried across the river to Grant's headquarters. Because officers had access to the wire, it is not inconceivable that Dwight's commanding officer, knowing of his mother's concern for him, might have convinced an operator to punch through a message to her. The message would have told her that Dwight was ill with a fever or that he had died.

Soldiers' bodies were often hauled to Mound City to the new national cemetery for burial. Did Rachel wait in Cairo for Dwight's body to be delivered from New Madrid?

Hospitals were still-standing homes on the outskirts of New Madrid, away from the shelling. Besides the Bloomfield home, a hospital on the western flank, near where the 2nd Michigan Cavalry was located during the New Madrid fighting, was set up at the Newsome-Phillips farm. Dwight likely was admitted to a regimental hospital tent there and perhaps to the house itself.

Union soldiers enjoyed excellent communication to and from home. Although letters might take weeks to travel, the big-city newspapers arrived daily, and letters from home seemed to find their recipients even when the men were on the march and fighting battles in new locations. Perhaps mother and son communicated through letters.

Rachel could have crossed the river at Cairo and gone to Charleston, Missouri. From Charleston a railroad ran to Buffington, near present-day Sikeston, about twenty miles north of New Madrid. Rachel then could have taken the King's Highway to New Madrid. However, the railroad was in disrepair from Union troopers removing ties and tearing up the tracks. Also, the road would have been in poor condition due to bad weather, flooding, and the land march of Pope's huge army with its artillery and supply wagons.

My notebook pages fill rapidly while listening to Lynn Bock discuss these and other possible outcomes.

That night I eat an Arby's salad in my motel room at the Super 8. The parts of the puzzle are coming together at last. Based on what I know thus far, I may construct the novel in this manner:

Rachel receives a telegram from Dwight's commanding officer in late March of 1862. The message is that Dwight is seriously ill and might not live. In her reply, Rachel says she will board the first available train and requests passage through war zone lines to be with her son.

Three days are needed to drive her wagon and team of horses thirty-plus miles from Rachel's farm to Battle Creek. She spends a night near Kalamo at a hotel or at the home of a farm family along the Ionia Trail. She stays the next night in a Bellevue hotel. On Day Three she puts up her team at a Battle Creek livery and boards the Michigan Central to Chicago. The next day she buys a ticket on the Illinois Central and arrives in Cairo. I now have the timetables and fares for both trains.

Advised that passage is not possible via the river due to the Confederates' fortified position on Island No. 10, she weighs the possibility of crossing the flooded river and going to New Madrid by way of Charleston to Buffington. Told that the road is impassable and that all wagons and horses have been pressed into Union service, she waits in Cairo for news of Island No. 10's fall. While trapped in Cairo, fearing she will never see her son again, she hears and reads news of the bloody fighting at Shiloh April 6 and 7.

During the early morning of April 8, Rebels surrender

the island, freeing Rachel to travel downriver. The *Arago* is carrying munitions and supplies for Commodore Foote's gunboat fleet, and Rachel secures passage on this packet. She reaches Dwight that evening and cares for him until he passes five or six days later. Rachel then arranges for her son's body to be embalmed before taking it on the long journey home. She arrives home after an absence of three weeks and buries Dwight on Sunday, April 20.

Thursday, October 21

IT IS NOW TIME TO go home myself. I awaken at 3:30 a.m., shower, pack, and walk over to Arby's—past the diesel long-haulers with their grumbling engines belching blue smoke—and pick up an extra-large coffee and turkey wrap. Back at the motel, the Bootheel Area Rapid Transit (BART) van picks me up at 4:15. Steve, the driver, and I make small talk on our way to Sikeston to pick up another fare.

Steve looks to be in his sixties. After thirty years with Proctor & Gamble where he worked as a packaging expert, he retired four years ago to work part-time for BART. At Sikeston, we pick up Pat, an older woman who is flying to North Carolina from the St. Louis airport. I'm surprised Steve can find her home on a darkened cul-de-sac in a nondescript neighborhood. At Cape Girardeau, we gather another woman passenger at the BART office. She, too, is going to the airport.

The three-hour ride goes smoothly, and I arrive at the Amtrak station in St. Louis a half-hour ahead of schedule. The station, much smaller than one would expect, is about the same size as the Amtrak depot at Carbondale. Another lucky day because I get to ride in style in a two-tier Super-liner. On the long, slow haul out of St. Louis, I see the famous arch before we drone past a gray parade of industrial plants and factories: Grossman Iron & Steel, Heinz Steel, Phillips Metal, and various redi-mix and cement plants. Field after field of towering Illinois corn all the way to the Chicago suburbs are broken up by Alton, Springfield, Lincoln, Bloomington-Normal, Pontiac, and Joliet.

A morning paper carries this headline on the bottom of the front page: "Bootheel girls thrown 300 feet by tornado return to scene of death." It's a moving story about a trio of Cooter, Missouri, kids who survived the Monday night twister that killed three people. The girls hid in the closet of a modular home while the tornado roared through. Although one suffered a cut requiring stitches, all three escaped serious injury by landing in a pile of pink home insulation. I clip the news article, thinking I may reference it somewhere in my novel.

Arriving in Chicago five minutes late at 2:30 p.m., I walk a few blocks east to the Berghoff, a Chicago brewery and restaurant dating to 1898. Original owner Herman Joseph Berghoff sold beer for five cents a glass and offered a free sandwich to go with it. To this day Berghoff makes its own beer and root beer. I order a stein of dark and a plate of sauerbraten, thin slices of beef drowning in a dark freight of sweet-and-sour gravy. The sides of spaetzle and sauerkraut make my day, prompting a second mug of beer.

Shouldering my backpack and lugging the laptop, I walk off the beer buzz on the hike back to Union Station. The expansive feeling grows to magnanimity, prompting me to drop dollar bills into the hands of two wheelchair-bound beggars. A young man of twenty or so is wrapped in a dirty blanket. He holds a brown cardboard sign with uneven lettering—"Hungry and cold. Please help me." Leaning against a cement step next to the Chicago River, the youth takes long, determined drags on a final inch of cigarette and stares into nothing through deep-set eyes of aquamarine.

I wonder why he is desperate. Is it mental illness? Some other misfortune, or merely sloth and indifference? It doesn't matter; he needs help. I give him the blanket from my backpack. He looks up: "God bless you, man," he says.

"Stay warm tonight," I reply. "Be careful." And slip him a five-dollar bill. I don't know why I do this spontaneous act of generosity. I do recognize this same fellow I saw three days earlier in the same place, with the same look on his face. I wonder if Dwight Barnum looked like him—blue eyes, brown hair, fair complexion. Rather than try to explain my own motivations, I'd rather analyze Rachel's.

On the final Amtrak leg to Battle Creek and my waiting pickup, I ponder a line from *The Hobbitt*: "All who wander are not lost." Rachel was not lost although she had no clue how the mission to bring her son home, one way or another, would unfold. I believe her determination was fueled by more than a mother's love. I wonder if within Rachel's subconscious stirred the need to assuage loss: her twin sister Helen, three months before the girls turned four in New Jersey; the passing of their mother, in New York City when Rachel was ten; the death of her first husband Willis, when she was thirty-six and he forty.

She had no control over these terrible losses. Given her Dutch upbringing and her steadfast character, I think adult Rachel held fast to what remained in her life and needed to control outcomes as much as she could. That's why she carved out a family burial place from her farm and laid Willis to rest where she could see his gravestone from her kitchen window. Were it not for Rachel's Christian faith and the love of an itinerate worker who became her second husband, she could not have carried the burden few others could bear.

When I first visited the Welch Cemetery, maintained to this day by Sunfield Township, two huge white cedars towered over the plot containing six graves of the original Barnum family. Curious about how old the trees were, in 2004 Lindsay Welch and I enlisted a forester friend to take a core sample from one. The number of rings suggested the tree was around ninety years old. When Rachel died in 1918, she was almost ninety-six, and her closest living heir was Perry John Welch, Lindsay's great-grandfather and the sole offspring of Rachel and John Welch, who died in 1907. Lindsay and I think son PJ, as he was known, could have planted those cedars as a tribute to his mother. My novel nearing completion, I returned to the Welch Cemetery in May of 2025 and learned the cedars were gone.

I hope this book will take their place. The courage and fortitude of Rachel van Houten Barnum Welch are an inspiration to all. In telling her story, I needed to be accurate while allowing fictional narrative to play its part. *The Woman She Left Behind* covers less than a month of Rachel's long life. There is much more to tell; I am writing the rest of her story now.

Tom Huggler
Sunfield, Michigan

ACKNOWLEDGMENTS

No one writes a book without help from others. I am indebted to many.

First, to my wife Laura Huggler, who offered emotional support during the more than twenty years of fits and starts the effort took and whose insights as a psychoanalyst helped to explain Rachel's motivations and to shape her character.

To Lindsay Welch, Rachel's great-great grandson, for sharing *"Myrte's Memories,"* a family journal written by his grandmother (Rachel's granddaughter-in-law), and which sparked my interest in telling Rachel's story. A special thanks to Lindsay for sharing Rachel's family photos (see "Author's Notes.)"

To Larry J. Daniel and Lynn N. Bock, coauthors of *The Battle for Island No. 10,* the definitive treatise on this critical Mississippi River struggle that occurred during the epic Battle of Shiloh and has been relegated to historical footnote as a result.

To those who helped me retrace Rachel's journey, mile

by mile: Amishman John Miller from Vermontville, Michigan; my neighbor and small-plane pilot Kerry Haynor; Mickey Blackburn of the Cairo Chamber of Commerce; Cairo historian Russel Ogg and his wife Virginia; Margaret Palmer of the New Madrid Area C of C; New Madrid Museum curator Harriet Porter; Mike Comer, Missouri DNR administrator of the Hunter-Dawson Historic site; Martha Hunter and Jerrie Ruth Palmer of the New Madrid Public Library; and Cairo friends Bob Conroy, Don Turner, and David Barkett who teamed up to take me down the Mississippi to New Madrid.

To novelists Larry Sommers and Christine DeSmet for their first-draft advice which helped to set the course. To beta readers Tom Carney, Bob DeMott, Jerry Dennis, Dr. Jim Gilsdorf, Mary Jo Kietsman, and Zieva Konvisser; to developmental editor Samantha Wekstein of the Thompson Literary Agency; to Friesen Press for editorial evaluation; and to fellow members of Ray's Writing Group: Kelly Gruner, Robert Nelson, Rick Rashid, Esther Reed, Paul Ross, the late Carol Scot, and Jim Weaver. The encouragement and insights from these friends and colleagues were beyond helpful and provided the book's lifeblood.

A special thanks to editor Art DeLaurier, for his keen interest in Rachel's story, critical eye during several drafts, and deep research into Civil War-era newspapers invaluable to getting the story right.

To my daughter Jennifer Kruis for creating the AI-inspired book's cover art, to Nat Case of incasellc.com for map design, and to Marj Charlier of Sunacumen Press for proofreading, cover and book design, formatting, and myriad other details to prepare the novel for publication.

My sincere thanks to all and to those I may have inadvertently omitted.

Note: The reader may have noticed this book contains few blurbs of praise from successful authors of renown. As always, the reader has the last word.